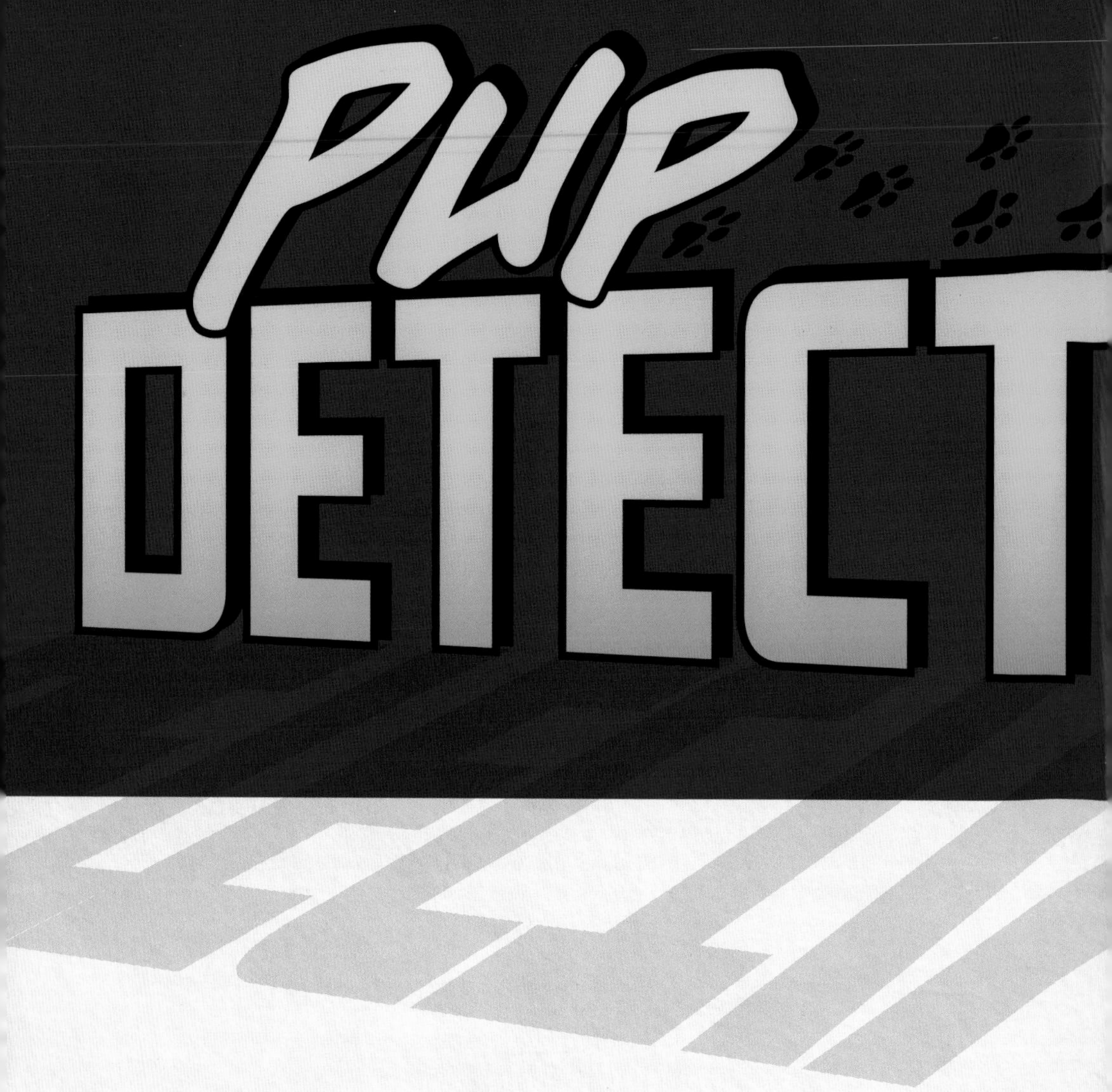
PUP
DETECT

IVES

GHOSTS, GOBLINS, AND NINJAS!

Written by FELIX GUMPAW
Illustrated by WALMIR ARCHANJO
at GLASS HOUSE GRAPHICS

 LITTLE SIMON
NEW YORK   LONDON   TORONTO   SYDNEY   NEW DELHI

LITTLE SIMON
AN IMPRINT OF SIMON & SCHUSTER CHILDREN'S PUBLISHING DIVISION
1230 AVENUE OF THE AMERICAS, NEW YORK, NEW YORK 10020
FIRST LITTLE SIMON EDITION JULY 2021
COPYRIGHT © 2021 BY SIMON & SCHUSTER, INC.
ALL RIGHTS RESERVED, INCLUDING THE RIGHT OF REPRODUCTION IN WHOLE OR IN PART IN ANY FORM. LITTLE SIMON IS A REGISTERED TRADEMARK OF SIMON & SCHUSTER, INC., AND ASSOCIATED COLOPHON IS A TRADEMARK OF SIMON & SCHUSTER, INC. FOR INFORMATION ABOUT SPECIAL DISCOUNTS FOR BULK PURCHASES, PLEASE CONTACT SIMON & SCHUSTER SPECIAL SALES AT 1-866-506-1949 OR BUSINESS@SIMONANDSCHUSTER.COM. ART BY WALMIR ARCHANJO AND JOÃO ZOD • COLORING BY WALMIR ARCHANJO, JOÃO ZOD, LELO ALVES, HUGO CARVALHO, ADJAIR FRANÇA AND IZAAC BRITO • LETTERING BY MARCOS MASSÃO INOUE • SUPERVISION BY MJ MACEDO/ANCIENT BLACK • ART SERVICES BY GLASS HOUSE GRAPHICS • THE SIMON & SCHUSTER SPEAKERS BUREAU CAN BRING AUTHORS TO YOUR LIVE EVENT. FOR MORE INFORMATION OR TO BOOK AN EVENT CONTACT THE SIMON & SCHUSTER SPEAKERS BUREAU AT 1-866-248-3049 OR VISIT OUR WEBSITE AT WWW.SIMONSPEAKERS.COM.
DESIGNED BY NICHOLAS SCIACCA
MANUFACTURED IN CHINA 0421 SCP
10 9 8 7 6 5 4 3 2 1
LIBRARY OF CONGRESS CATALOGING-IN-PUBLICATION DATA
NAMES: GUMPAW, FELIX, AUTHOR. I GLASS HOUSE GRAPHICS, ILLUSTRATOR. TITLE: GHOSTS, GOBLINS, AND NINJAS / BY FELIX GUMPAW ; ILLUSTRATED BY GLASS HOUSE GRAPHICS. DESCRIPTION: FIRST LITTLE SIMON EDITION. I NEW YORK : LITTLE SIMON, 2021. I SERIES: PUP DETECTIVES ; 4 I AUDIENCE: AGES 5-9 I AUDIENCE: GRADES K-1 I SUMMARY: "DURING A MARTIAL ARTS EXPO AT PAWSTON ELEMENTARY, THE SACRED SCROLL OF BARK-JITSU IS STOLEN. THE PUP DETECTIVES SET OUT TO CRACK THEIR MOST PUZZLING CASE YET... BECAUSE THIS ONE INVOLVES GHOSTS, GOBLINS, AND A SUPER STEALTHY NINJA"—PROVIDED BY PUBLISHER. IDENTIFIERS: LCCN 2020027929 (PRINT) I LCCN 2020027930 (EBOOK) I ISBN 9781534478725 (PAPERBACK) I ISBN 9781534478732 (HARDCOVER) I ISBN 9781534478749 (EBOOK) SUBJECTS: LCSH: GRAPHIC NOVELS. I CYAC: GRAPHIC NOVELS. I MYSTERY AND DETECTIVE STORIES. I DOG—FICTION. CLASSIFICATION: LCC PZ7.7.G858 GH 2021 (PRINT) I LCC PZ7.7.G858 (EBOOK) I DDC 741.5/973—DC23. LC RECORD AVAILABLE AT HTTPS://LCCN.LOC.GOV/2020027929. LC EBOOK RECORD AVAILABLE AT HTTPS://LCCN.LOC.GOV/2020027930

CONTENTS

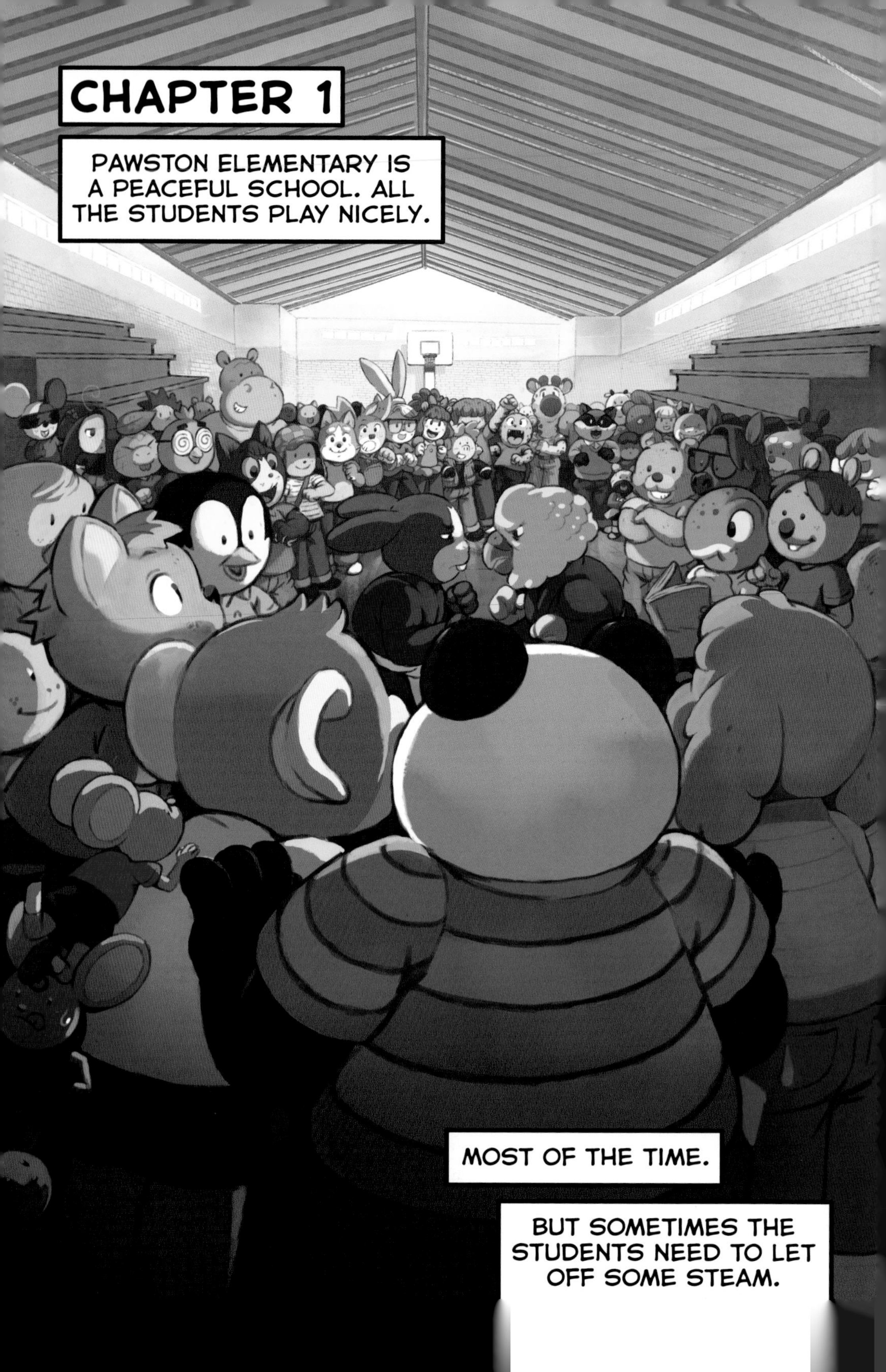
CHAPTER 1
PAWSTON ELEMENTARY IS A PEACEFUL SCHOOL. ALL THE STUDENTS PLAY NICELY.
MOST OF THE TIME.
BUT SOMETIMES THE STUDENTS NEED TO LET OFF SOME STEAM.

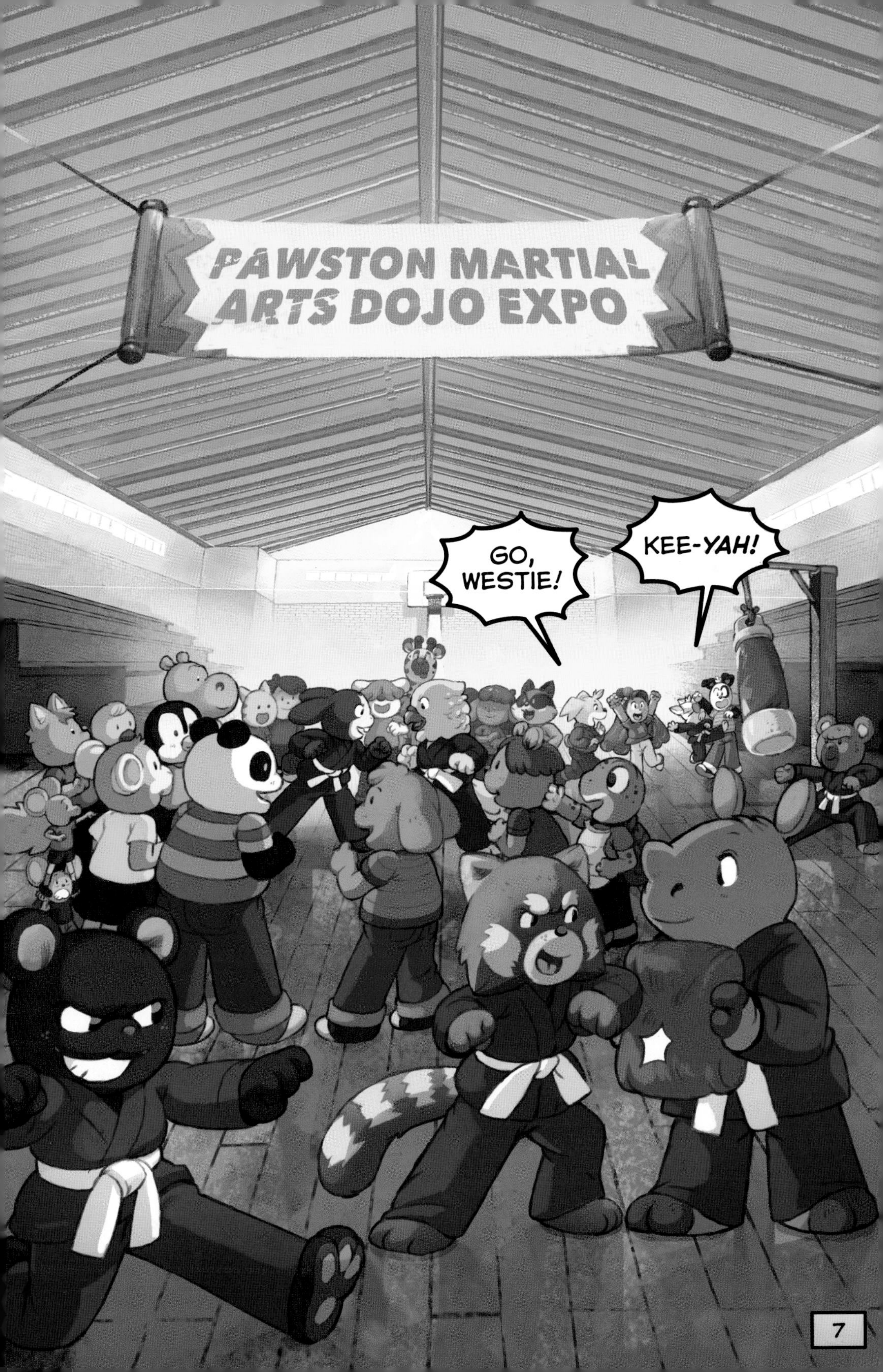
PAWSTON MARTIAL ARTS DOJO EXPO
GO, WESTIE!
KEE-YAH!

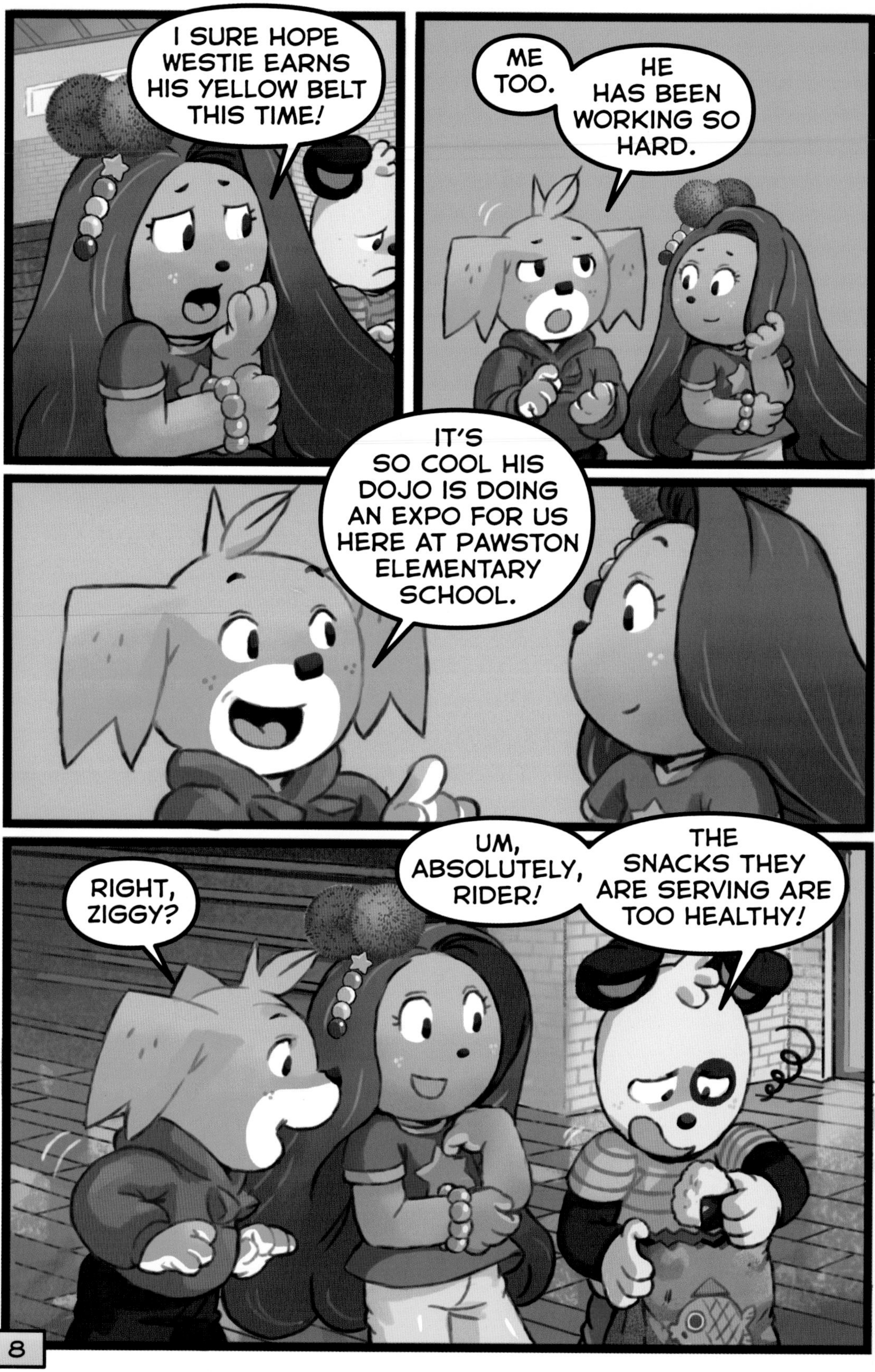
I SURE HOPE WESTIE EARNS HIS YELLOW BELT THIS TIME!
ME TOO.
HE HAS BEEN WORKING SO HARD.
IT'S SO COOL HIS DOJO IS DOING AN EXPO FOR US HERE AT PAWSTON ELEMENTARY SCHOOL.
RIGHT, ZIGGY?
UM, ABSOLUTELY, RIDER!
THE SNACKS THEY ARE SERVING ARE TOO HEALTHY!

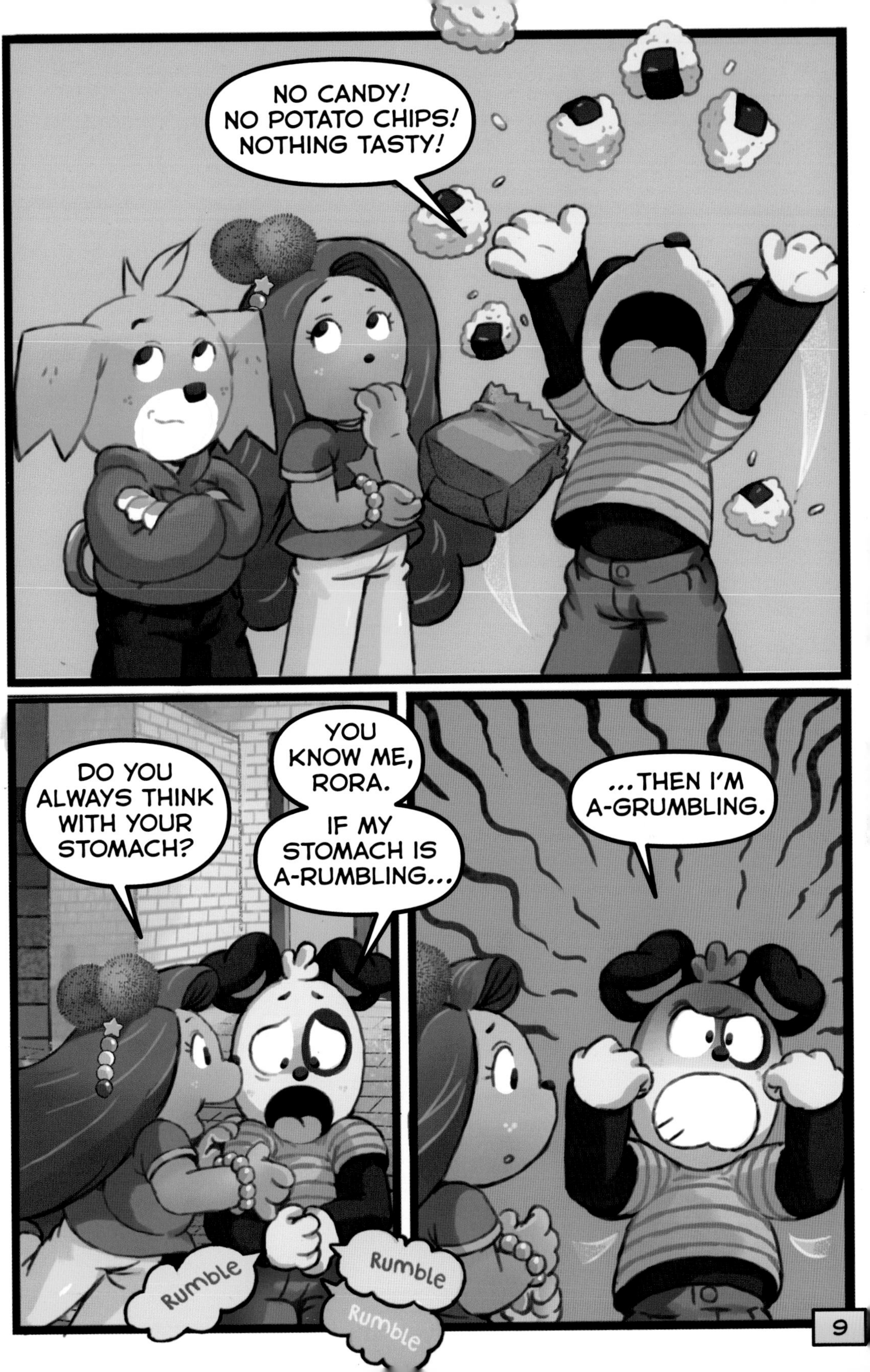
NO CANDY! NO POTATO CHIPS! NOTHING TASTY!
DO YOU ALWAYS THINK WITH YOUR STOMACH?
YOU KNOW ME, RORA.
IF MY STOMACH IS A-RUMBLING...
Rumble
Rumble
Rumble
...THEN I'M A-GRUMBLING.

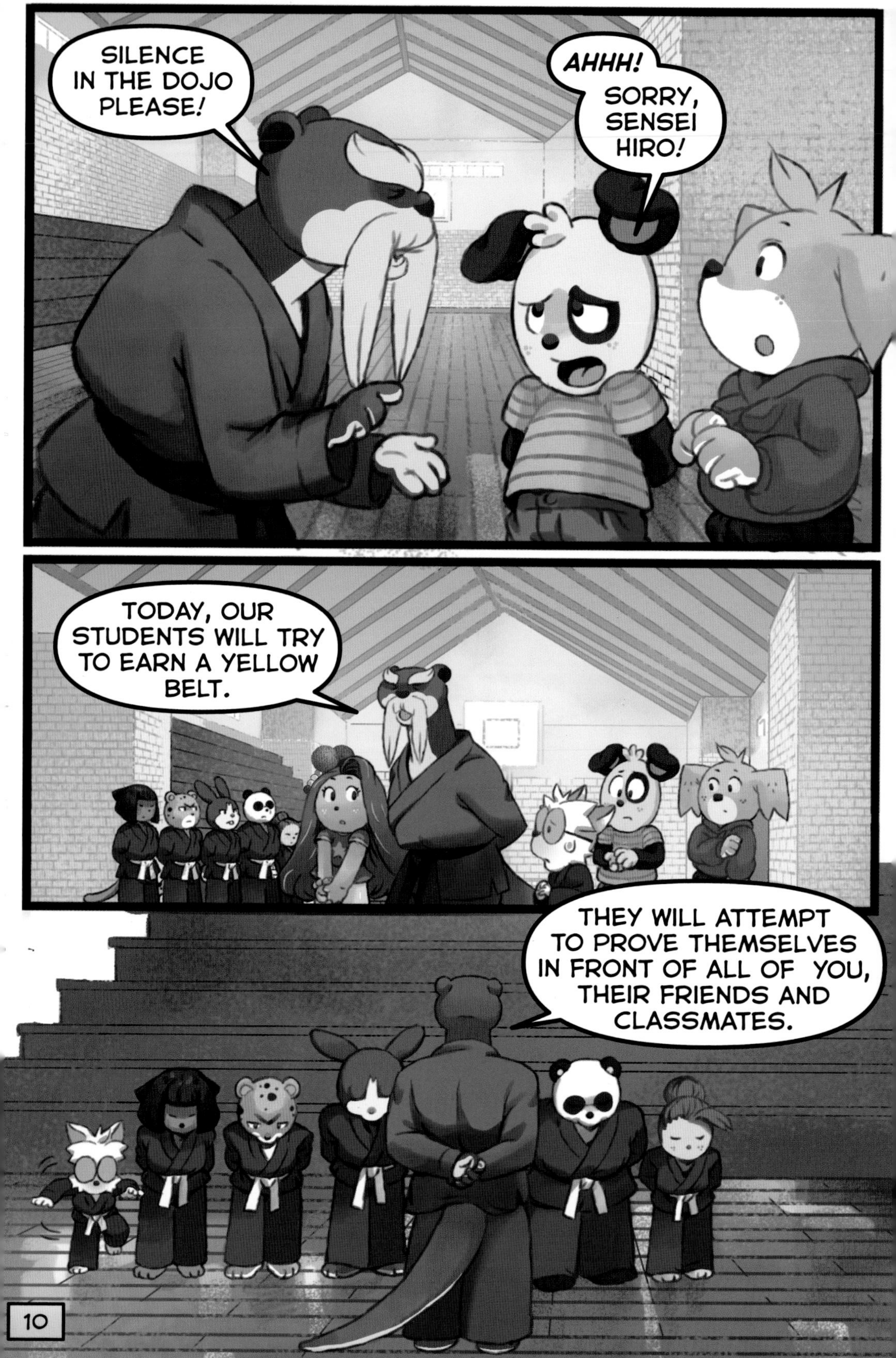
SILENCE IN THE DOJO PLEASE!
AHHH!
SORRY, SENSEI HIRO!
TODAY, OUR STUDENTS WILL TRY TO EARN A YELLOW BELT.
THEY WILL ATTEMPT TO PROVE THEMSELVES IN FRONT OF ALL OF YOU, THEIR FRIENDS AND CLASSMATES.

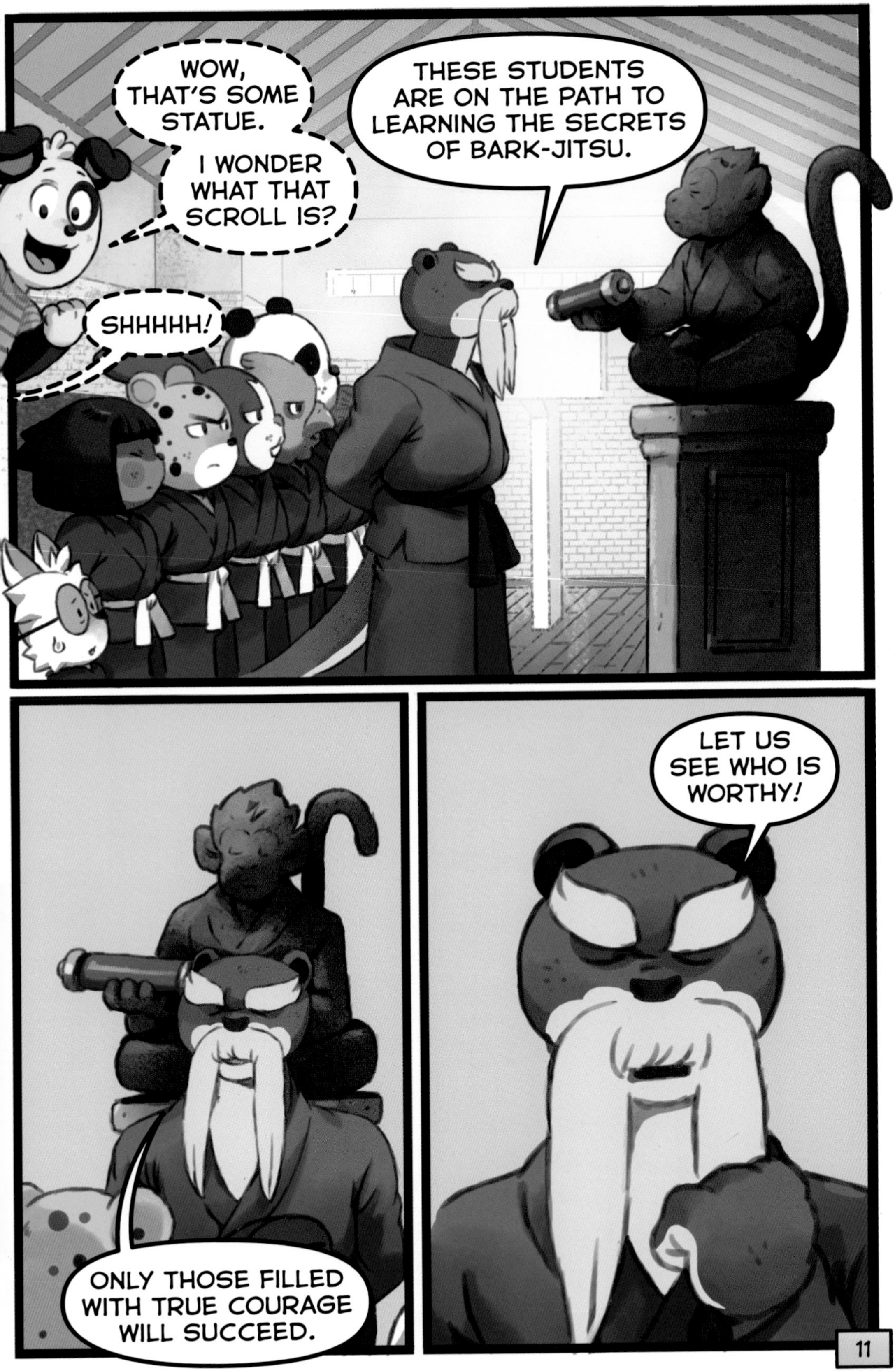
WOW, THAT'S SOME STATUE.
I WONDER WHAT THAT SCROLL IS?
THESE STUDENTS ARE ON THE PATH TO LEARNING THE SECRETS OF BARK-JITSU.
SHHHHH!
ONLY THOSE FILLED WITH TRUE COURAGE WILL SUCCEED.
LET US SEE WHO IS WORTHY!

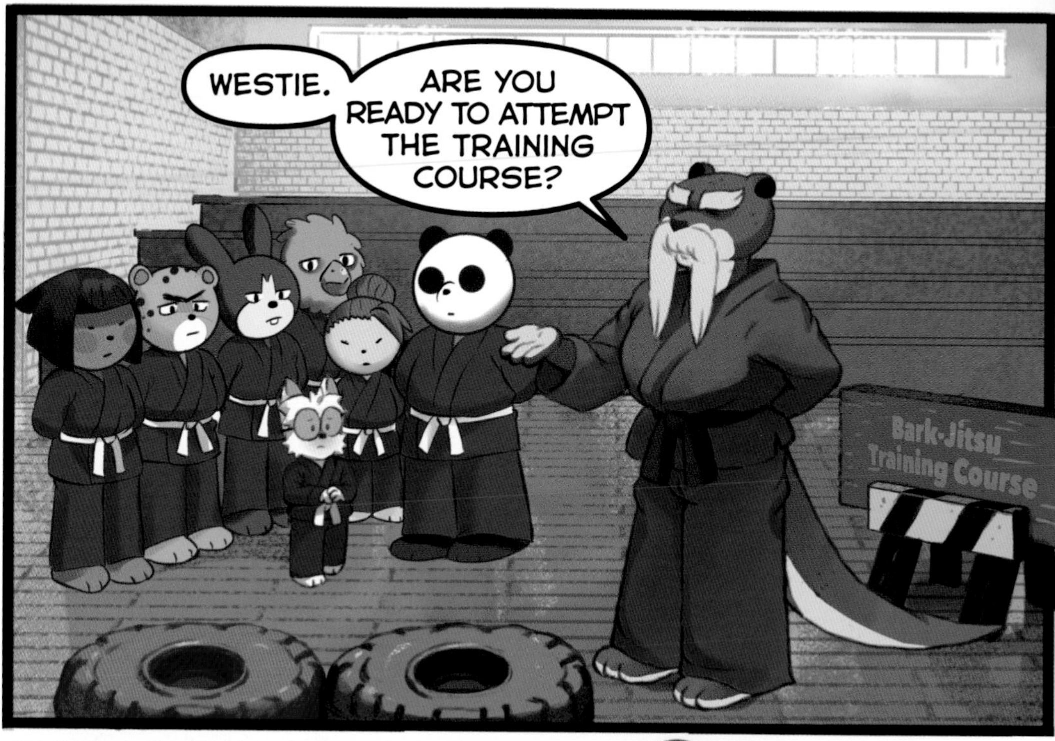
WESTIE.
ARE YOU READY TO ATTEMPT THE TRAINING COURSE?
Bark-Jitsu Training Course

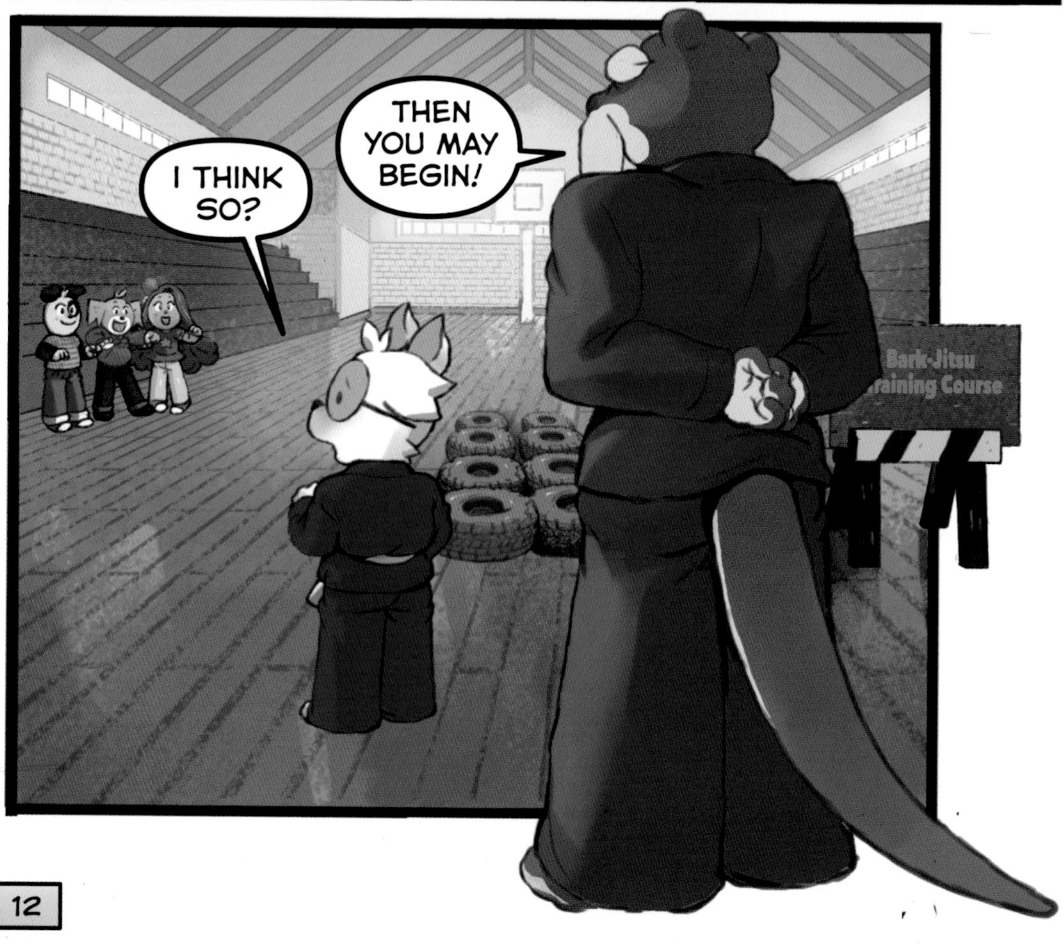
THEN YOU MAY BEGIN!
I THINK SO?
Bark-Jitsu Training Course

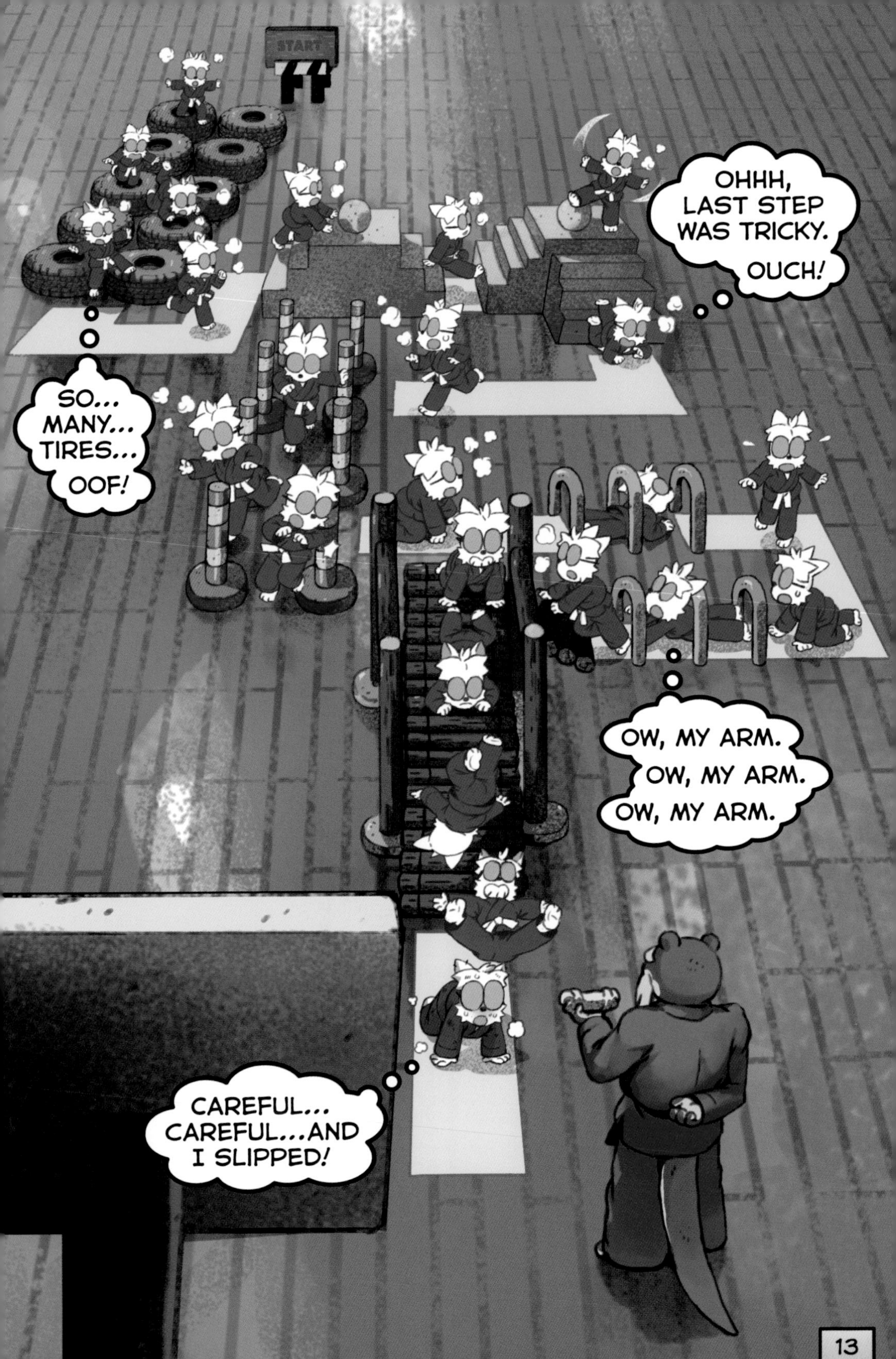
START
OHHH, LAST STEP WAS TRICKY. OUCH!
SO... MANY... TIRES... OOF!
OW, MY ARM. OW, MY ARM. OW, MY ARM.
CAREFUL... CAREFUL...AND I SLIPPED!

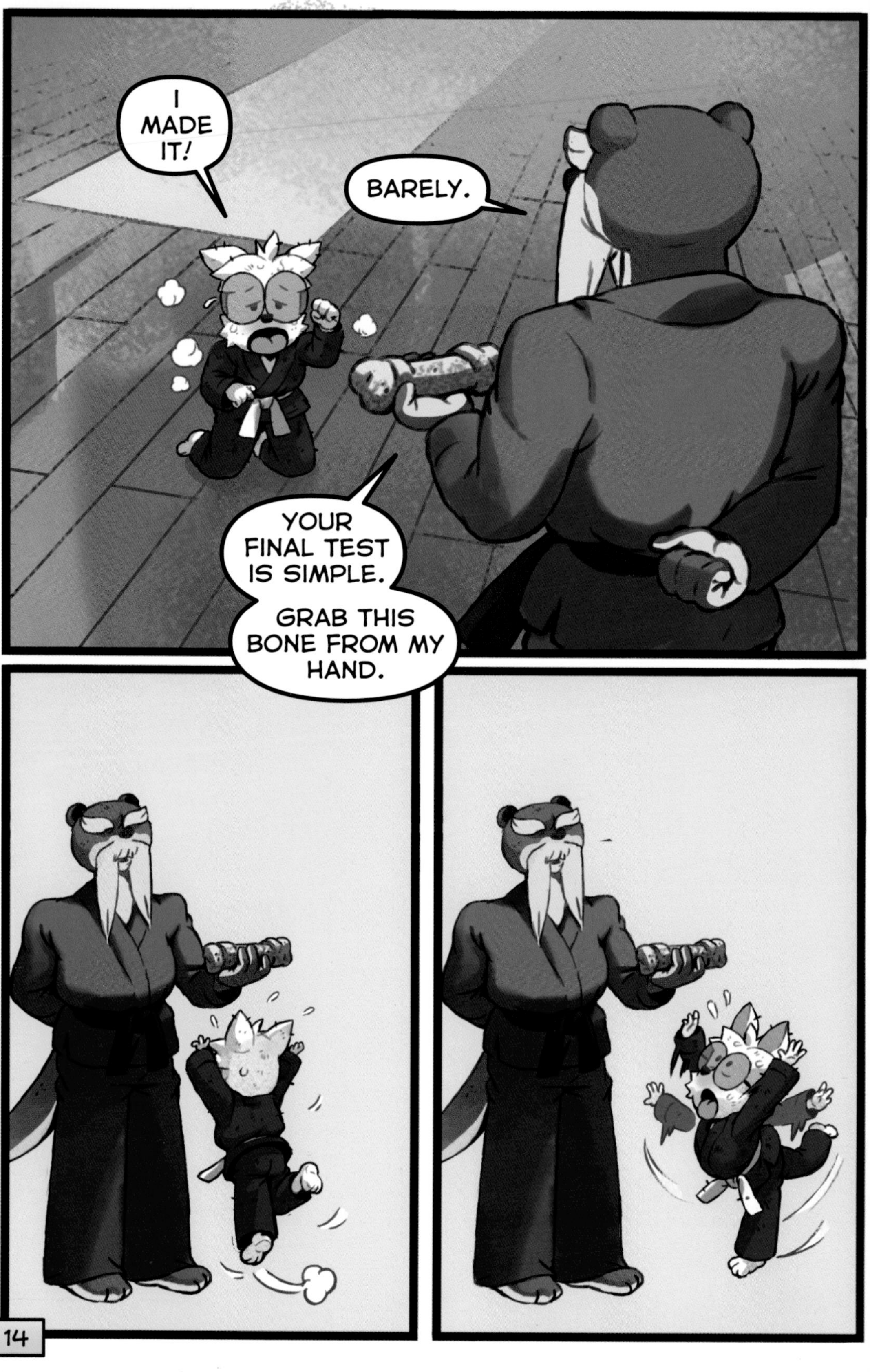
I MADE IT!
BARELY.
YOUR FINAL TEST IS SIMPLE.
GRAB THIS BONE FROM MY HAND.

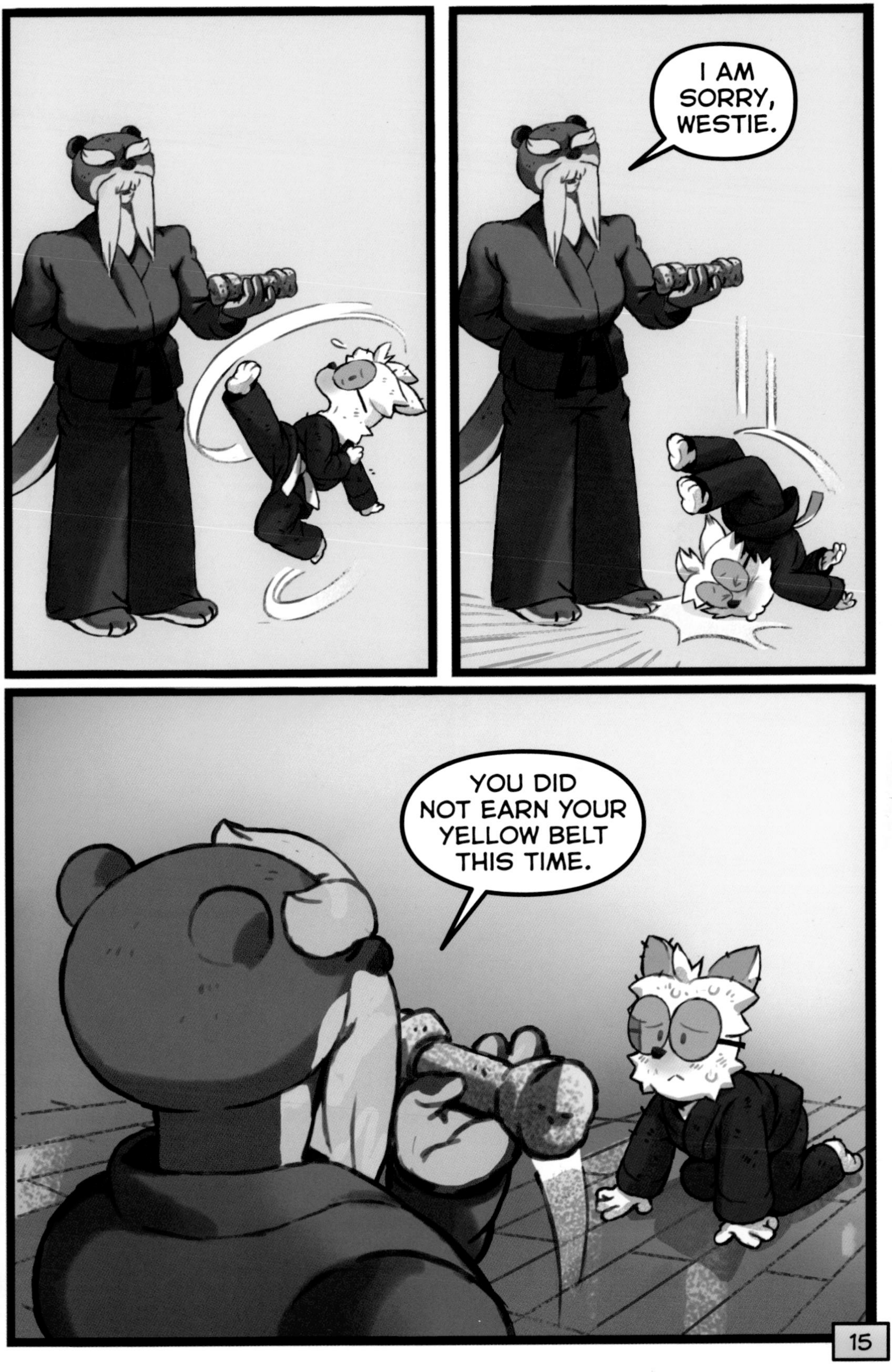
I AM SORRY, WESTIE.
YOU DID NOT EARN YOUR YELLOW BELT THIS TIME.

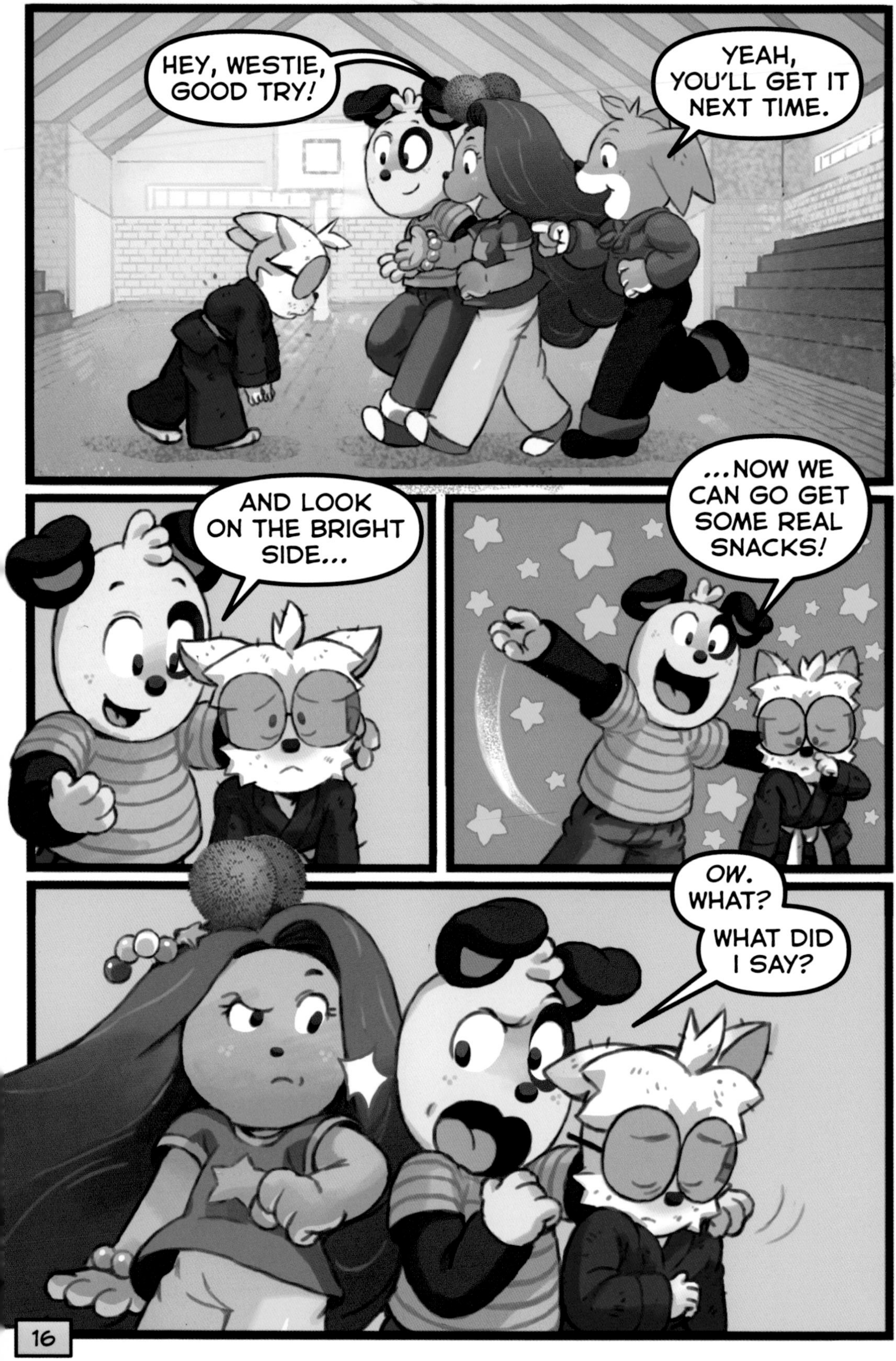
HEY, WESTIE, GOOD TRY!
YEAH, YOU'LL GET IT NEXT TIME.
AND LOOK ON THE BRIGHT SIDE...
...NOW WE CAN GO GET SOME REAL SNACKS!
OW. WHAT?
WHAT DID I SAY?

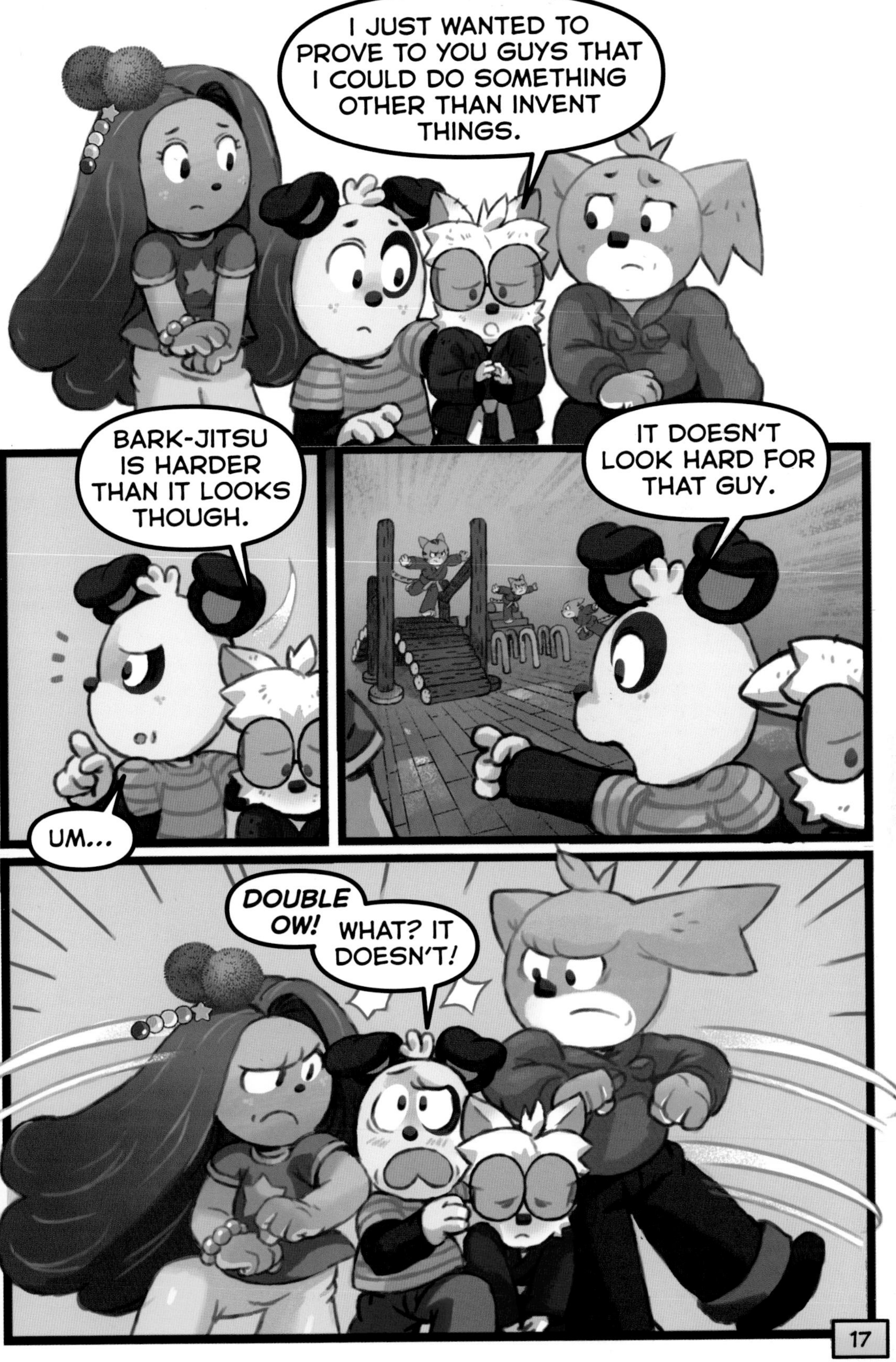
I JUST WANTED TO PROVE TO YOU GUYS THAT I COULD DO SOMETHING OTHER THAN INVENT THINGS.
BARK-JITSU IS HARDER THAN IT LOOKS THOUGH.
UM...
IT DOESN'T LOOK HARD FOR THAT GUY.
DOUBLE OW!
WHAT? IT DOESN'T!

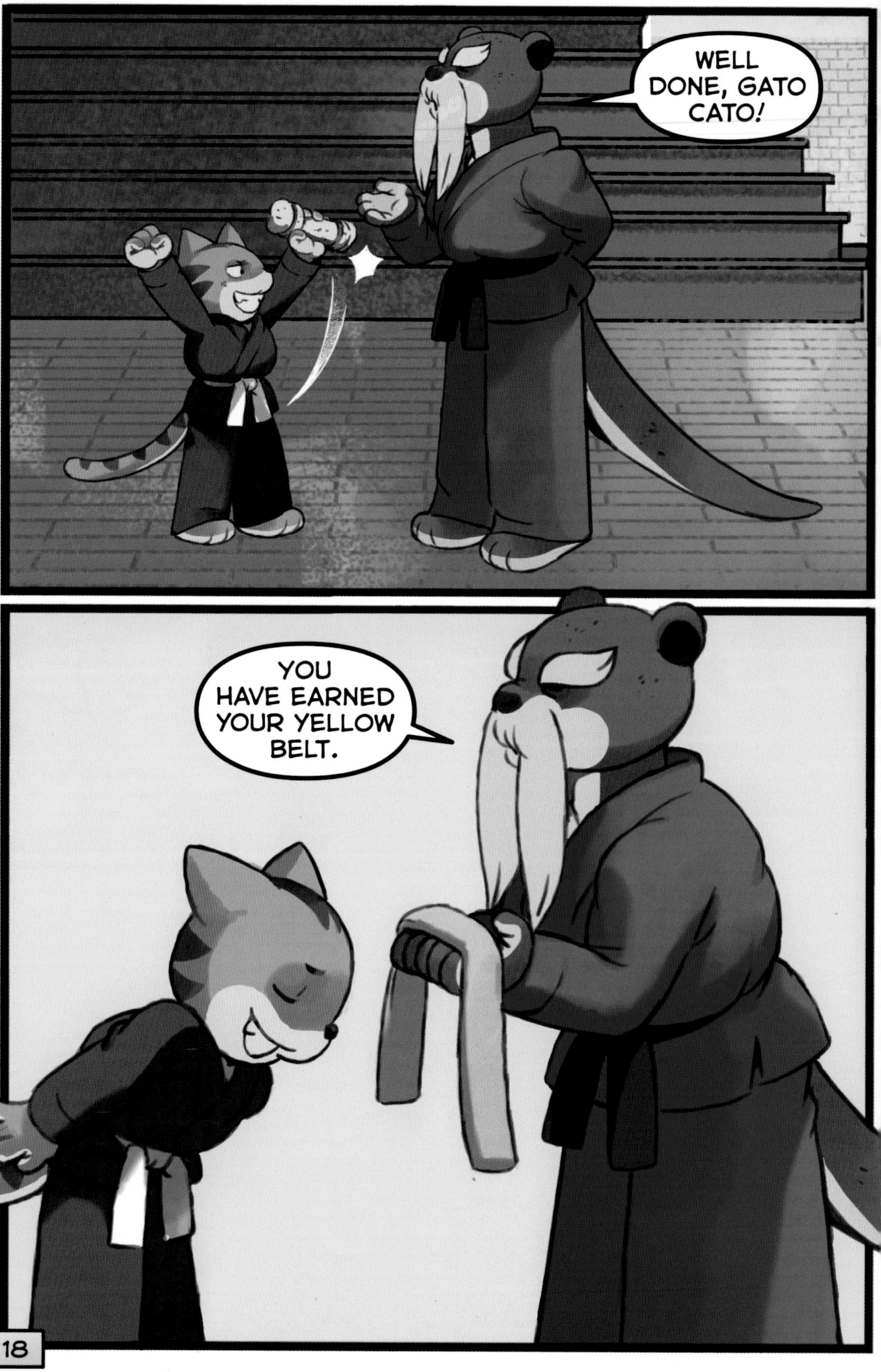
WELL DONE, GATO CATO!
YOU HAVE EARNED YOUR YELLOW BELT.

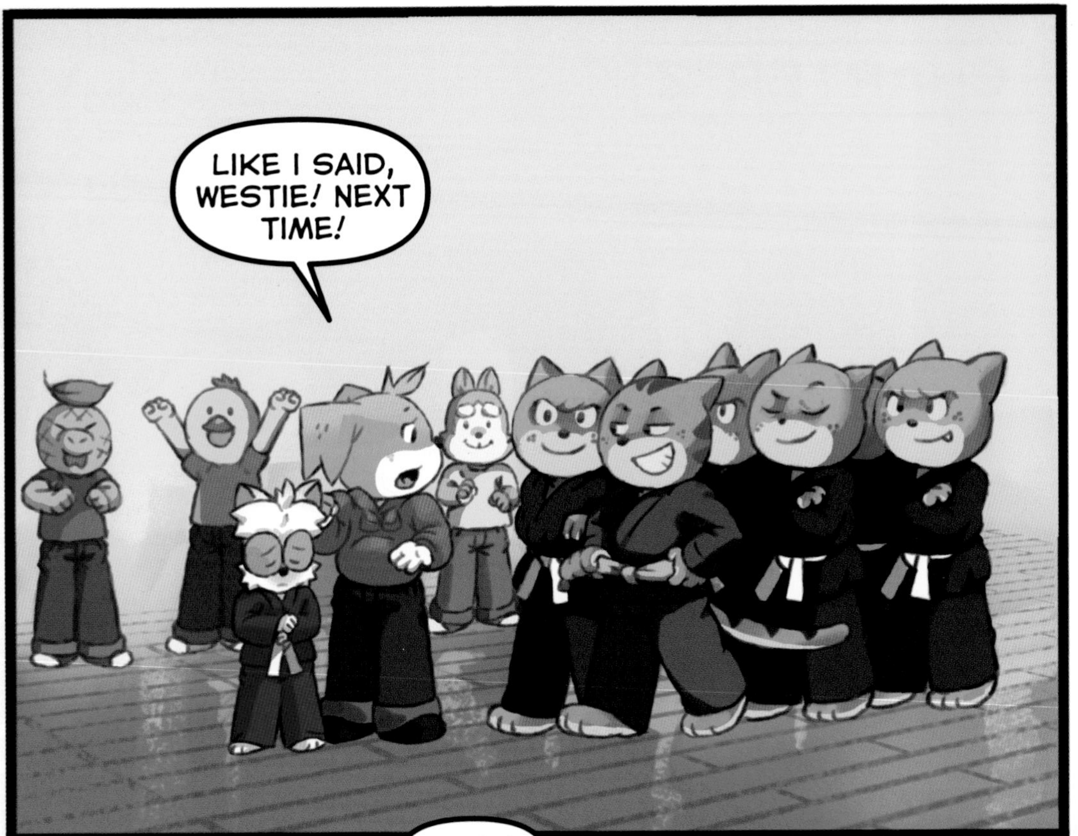
LIKE I SAID, WESTIE! NEXT TIME!

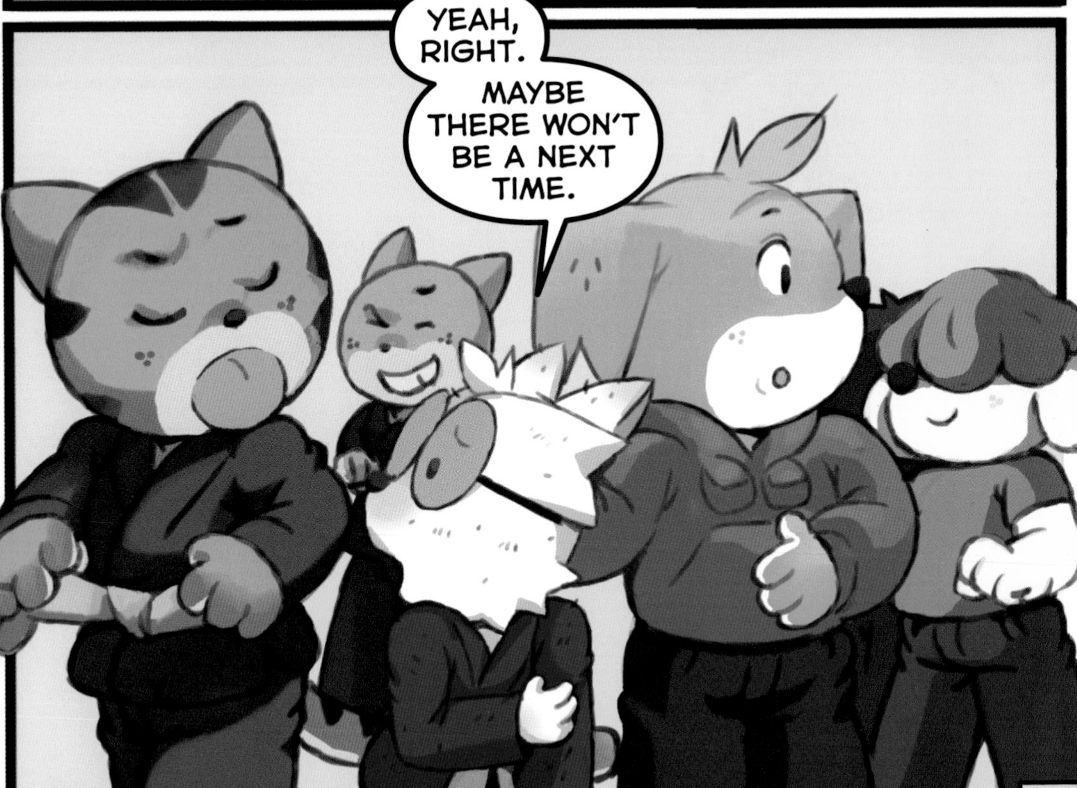
YEAH, RIGHT.
MAYBE THERE WON'T BE A NEXT TIME.

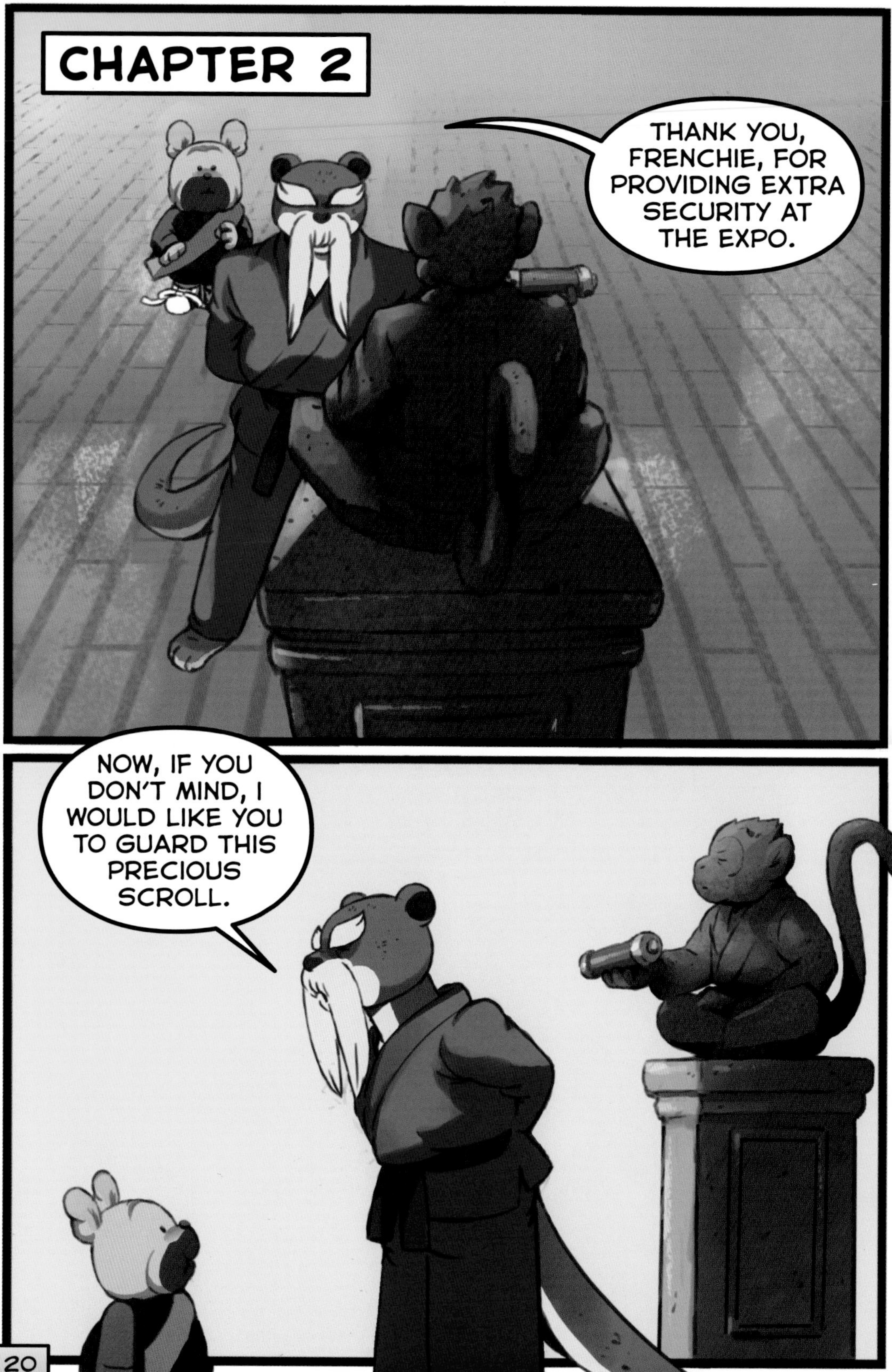
CHAPTER 2
THANK YOU, FRENCHIE, FOR PROVIDING EXTRA SECURITY AT THE EXPO.
NOW, IF YOU DON'T MIND, I WOULD LIKE YOU TO GUARD THIS PRECIOUS SCROLL.

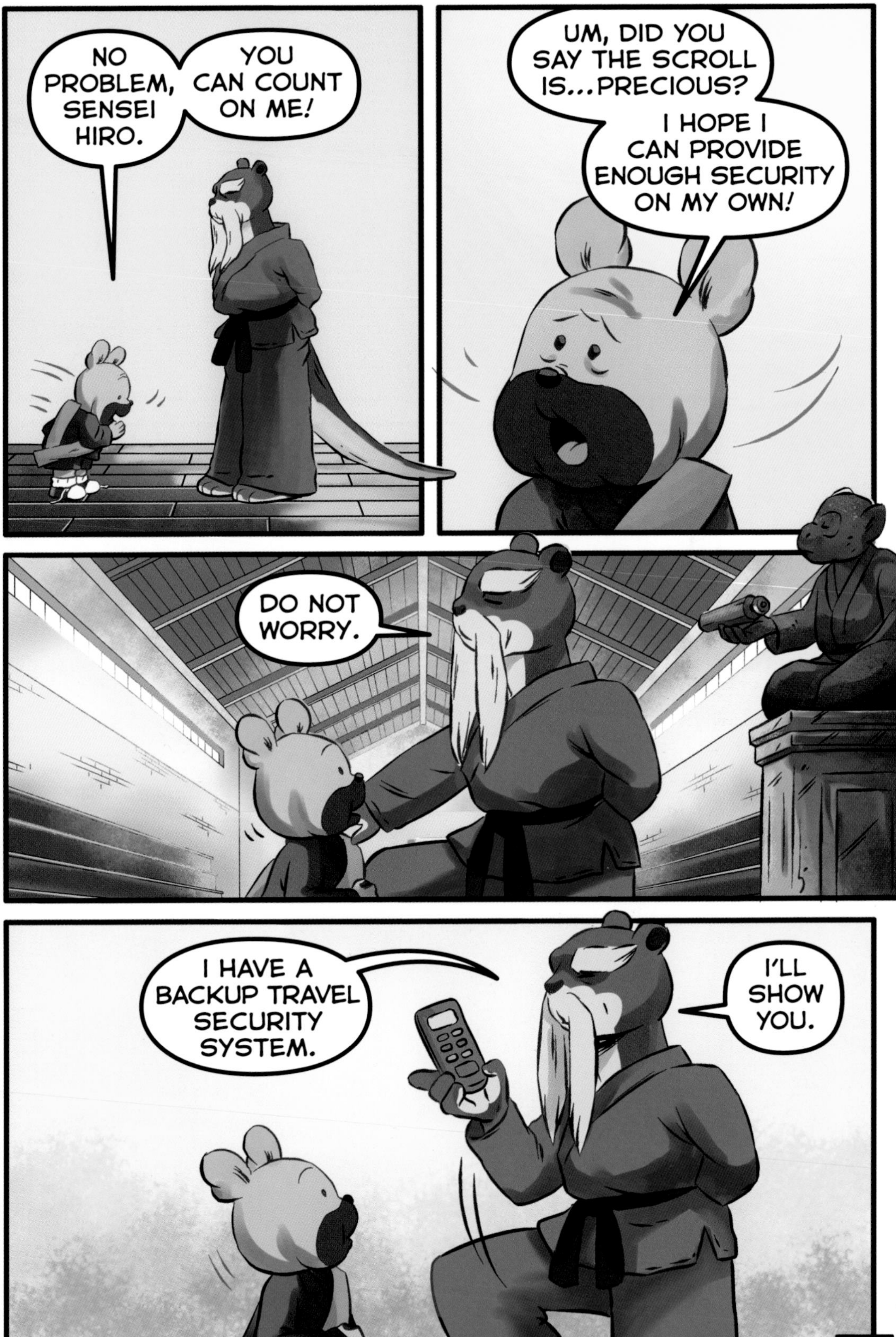
NO PROBLEM, SENSEI HIRO.
YOU CAN COUNT ON ME!
UM, DID YOU SAY THE SCROLL IS...PRECIOUS?
I HOPE I CAN PROVIDE ENOUGH SECURITY ON MY OWN!
DO NOT WORRY.
I HAVE A BACKUP TRAVEL SECURITY SYSTEM.
I'LL SHOW YOU.

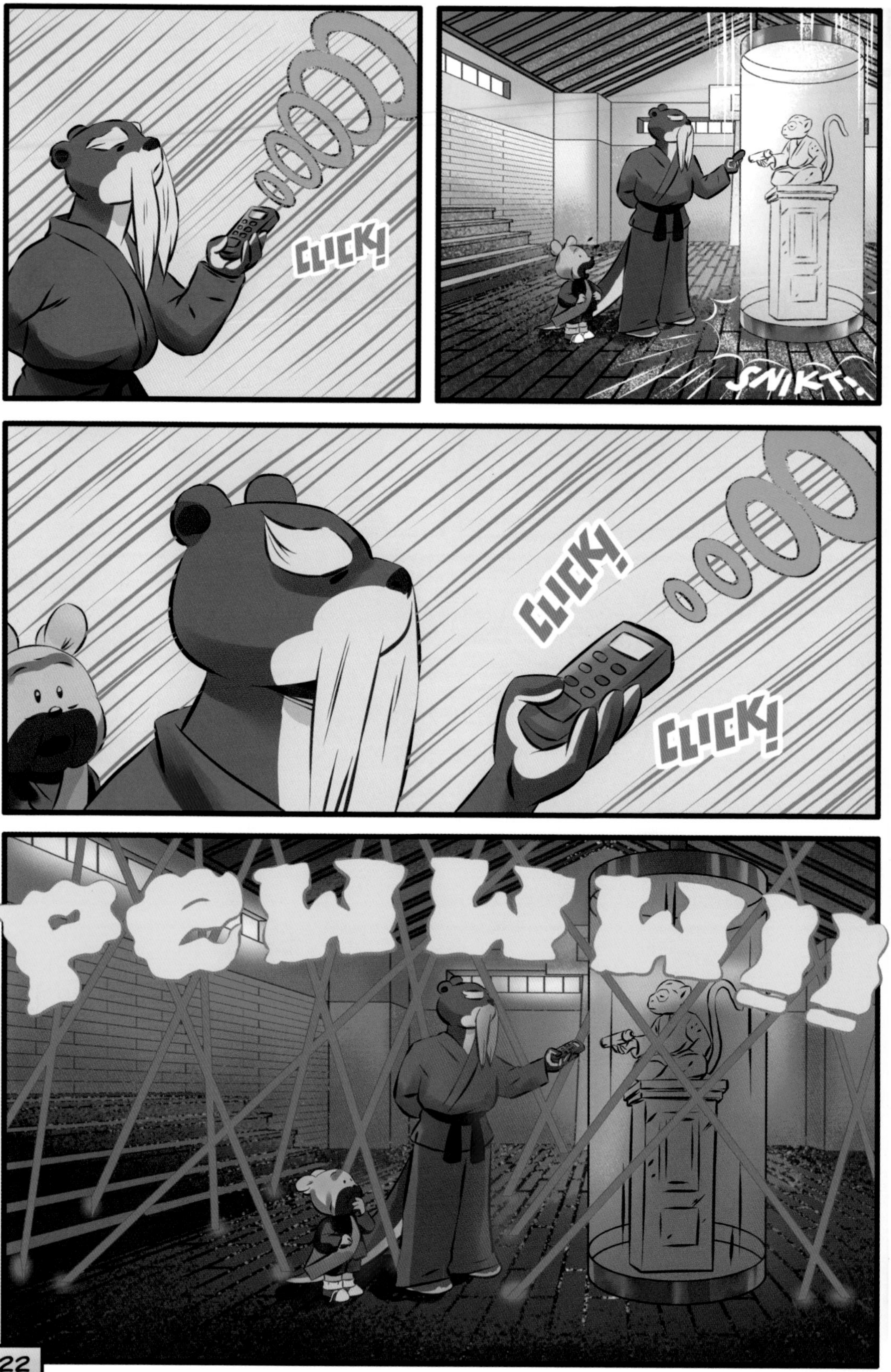
CLICK!
SNIKT!
CLICK!
CLICK!
PEWWW!!

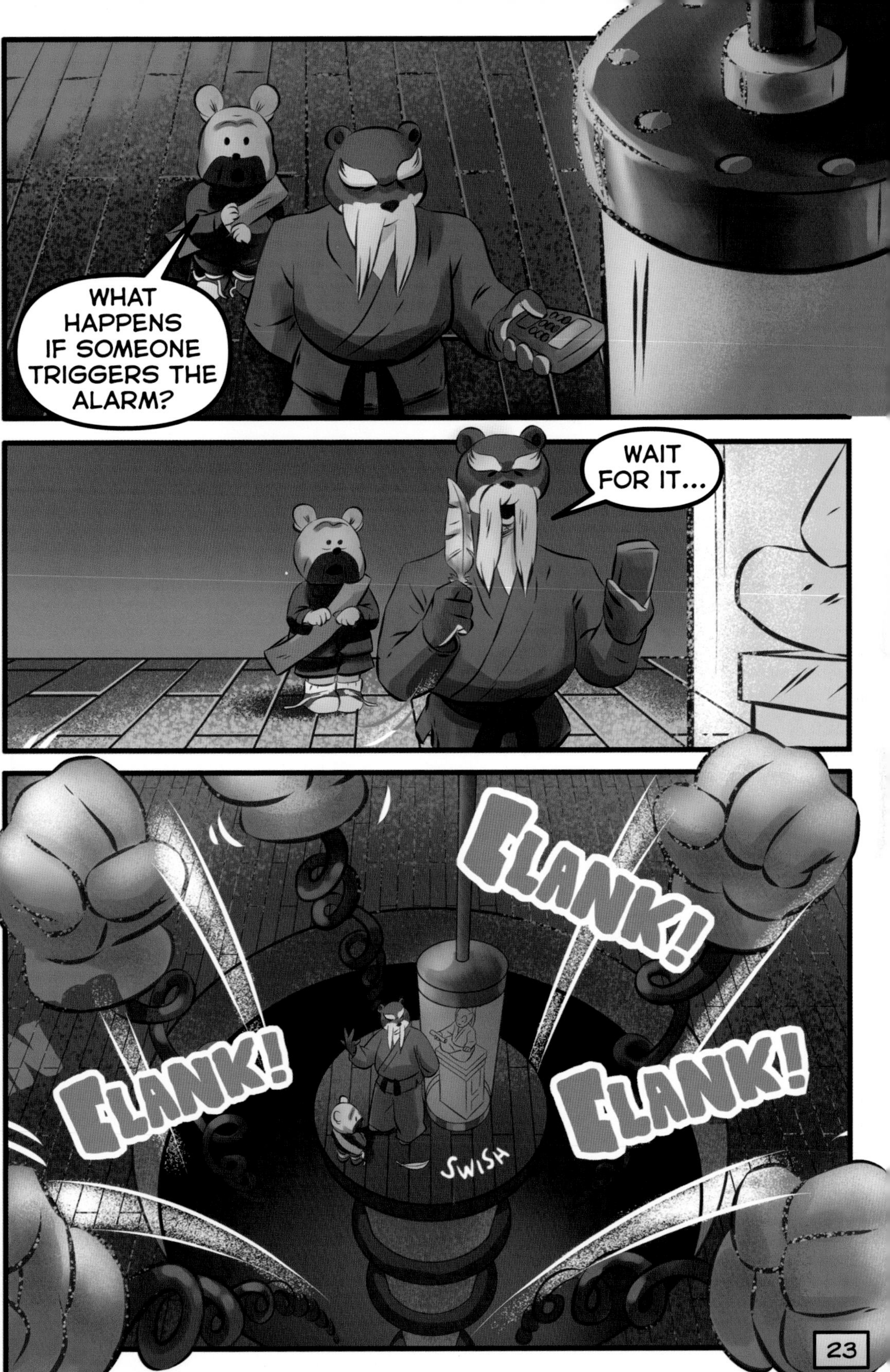
WHAT HAPPENS IF SOMEONE TRIGGERS THE ALARM?
WAIT FOR IT...
CLANK!
CLANK!
CLANK!
SWISH

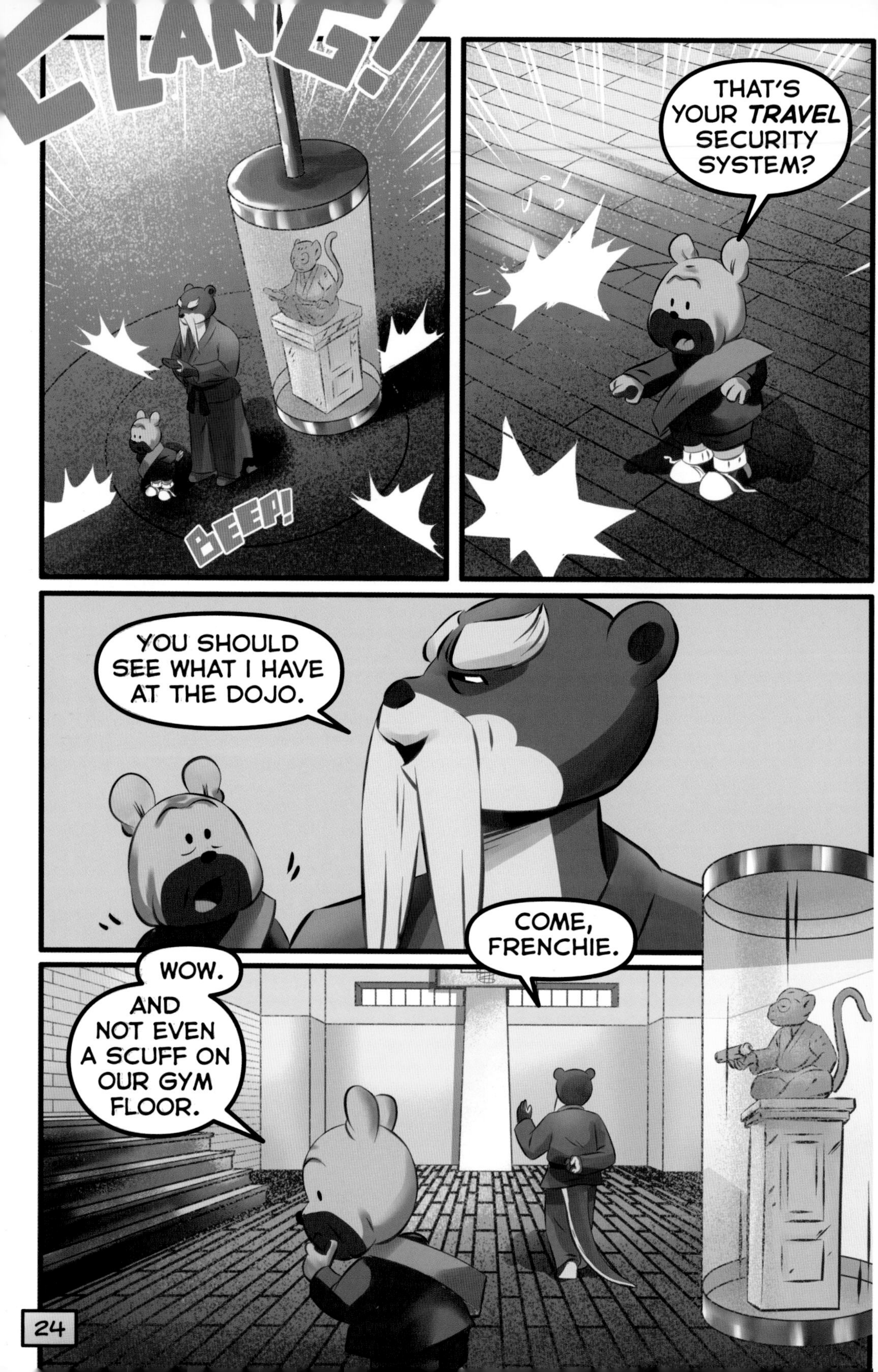

CLANG!
BEEP!
THAT'S YOUR *TRAVEL* SECURITY SYSTEM?
YOU SHOULD SEE WHAT I HAVE AT THE DOJO.
COME, FRENCHIE.
WOW.
AND NOT EVEN A SCUFF ON OUR GYM FLOOR.

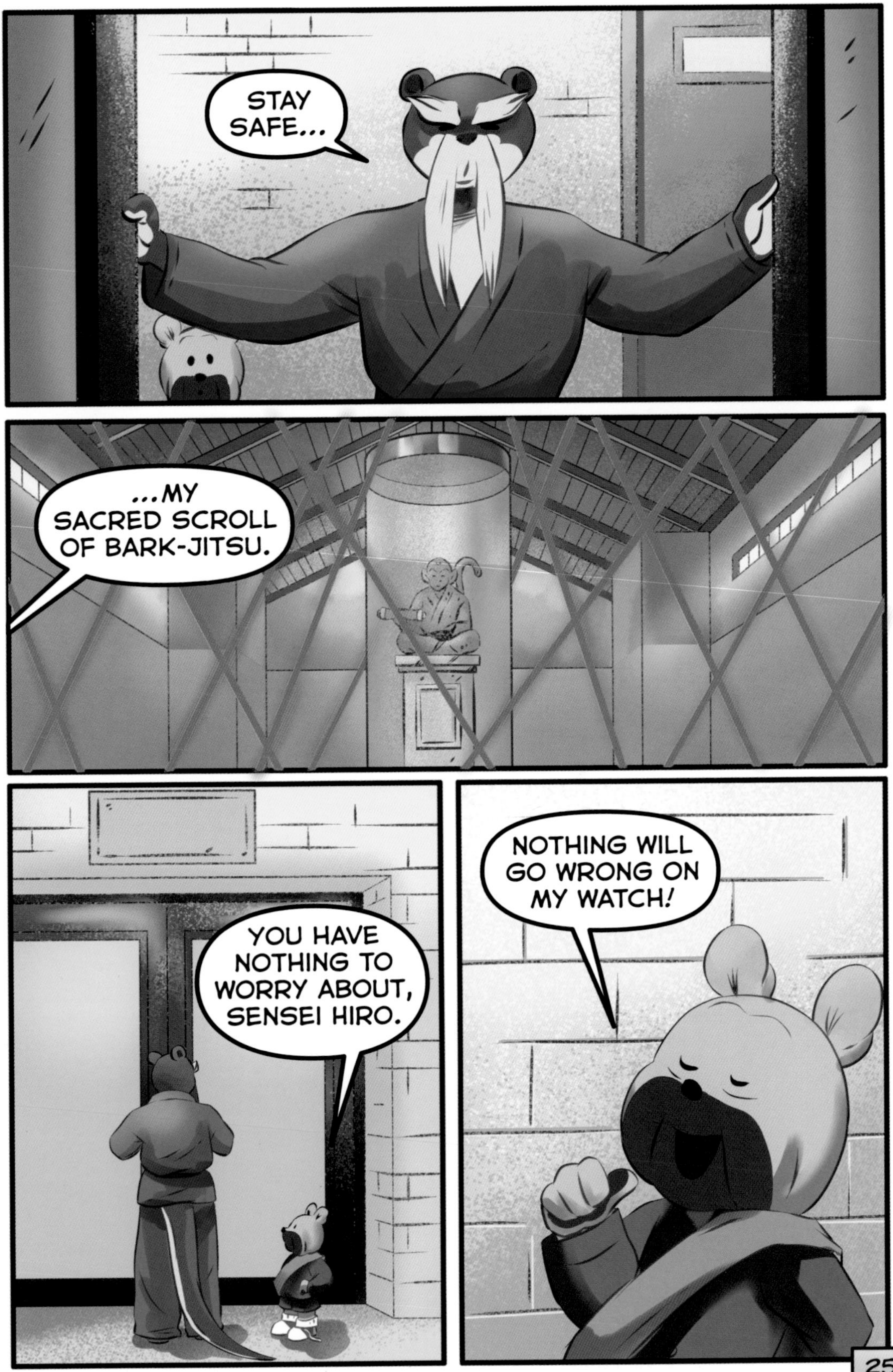
STAY SAFE...
...MY SACRED SCROLL OF BARK-JITSU.
YOU HAVE NOTHING TO WORRY ABOUT, SENSEI HIRO.
NOTHING WILL GO WRONG ON MY WATCH!

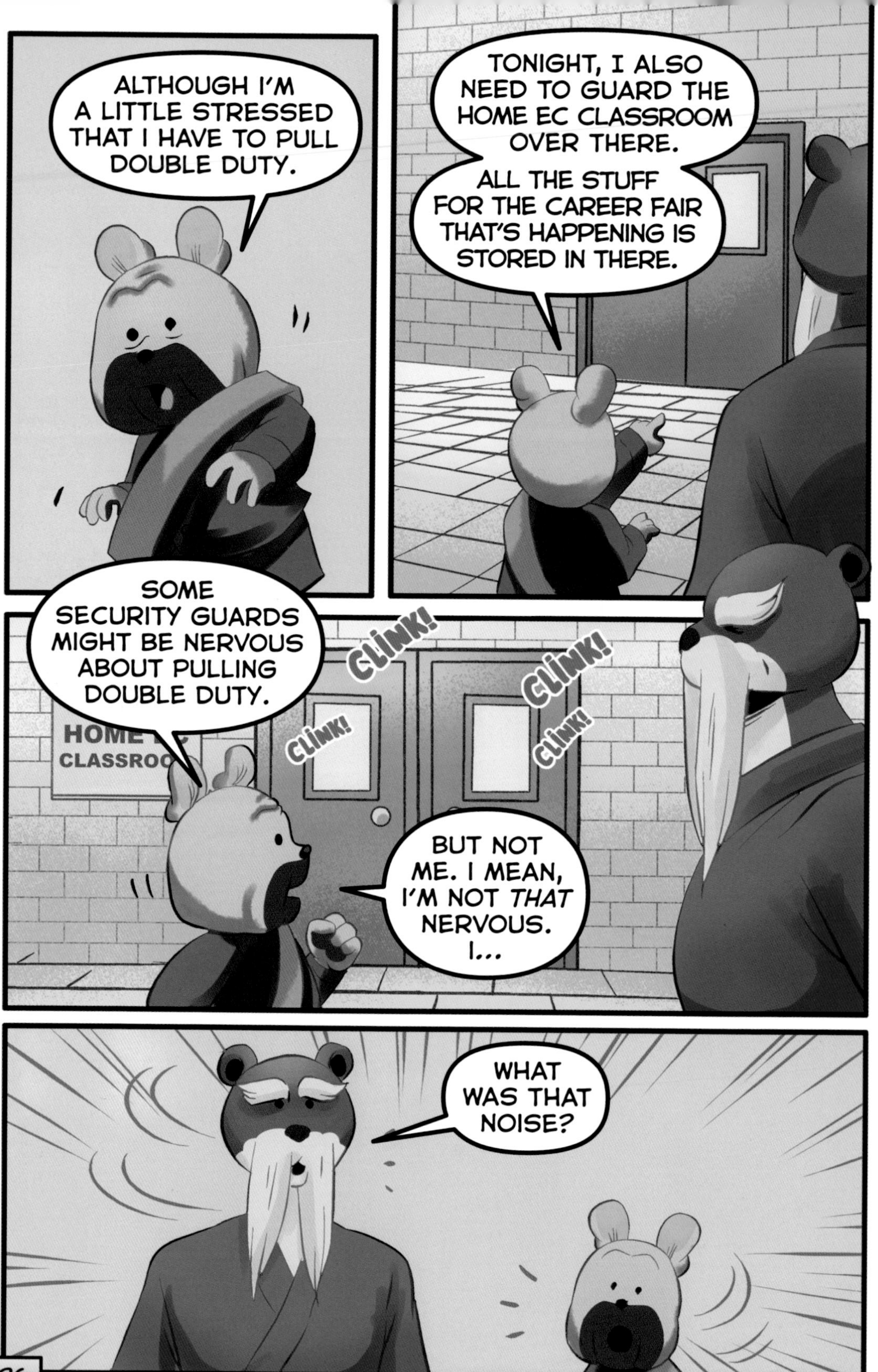
ALTHOUGH I'M A LITTLE STRESSED THAT I HAVE TO PULL DOUBLE DUTY.
TONIGHT, I ALSO NEED TO GUARD THE HOME EC CLASSROOM OVER THERE.
ALL THE STUFF FOR THE CAREER FAIR THAT'S HAPPENING IS STORED IN THERE.
SOME SECURITY GUARDS MIGHT BE NERVOUS ABOUT PULLING DOUBLE DUTY.
CLINK!
CLINK!
CLINK!
CLINK!
BUT NOT ME. I MEAN, I'M NOT *THAT* NERVOUS. I...
WHAT WAS THAT NOISE?

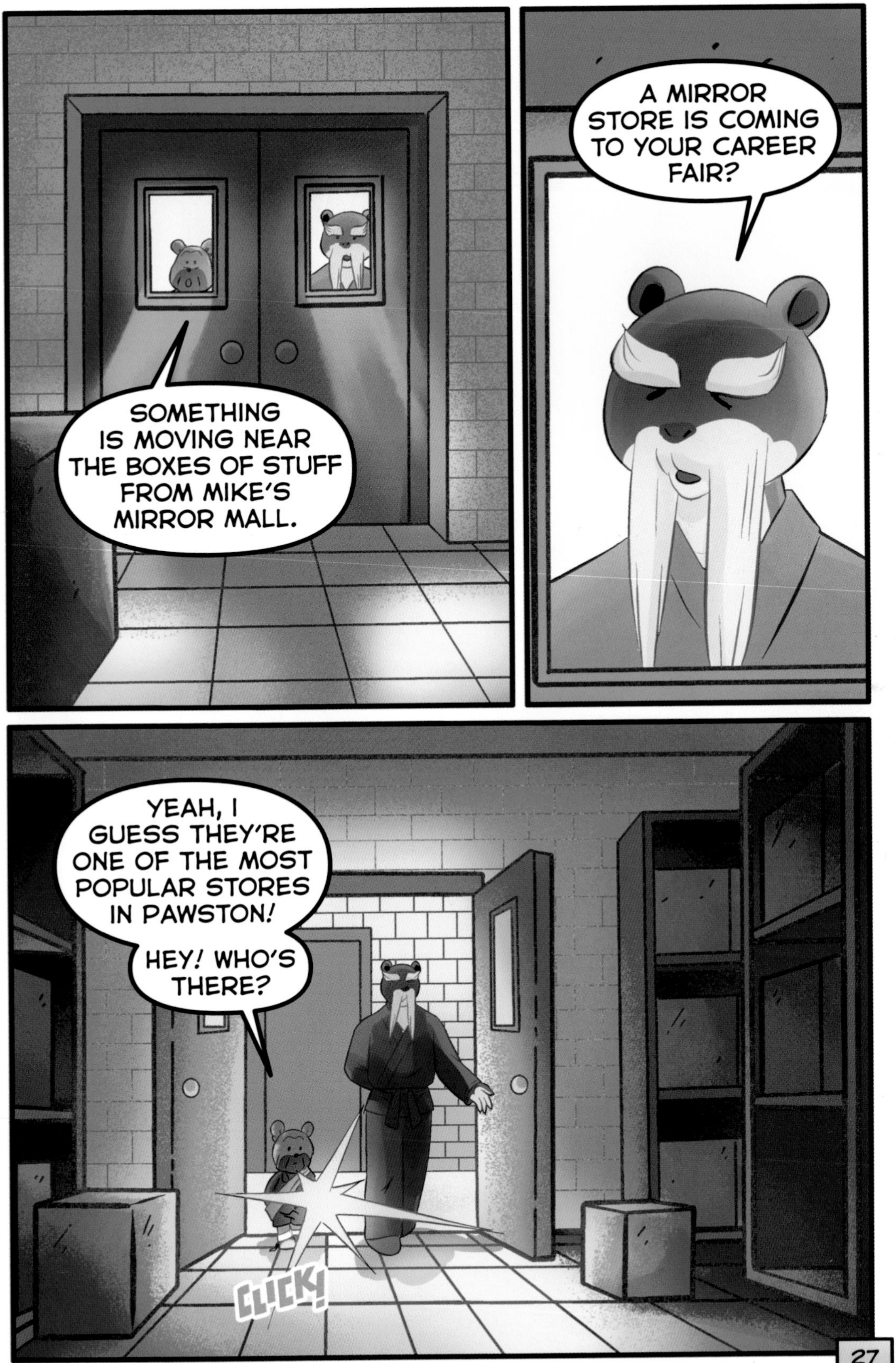

SOMETHING IS MOVING NEAR THE BOXES OF STUFF FROM MIKE'S MIRROR MALL.
A MIRROR STORE IS COMING TO YOUR CAREER FAIR?
YEAH, I GUESS THEY'RE ONE OF THE MOST POPULAR STORES IN PAWSTON!
HEY! WHO'S THERE?
CLICK!

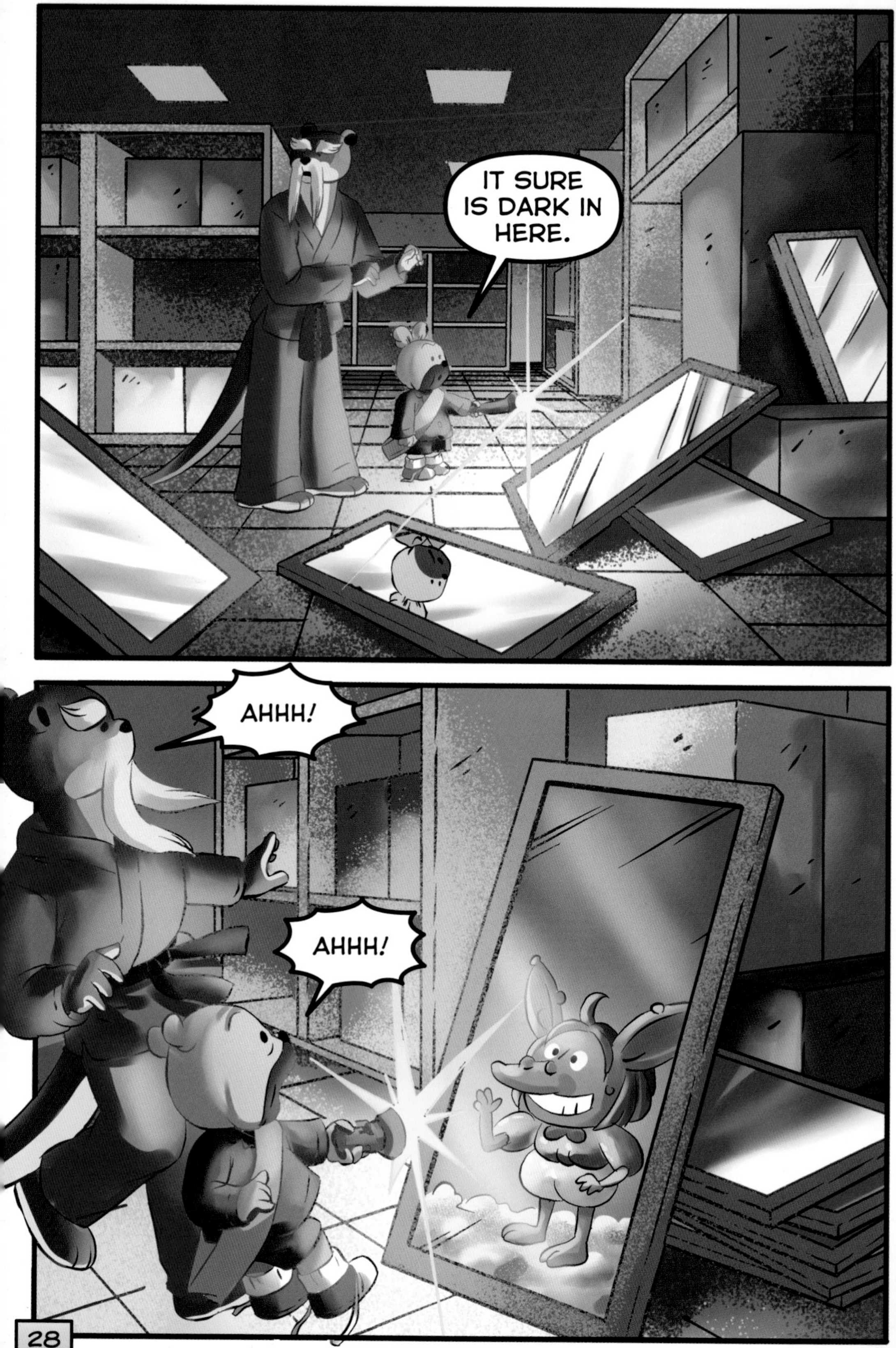
IT SURE IS DARK IN HERE.
AHHH!
AHHH!

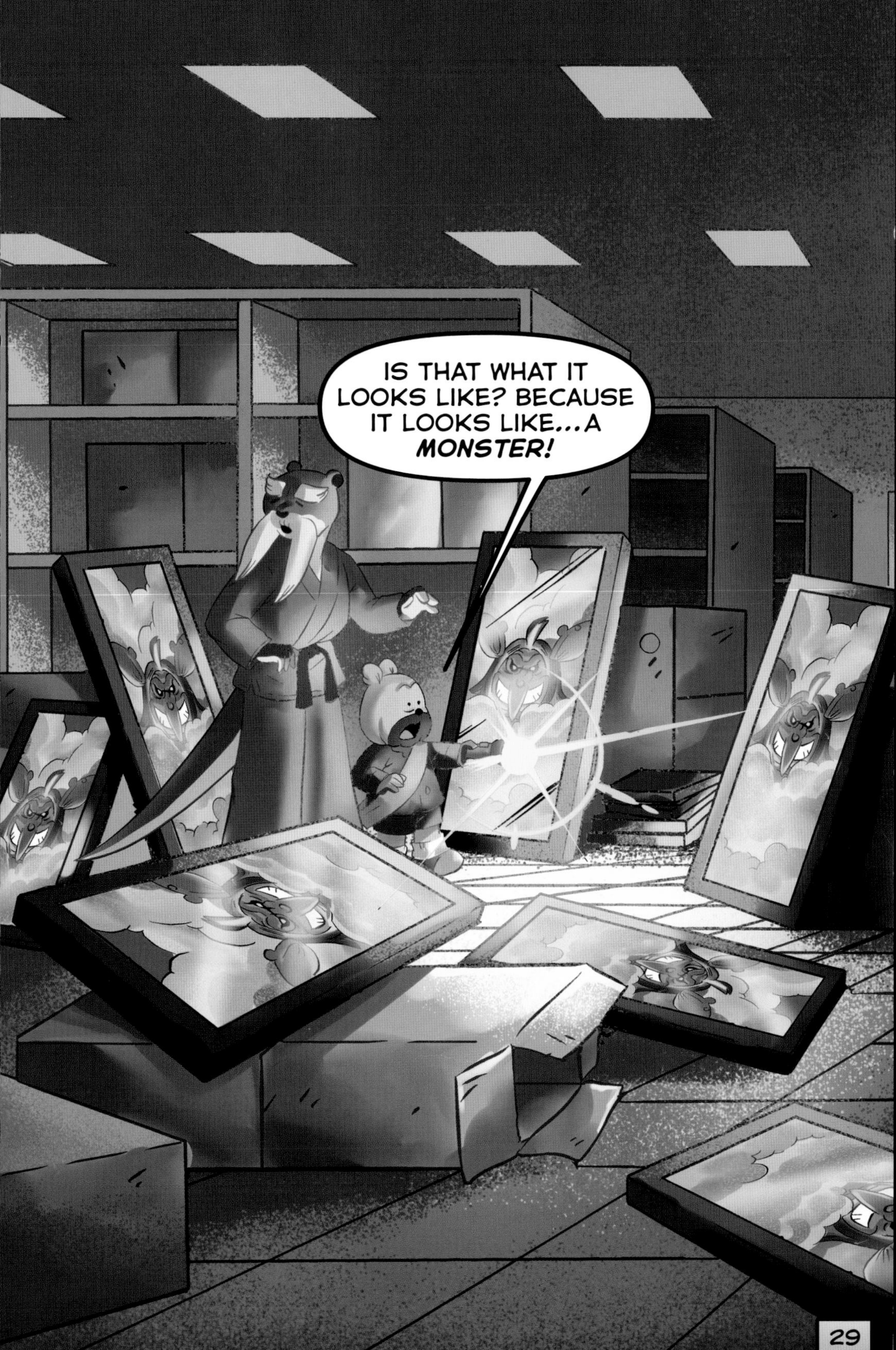
IS THAT WHAT IT LOOKS LIKE? BECAUSE IT LOOKS LIKE...A *MONSTER!*

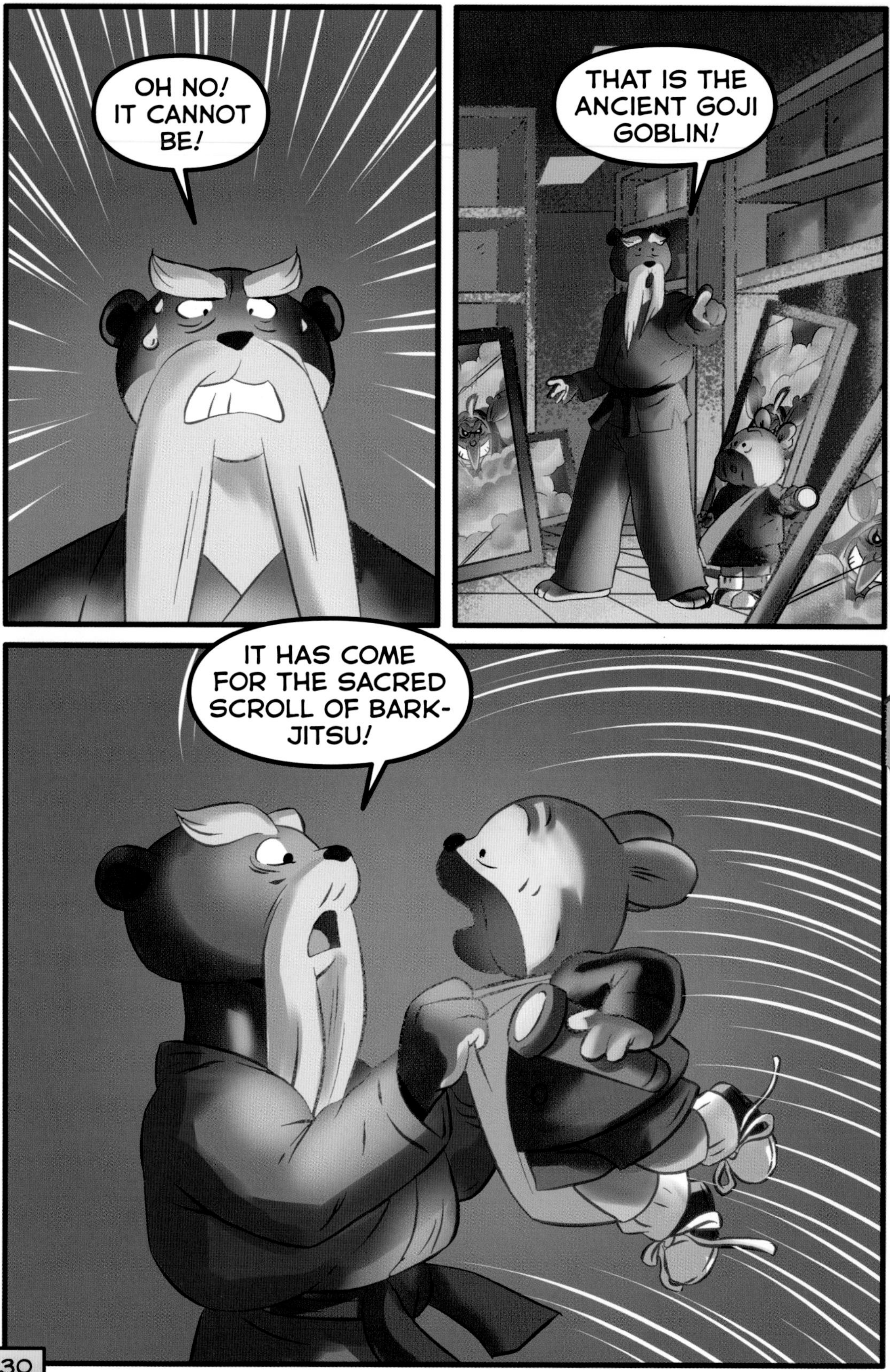
OH NO! IT CANNOT BE!
THAT IS THE ANCIENT GOJI GOBLIN!
IT HAS COME FOR THE SACRED SCROLL OF BARK-JITSU!

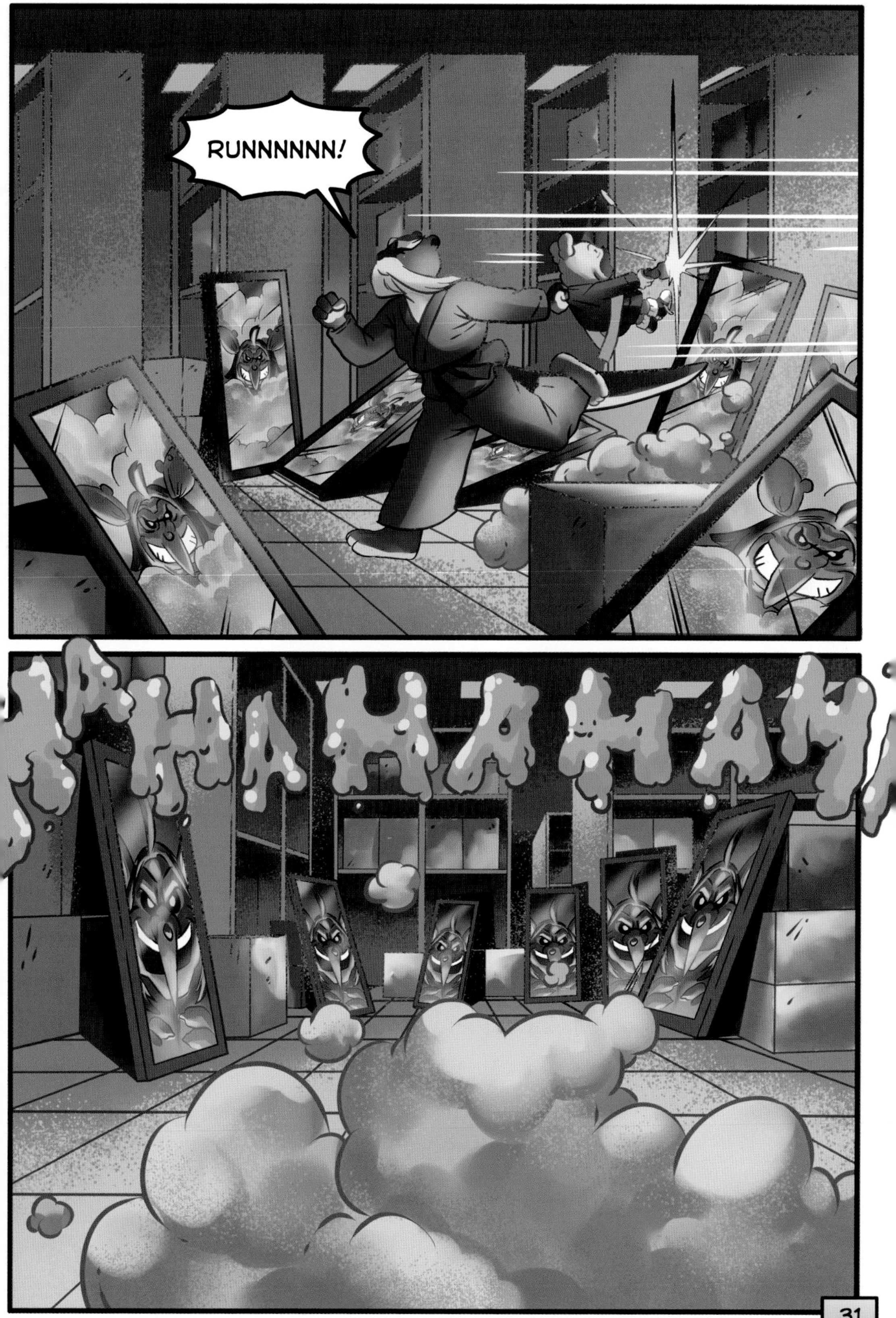
RUNNNNNN!
HAHAHAHA

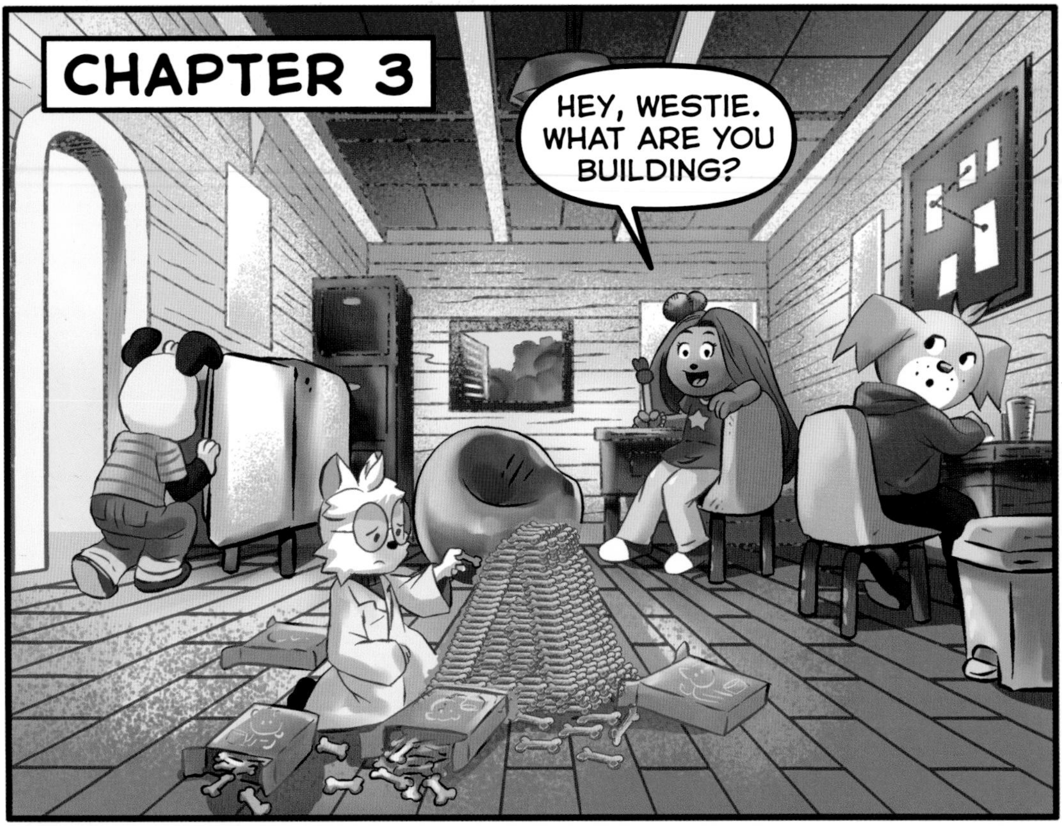
CHAPTER 3
HEY, WESTIE. WHAT ARE YOU BUILDING?

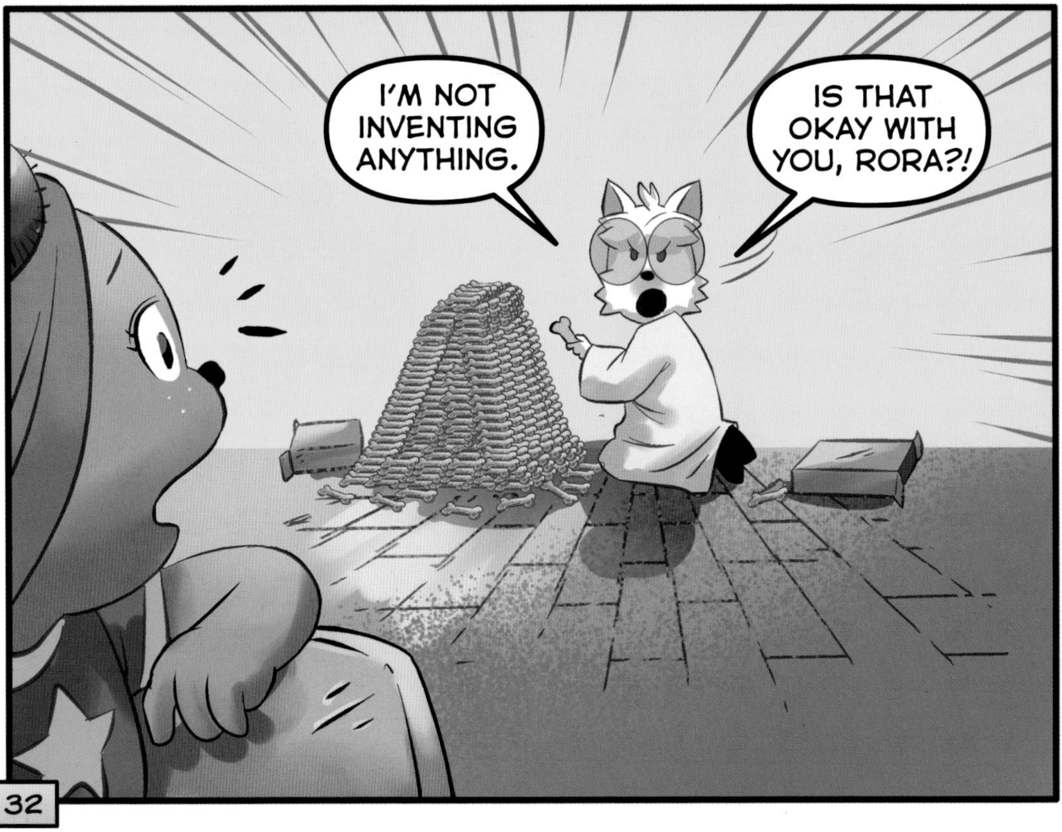
I'M NOT INVENTING ANYTHING.
IS THAT OKAY WITH YOU, RORA?!

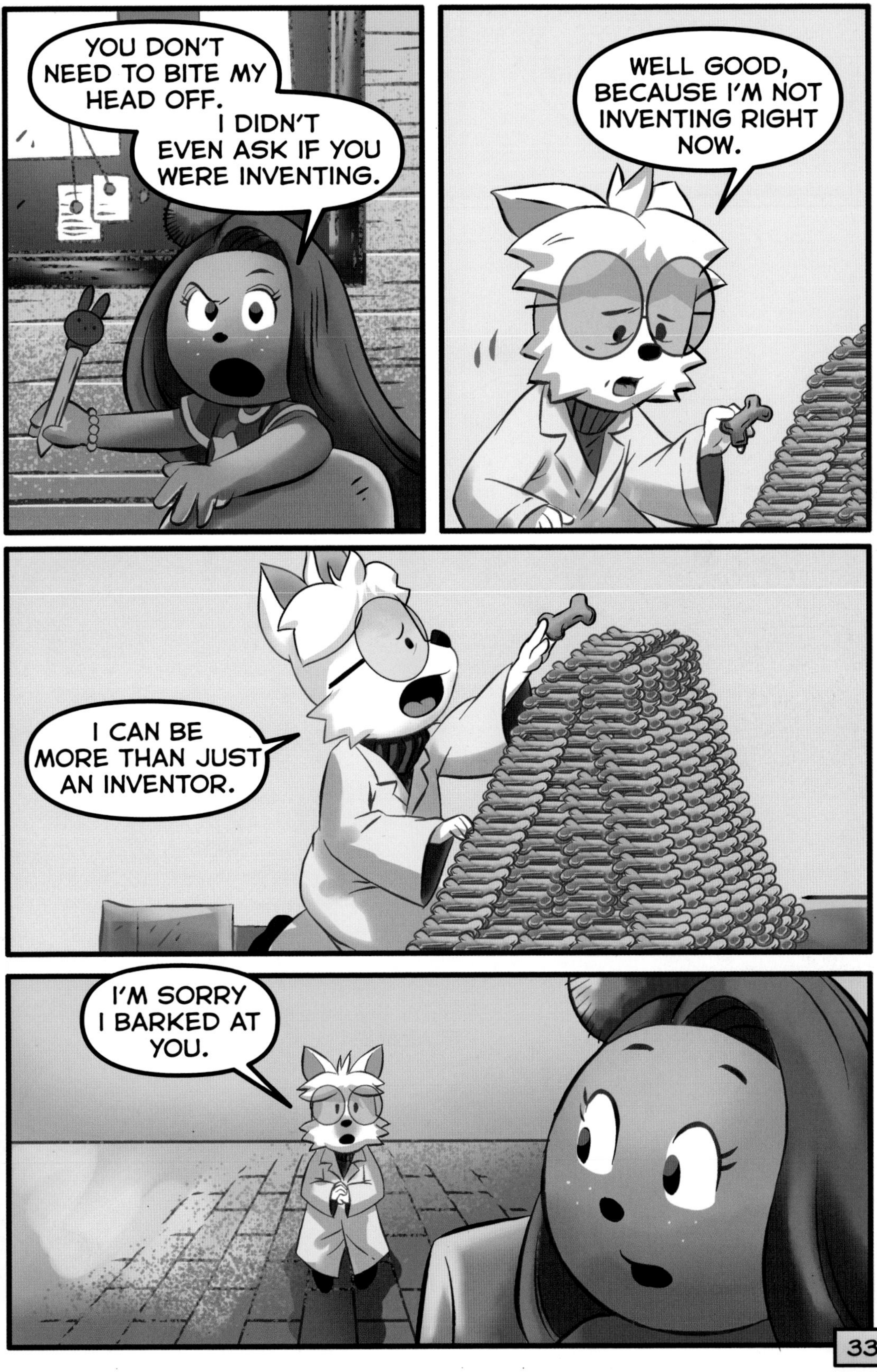
YOU DON'T NEED TO BITE MY HEAD OFF.
I DIDN'T EVEN ASK IF YOU WERE INVENTING.
WELL GOOD, BECAUSE I'M NOT INVENTING RIGHT NOW.
I CAN BE MORE THAN JUST AN INVENTOR.
I'M SORRY I BARKED AT YOU.

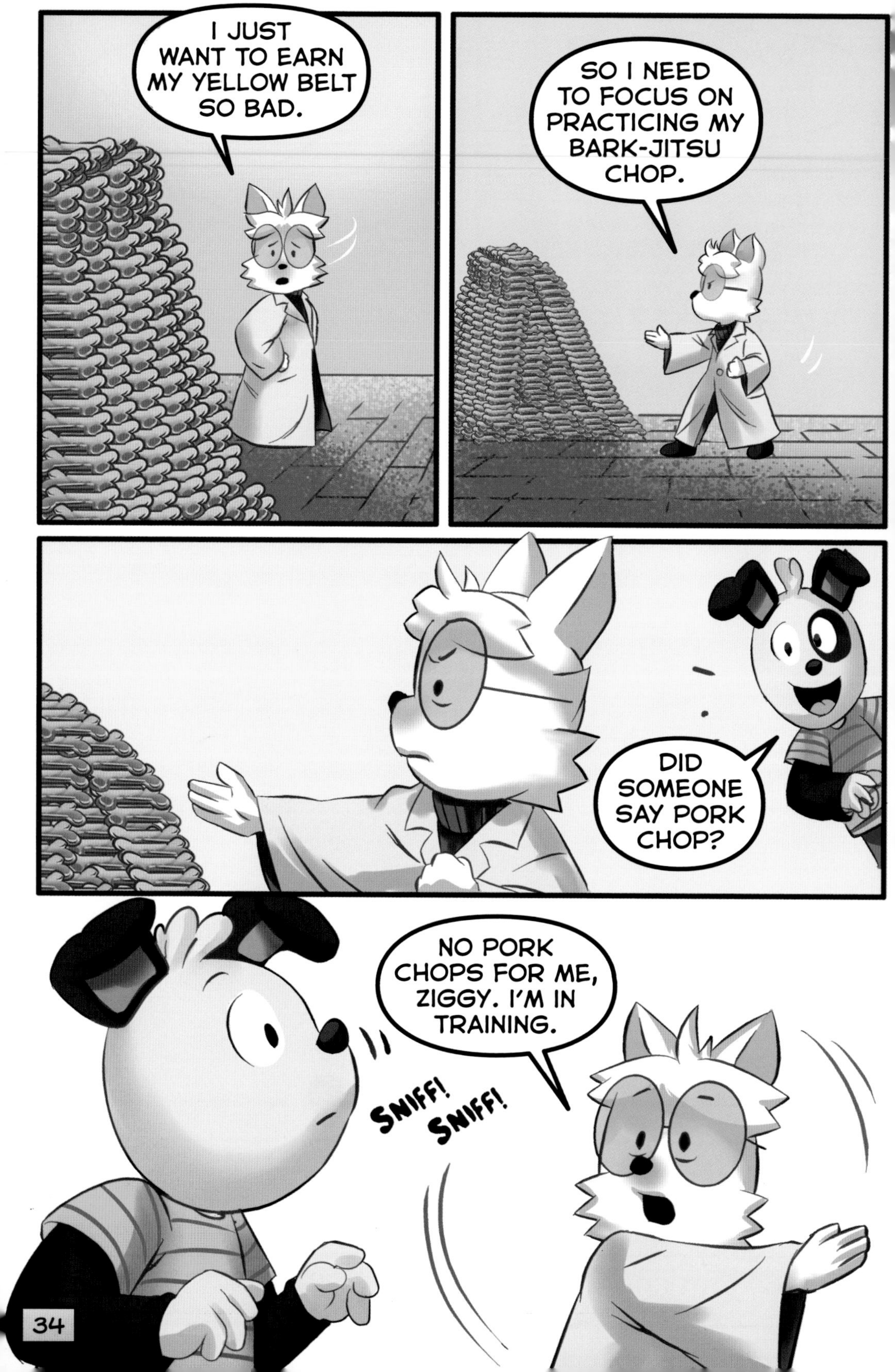
I JUST WANT TO EARN MY YELLOW BELT SO BAD.
SO I NEED TO FOCUS ON PRACTICING MY BARK-JITSU CHOP.
DID SOMEONE SAY PORK CHOP?
NO PORK CHOPS FOR ME, ZIGGY. I'M IN TRAINING.
SNIFF! SNIFF!

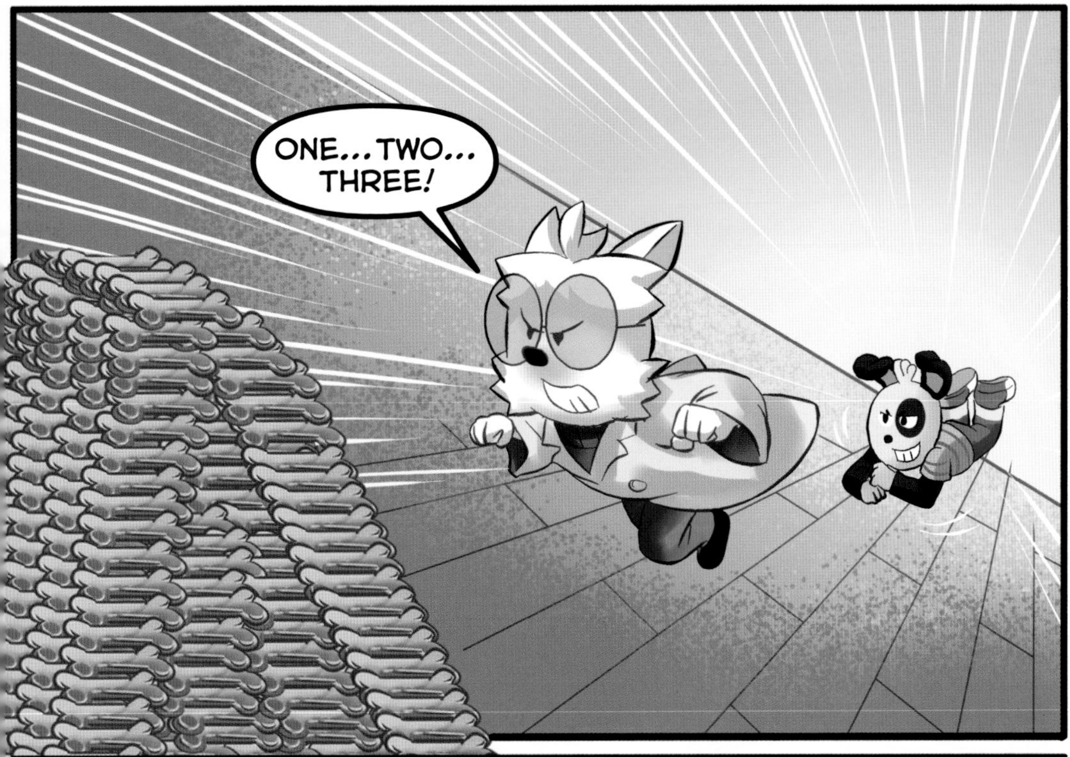
ONE... TWO... THREE!

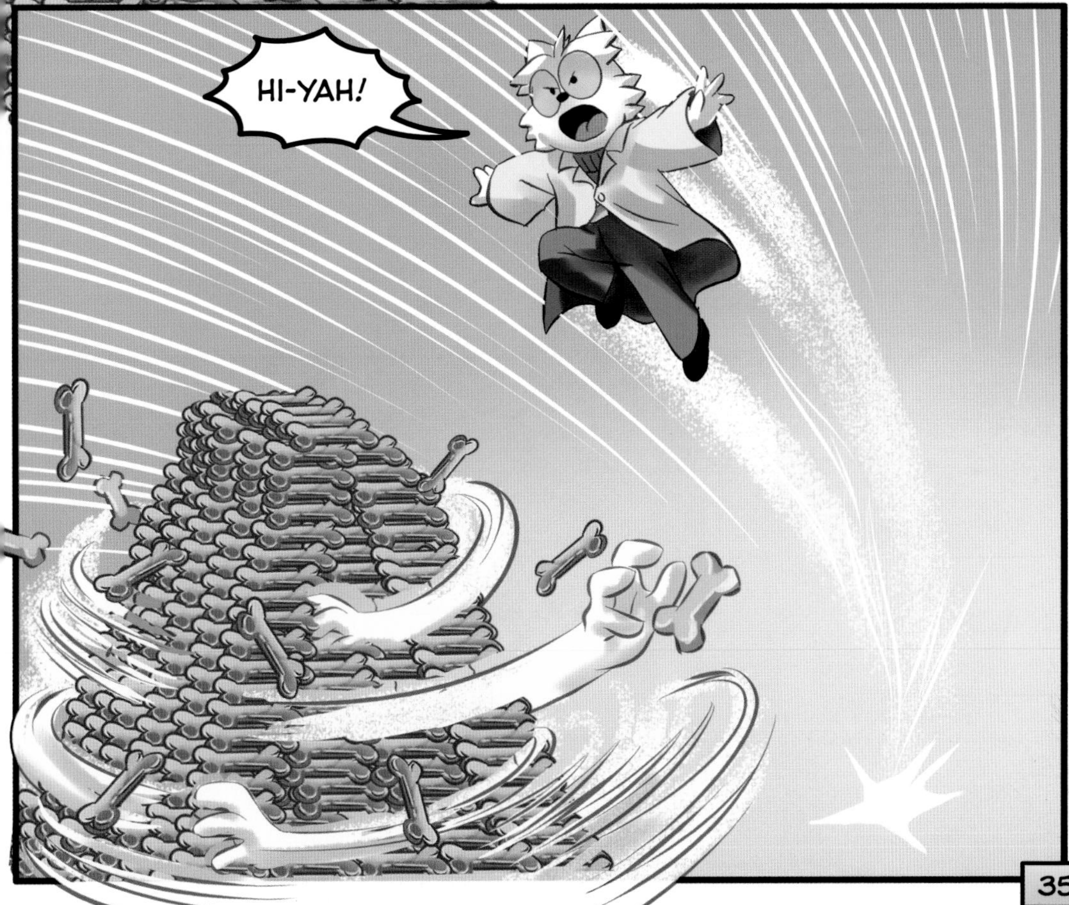
HI-YAH!

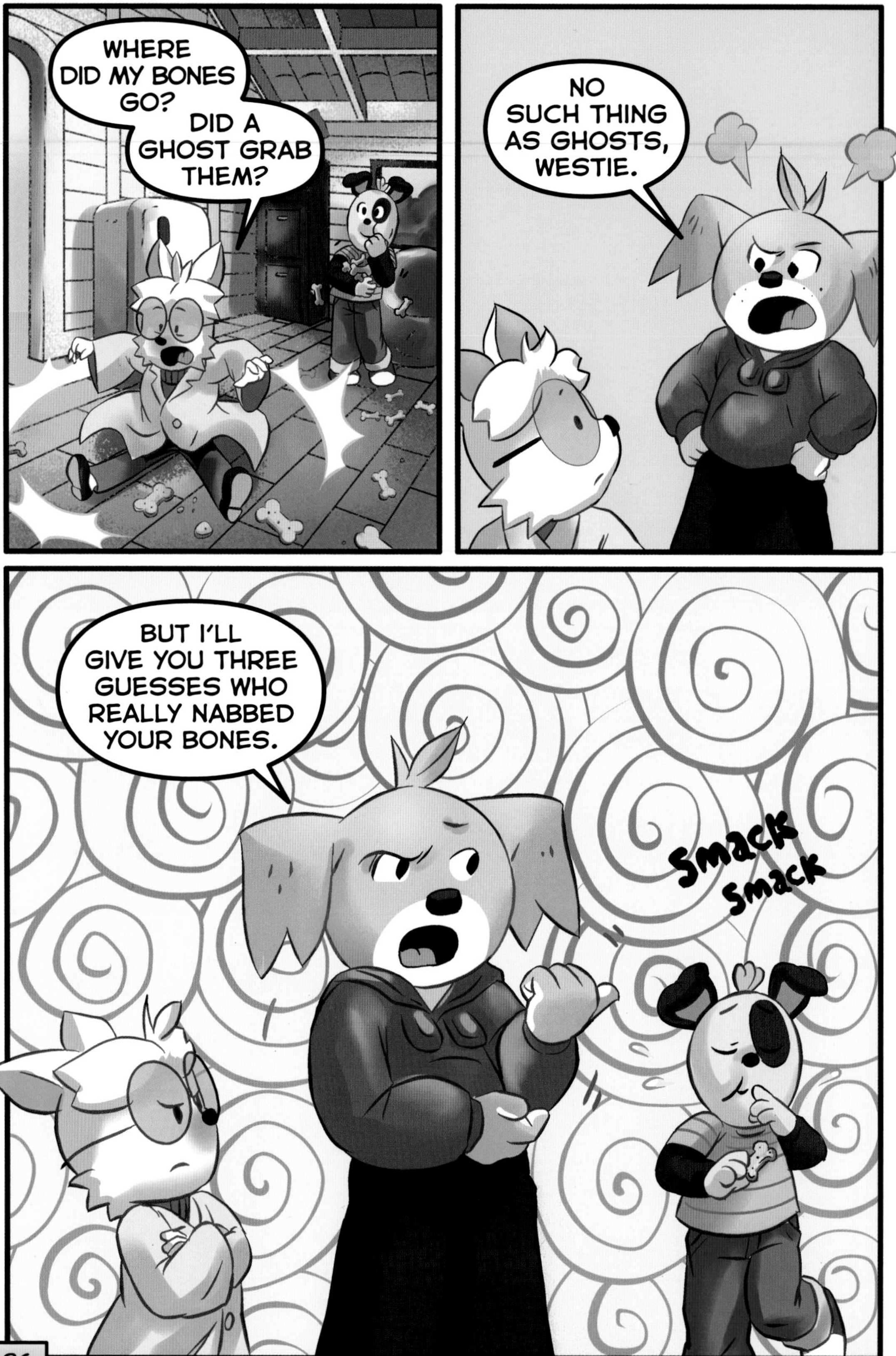
WHERE DID MY BONES GO?
DID A GHOST GRAB THEM?
NO SUCH THING AS GHOSTS, WESTIE.
BUT I'LL GIVE YOU THREE GUESSES WHO REALLY NABBED YOUR BONES.
Smack Smack

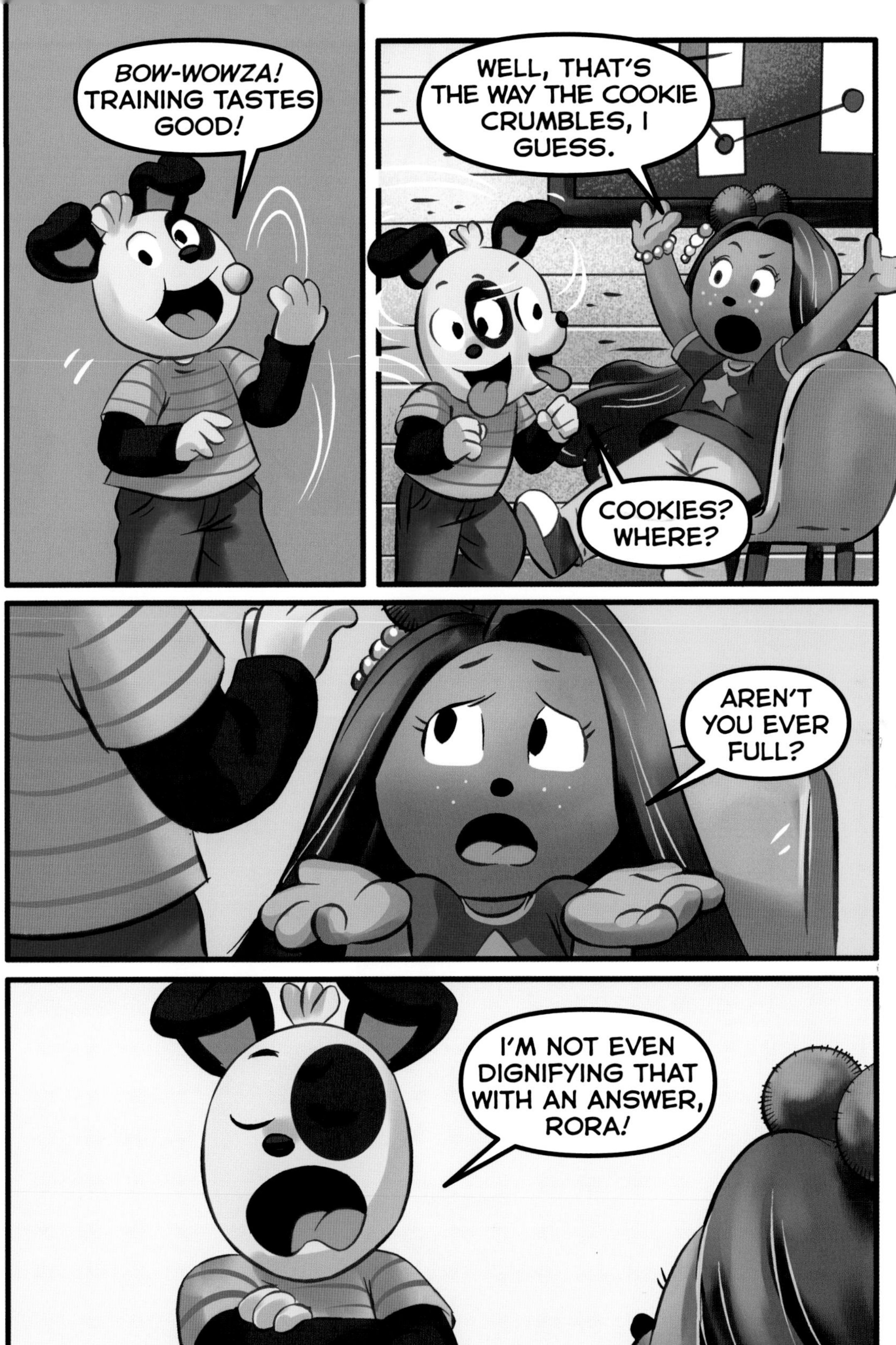
BOW-WOWZA! TRAINING TASTES GOOD!
WELL, THAT'S THE WAY THE COOKIE CRUMBLES, I GUESS.
COOKIES? WHERE?
AREN'T YOU EVER FULL?
I'M NOT EVEN DIGNIFYING THAT WITH AN ANSWER, RORA!

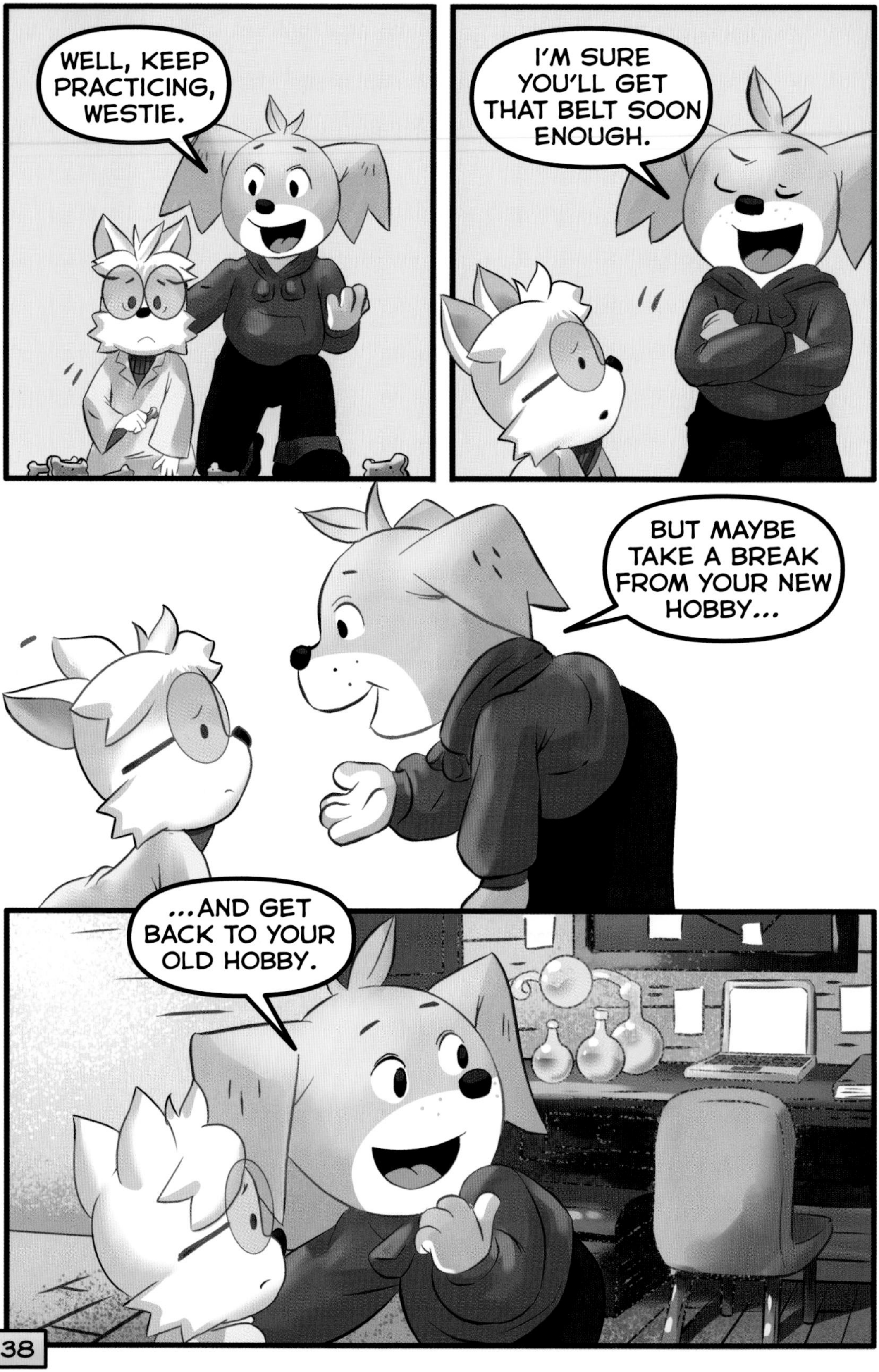
WELL, KEEP PRACTICING, WESTIE.
I'M SURE YOU'LL GET THAT BELT SOON ENOUGH.
BUT MAYBE TAKE A BREAK FROM YOUR NEW HOBBY...
...AND GET BACK TO YOUR OLD HOBBY.

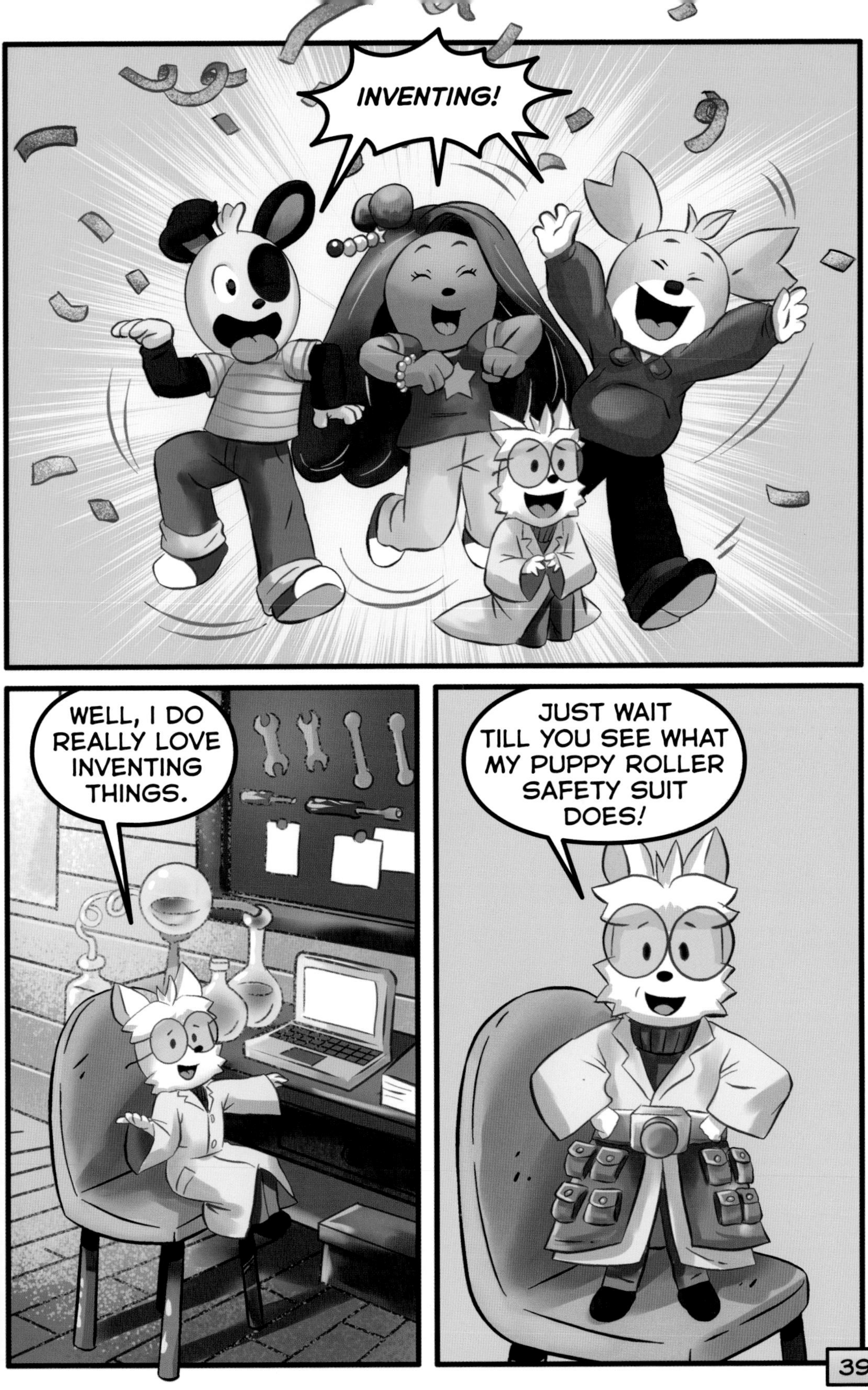
INVENTING!
WELL, I DO REALLY LOVE INVENTING THINGS.
JUST WAIT TILL YOU SEE WHAT MY PUPPY ROLLER SAFETY SUIT DOES!

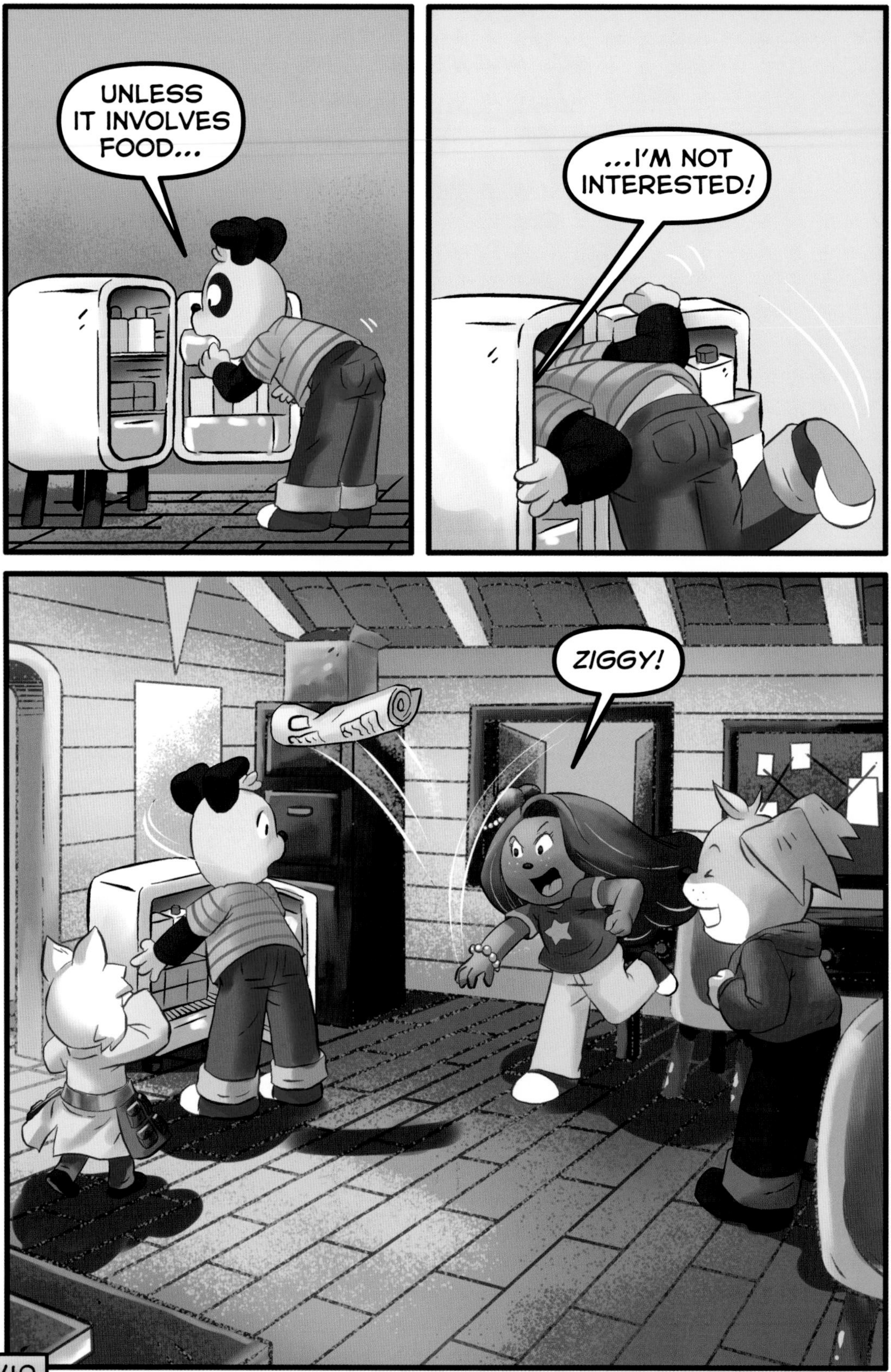
UNLESS IT INVOLVES FOOD...
...I'M NOT INTERESTED!
ZIGGY!

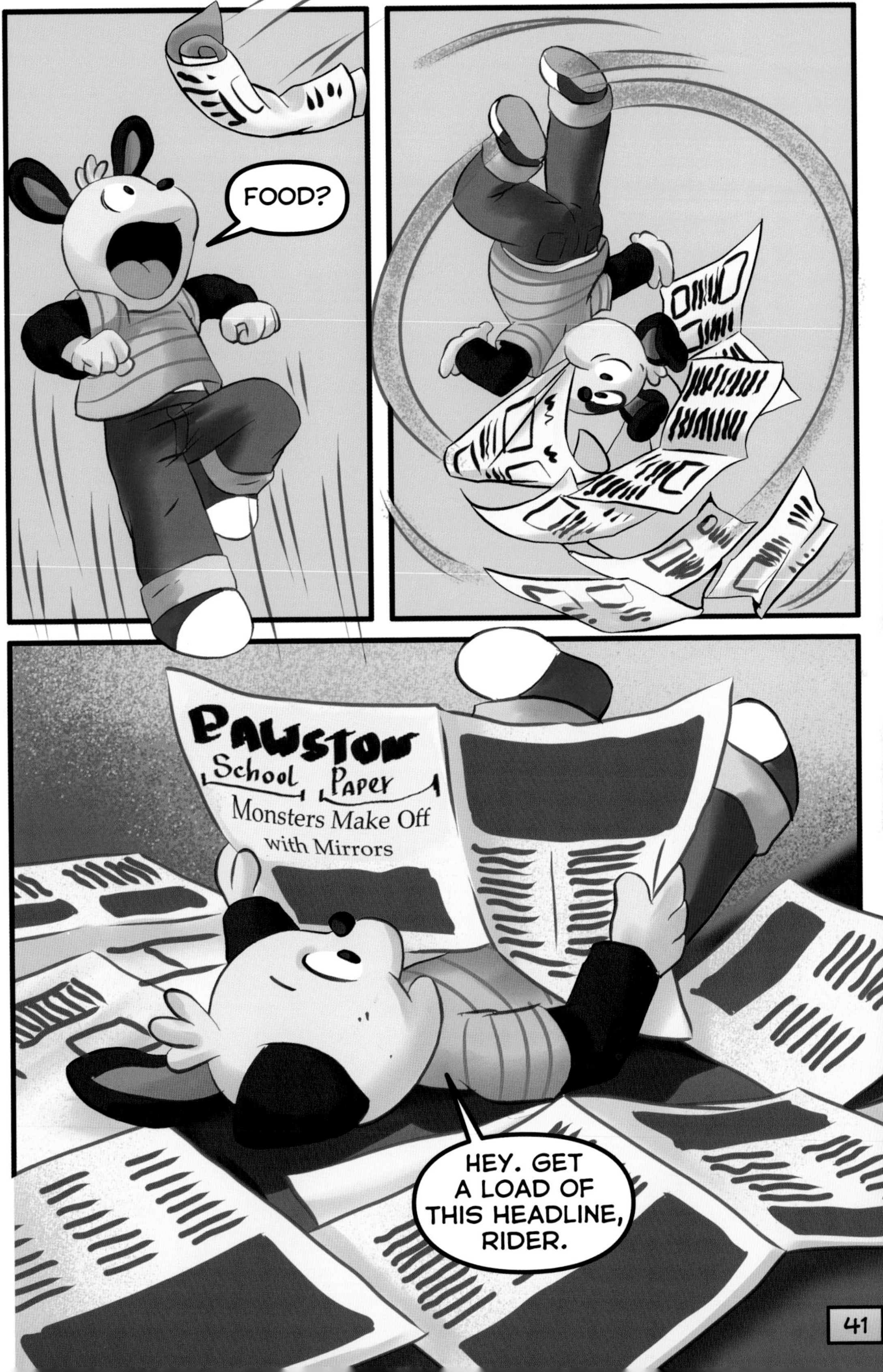
FOOD?
PAWSTON School Paper
Monsters Make Off with Mirrors
HEY. GET A LOAD OF THIS HEADLINE, RIDER.

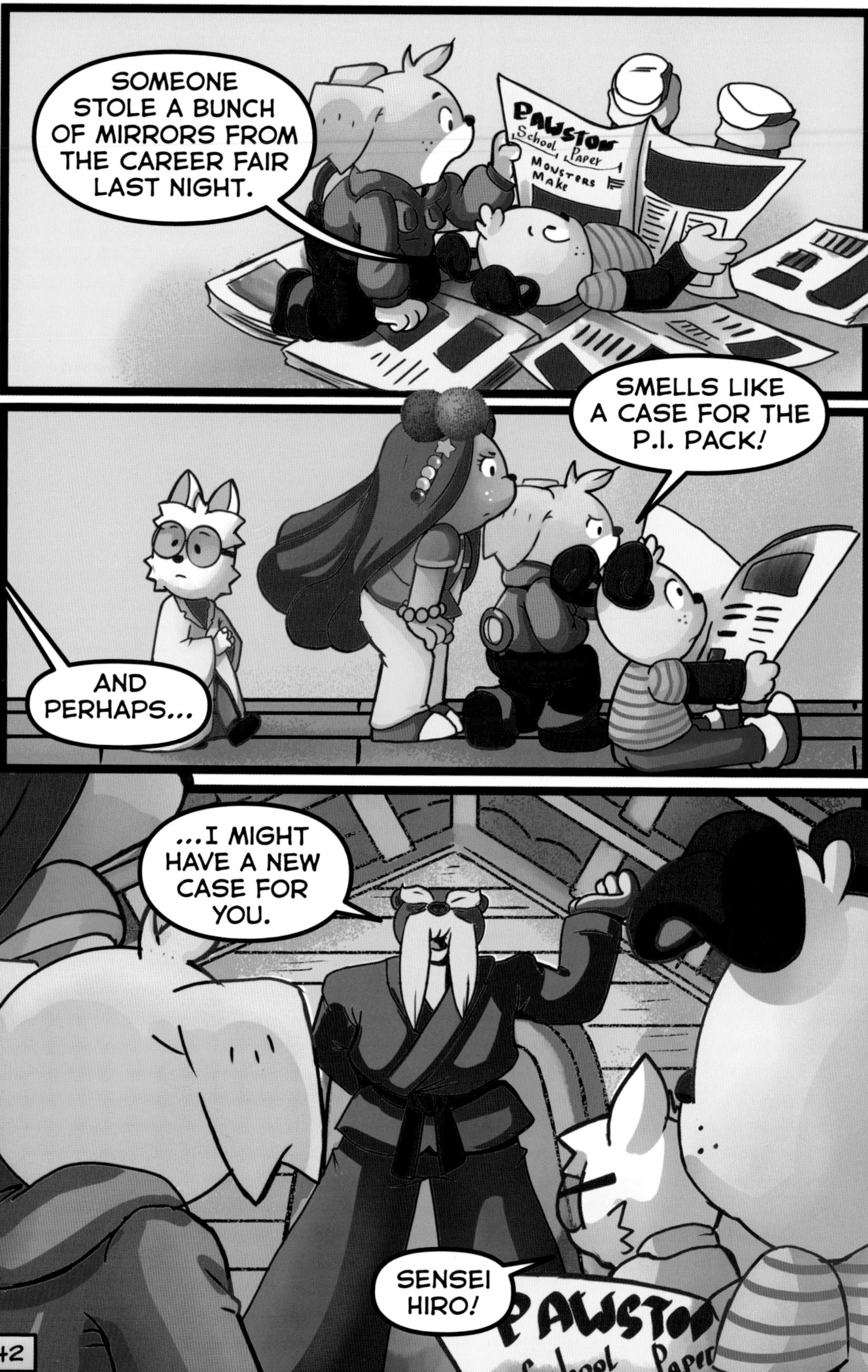
SOMEONE STOLE A BUNCH OF MIRRORS FROM THE CAREER FAIR LAST NIGHT.
PAWSTON School Paper
MONSTERS Make
SMELLS LIKE A CASE FOR THE P.I. PACK!
AND PERHAPS...
...I MIGHT HAVE A NEW CASE FOR YOU.
SENSEI HIRO!
PAWSTON School Paper

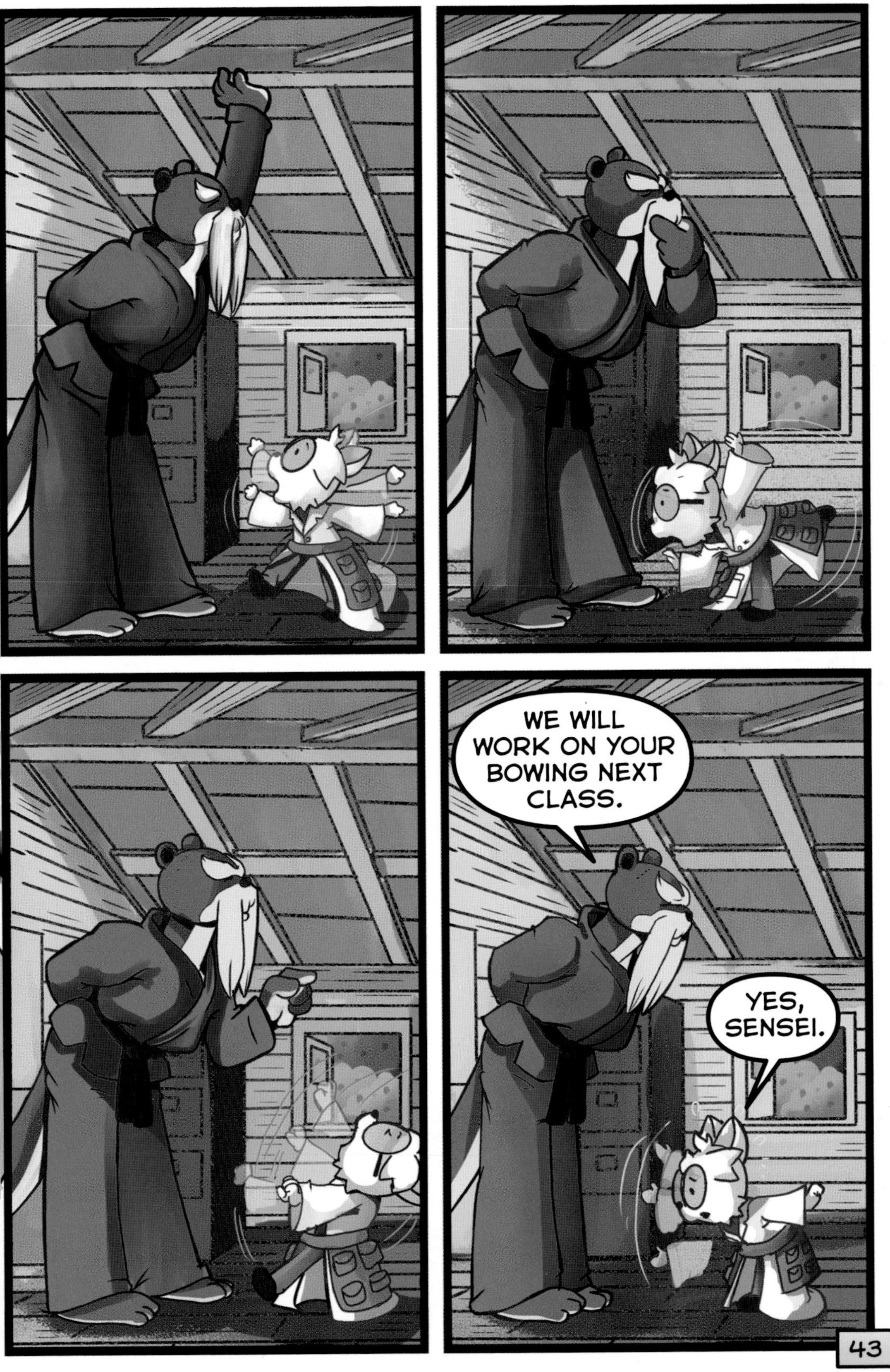
WE WILL WORK ON YOUR BOWING NEXT CLASS.
YES, SENSEI.

CHAPTER 4

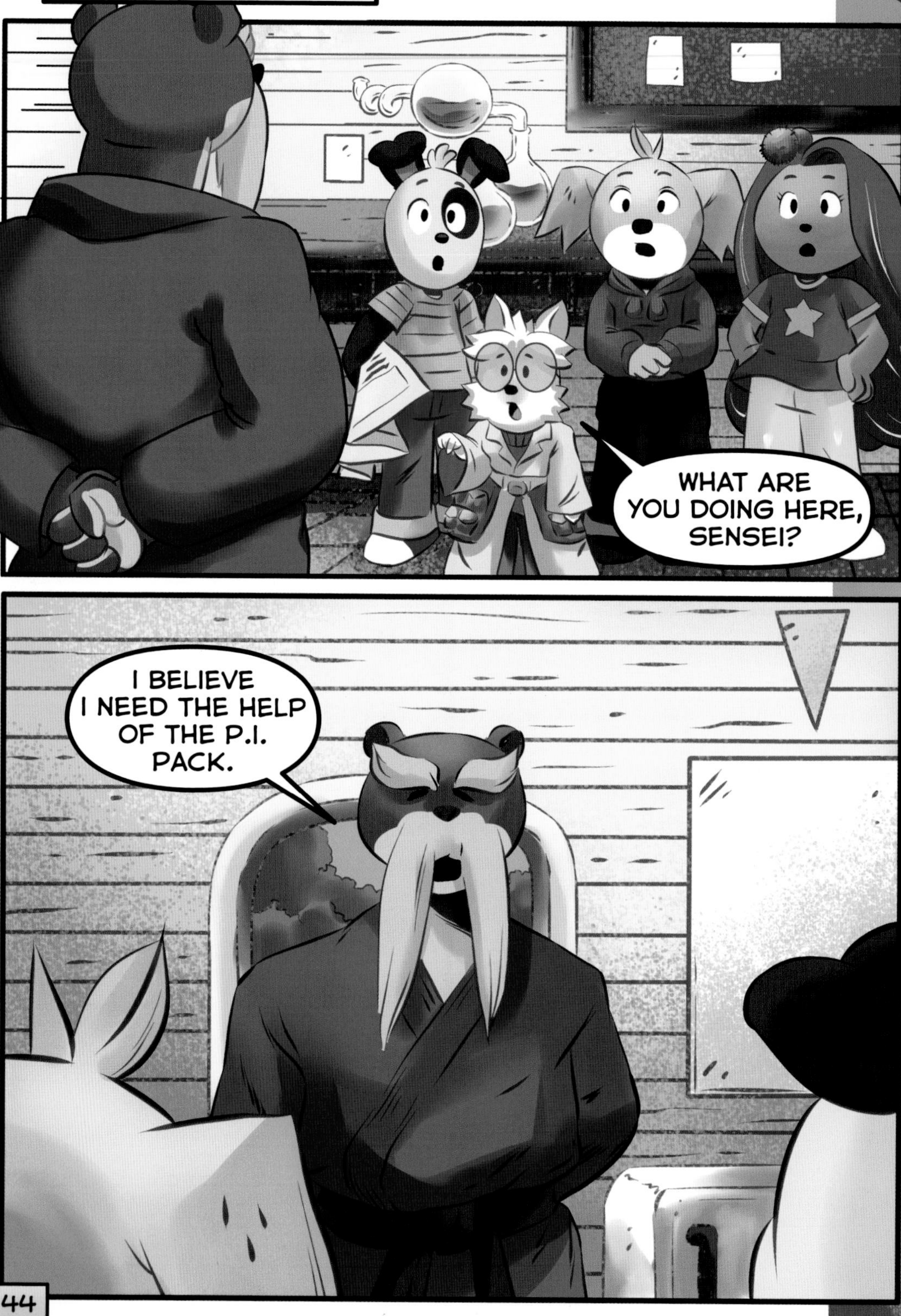

WHAT ARE YOU DOING HERE, SENSEI?
I BELIEVE I NEED THE HELP OF THE P.I. PACK.

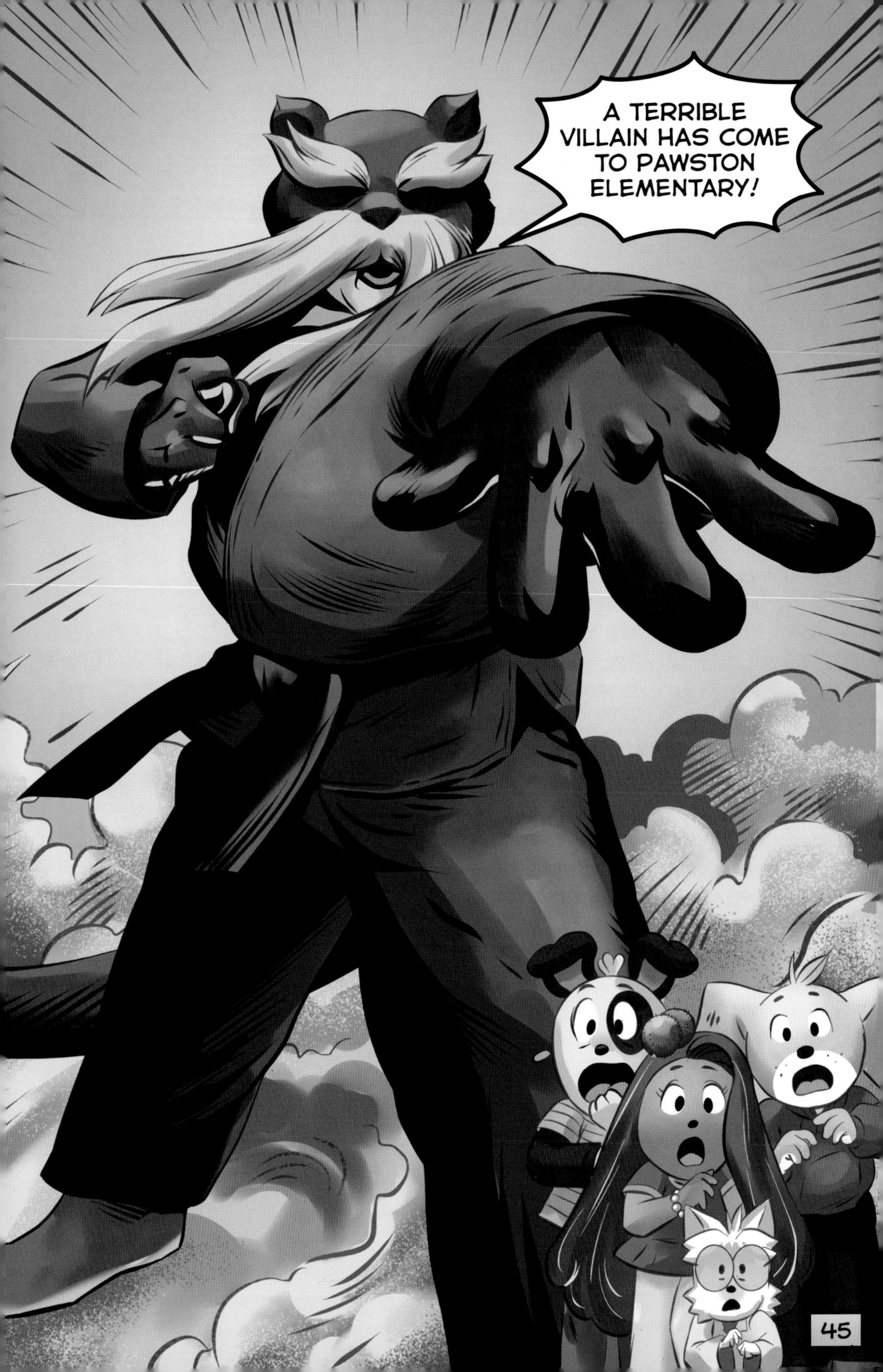
A TERRIBLE VILLAIN HAS COME TO PAWSTON ELEMENTARY!

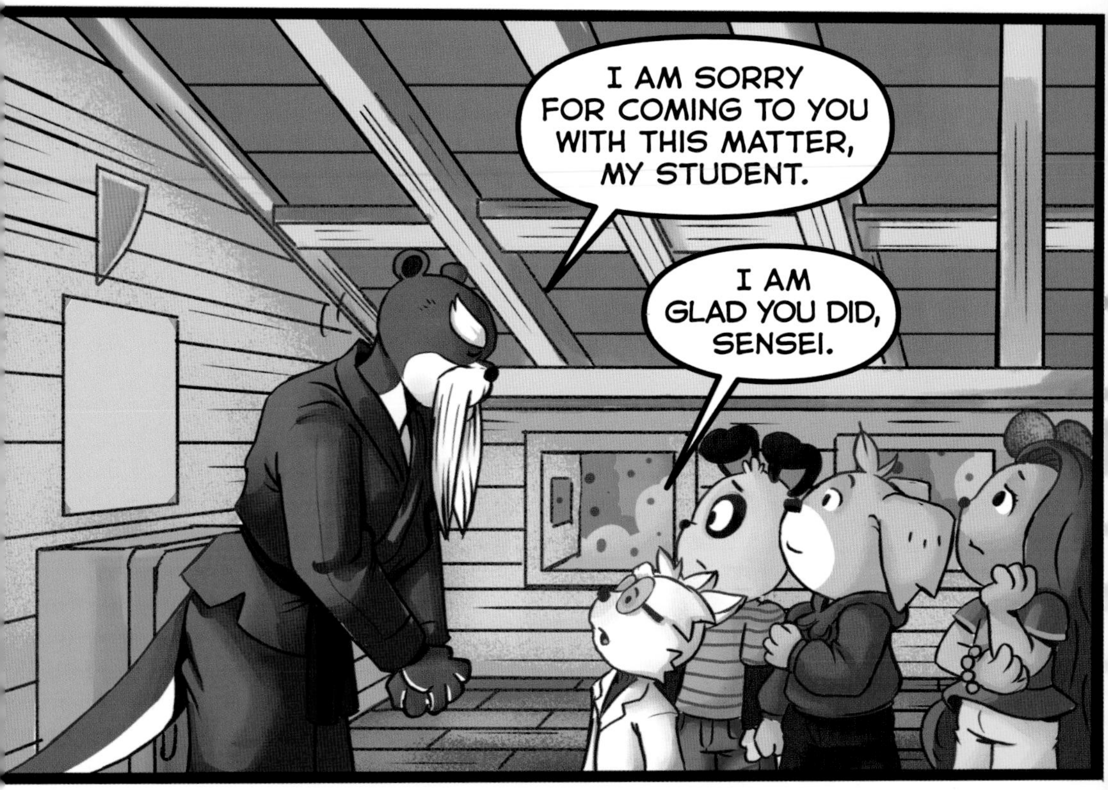
I AM SORRY FOR COMING TO YOU WITH THIS MATTER, MY STUDENT.
I AM GLAD YOU DID, SENSEI.

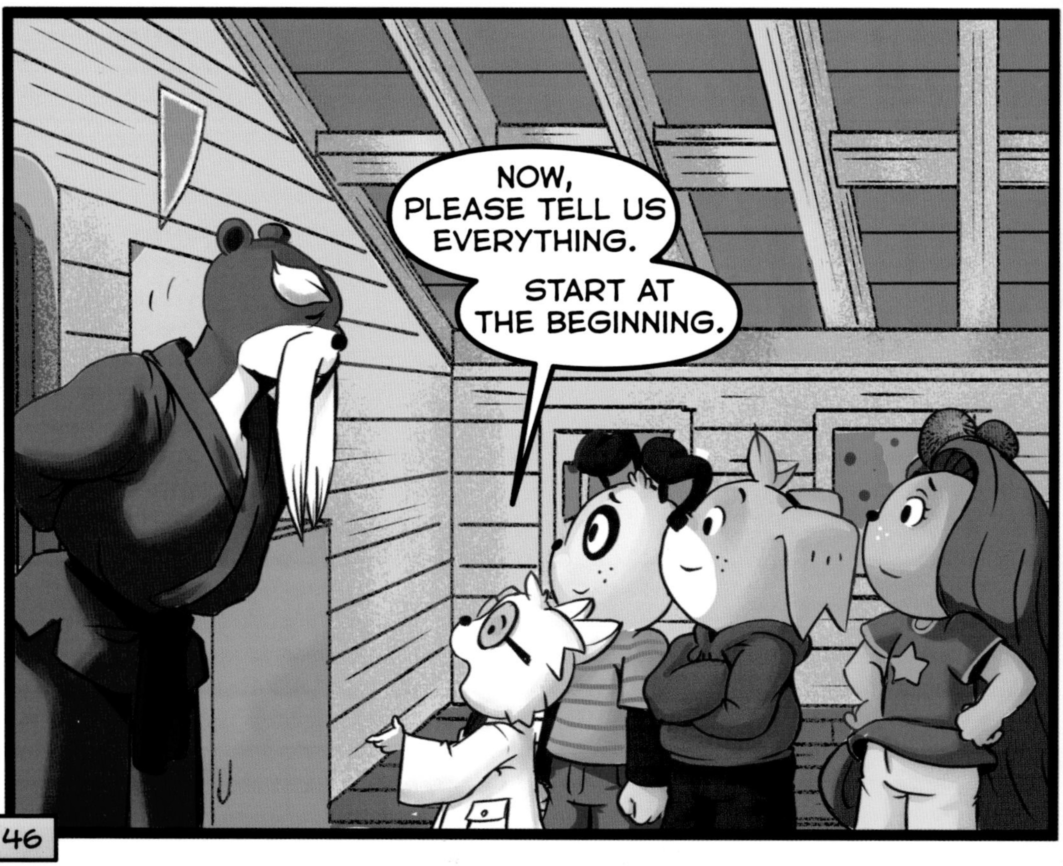
NOW, PLEASE TELL US EVERYTHING.
START AT THE BEGINNING.

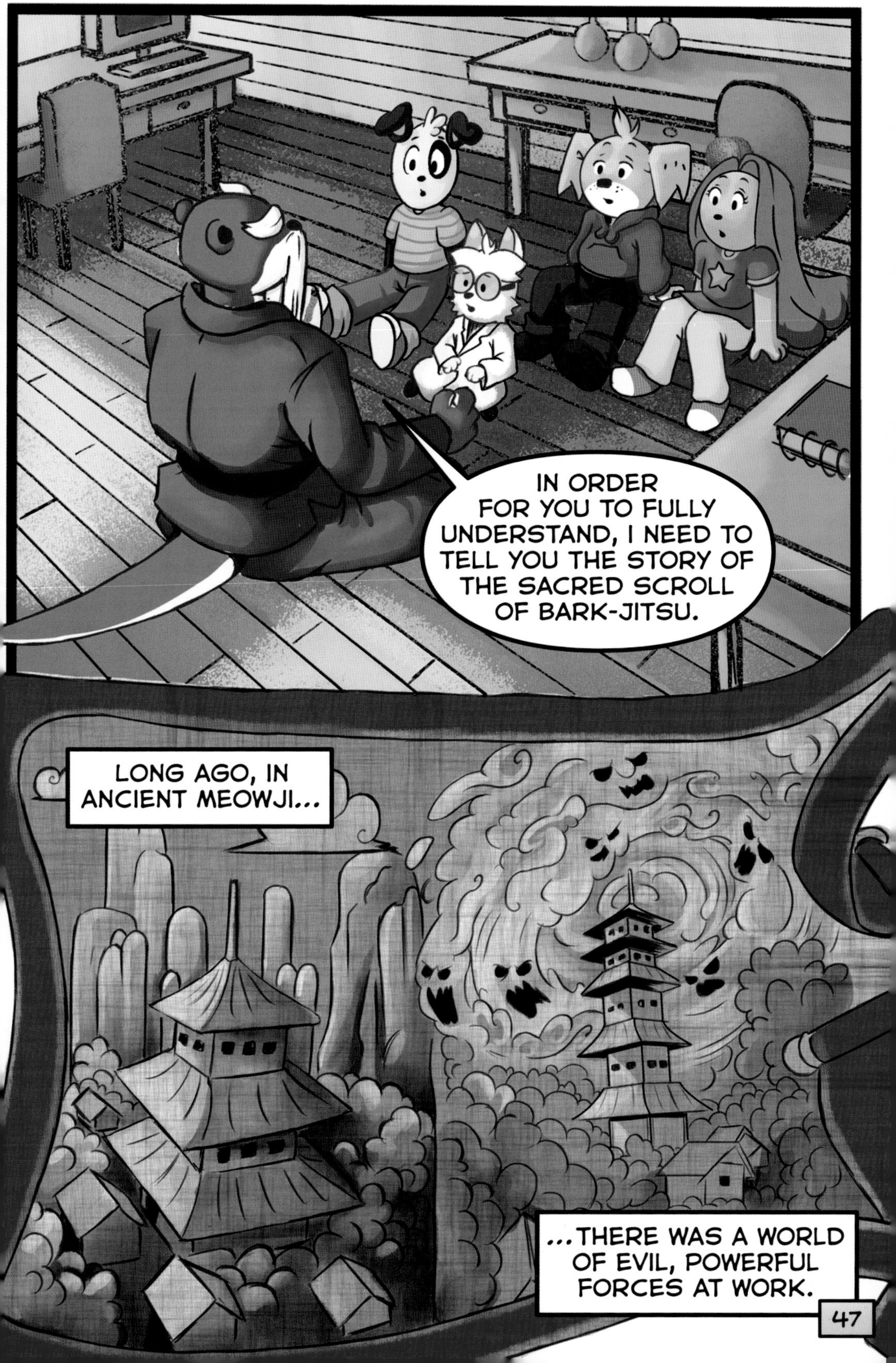
IN ORDER FOR YOU TO FULLY UNDERSTAND, I NEED TO TELL YOU THE STORY OF THE SACRED SCROLL OF BARK-JITSU.
LONG AGO, IN ANCIENT MEOWJI...
...THERE WAS A WORLD OF EVIL, POWERFUL FORCES AT WORK.

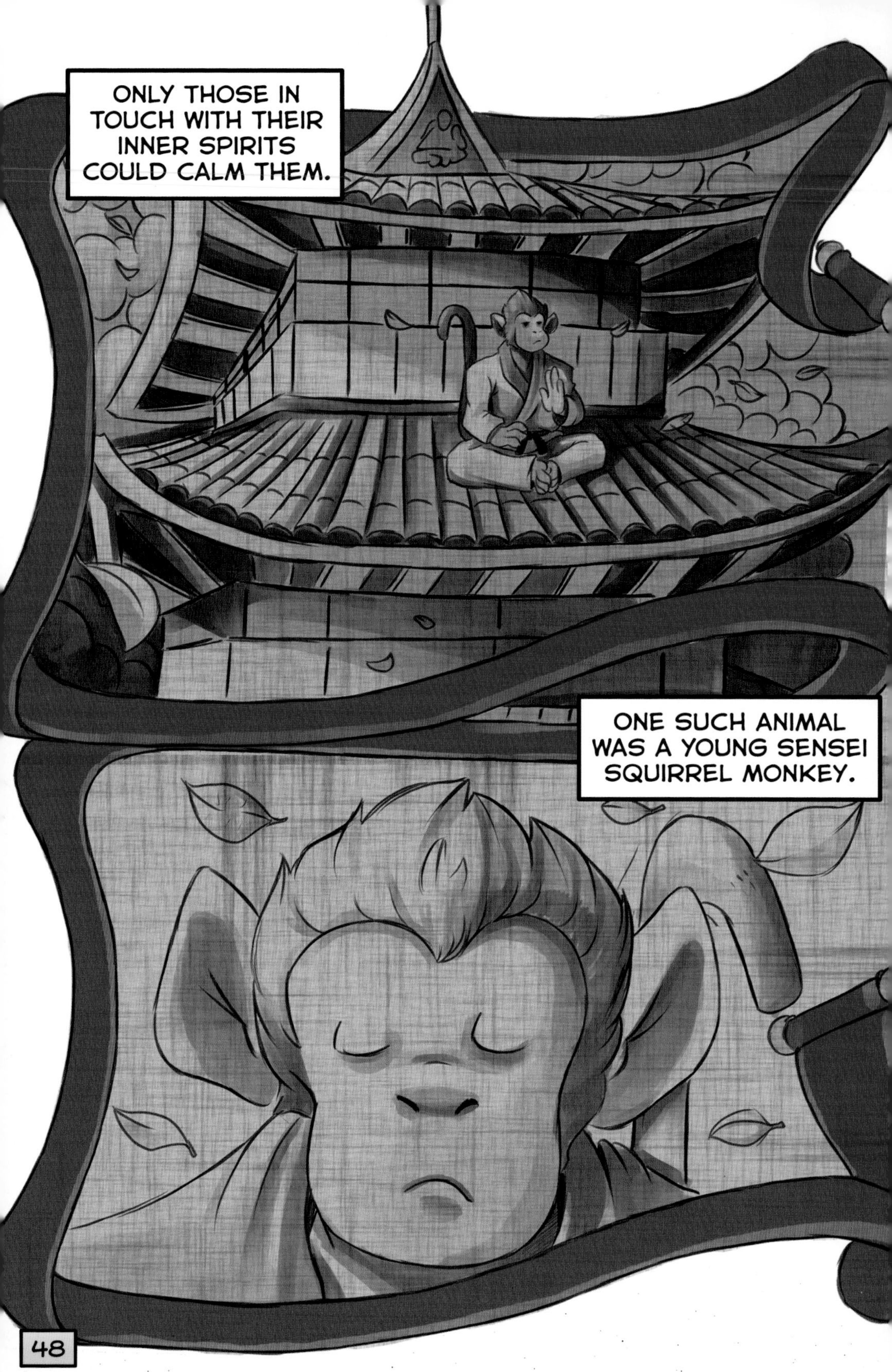
ONLY THOSE IN TOUCH WITH THEIR INNER SPIRITS COULD CALM THEM.
ONE SUCH ANIMAL WAS A YOUNG SENSEI SQUIRREL MONKEY.

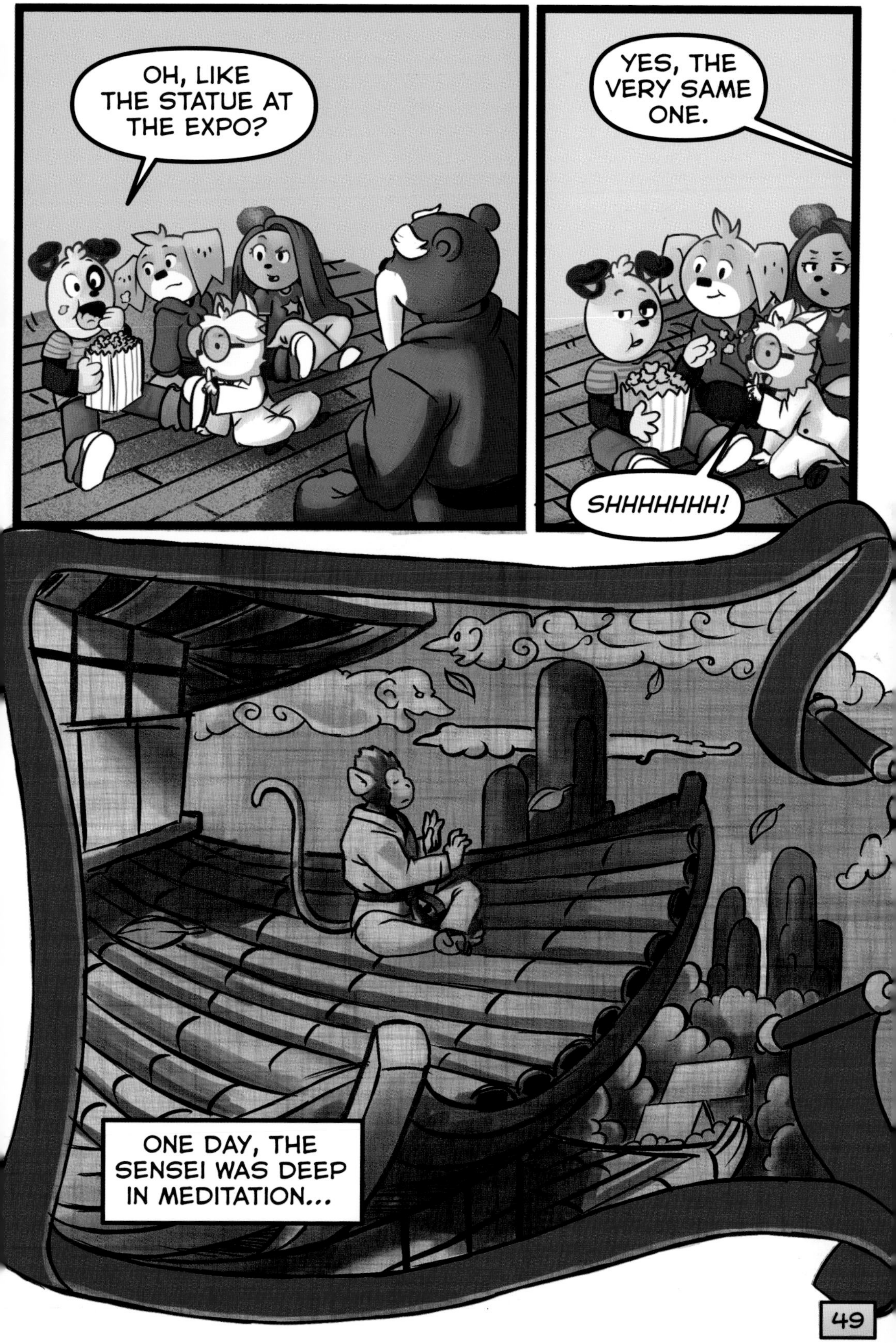
OH, LIKE THE STATUE AT THE EXPO?
YES, THE VERY SAME ONE.
SHHHHHHH!
ONE DAY, THE SENSEI WAS DEEP IN MEDITATION...

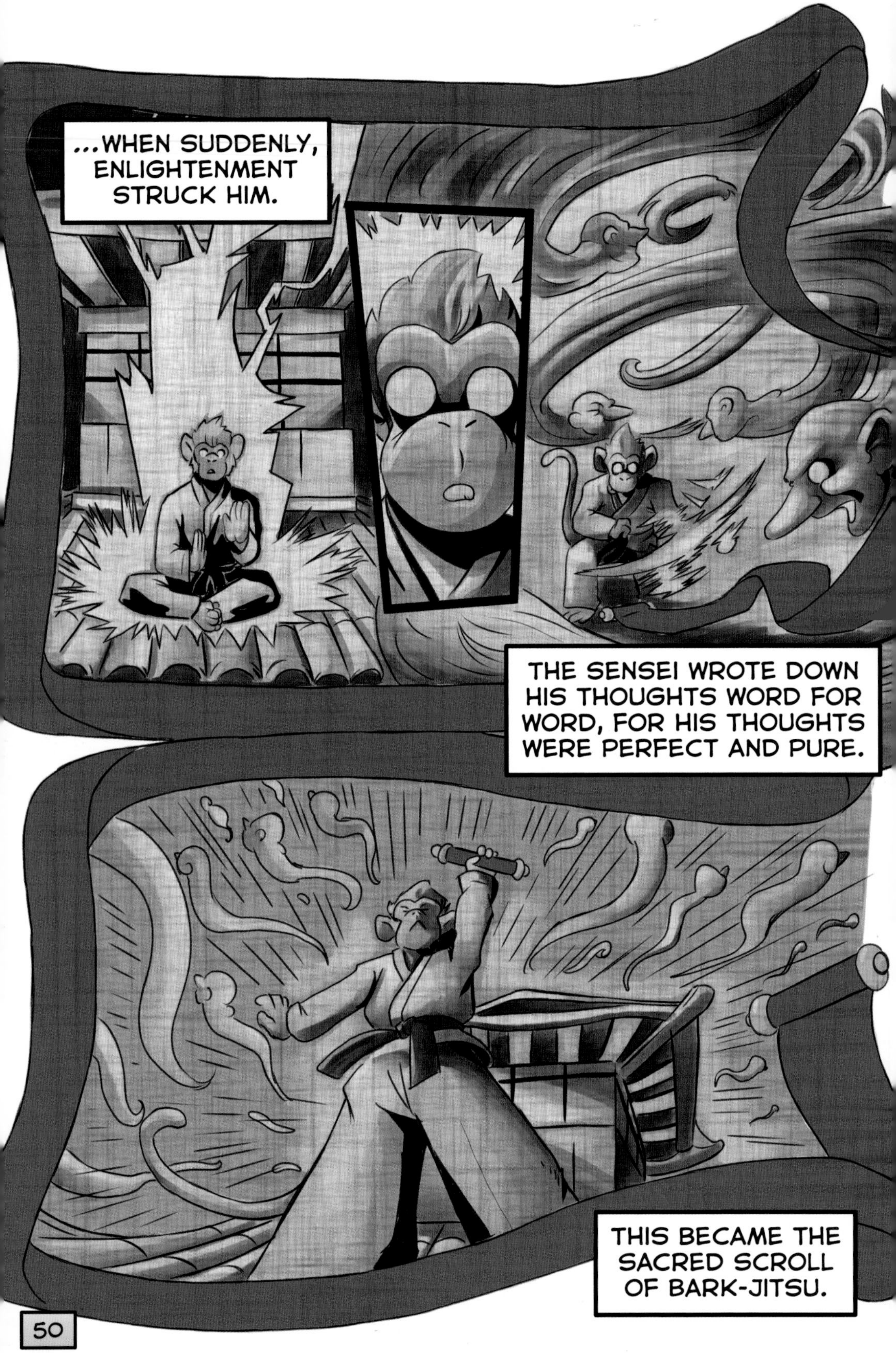
...WHEN SUDDENLY, ENLIGHTENMENT STRUCK HIM.
THE SENSEI WROTE DOWN HIS THOUGHTS WORD FOR WORD, FOR HIS THOUGHTS WERE PERFECT AND PURE.
THIS BECAME THE SACRED SCROLL OF BARK-JITSU.

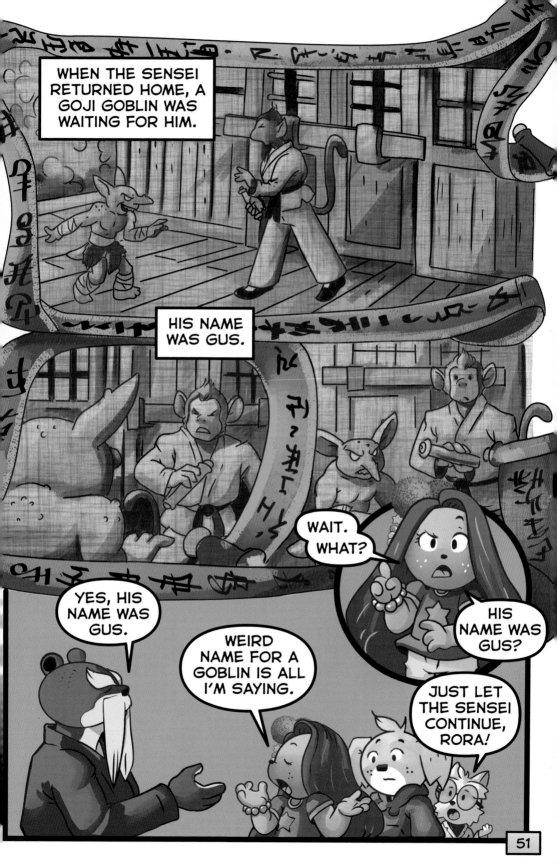

WHEN THE SENSEI RETURNED HOME, A GOJI GOBLIN WAS WAITING FOR HIM.

HIS NAME WAS GUS.

WAIT. WHAT?

YES, HIS NAME WAS GUS.

WEIRD NAME FOR A GOBLIN IS ALL I'M SAYING.

HIS NAME WAS GUS?

JUST LET THE SENSEI CONTINUE, RORA!

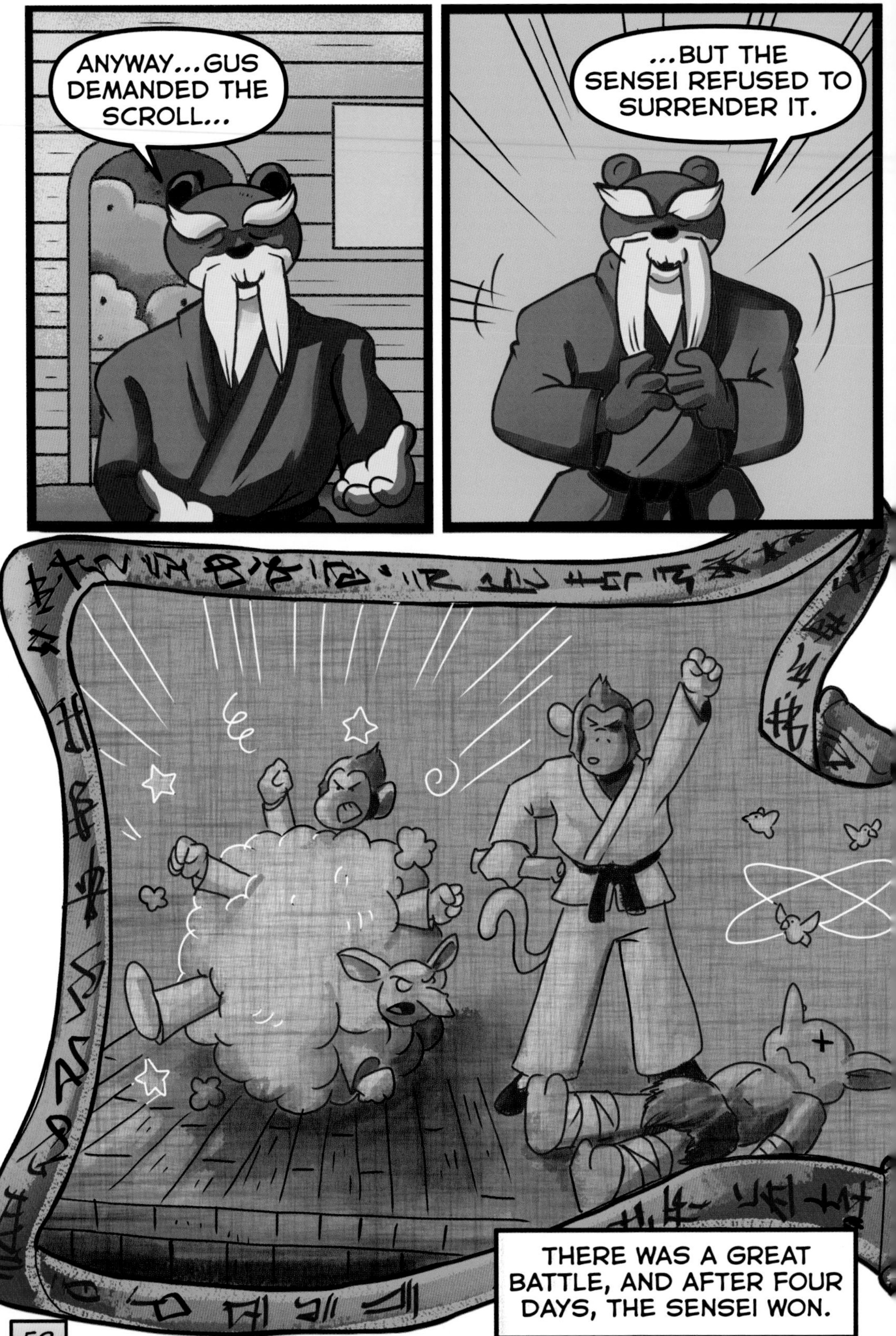
ANYWAY...GUS DEMANDED THE SCROLL...
...BUT THE SENSEI REFUSED TO SURRENDER IT.
THERE WAS A GREAT BATTLE, AND AFTER FOUR DAYS, THE SENSEI WON.

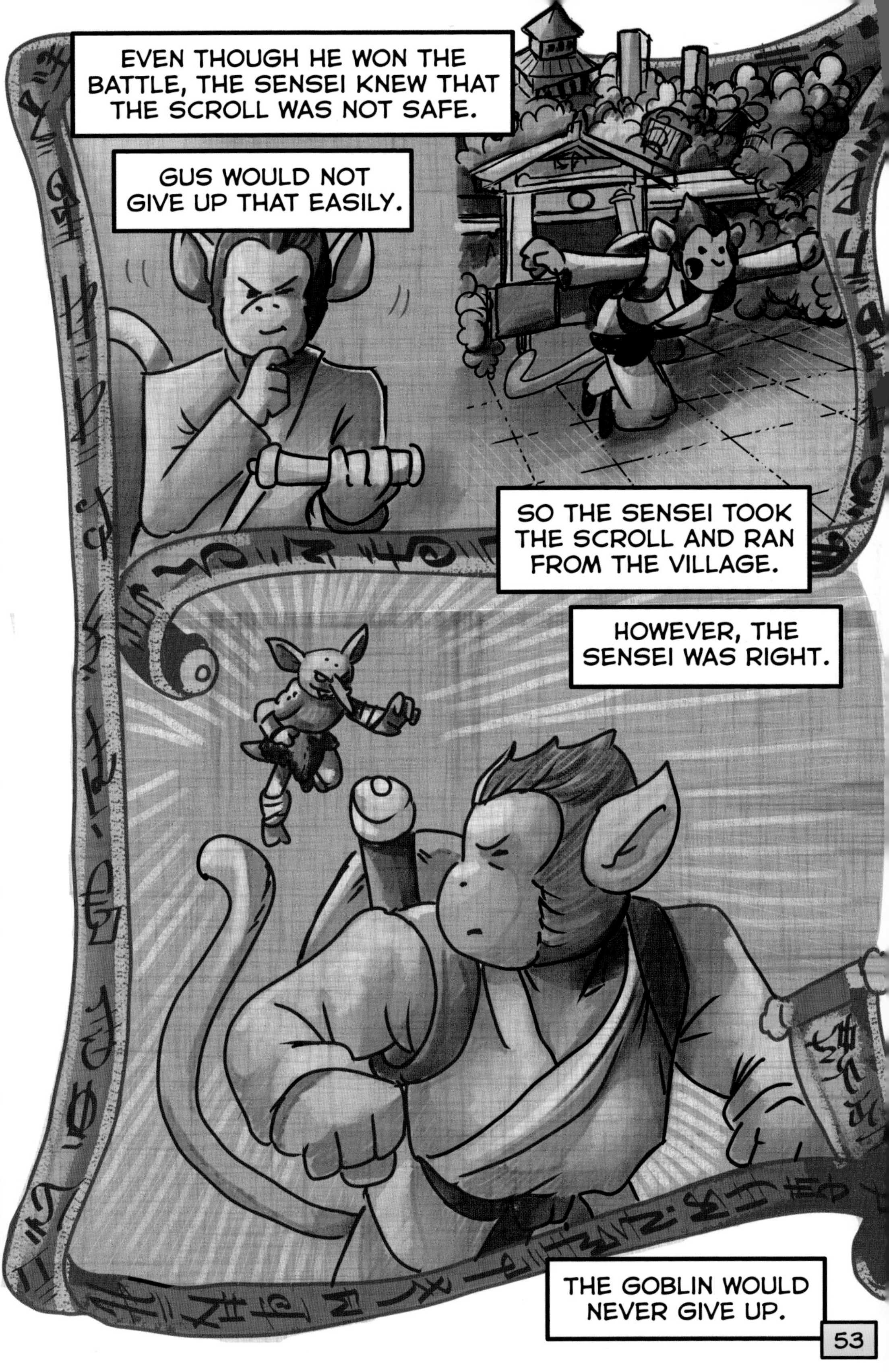
EVEN THOUGH HE WON THE BATTLE, THE SENSEI KNEW THAT THE SCROLL WAS NOT SAFE.
GUS WOULD NOT GIVE UP THAT EASILY.
SO THE SENSEI TOOK THE SCROLL AND RAN FROM THE VILLAGE.
HOWEVER, THE SENSEI WAS RIGHT.
THE GOBLIN WOULD NEVER GIVE UP.

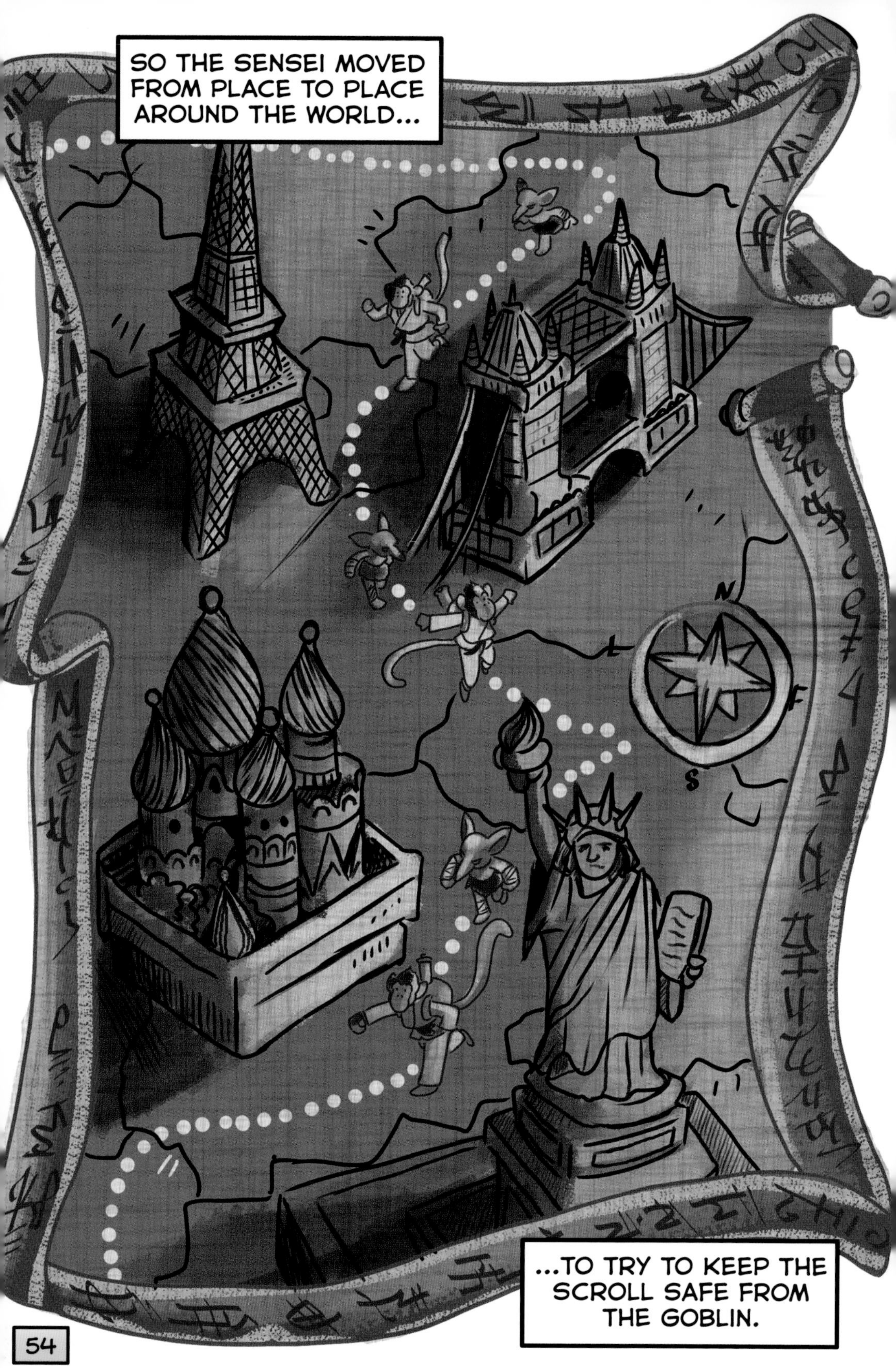
SO THE SENSEI MOVED FROM PLACE TO PLACE AROUND THE WORLD...
...TO TRY TO KEEP THE SCROLL SAFE FROM THE GOBLIN.

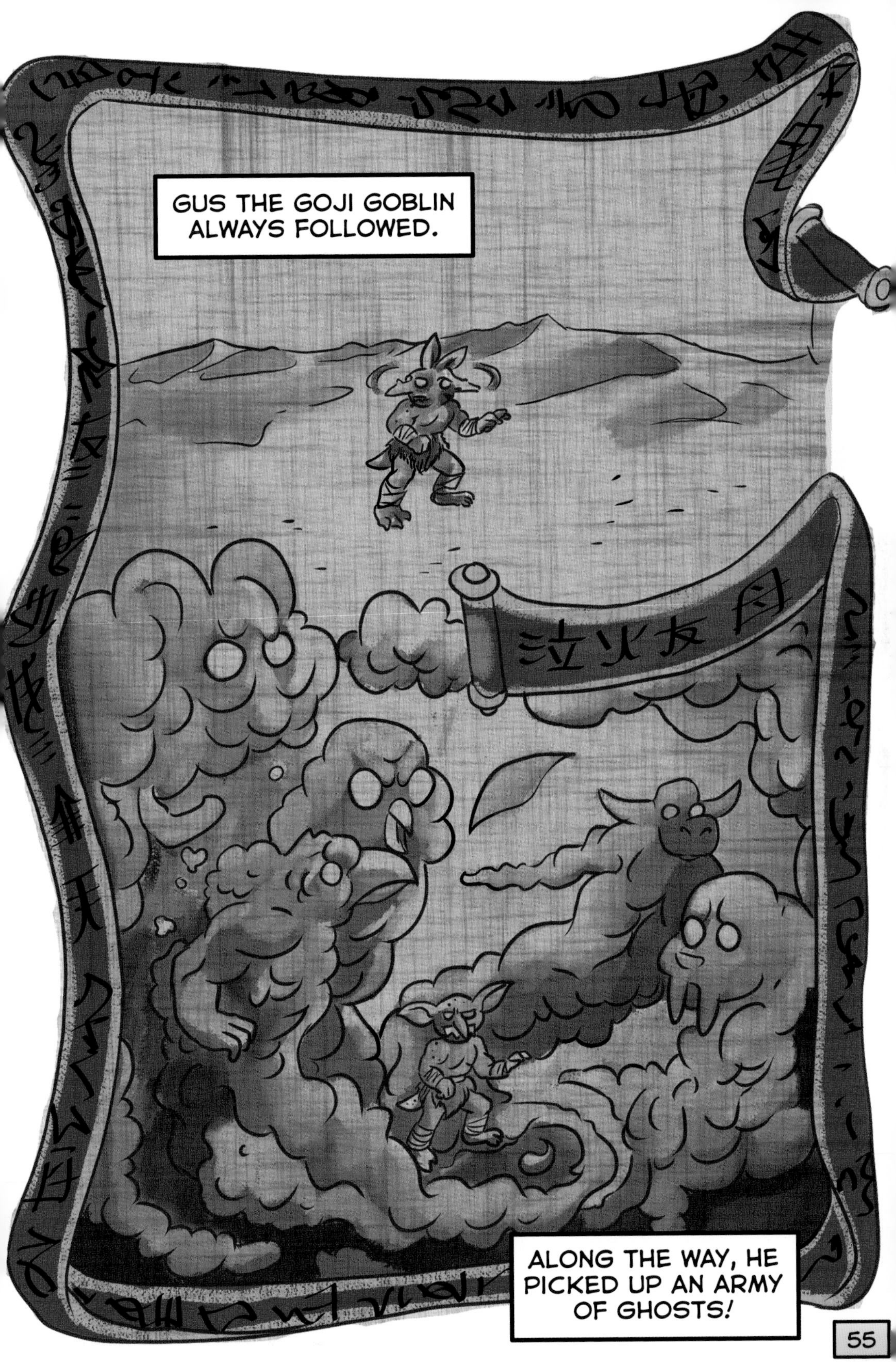
GUS THE GOJI GOBLIN ALWAYS FOLLOWED.
泣火友团
ALONG THE WAY, HE PICKED UP AN ARMY OF GHOSTS!

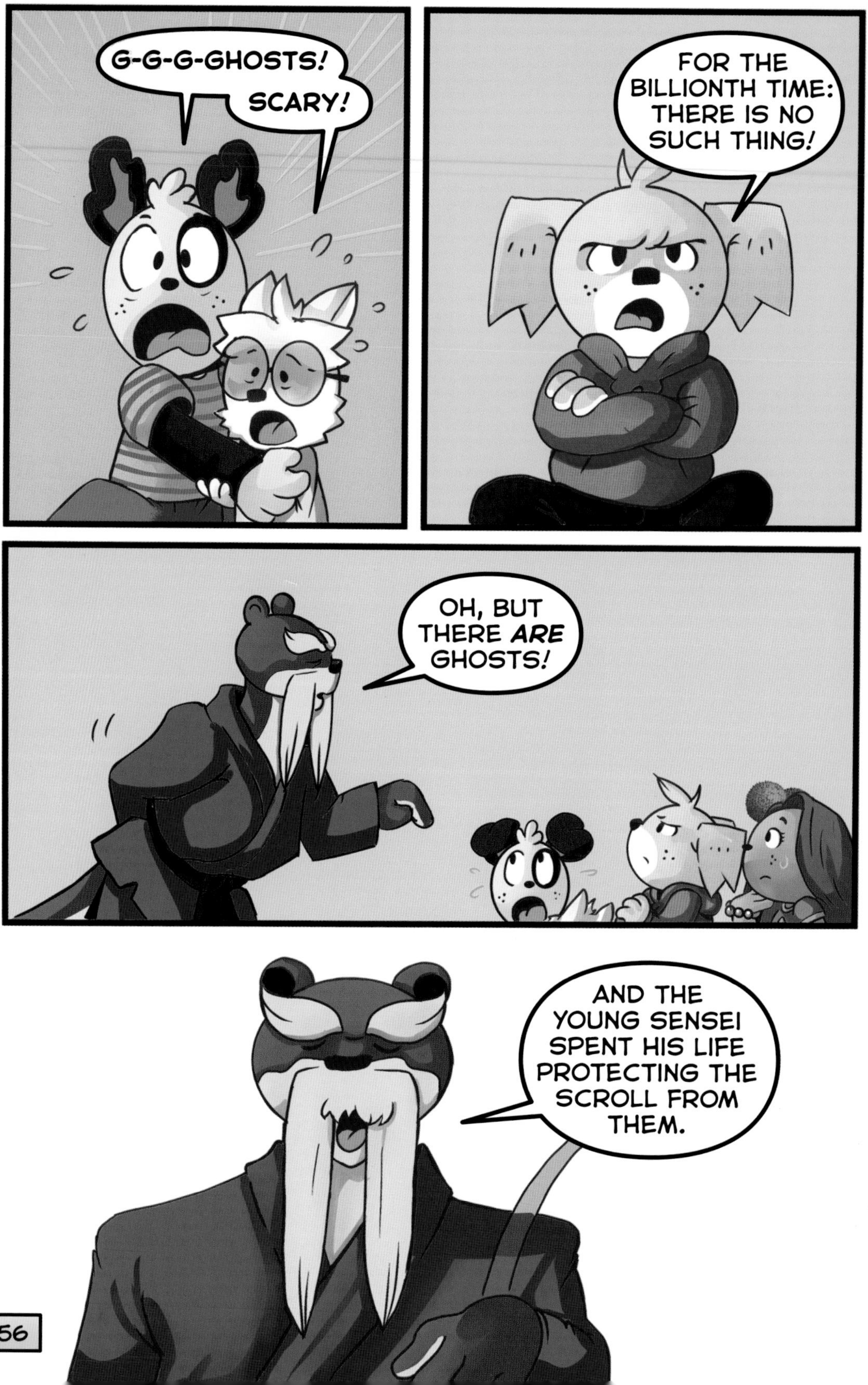
G-G-G-GHOSTS!
SCARY!
FOR THE BILLIONTH TIME: THERE IS NO SUCH THING!
OH, BUT THERE *ARE* GHOSTS!
AND THE YOUNG SENSEI SPENT HIS LIFE PROTECTING THE SCROLL FROM THEM.

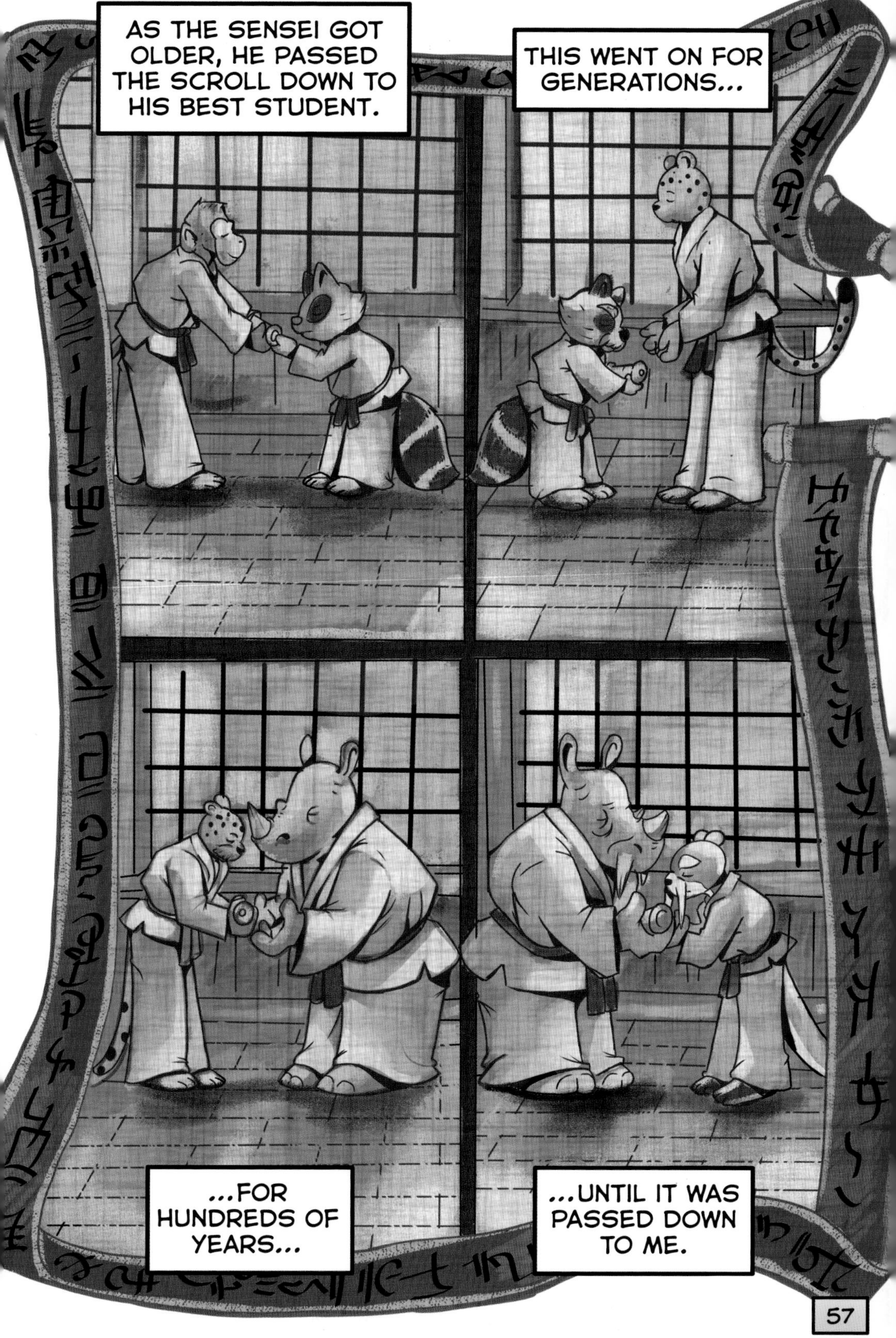
AS THE SENSEI GOT OLDER, HE PASSED THE SCROLL DOWN TO HIS BEST STUDENT.
THIS WENT ON FOR GENERATIONS...
...FOR HUNDREDS OF YEARS...
...UNTIL IT WAS PASSED DOWN TO ME.

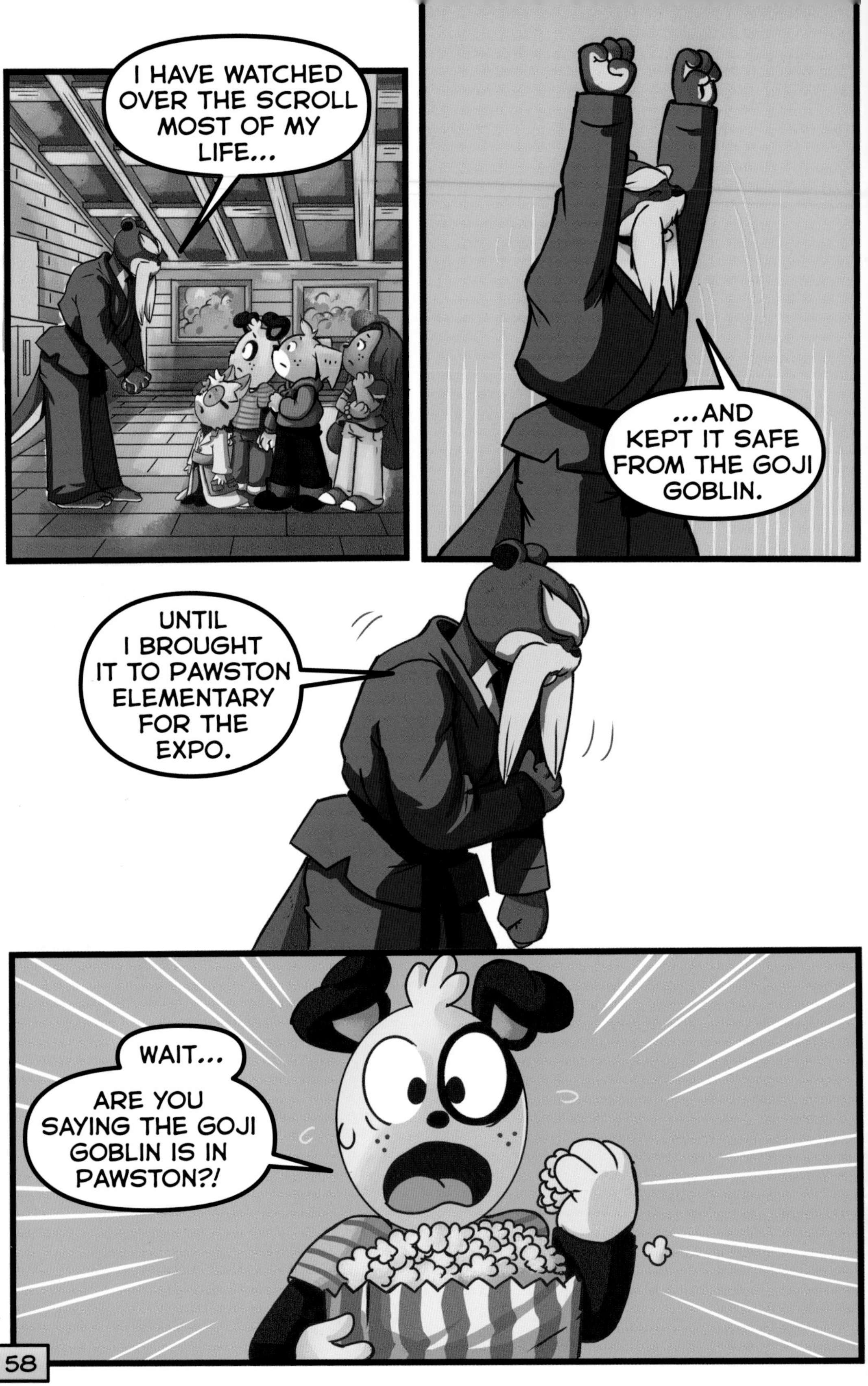
I HAVE WATCHED OVER THE SCROLL MOST OF MY LIFE...
...AND KEPT IT SAFE FROM THE GOJI GOBLIN.
UNTIL I BROUGHT IT TO PAWSTON ELEMENTARY FOR THE EXPO.
WAIT...
ARE YOU SAYING THE GOJI GOBLIN IS IN PAWSTON?!

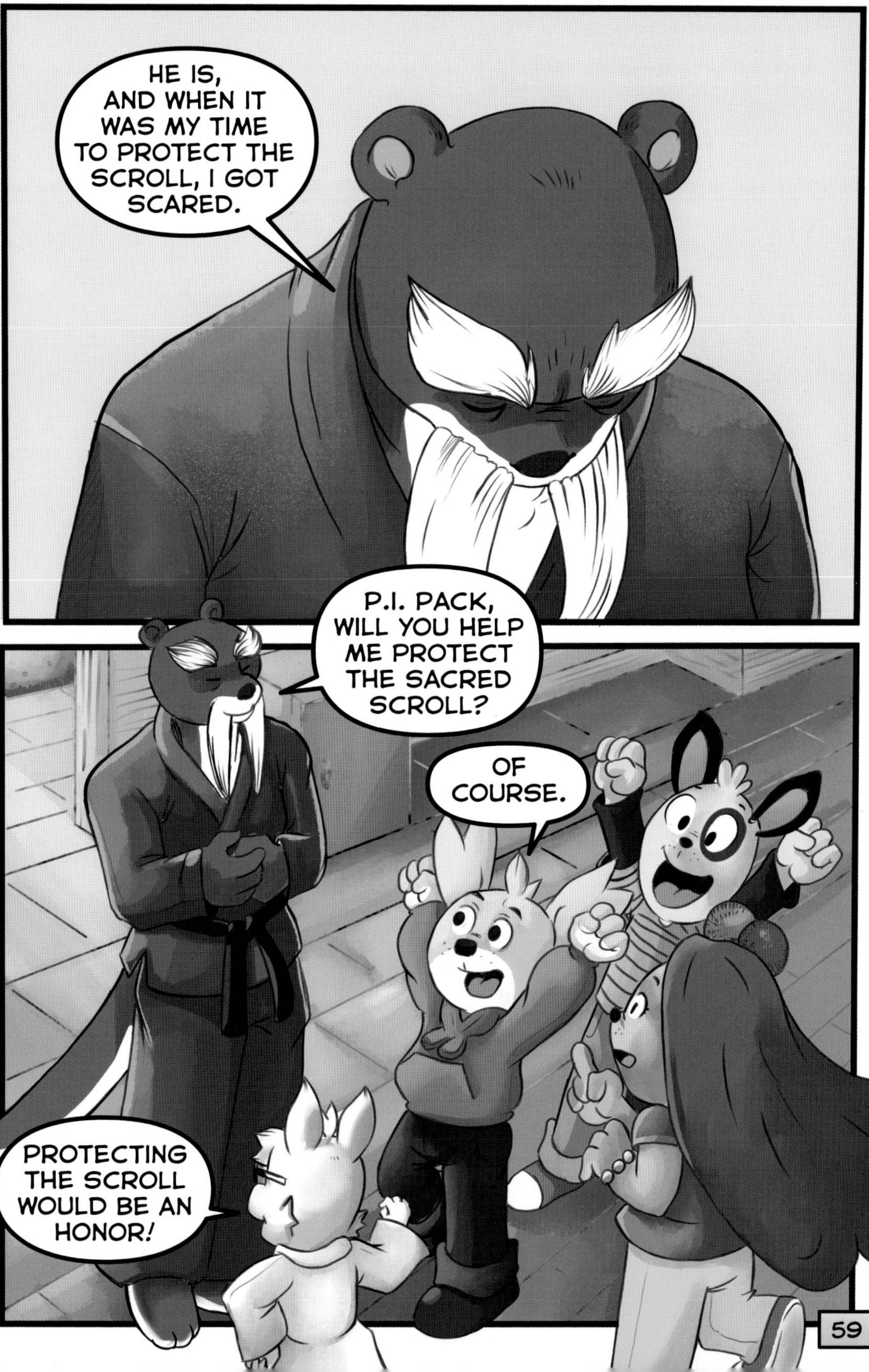
HE IS, AND WHEN IT WAS MY TIME TO PROTECT THE SCROLL, I GOT SCARED.
P.I. PACK, WILL YOU HELP ME PROTECT THE SACRED SCROLL?
OF COURSE.
PROTECTING THE SCROLL WOULD BE AN HONOR!

CHAPTER 5

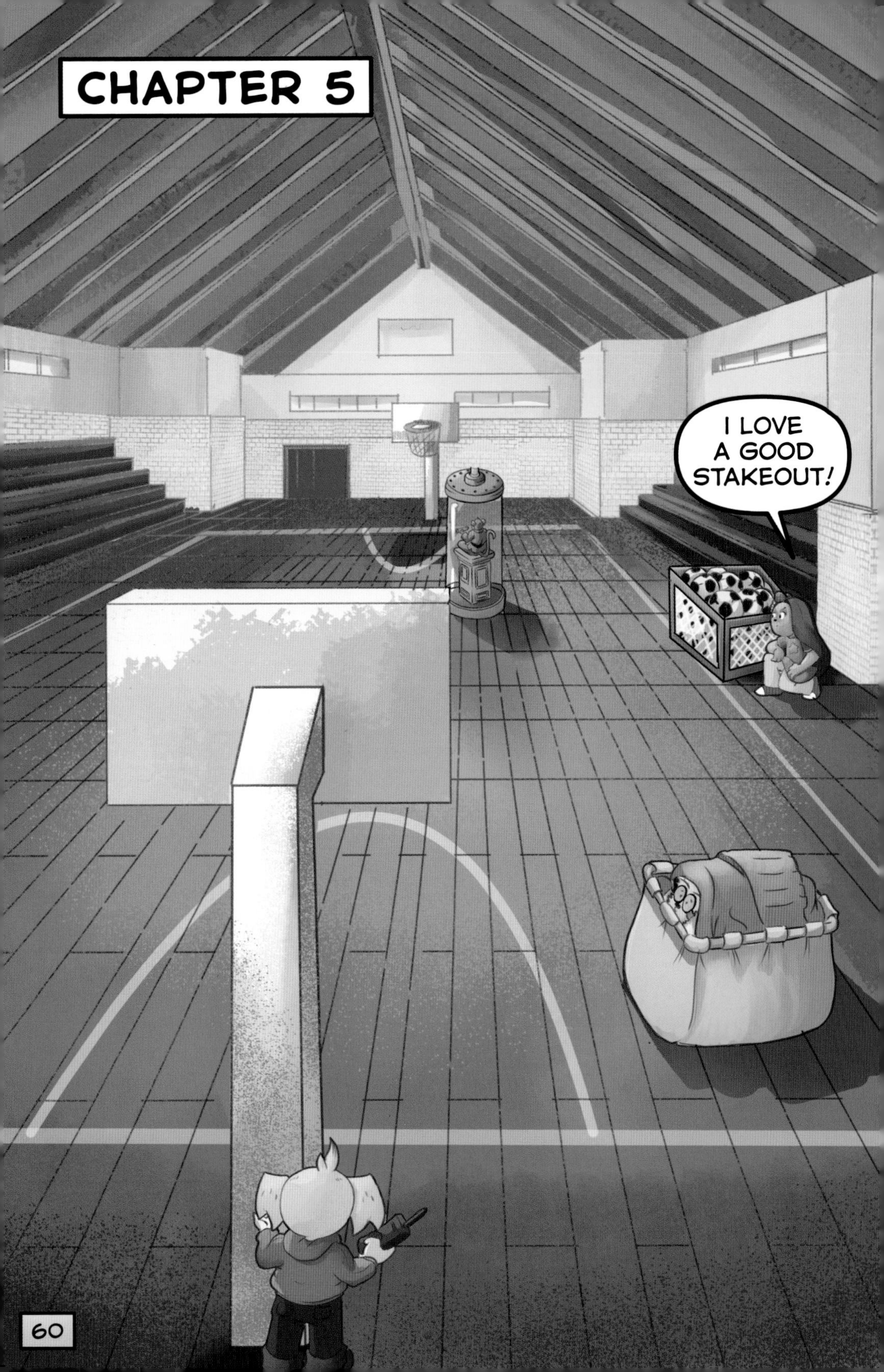
I LOVE A GOOD STAKEOUT!

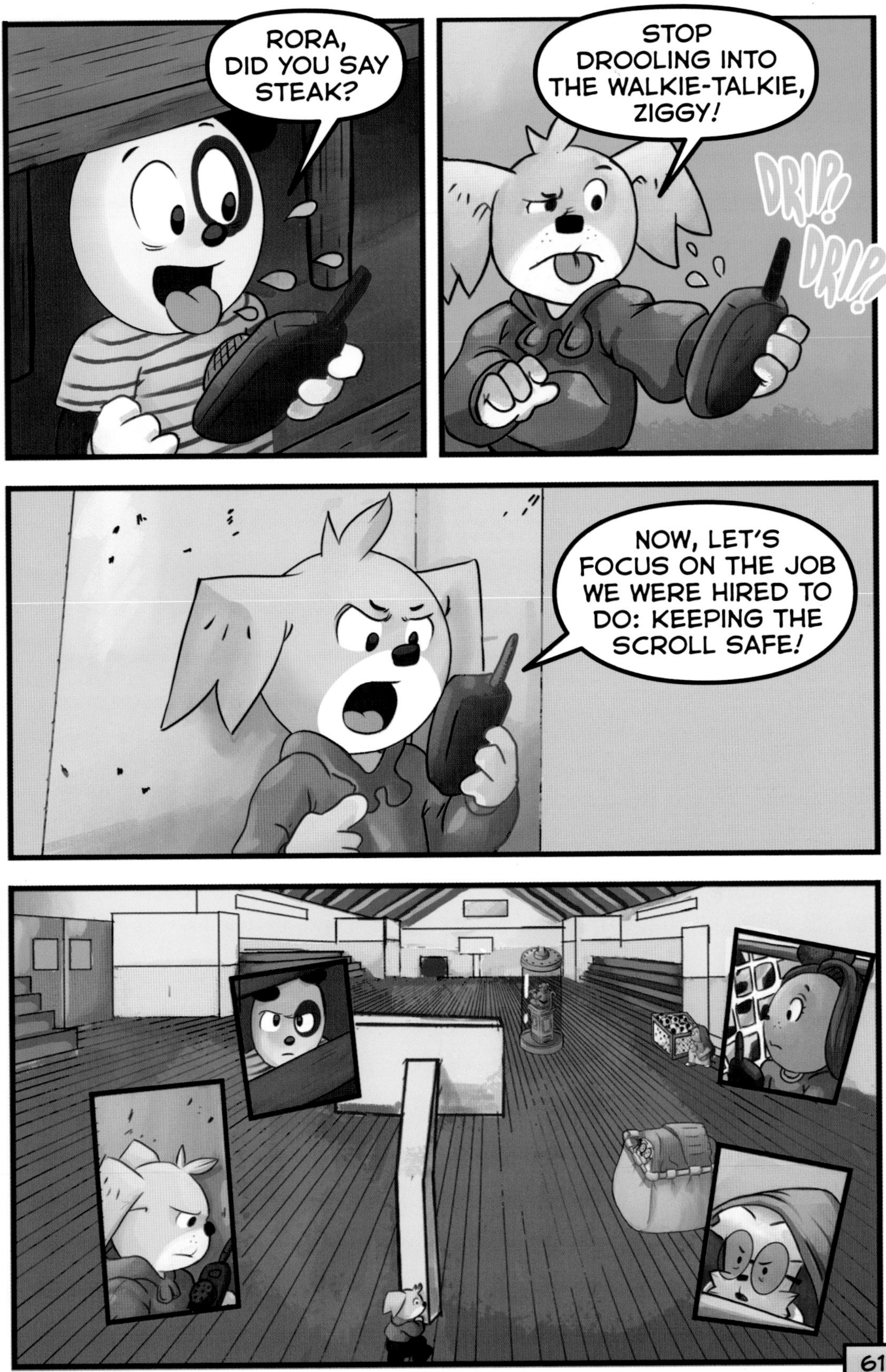
RORA, DID YOU SAY STEAK?
STOP DROOLING INTO THE WALKIE-TALKIE, ZIGGY!
DRIP! DRIP!
NOW, LET'S FOCUS ON THE JOB WE WERE HIRED TO DO: KEEPING THE SCROLL SAFE!

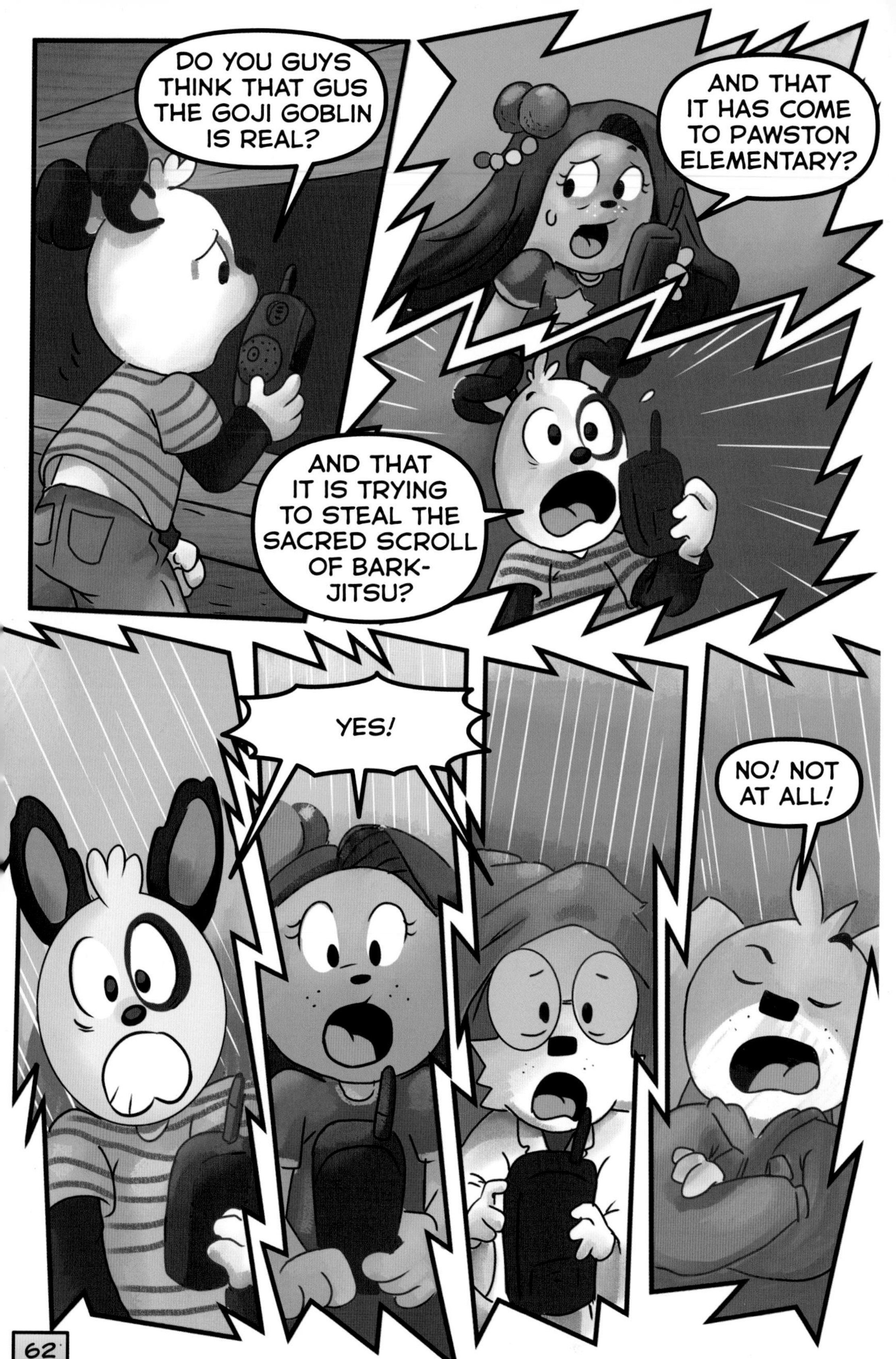
DO YOU GUYS THINK THAT GUS THE GOJI GOBLIN IS REAL?
AND THAT IT HAS COME TO PAWSTON ELEMENTARY?
AND THAT IT IS TRYING TO STEAL THE SACRED SCROLL OF BARK-JITSU?
YES!
NO! NOT AT ALL!

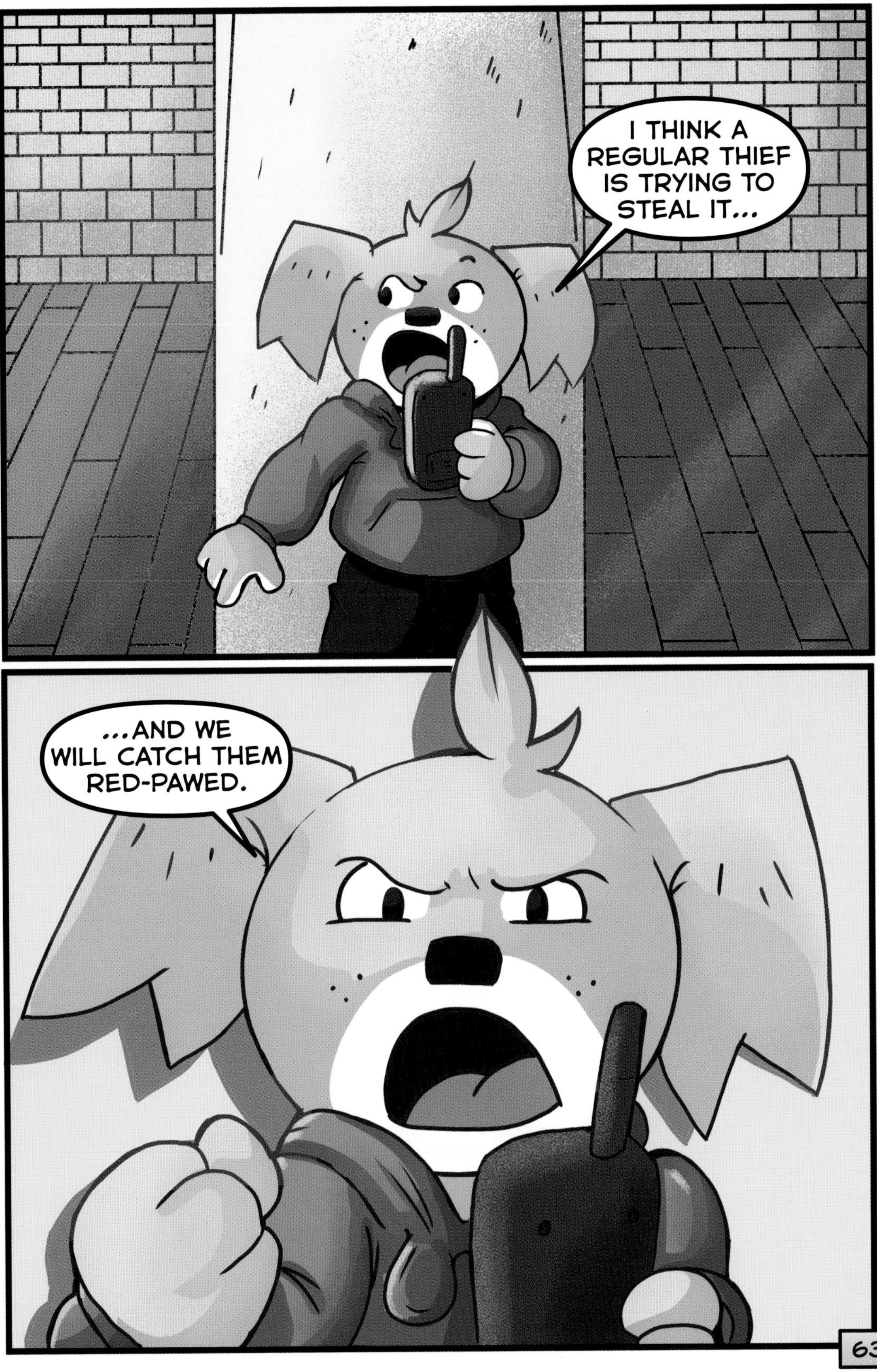
I THINK A REGULAR THIEF IS TRYING TO STEAL IT...
...AND WE WILL CATCH THEM RED-PAWED.

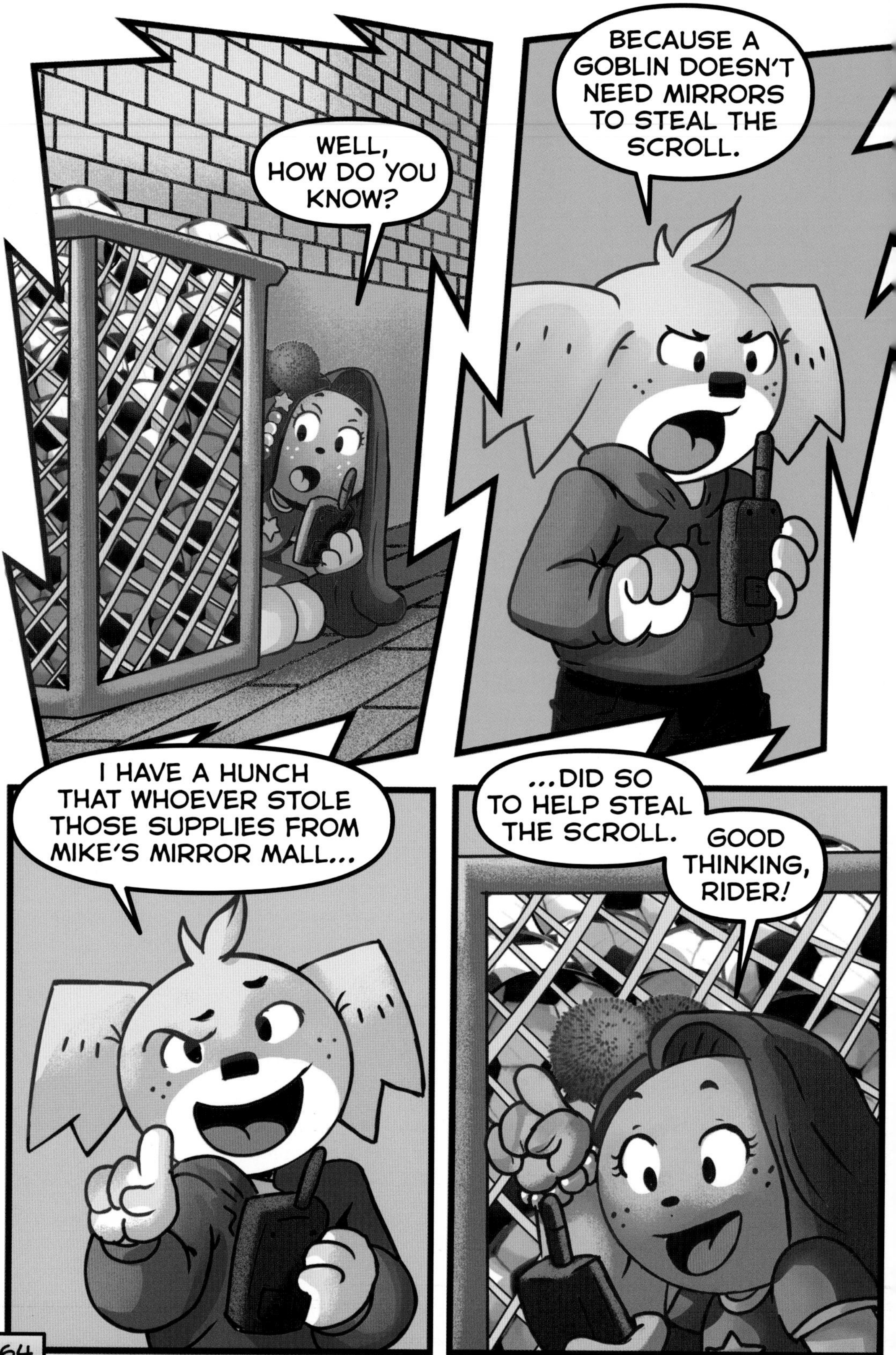
WELL, HOW DO YOU KNOW?
BECAUSE A GOBLIN DOESN'T NEED MIRRORS TO STEAL THE SCROLL.
I HAVE A HUNCH THAT WHOEVER STOLE THOSE SUPPLIES FROM MIKE'S MIRROR MALL...
...DID SO TO HELP STEAL THE SCROLL.
GOOD THINKING, RIDER!

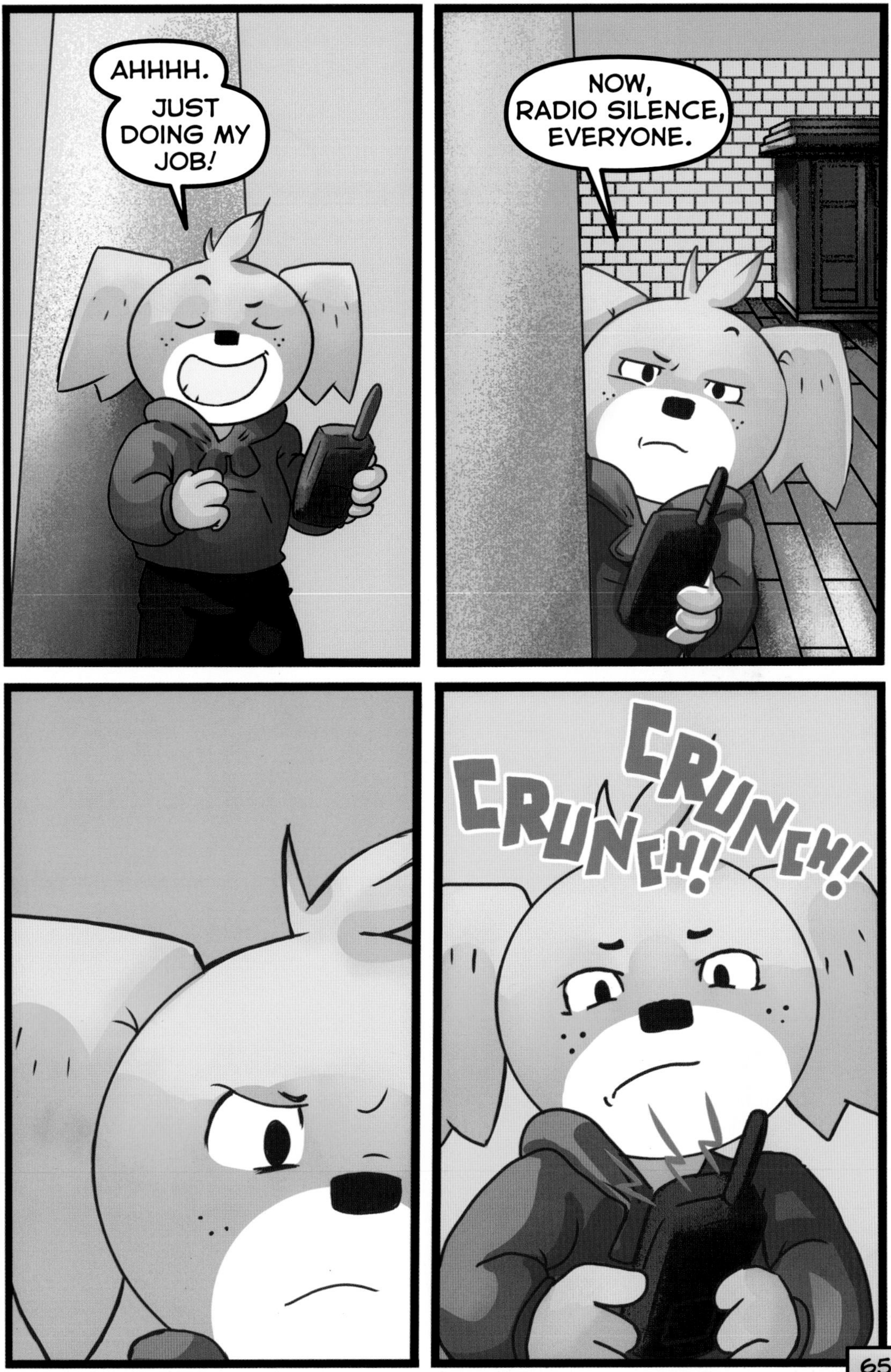
AHHHH.
JUST DOING MY JOB!
NOW, RADIO SILENCE, EVERYONE.
CRUNCH!
CRUNCH!

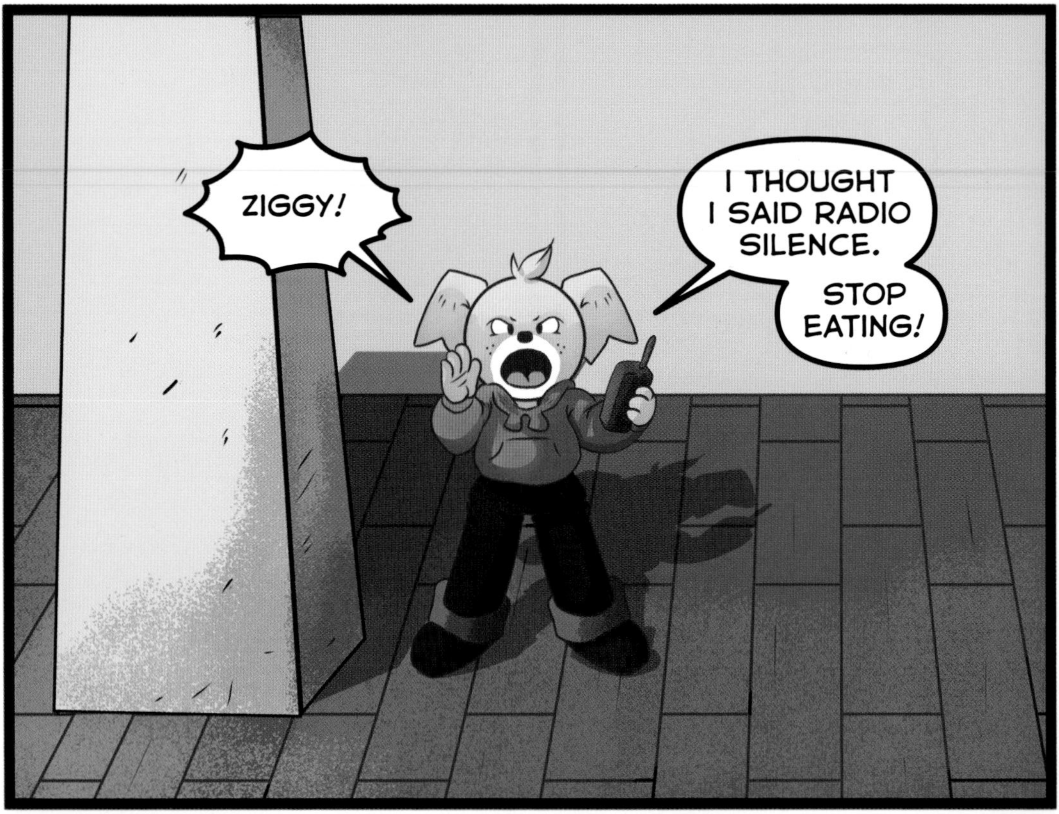
ZIGGY!
I THOUGHT I SAID RADIO SILENCE.
STOP EATING!

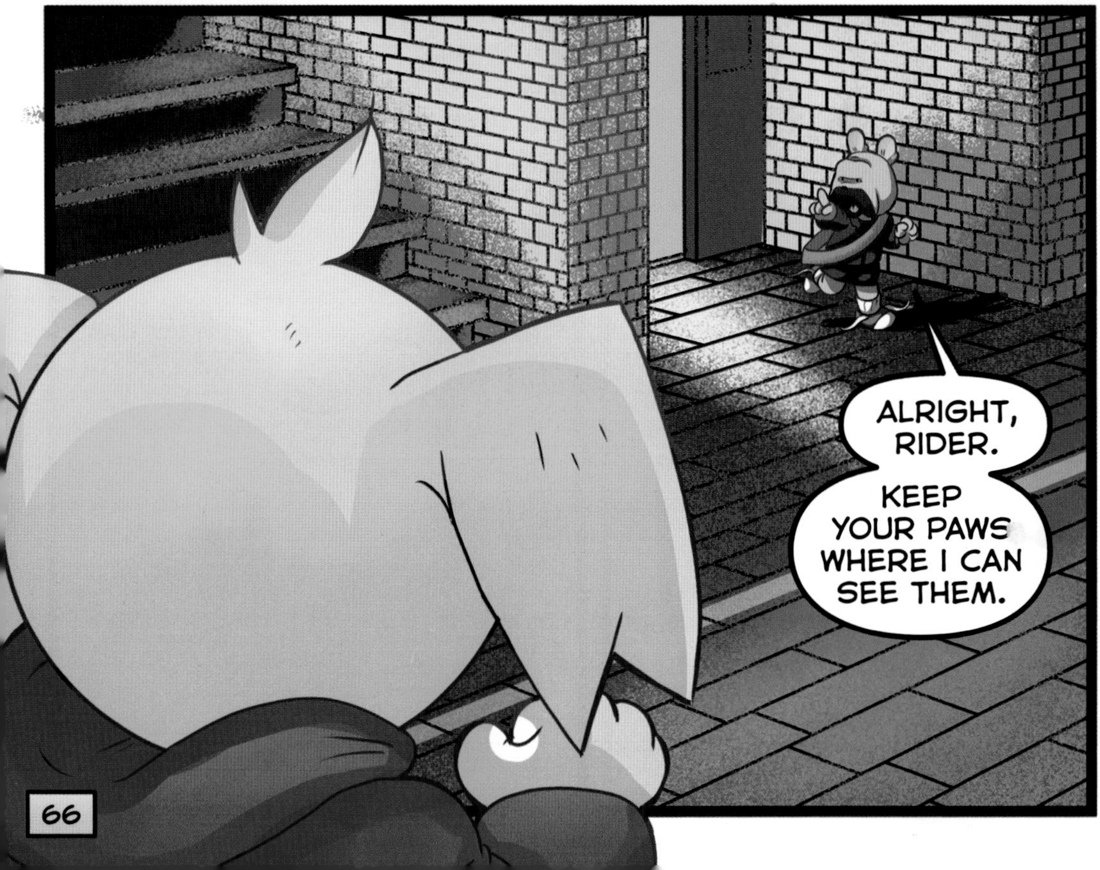
ALRIGHT, RIDER.
KEEP YOUR PAWS WHERE I CAN SEE THEM.

FRENCHIE, WHAT'S GOING ON HERE?

I'M SORRY, DETECTIVES.

I HAVE TO TAKE ALL OF YOU TO THE PRINCIPAL'S OFFICE.

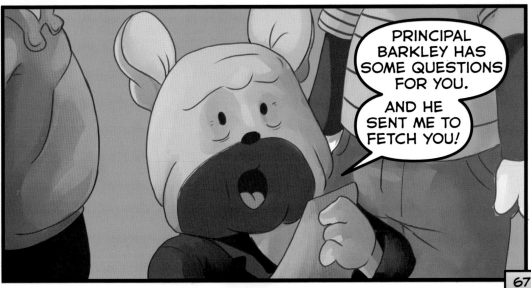

PRINCIPAL BARKLEY HAS SOME QUESTIONS FOR YOU.

AND HE SENT ME TO FETCH YOU!

OF COURSE, FRENCHIE.

WE ARE ALWAYS HAPPY TO HELP.

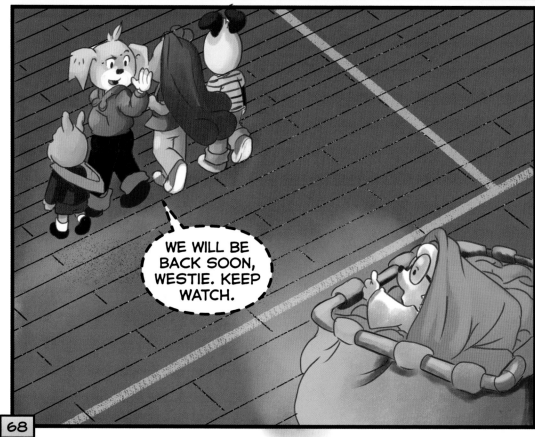

WE WILL BE BACK SOON, WESTIE. KEEP WATCH.

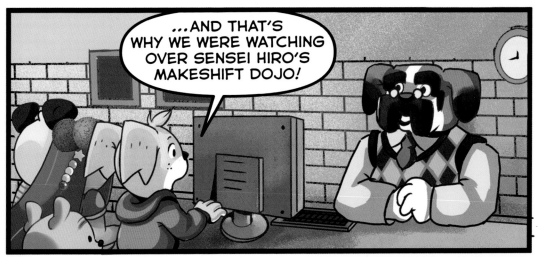

...AND THAT'S WHY WE WERE WATCHING OVER SENSEI HIRO'S MAKESHIFT DOJO!

SORRY ABOUT THAT, RIDER.

A CONCERNED STUDENT CALLED IN A TIP ABOUT SOME PUPS WHO APPEARED TO BE UP TO NO GOOD.

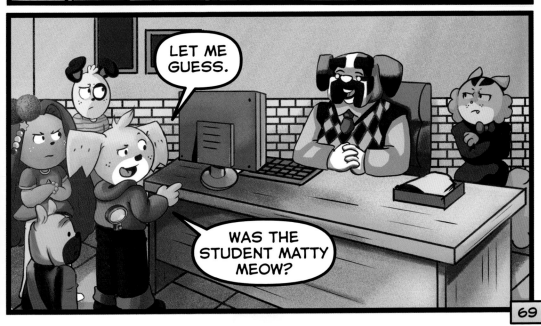

LET ME GUESS.

WAS THE STUDENT MATTY MEOW?

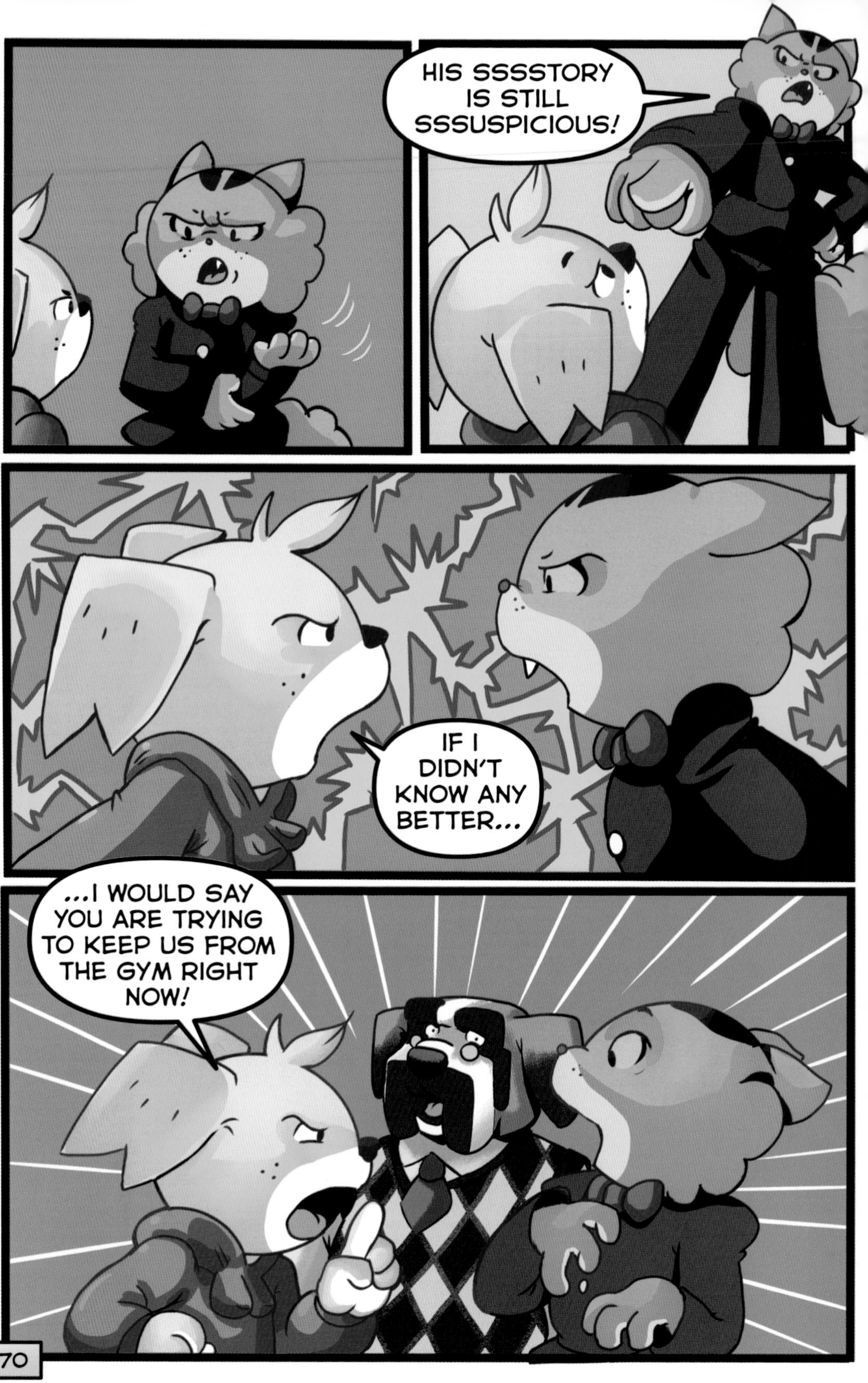
HIS SSSSTORY IS STILL SSSUSPICIOUS!
IF I DIDN'T KNOW ANY BETTER...
...I WOULD SAY YOU ARE TRYING TO KEEP US FROM THE GYM RIGHT NOW!

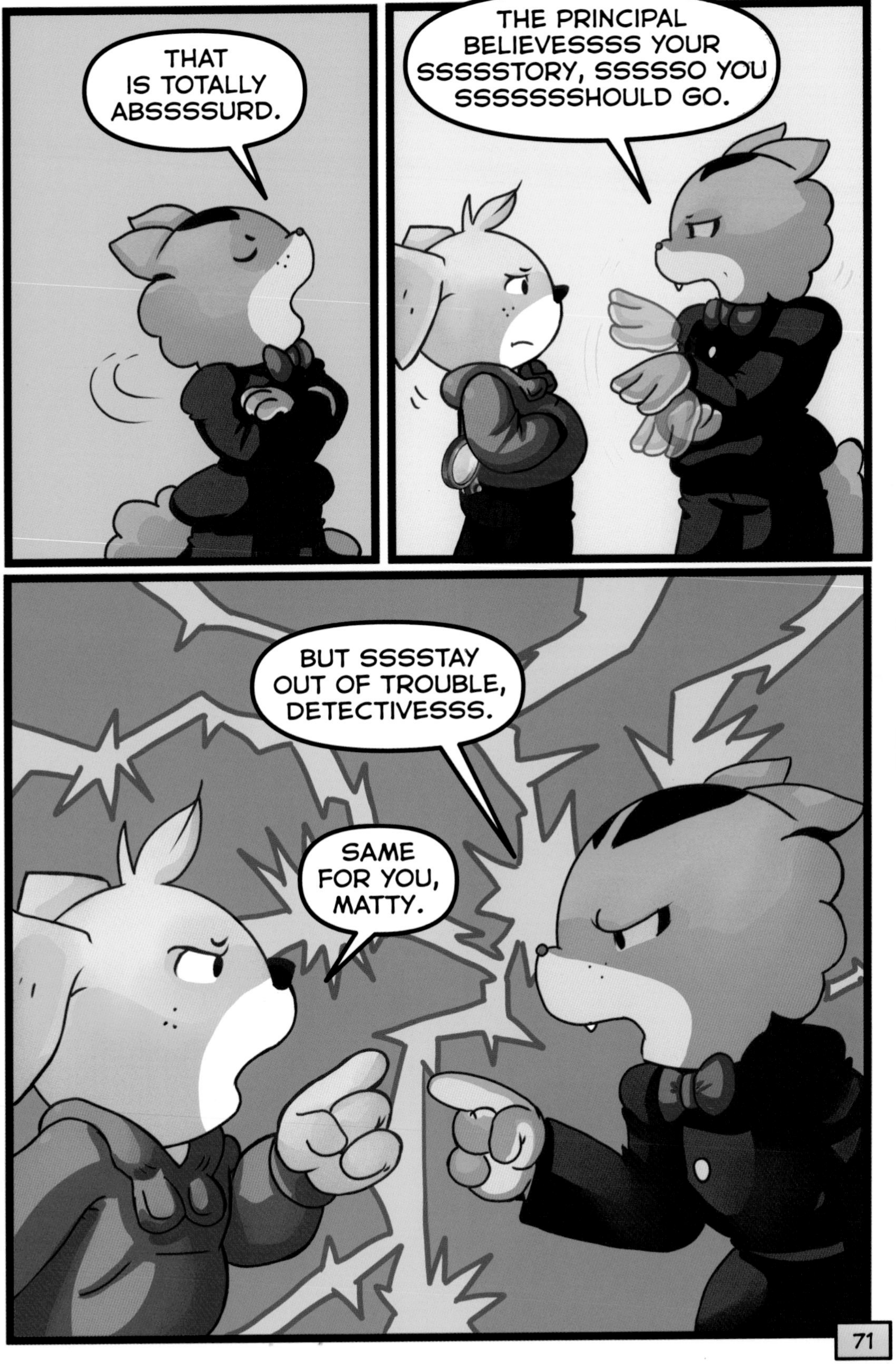
THAT IS TOTALLY ABSSSSURD.
THE PRINCIPAL BELIEVESSSS YOUR SSSSSTORY, SSSSSO YOU SSSSSSSHOULD GO.
BUT SSSSTAY OUT OF TROUBLE, DETECTIVESSS.
SAME FOR YOU, MATTY.

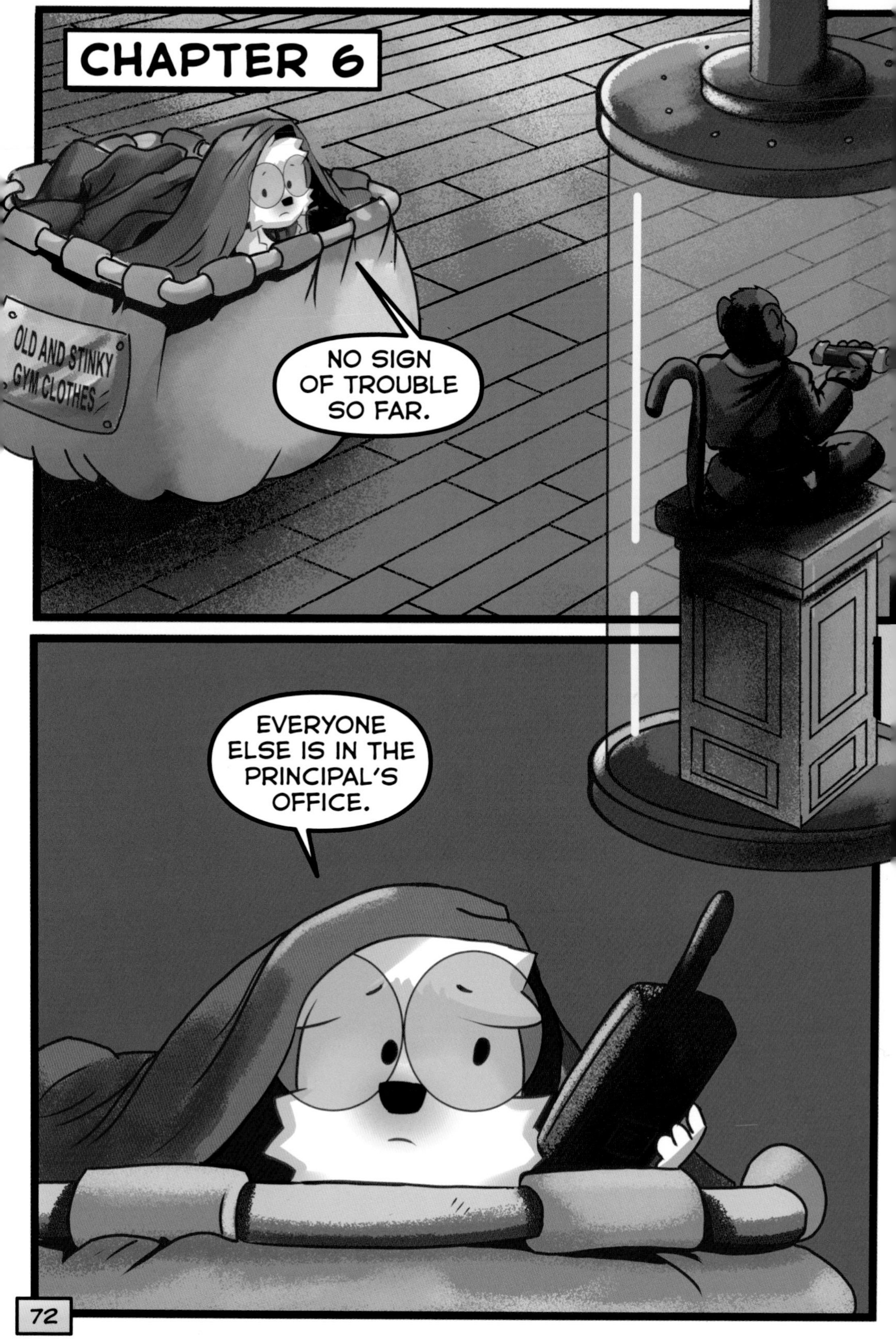
CHAPTER 6
OLD AND STINKY GYM CLOTHES
NO SIGN OF TROUBLE SO FAR.
EVERYONE ELSE IS IN THE PRINCIPAL'S OFFICE.

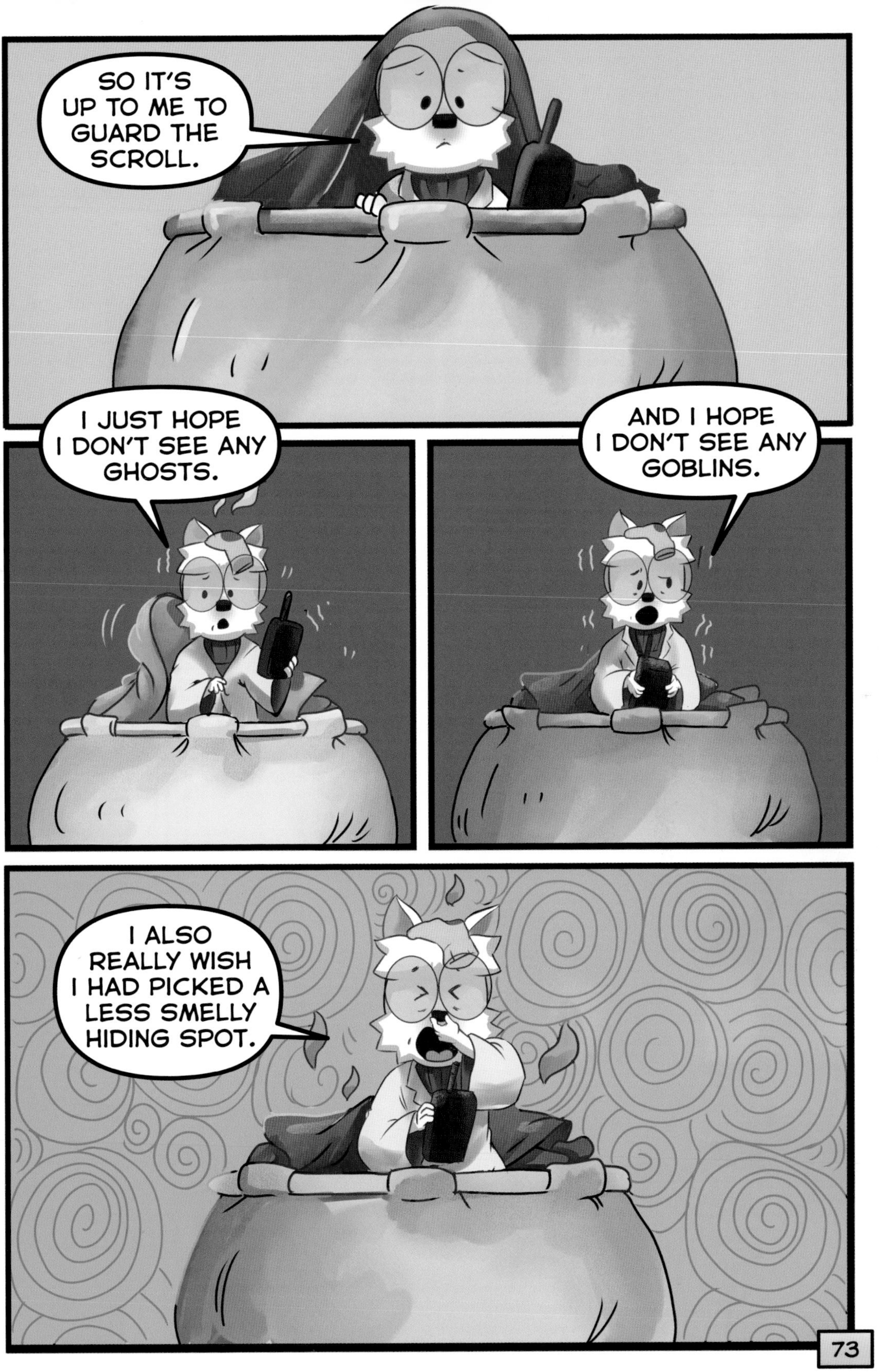
SO IT'S UP TO ME TO GUARD THE SCROLL.
I JUST HOPE I DON'T SEE ANY GHOSTS.
AND I HOPE I DON'T SEE ANY GOBLINS.
I ALSO REALLY WISH I HAD PICKED A LESS SMELLY HIDING SPOT.

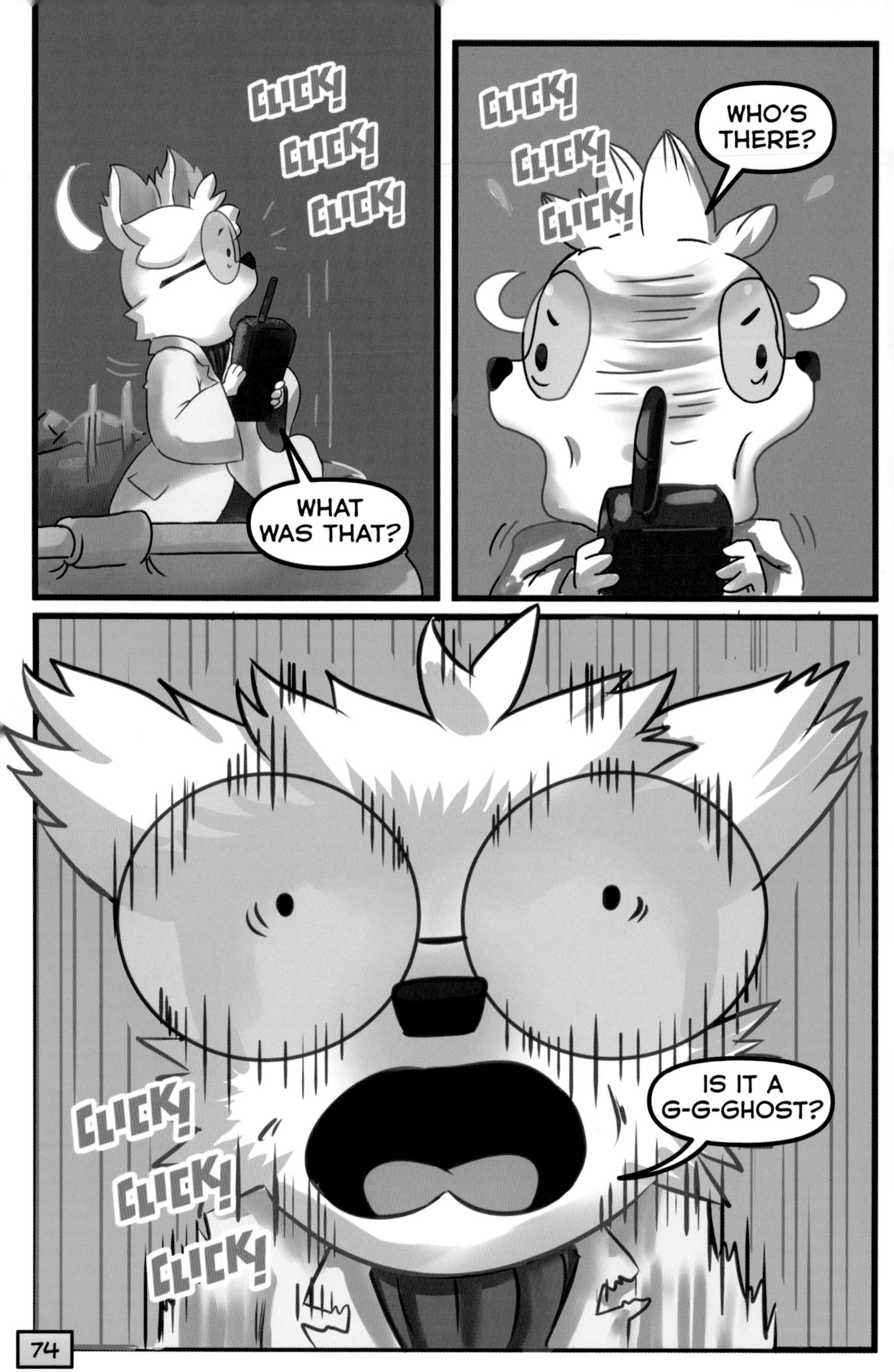
CLICK!
CLICK!
CLICK!
WHAT WAS THAT?
CLICK!
CLICK!
CLICK!
WHO'S THERE?
IS IT A G-G-GHOST?
CLICK!
CLICK!
CLICK!

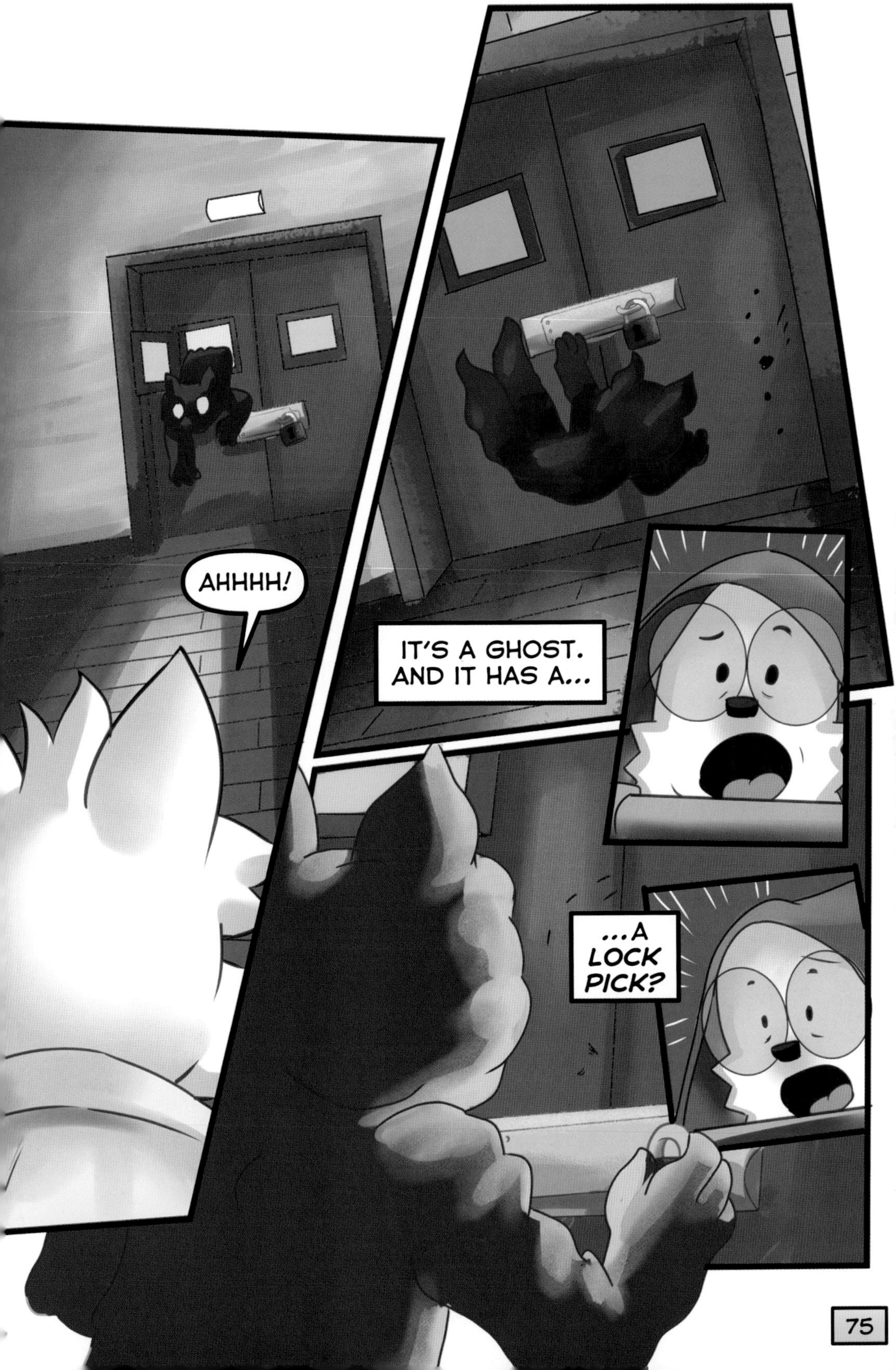
AHHHH!
IT'S A GHOST. AND IT HAS A...
...A LOCK PICK?

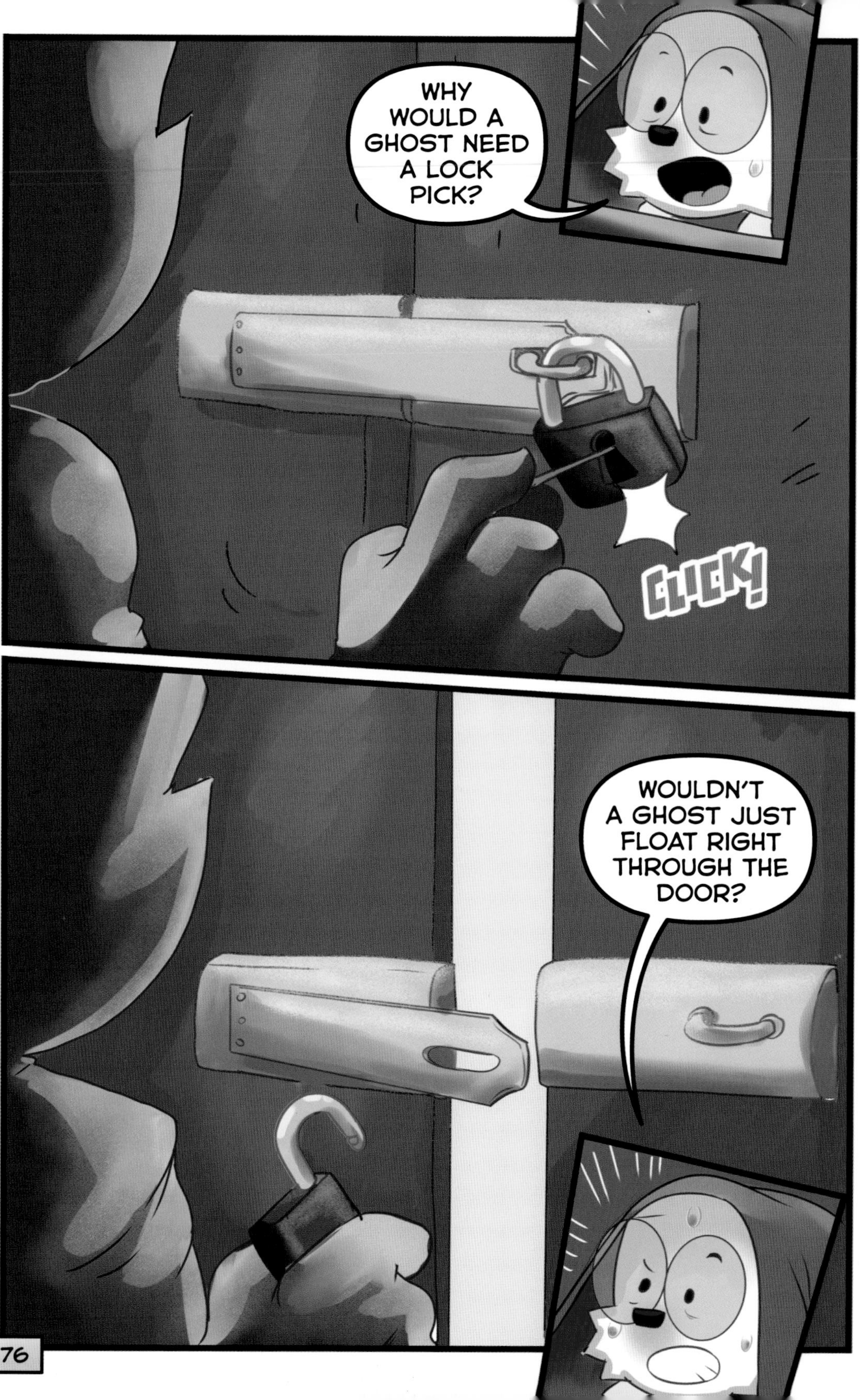
WHY WOULD A GHOST NEED A LOCK PICK?
CLICK!
WOULDN'T A GHOST JUST FLOAT RIGHT THROUGH THE DOOR?

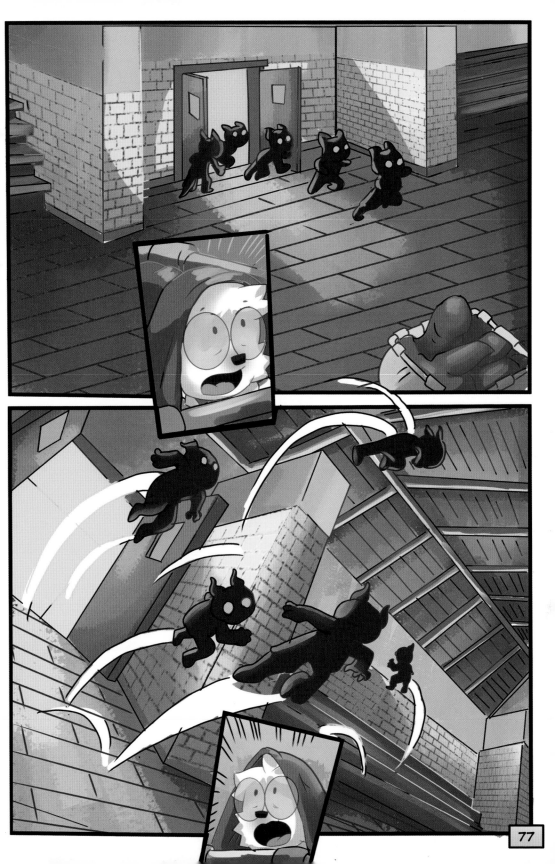

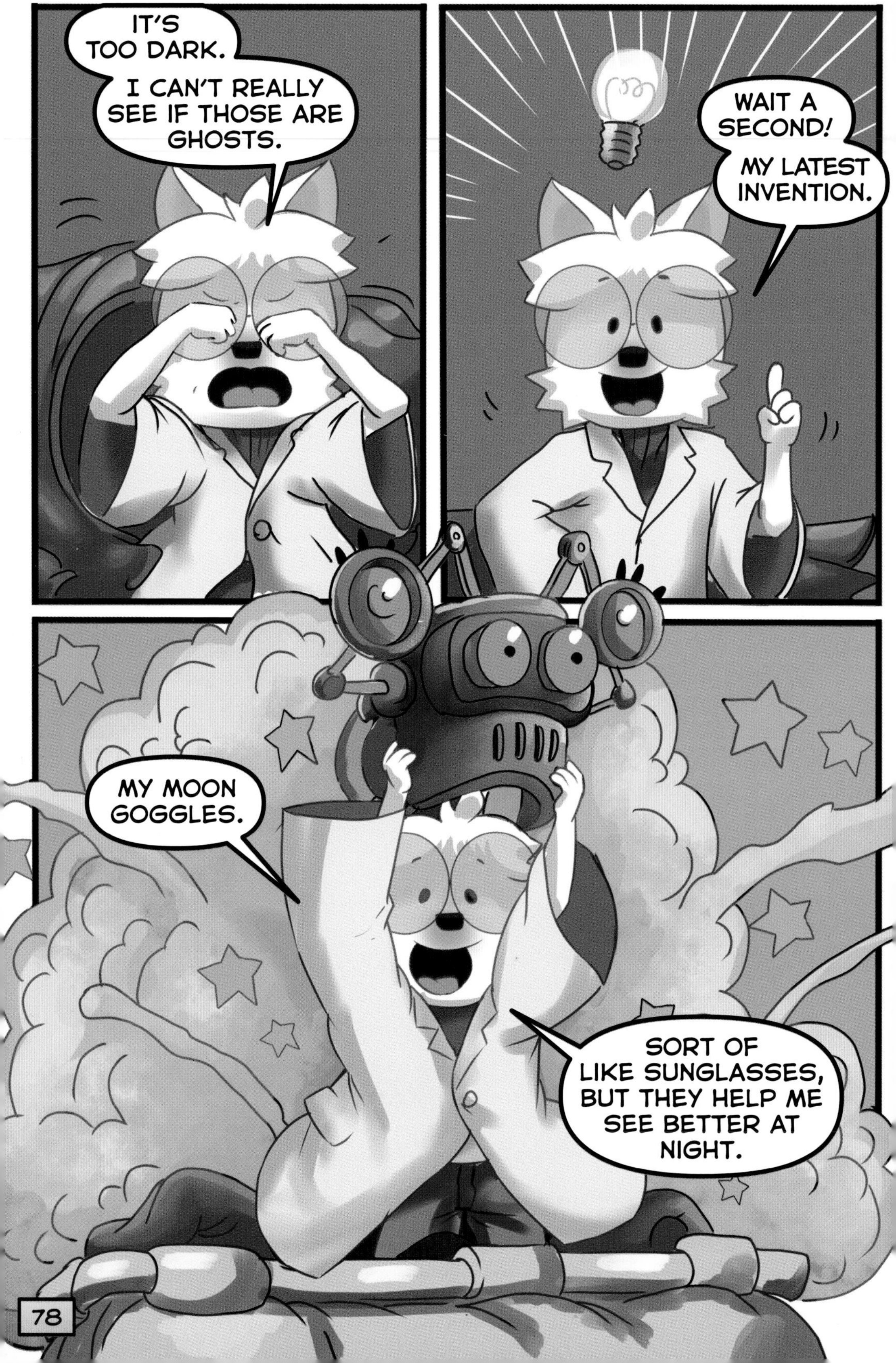
IT'S TOO DARK.
I CAN'T REALLY SEE IF THOSE ARE GHOSTS.
WAIT A SECOND!
MY LATEST INVENTION.
MY MOON GOGGLES.
SORT OF LIKE SUNGLASSES, BUT THEY HELP ME SEE BETTER AT NIGHT.

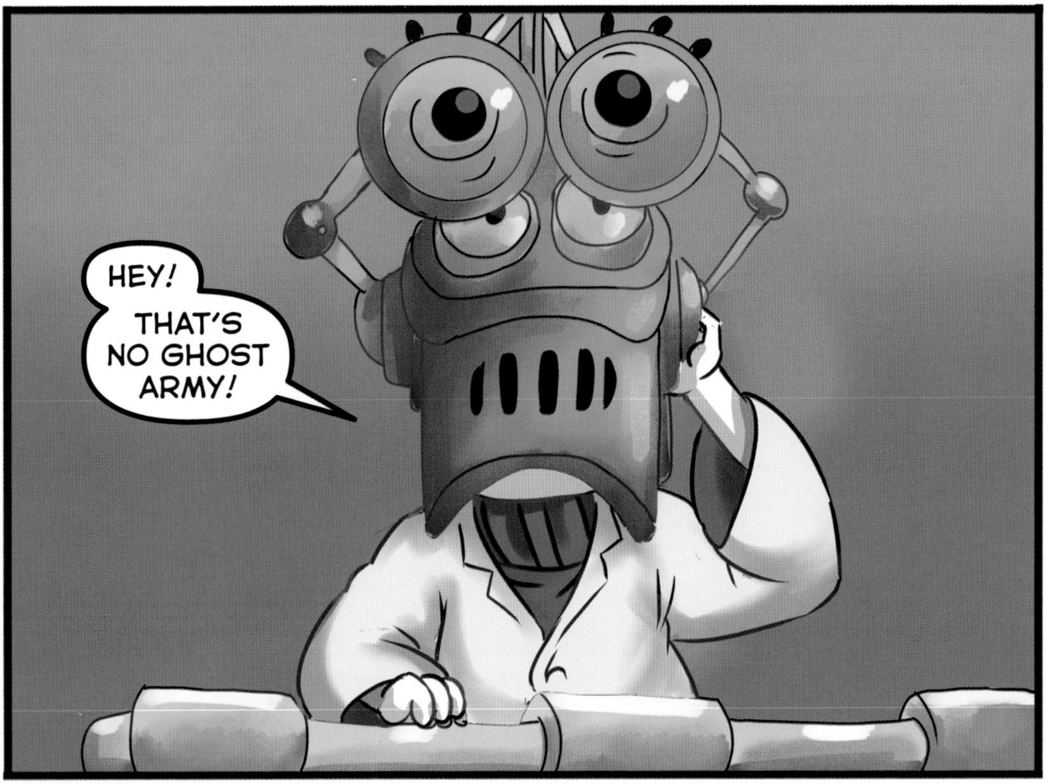
HEY!
THAT'S NO GHOST ARMY!

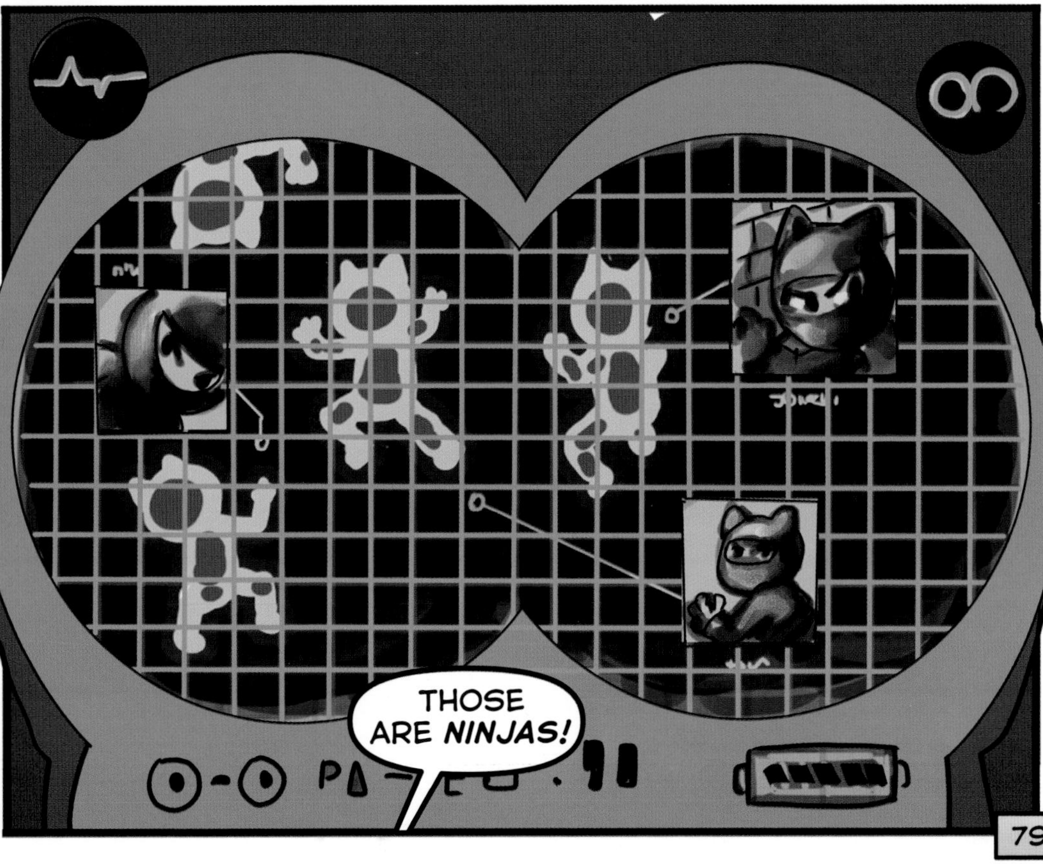
THOSE ARE *NINJAS!*

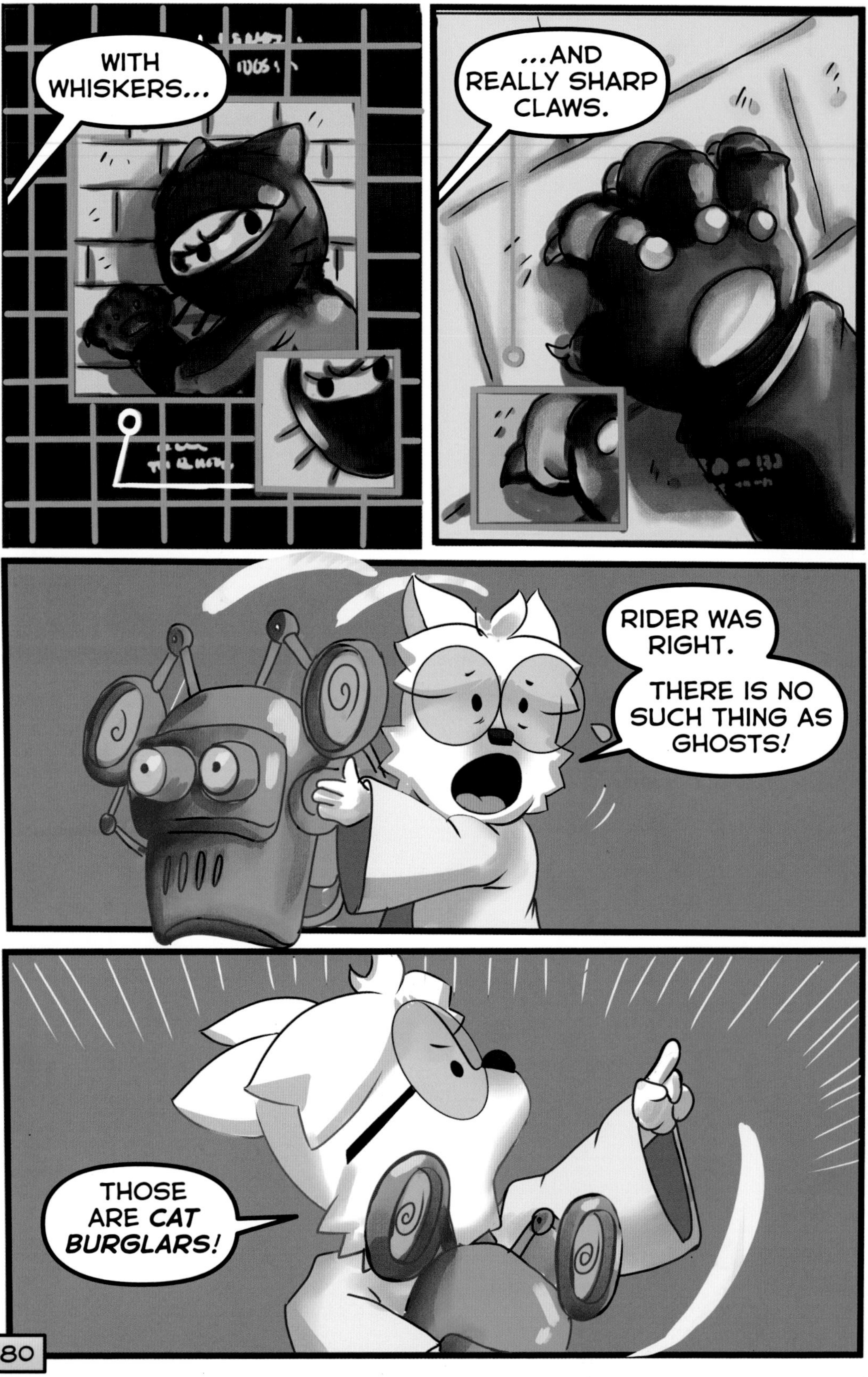
WITH WHISKERS...
...AND REALLY SHARP CLAWS.
RIDER WAS RIGHT.
THERE IS NO SUCH THING AS GHOSTS!
THOSE ARE *CAT BURGLARS*!

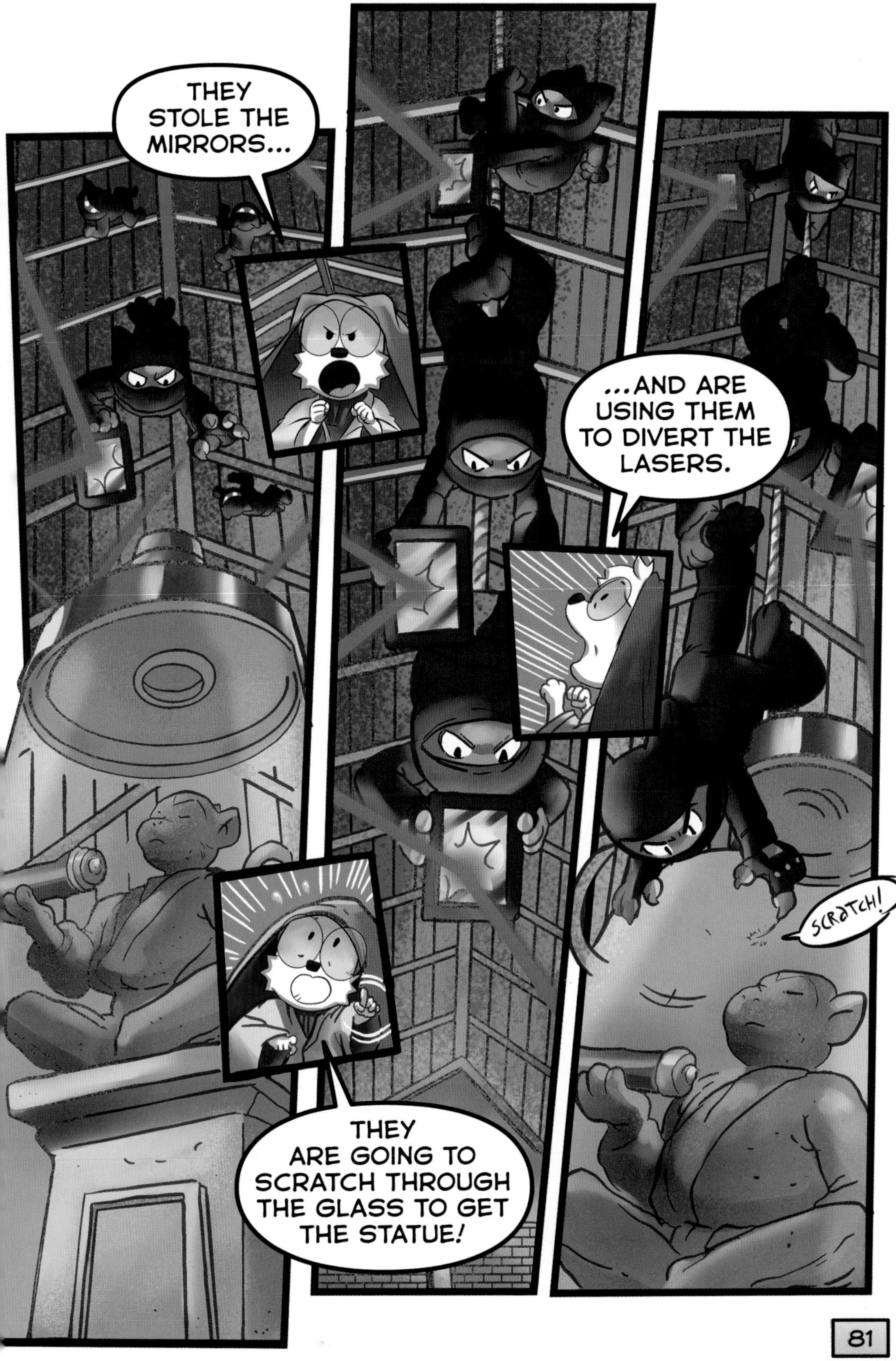
THEY STOLE THE MIRRORS...
...AND ARE USING THEM TO DIVERT THE LASERS.
THEY ARE GOING TO SCRATCH THROUGH THE GLASS TO GET THE STATUE!
SCRATCH!

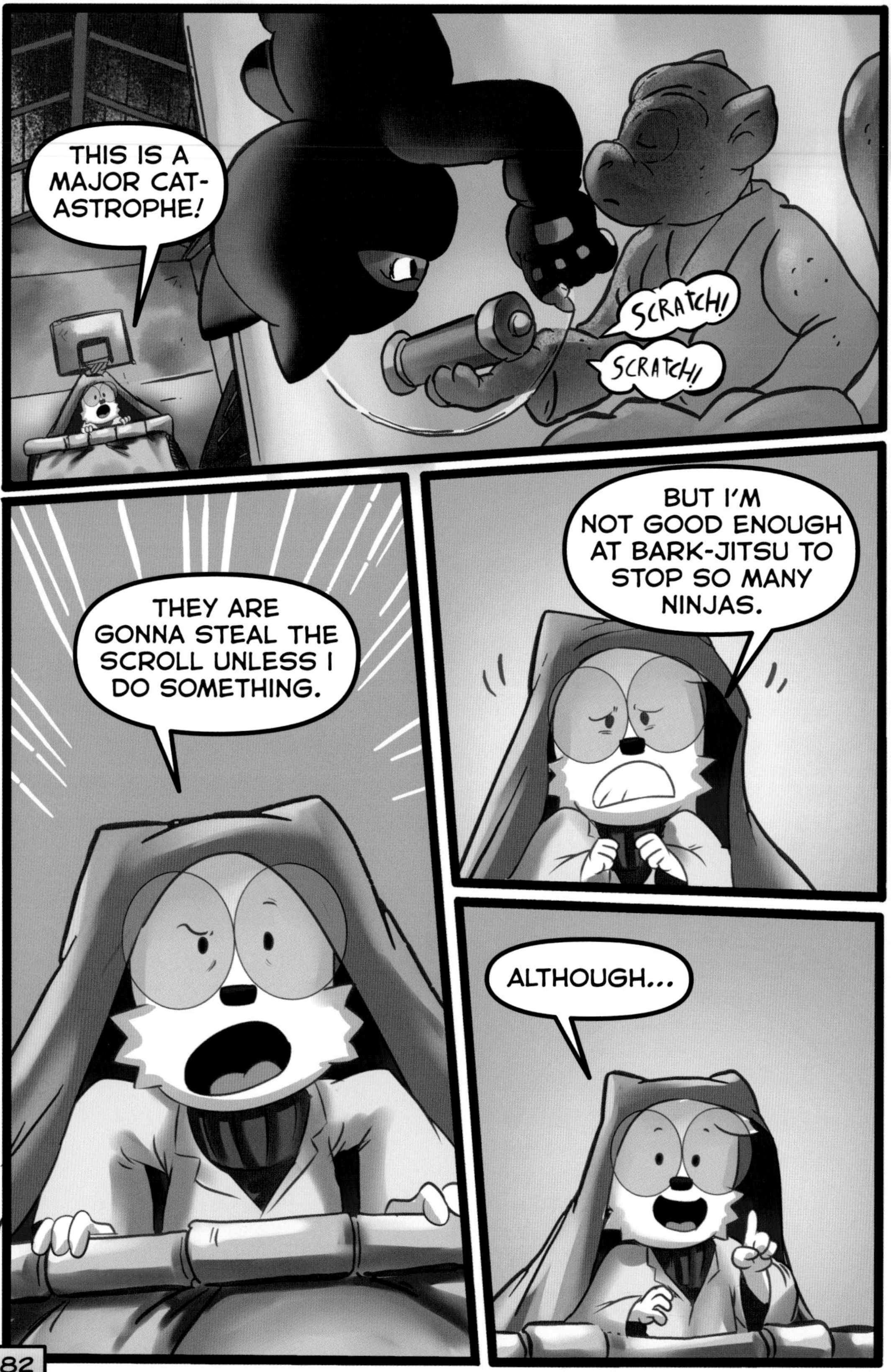
THIS IS A MAJOR CAT-ASTROPHE!
SCRATCH!
SCRATCH!
THEY ARE GONNA STEAL THE SCROLL UNLESS I DO SOMETHING.
BUT I'M NOT GOOD ENOUGH AT BARK-JITSU TO STOP SO MANY NINJAS.
ALTHOUGH...

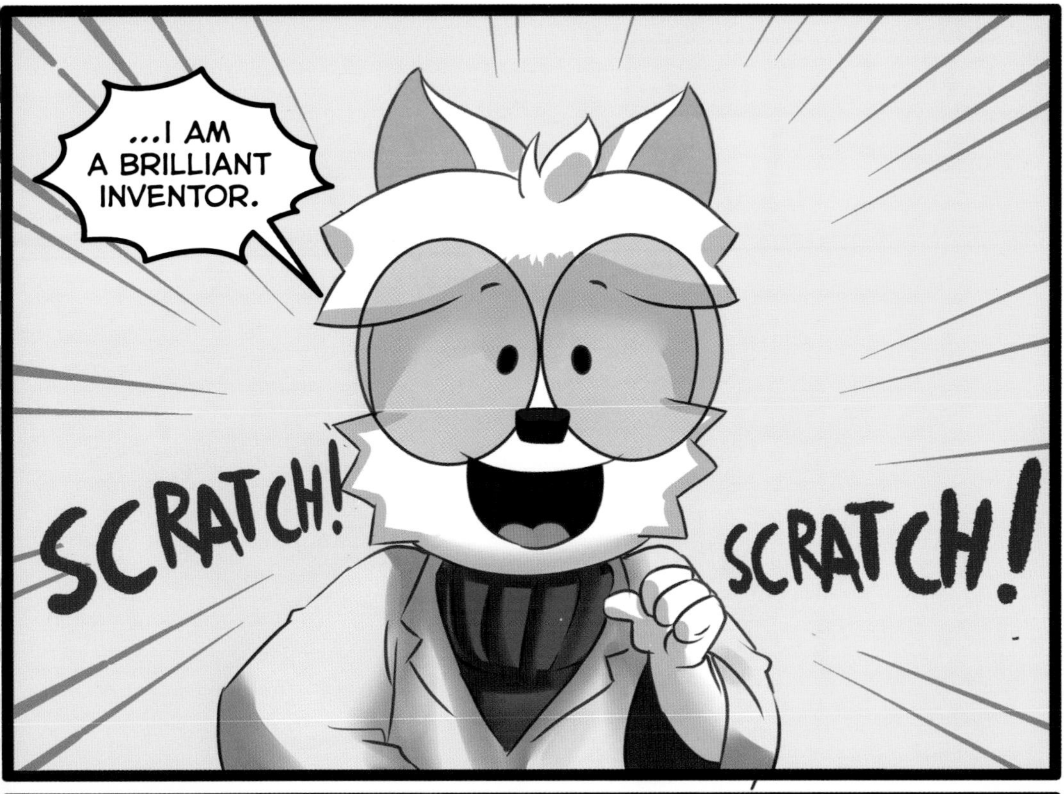
...I AM A BRILLIANT INVENTOR.
SCRATCH!
SCRATCH!

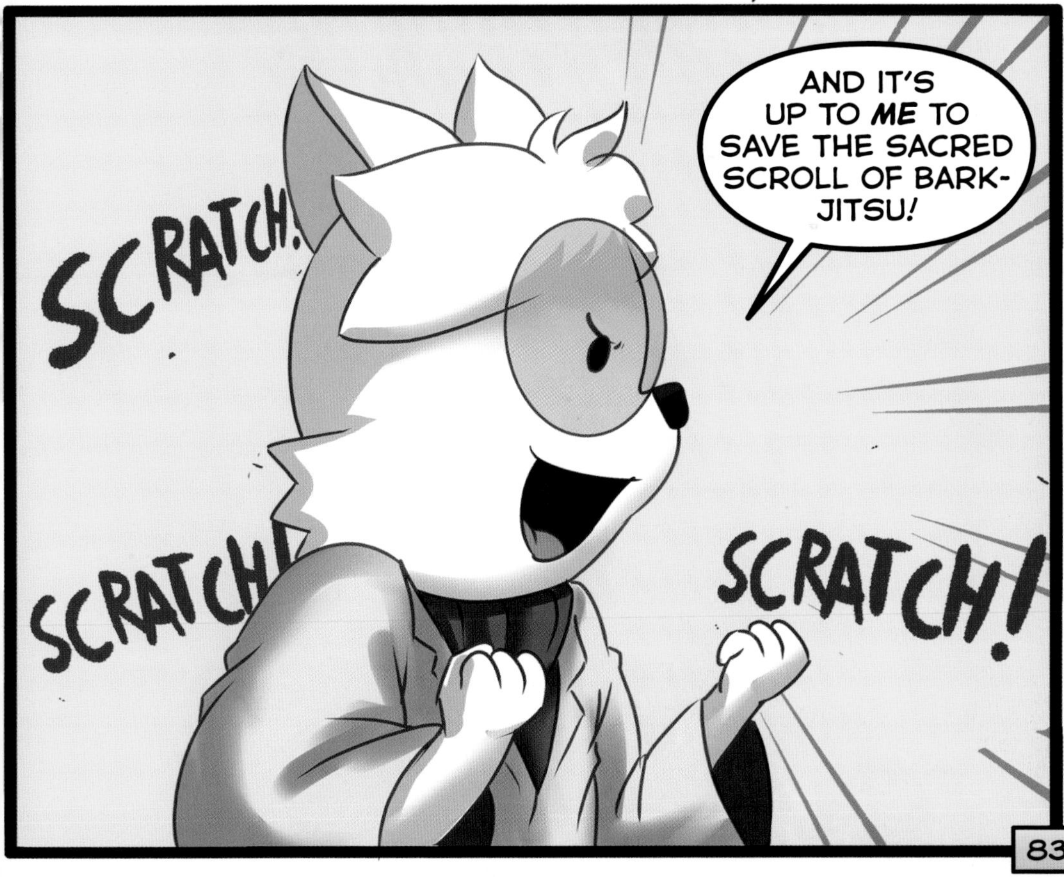
AND IT'S UP TO *ME* TO SAVE THE SACRED SCROLL OF BARK-JITSU!
SCRATCH!
SCRATCH!
SCRATCH!

CHAPTER 7

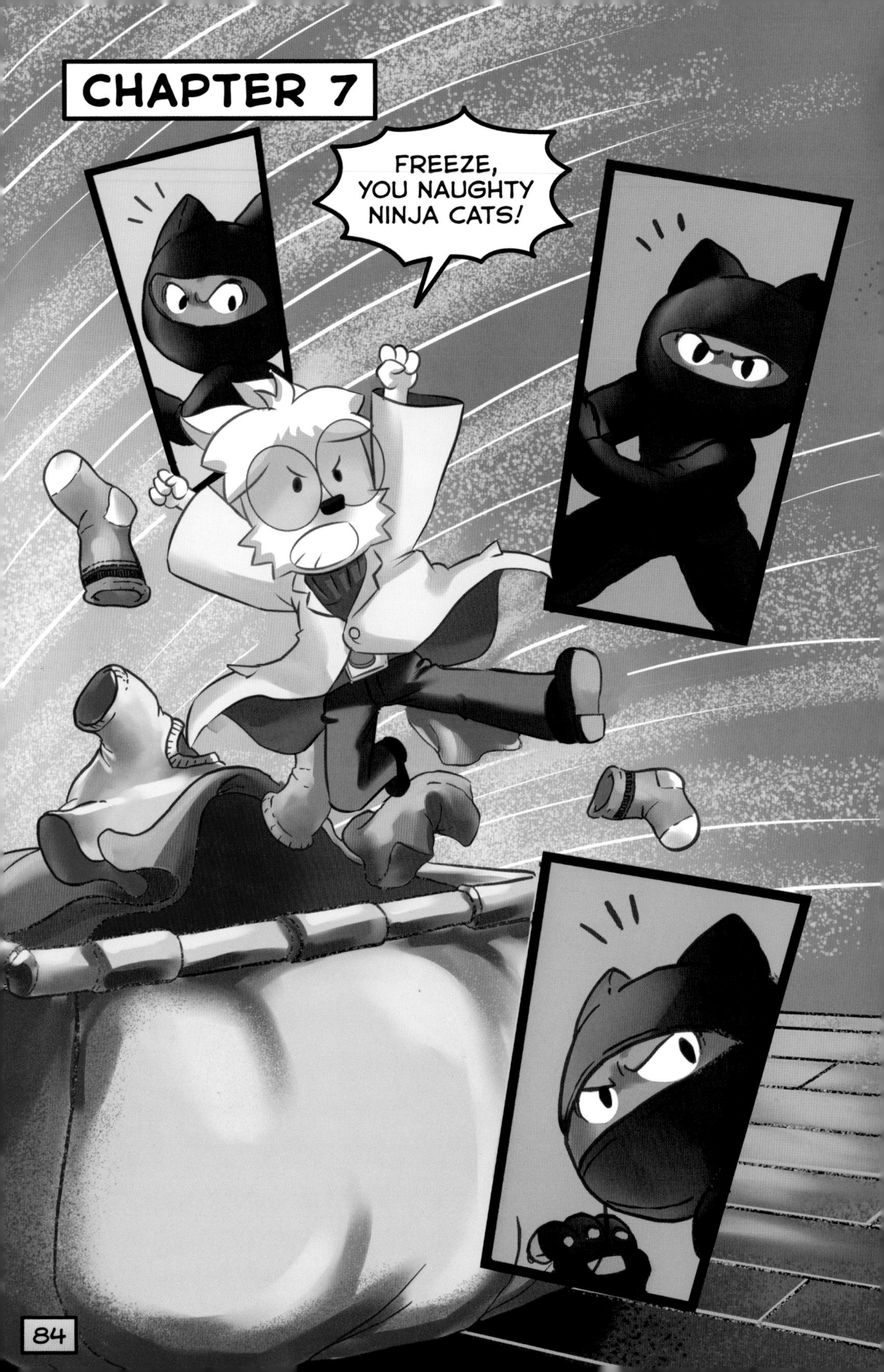
FREEZE, YOU NAUGHTY NINJA CATS!

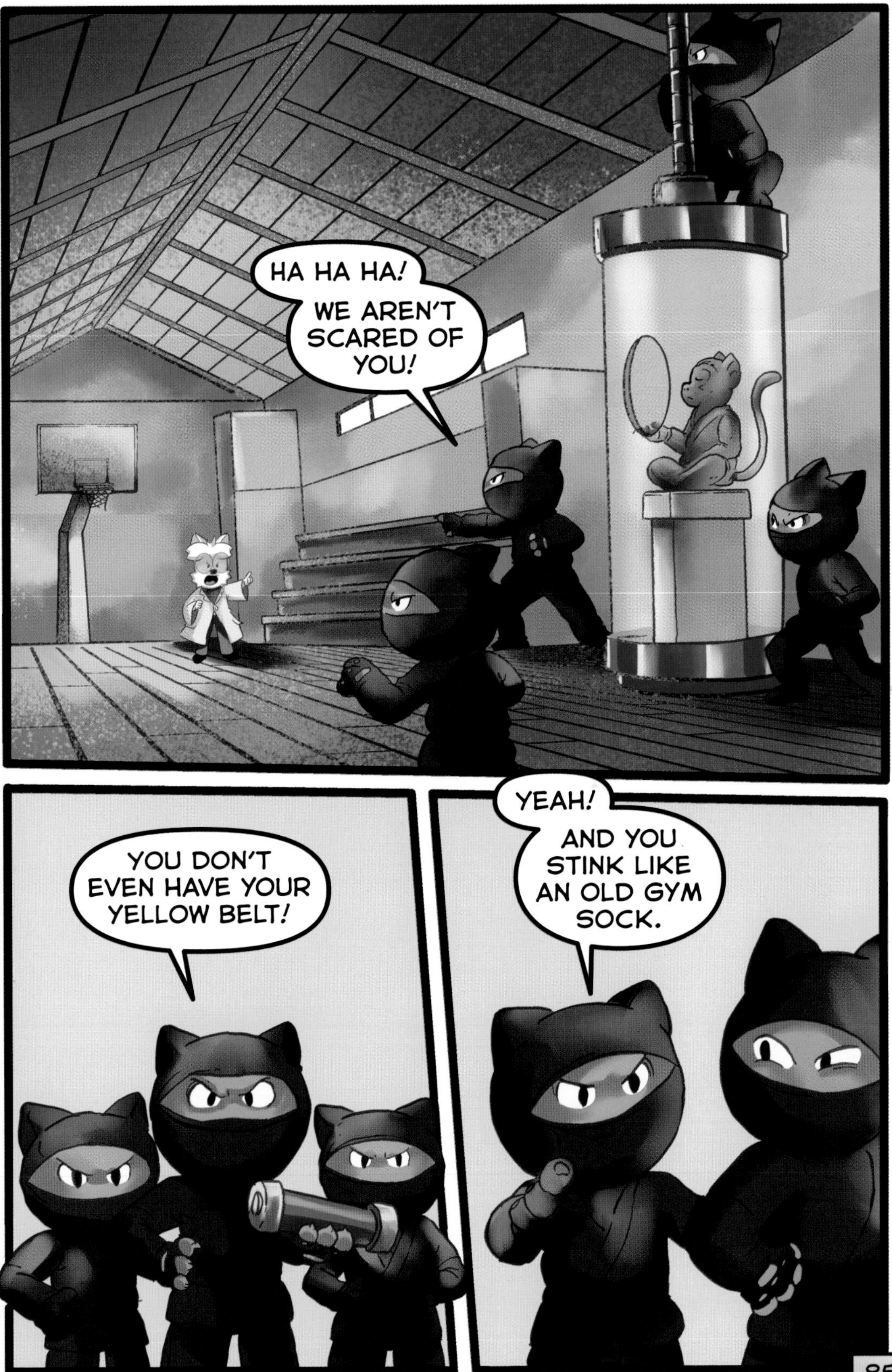
HA HA HA!
WE AREN'T SCARED OF YOU!
YOU DON'T EVEN HAVE YOUR YELLOW BELT!
YEAH!
AND YOU STINK LIKE AN OLD GYM SOCK.

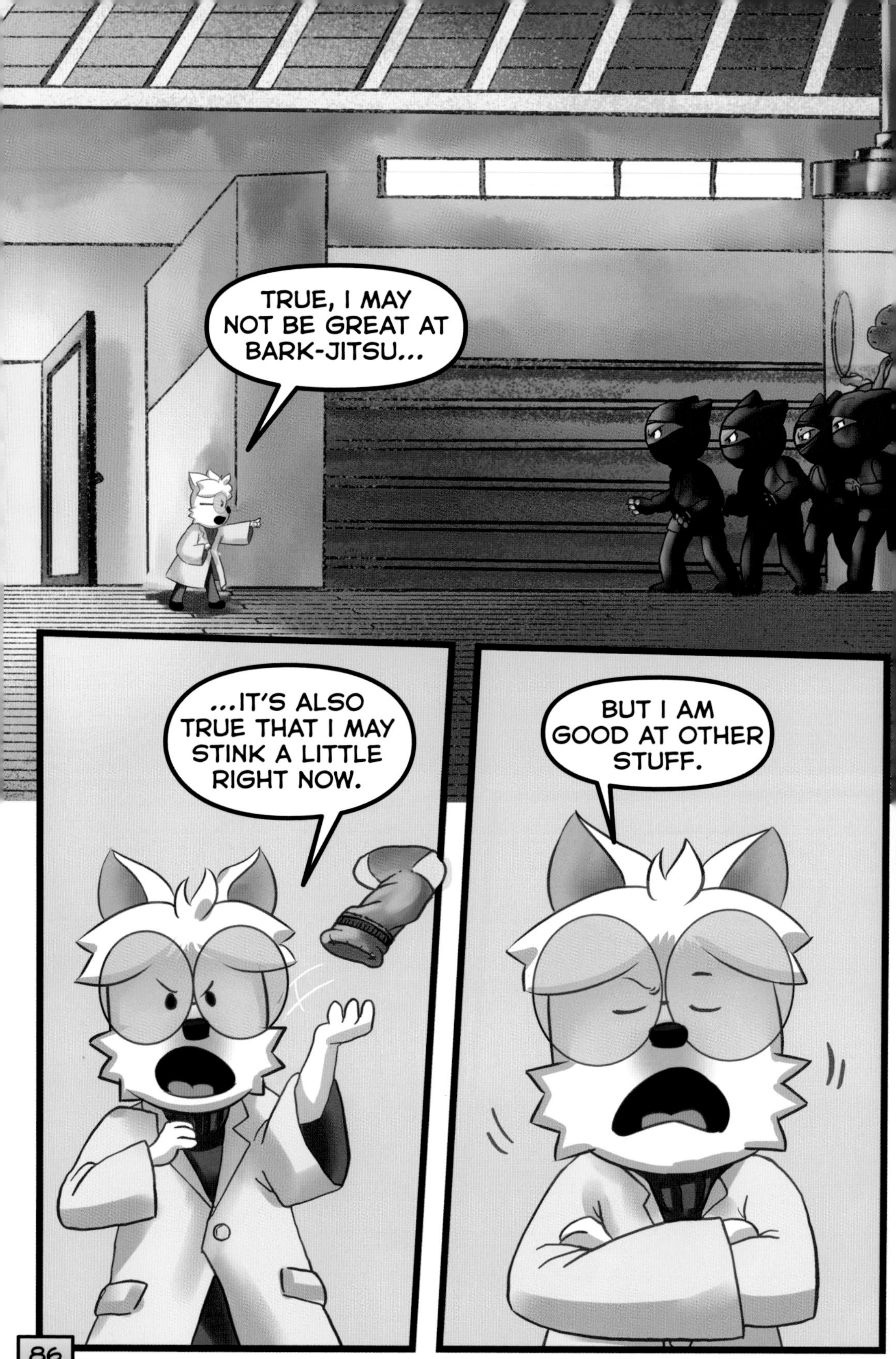
TRUE, I MAY NOT BE GREAT AT BARK-JITSU...
...IT'S ALSO TRUE THAT I MAY STINK A LITTLE RIGHT NOW.
BUT I AM GOOD AT OTHER STUFF.

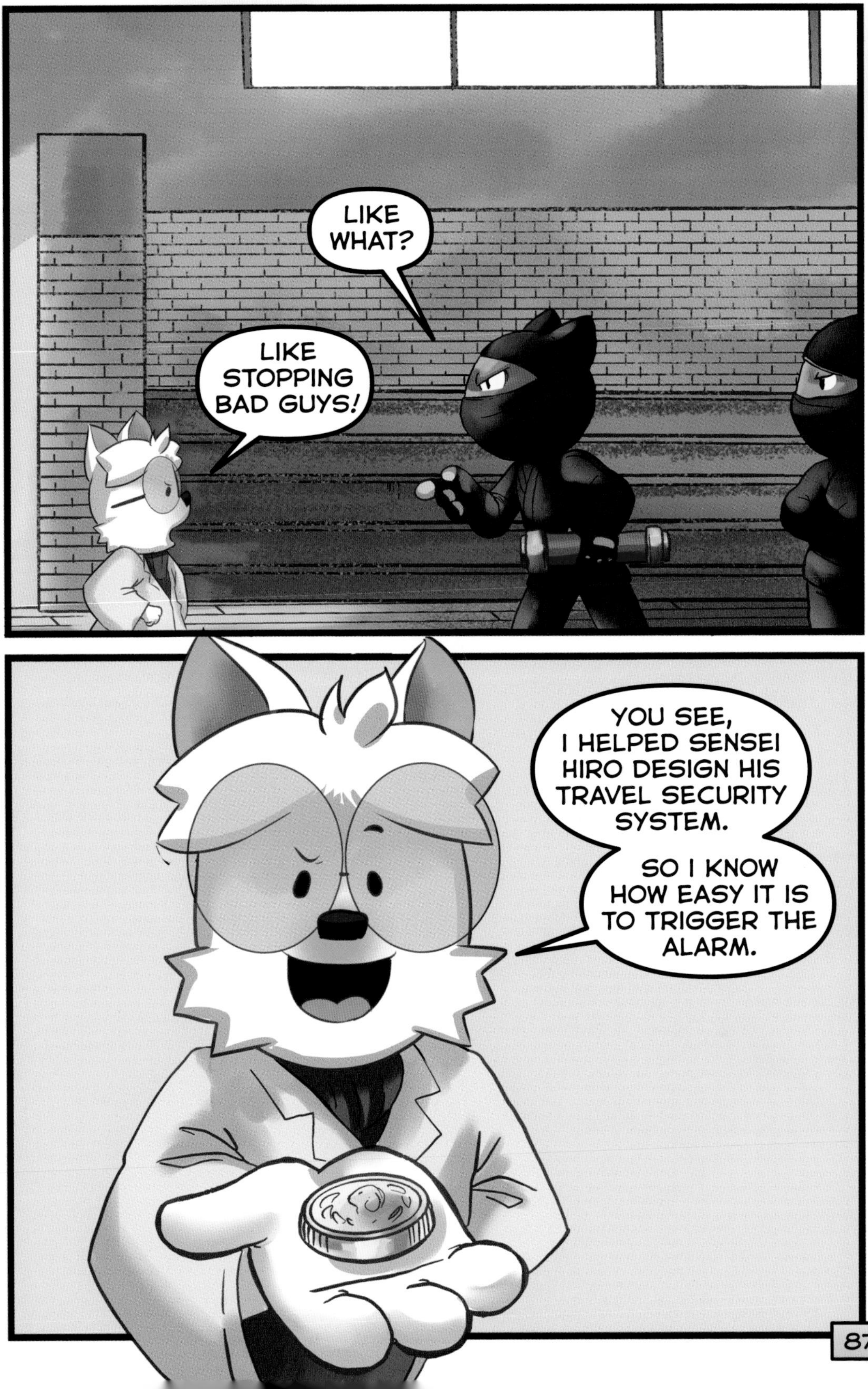
LIKE WHAT?
LIKE STOPPING BAD GUYS!
YOU SEE, I HELPED SENSEI HIRO DESIGN HIS TRAVEL SECURITY SYSTEM.
SO I KNOW HOW EASY IT IS TO TRIGGER THE ALARM.

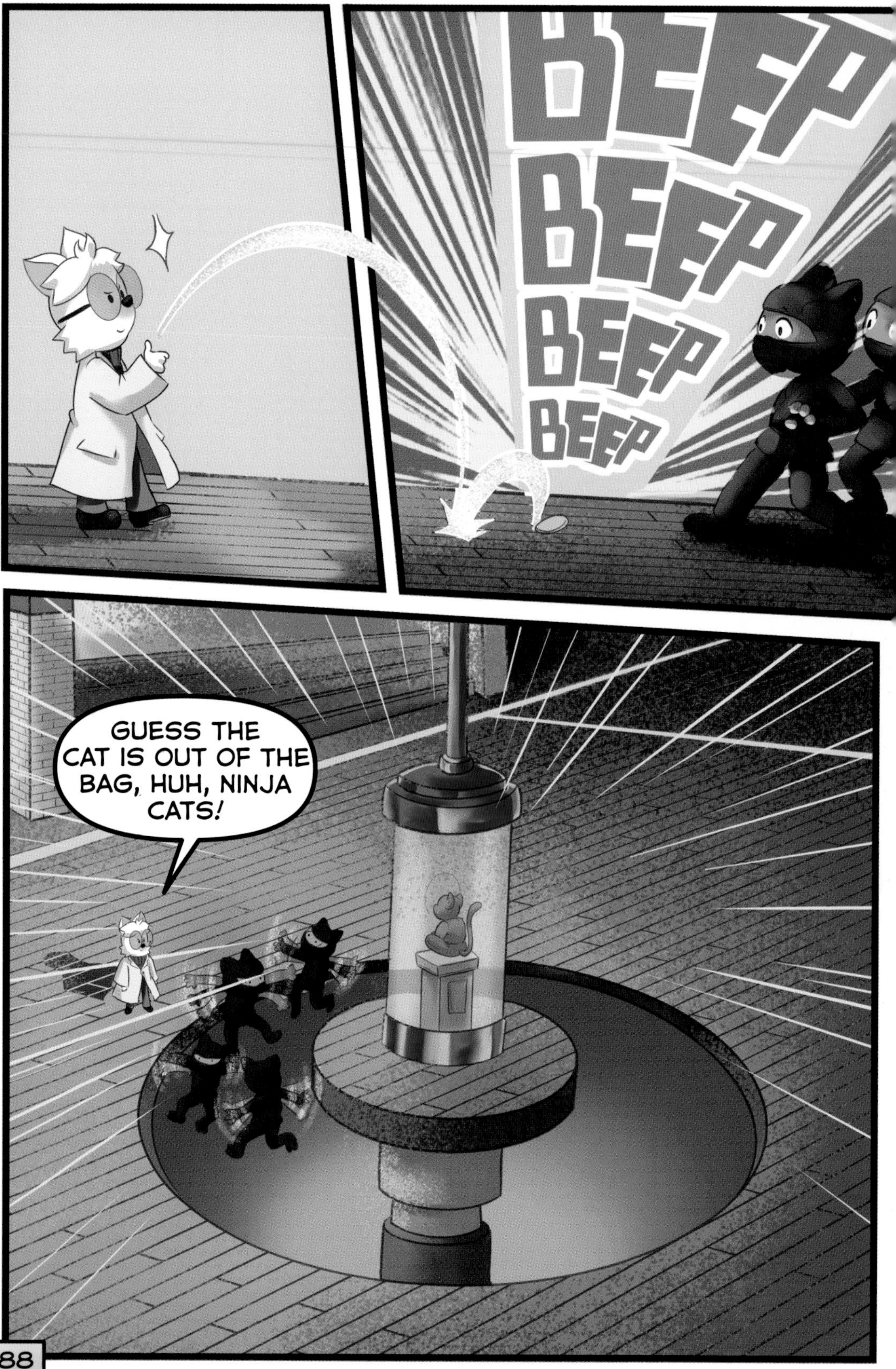
BEEP
BEEP
BEEP
BEEP
GUESS THE CAT IS OUT OF THE BAG, HUH, NINJA CATS!

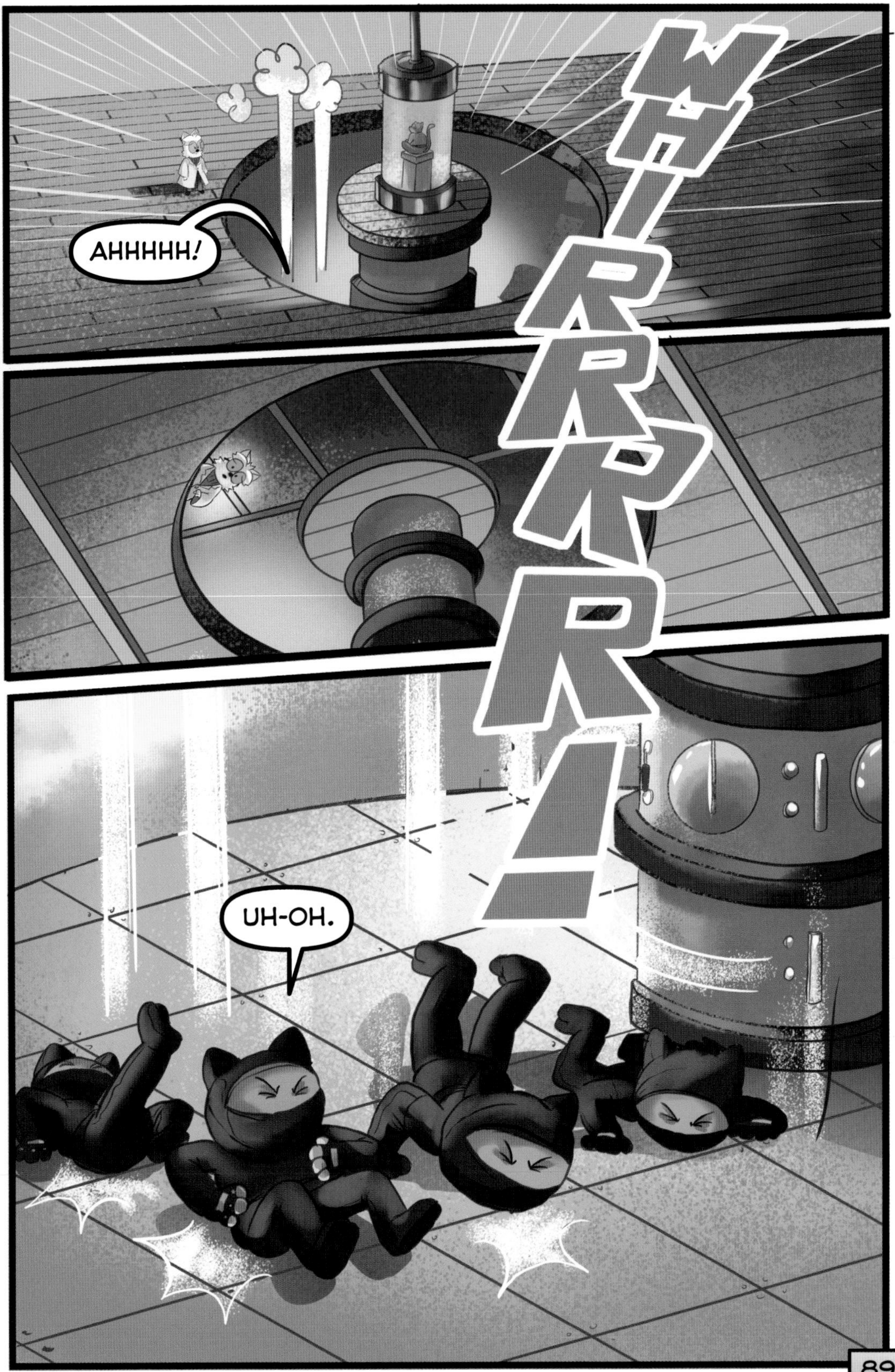
AHHHHH!
WHIRRRRR!
UH-OH.

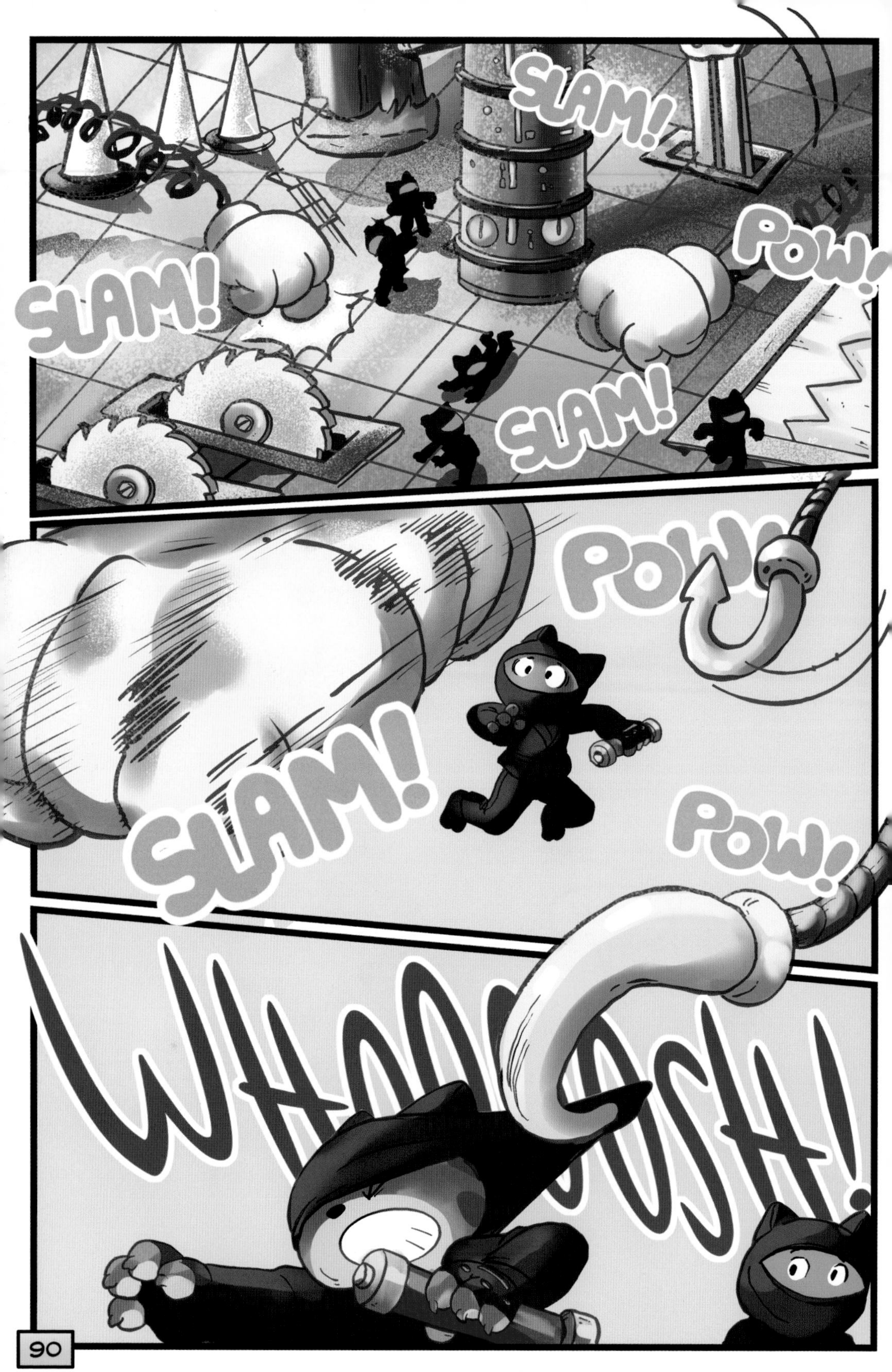
SLAM!
POW!
SLAM!
SLAM!
SLAM!
POW!
WHOOOOSH!

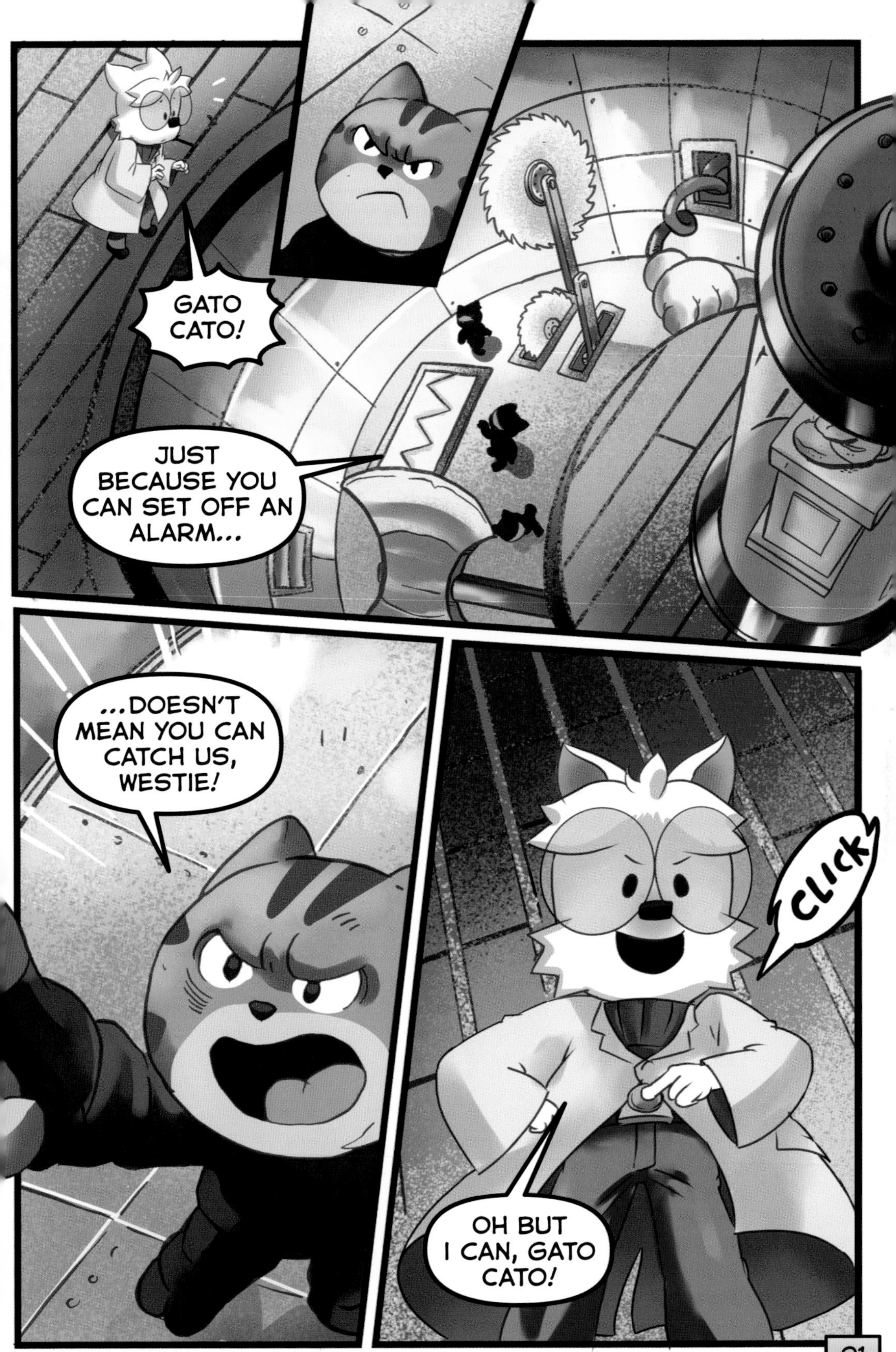
GATO CATO!
JUST BECAUSE YOU CAN SET OFF AN ALARM...
...DOESN'T MEAN YOU CAN CATCH US, WESTIE!
CLICK
OH BUT I CAN, GATO CATO!

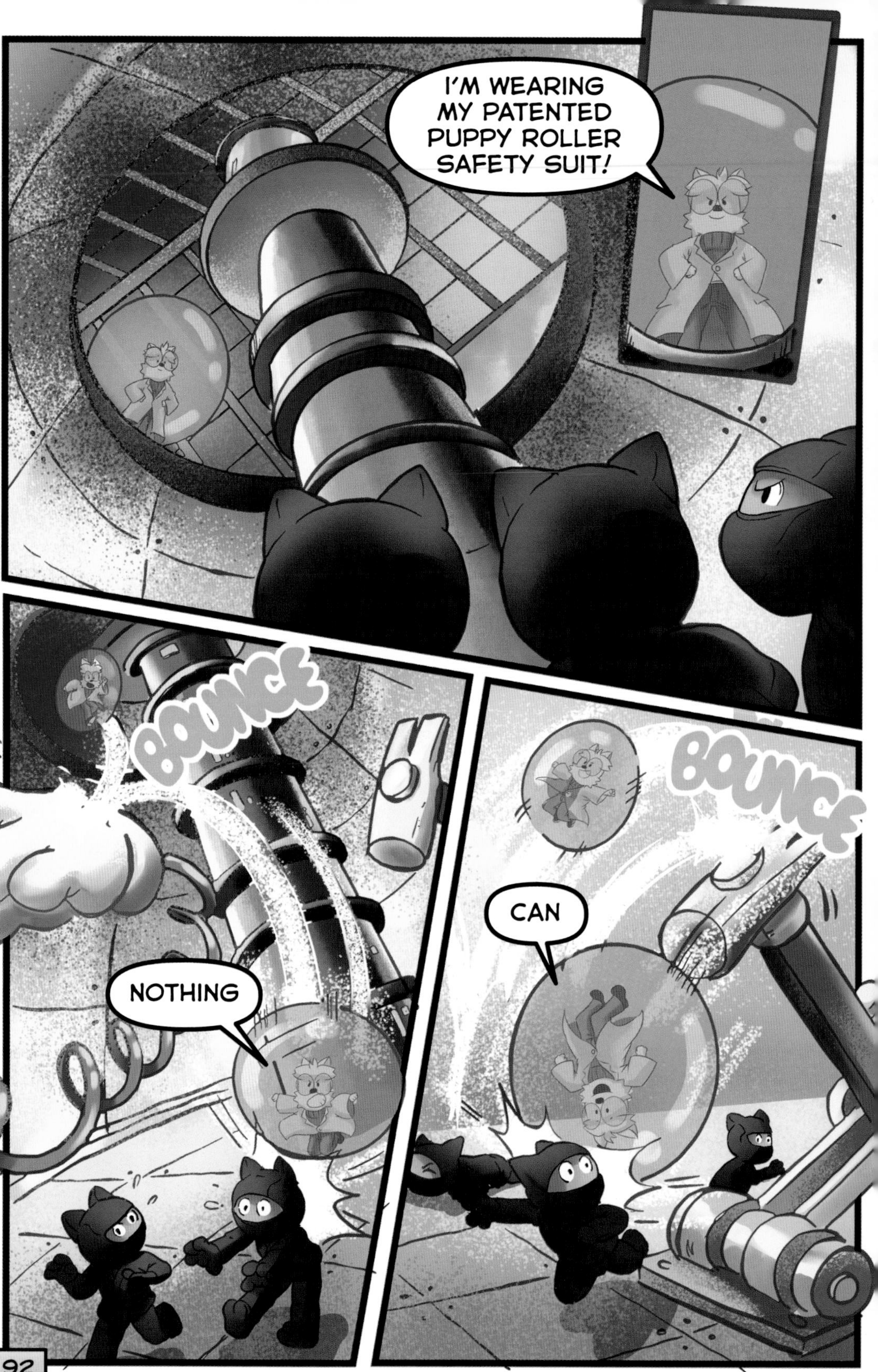
I'M WEARING MY PATENTED PUPPY ROLLER SAFETY SUIT!
BOUNCE
NOTHING
BOUNCE
CAN

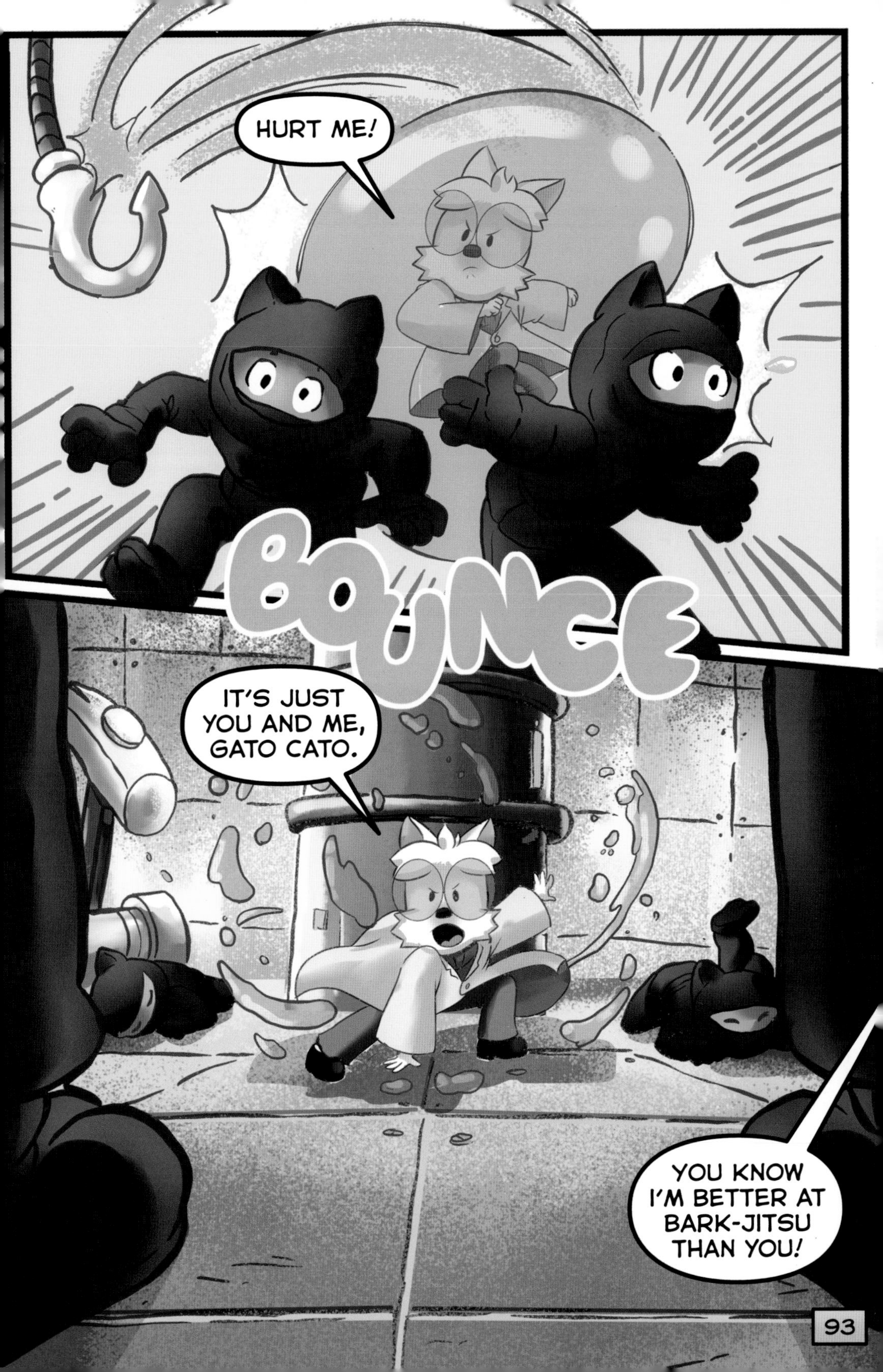
HURT ME!
BOUNCE
IT'S JUST YOU AND ME, GATO CATO.
YOU KNOW I'M BETTER AT BARK-JITSU THAN YOU!

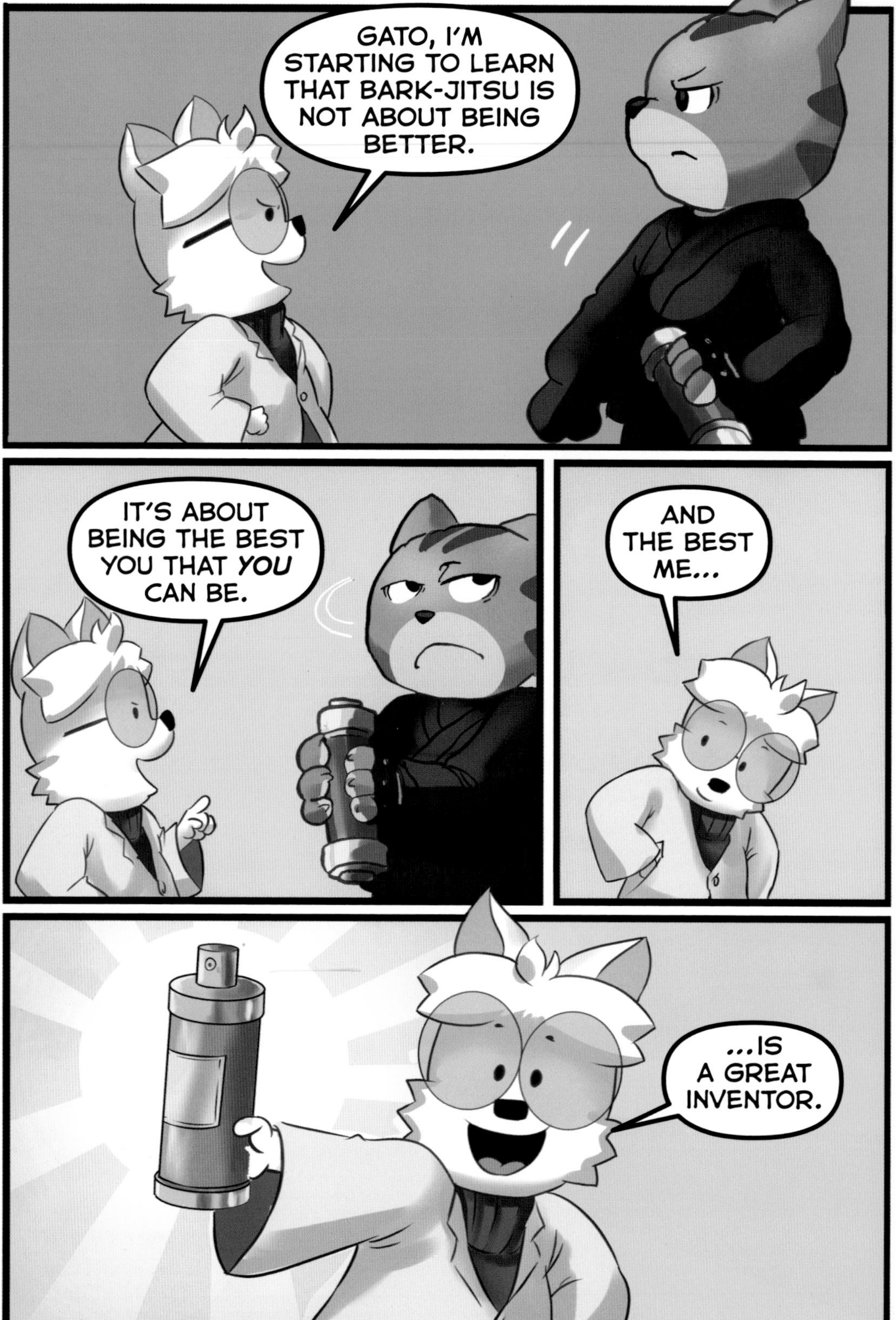
GATO, I'M STARTING TO LEARN THAT BARK-JITSU IS NOT ABOUT BEING BETTER.
IT'S ABOUT BEING THE BEST YOU THAT *YOU* CAN BE.
AND THE BEST ME...
...IS A GREAT INVENTOR.

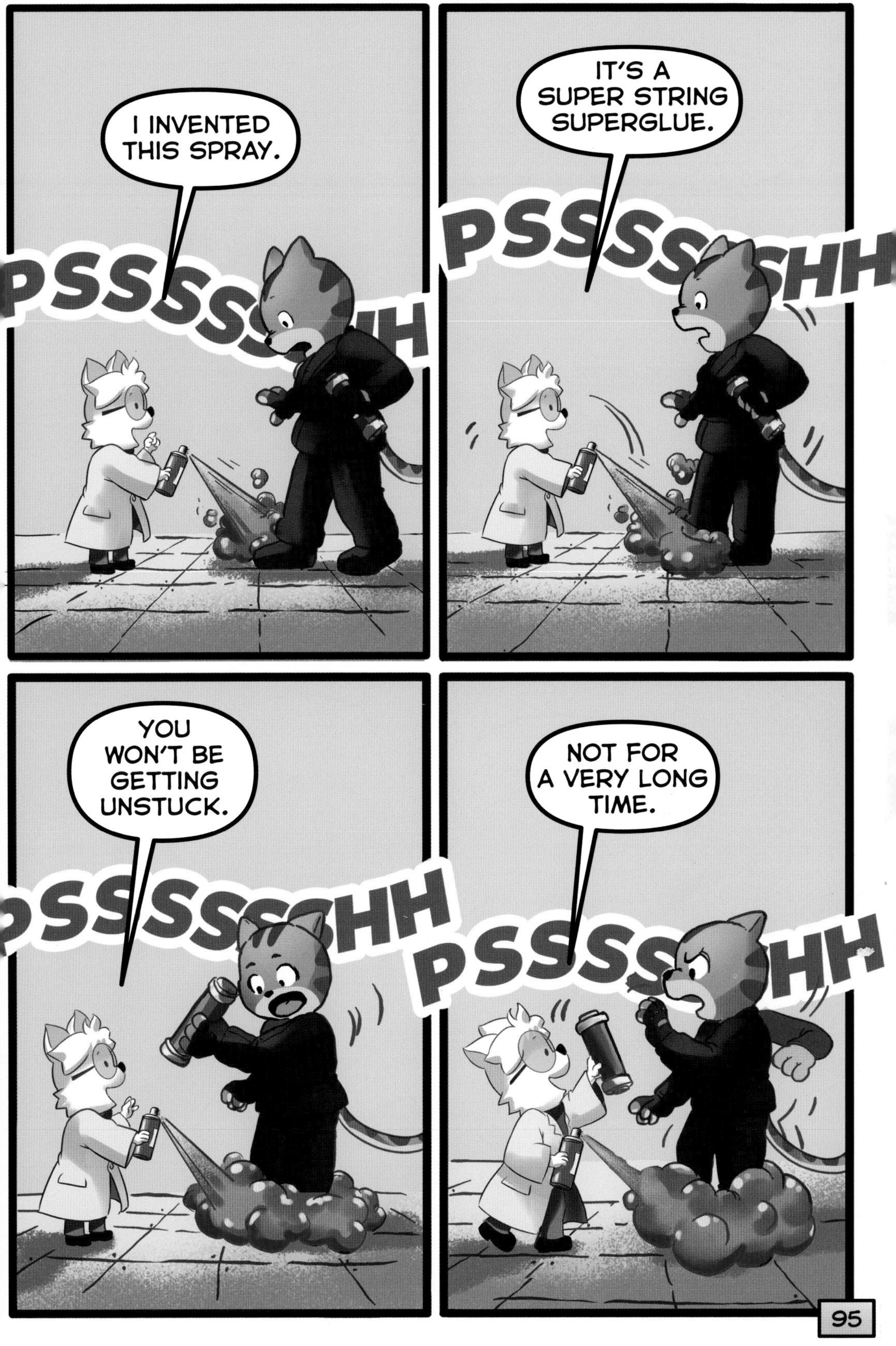

I INVENTED THIS SPRAY.
PSSSSSSHH
IT'S A SUPER STRING SUPERGLUE.
PSSSSSSHH
YOU WON'T BE GETTING UNSTUCK.
PSSSSSSHH
NOT FOR A VERY LONG TIME.
PSSSSSHH

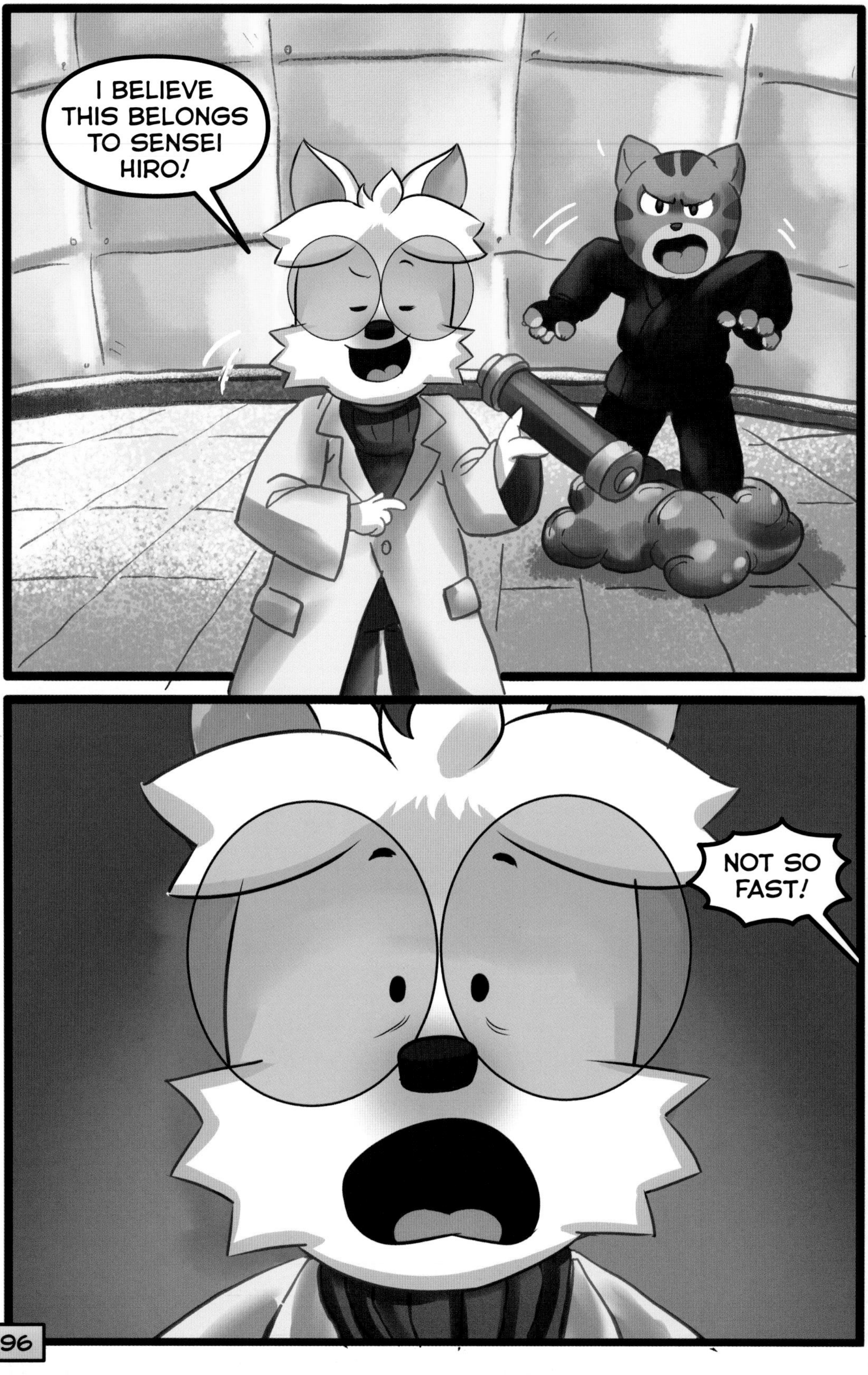
I BELIEVE THIS BELONGS TO SENSEI HIRO!
NOT SO FAST!

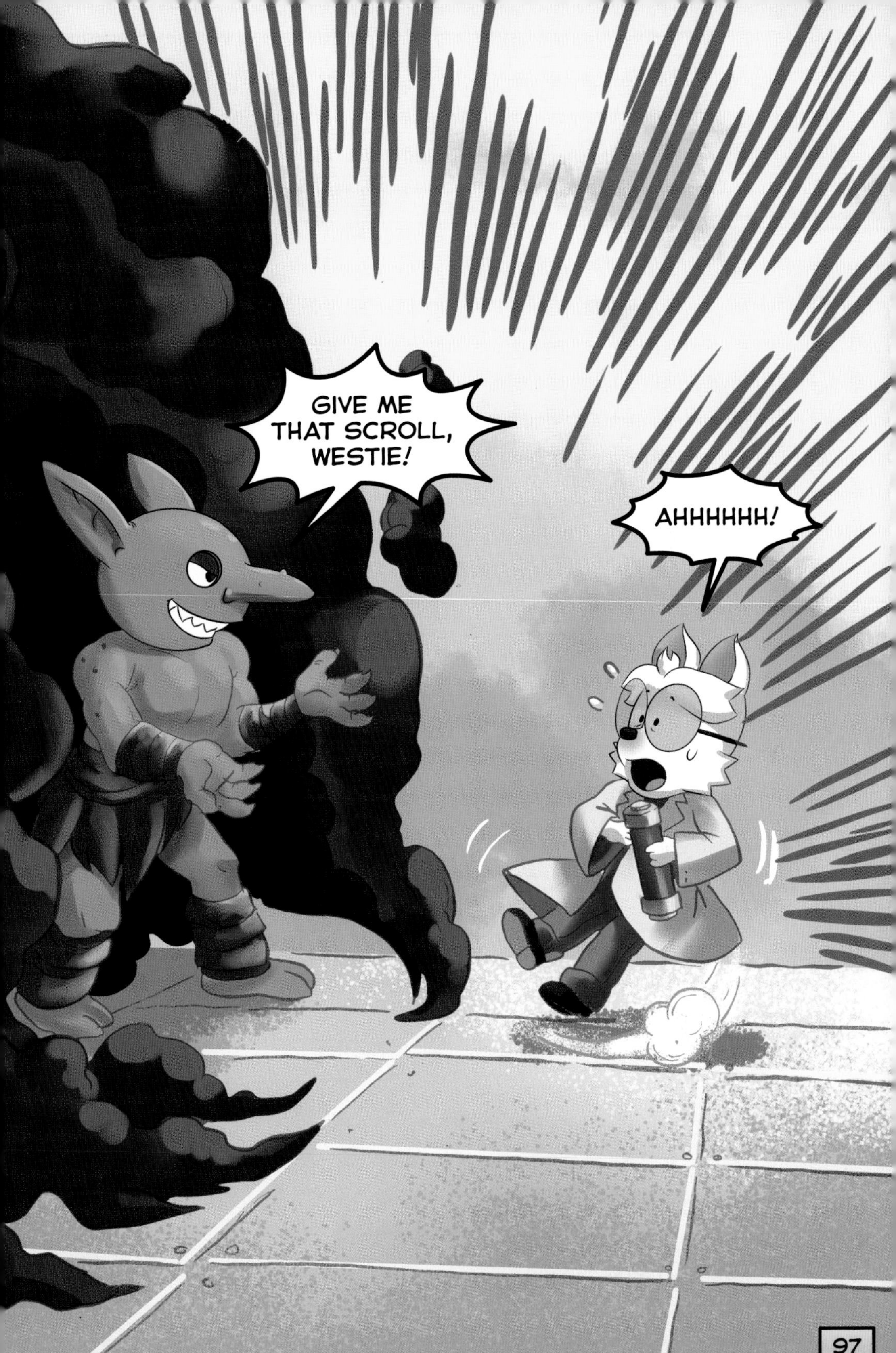
GIVE ME THAT SCROLL, WESTIE!
AHHHHHH!

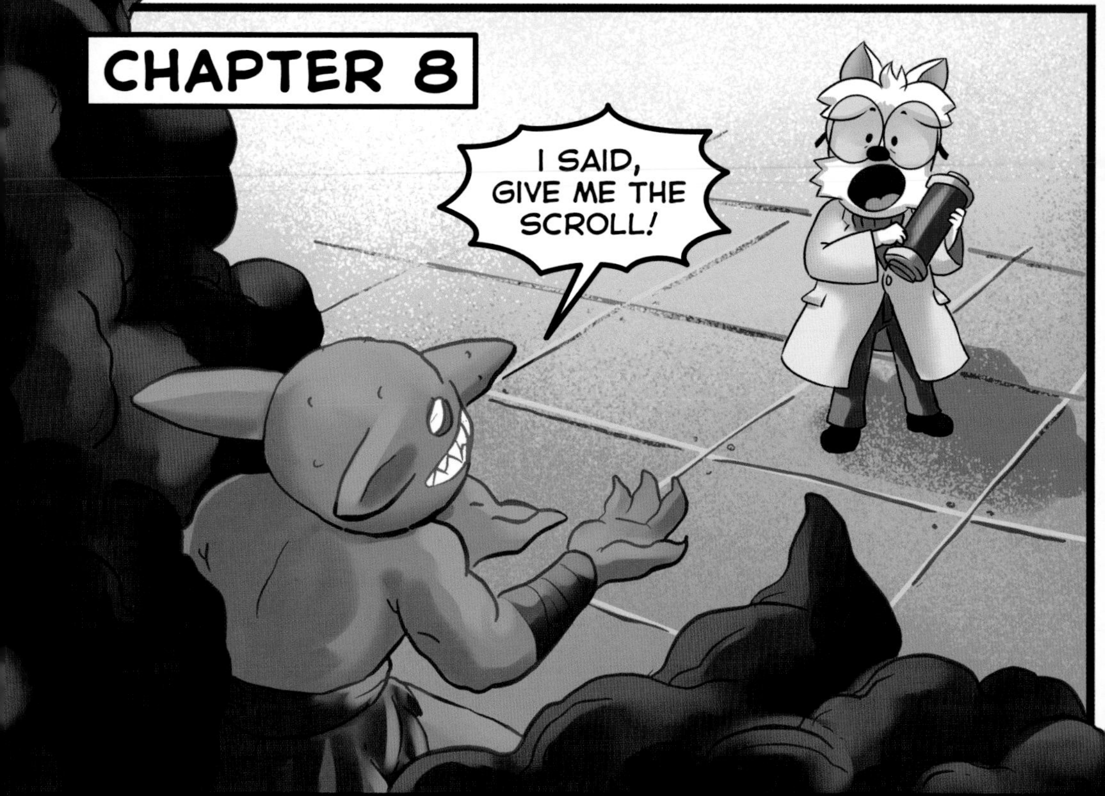
CHAPTER 8
I SAID, GIVE ME THE SCROLL!

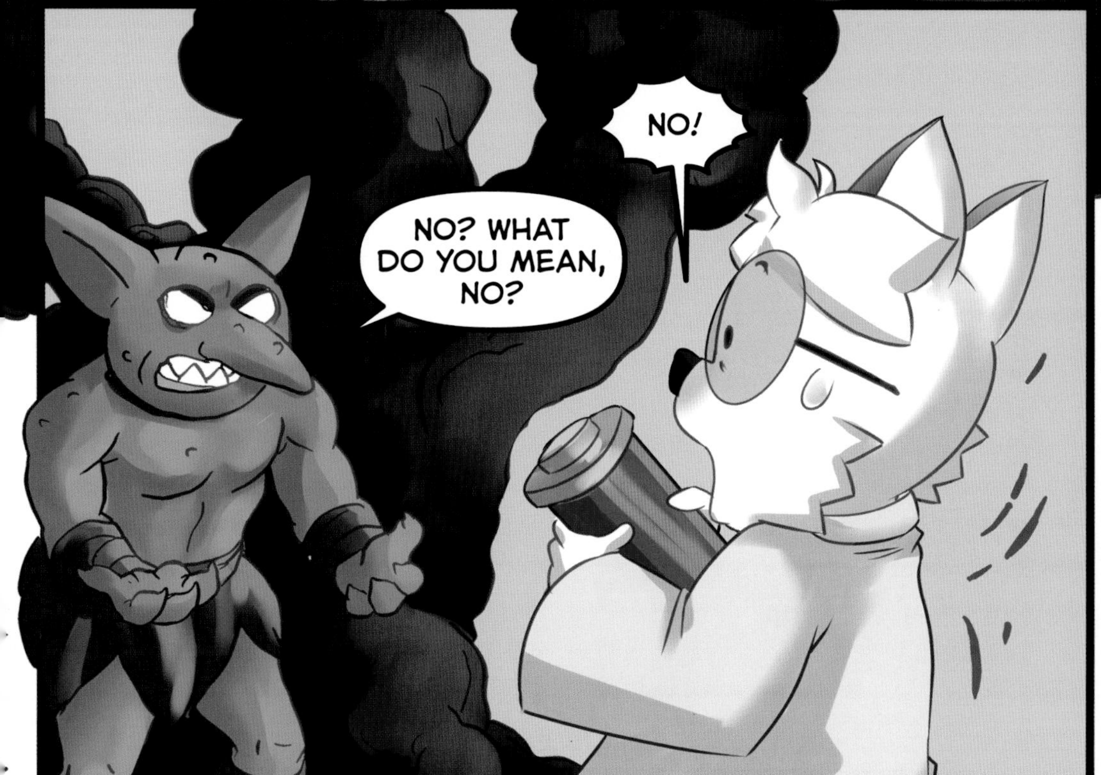
NO!
NO? WHAT DO YOU MEAN, NO?

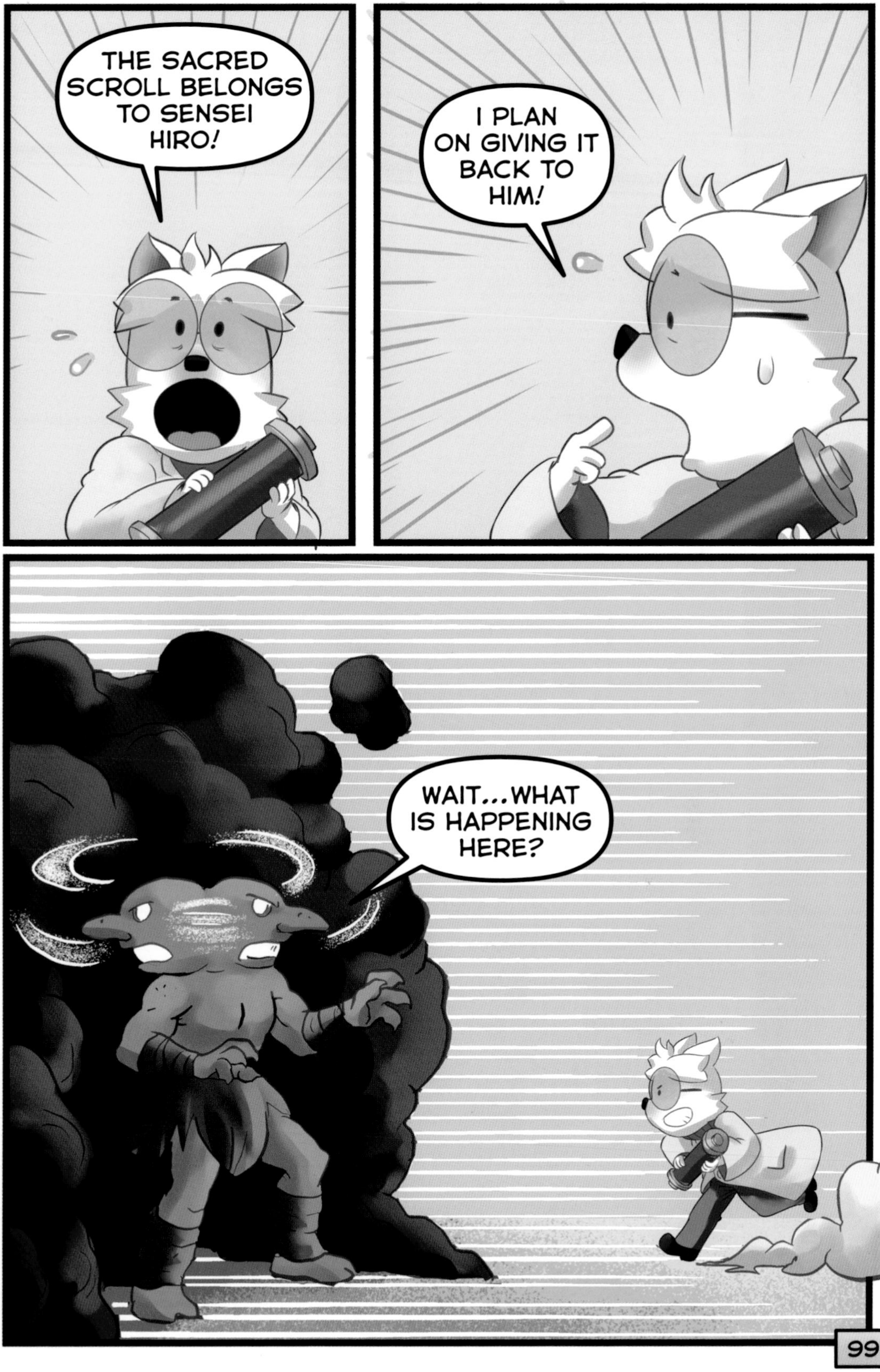
THE SACRED SCROLL BELONGS TO SENSEI HIRO!
I PLAN ON GIVING IT BACK TO HIM!
WAIT...WHAT IS HAPPENING HERE?

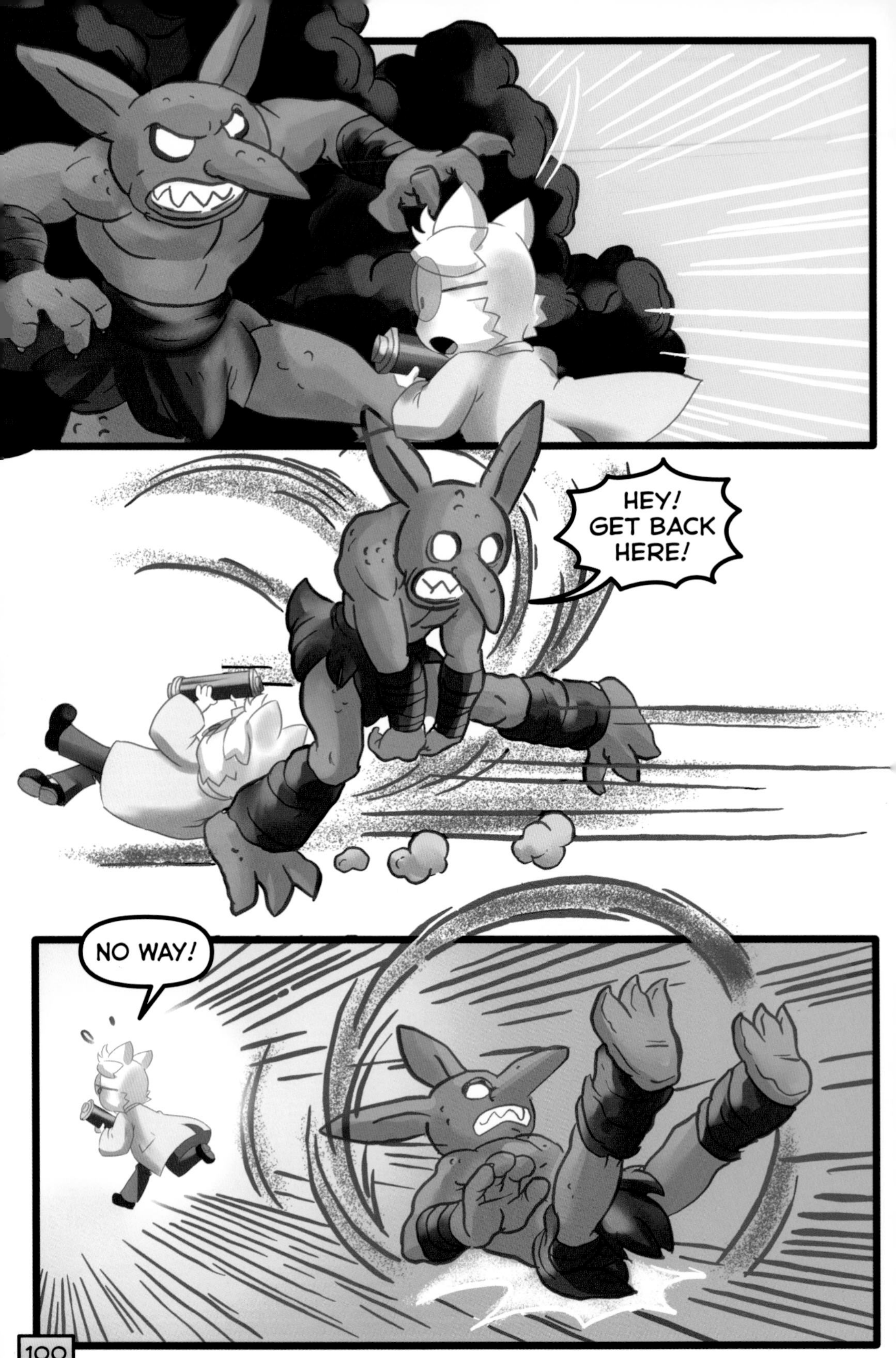
HEY! GET BACK HERE!
NO WAY!

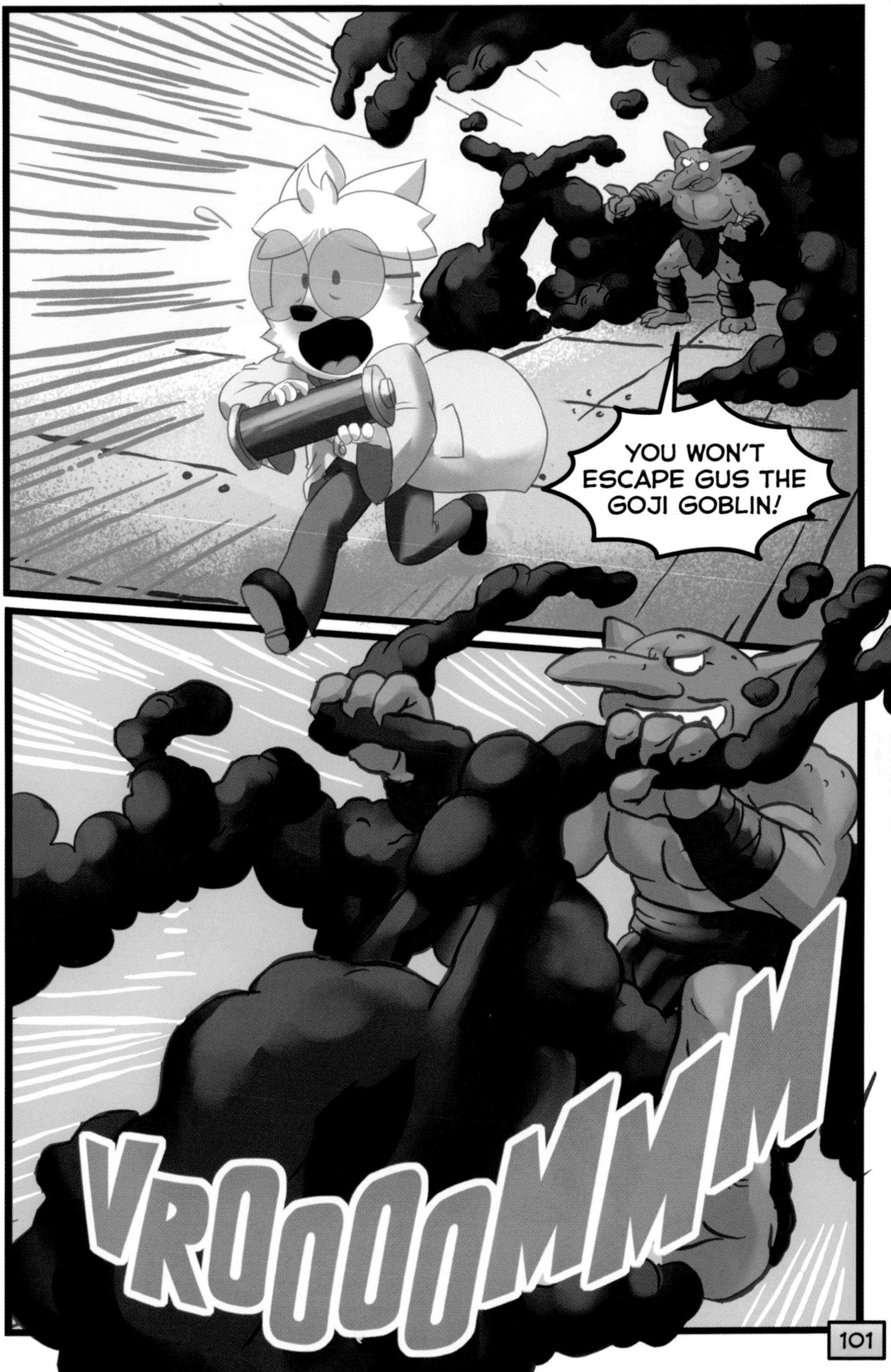
YOU WON'T ESCAPE GUS THE GOJI GOBLIN!
VROOOOOMMMM

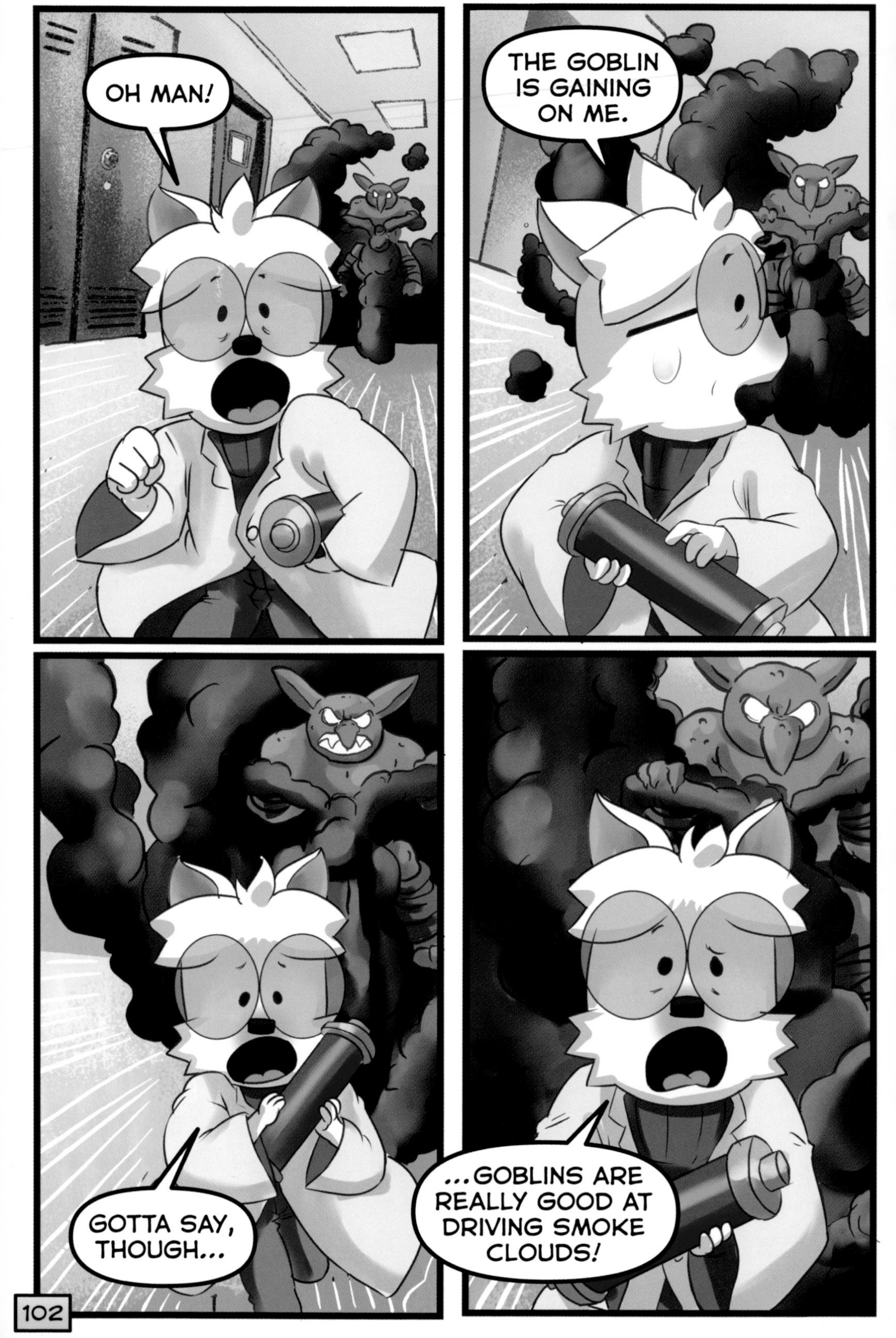
OH MAN!
THE GOBLIN IS GAINING ON ME.
GOTTA SAY, THOUGH...
...GOBLINS ARE REALLY GOOD AT DRIVING SMOKE CLOUDS!

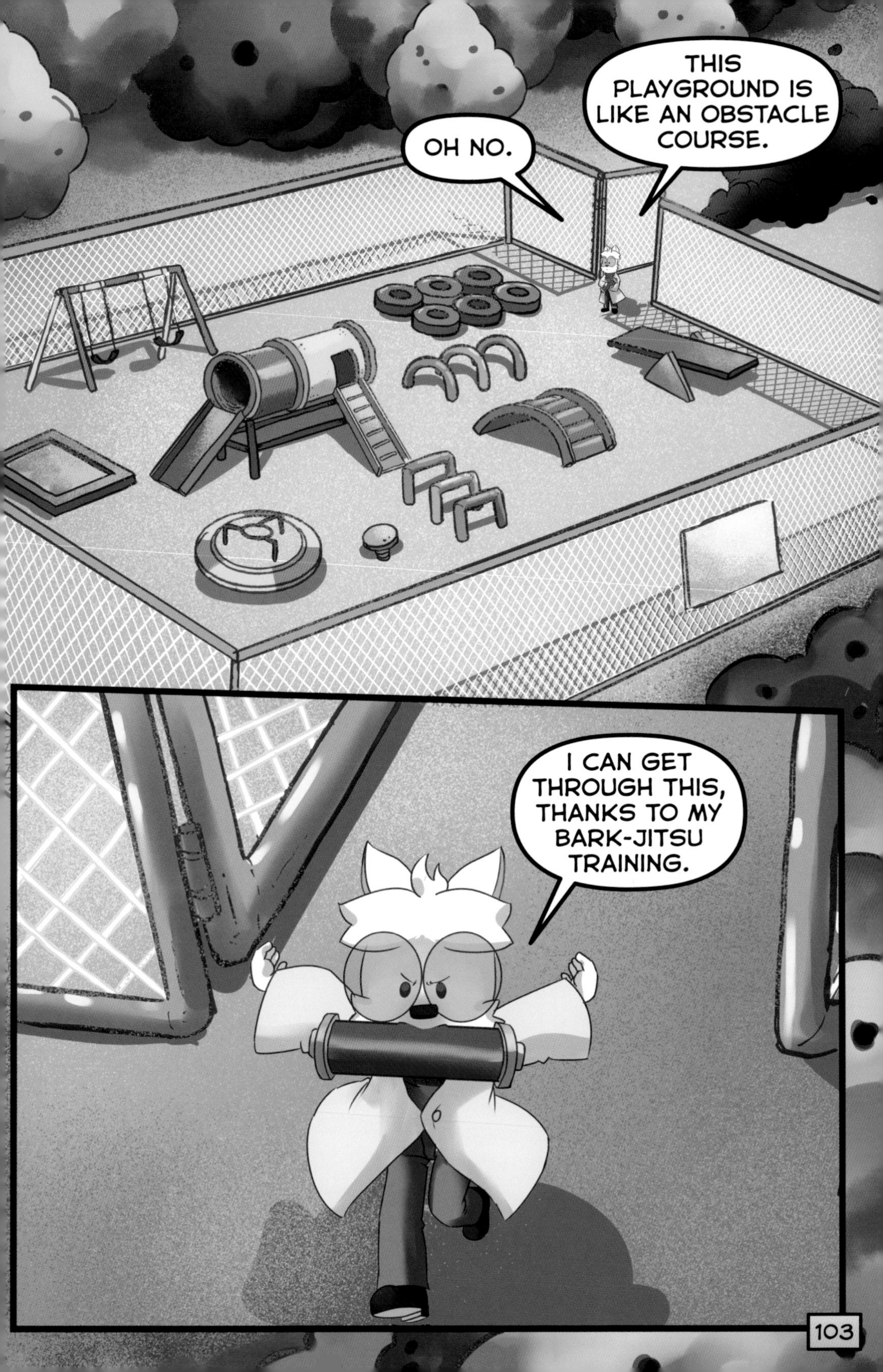
THIS PLAYGROUND IS LIKE AN OBSTACLE COURSE.
OH NO.
I CAN GET THROUGH THIS, THANKS TO MY BARK-JITSU TRAINING.

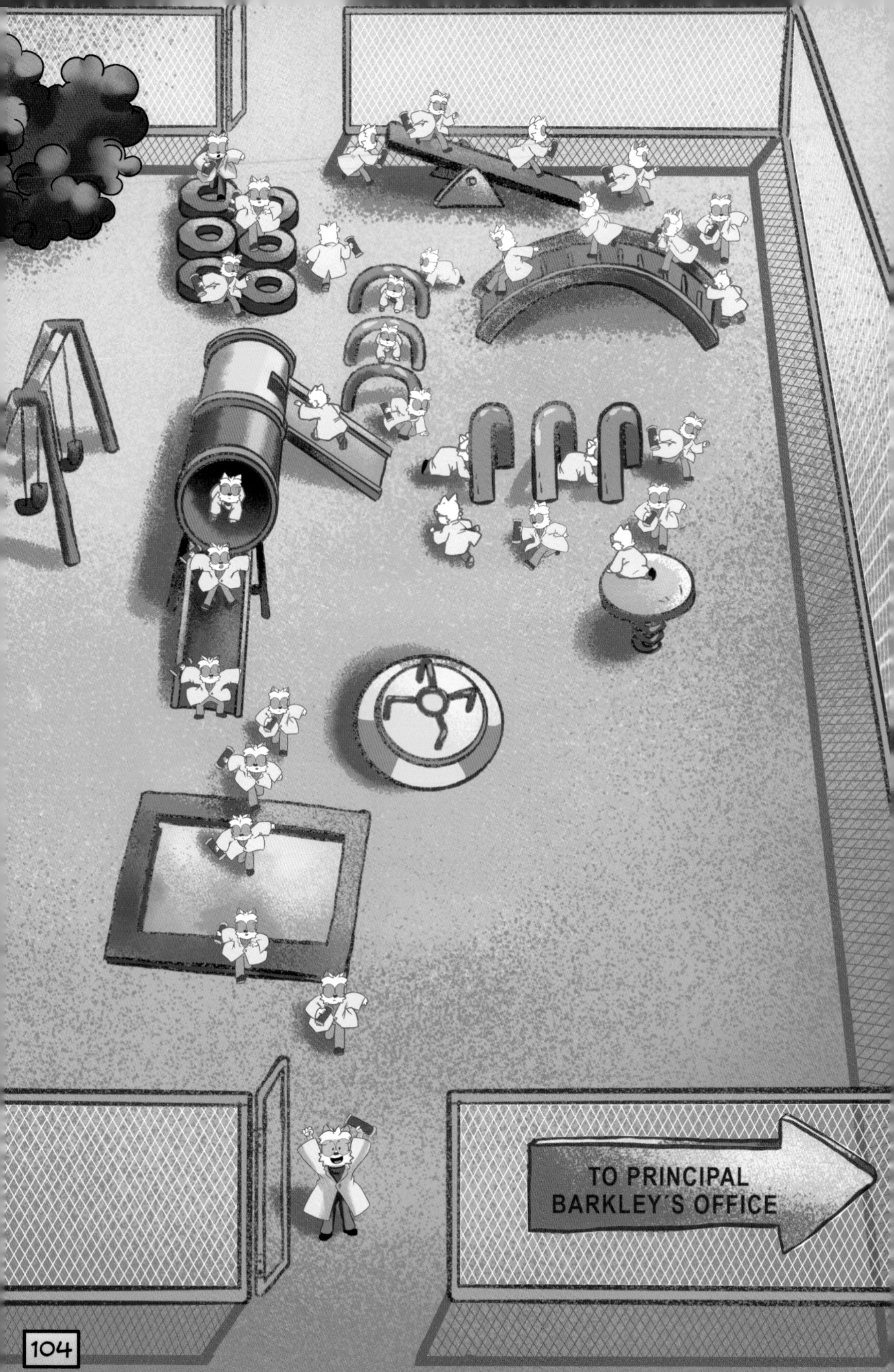
TO PRINCIPAL
BARKLEY´S OFFICE

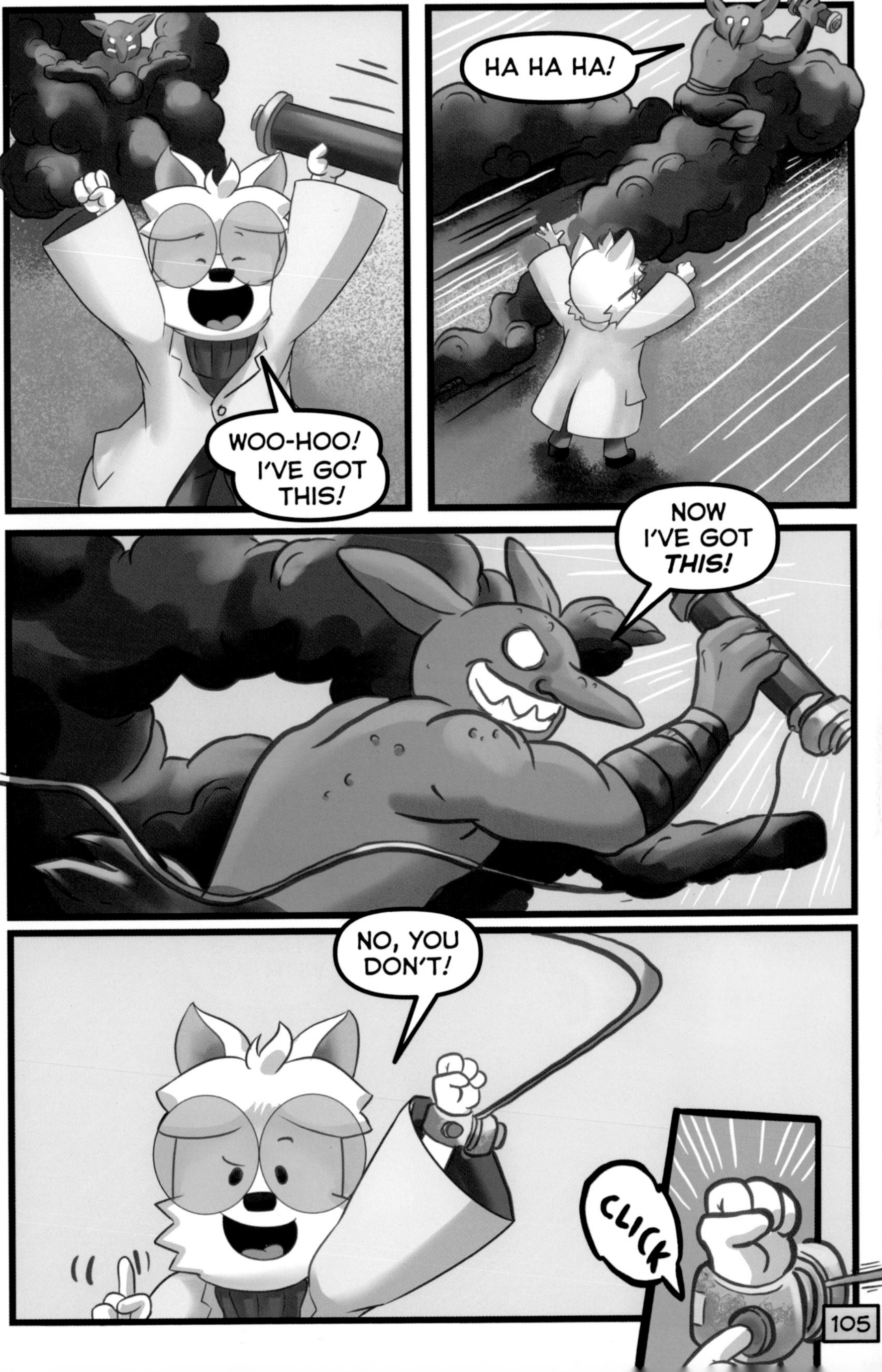
WOO-HOO! I'VE GOT THIS!
HA HA HA!
NOW I'VE GOT THIS!
NO, YOU DON'T!
CLICK

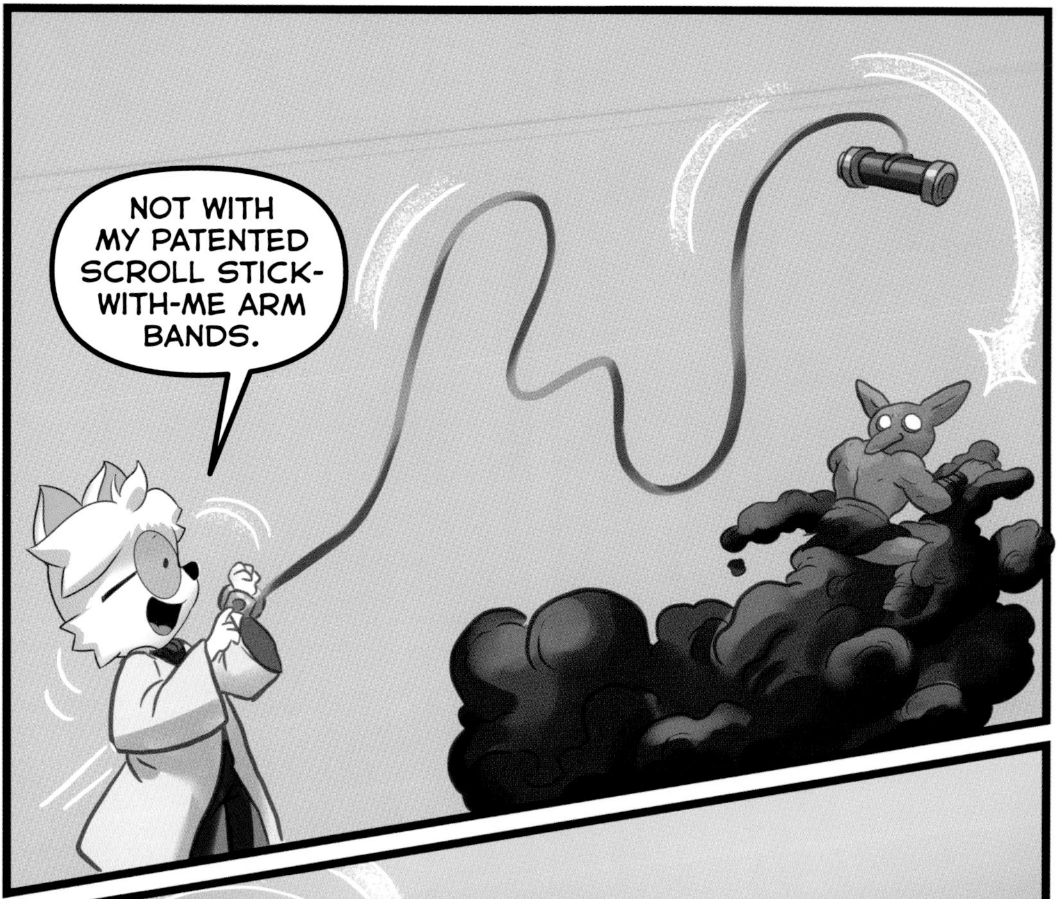
NOT WITH MY PATENTED SCROLL STICK-WITH-ME ARM BANDS.

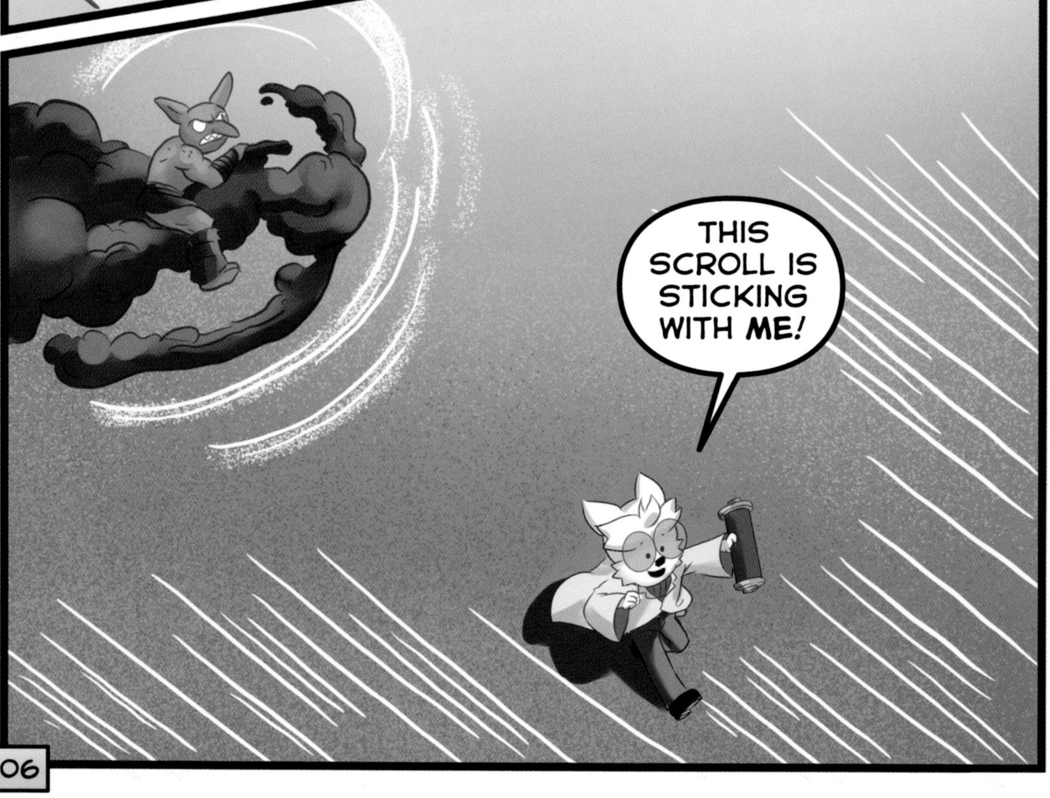
THIS SCROLL IS STICKING WITH ME!

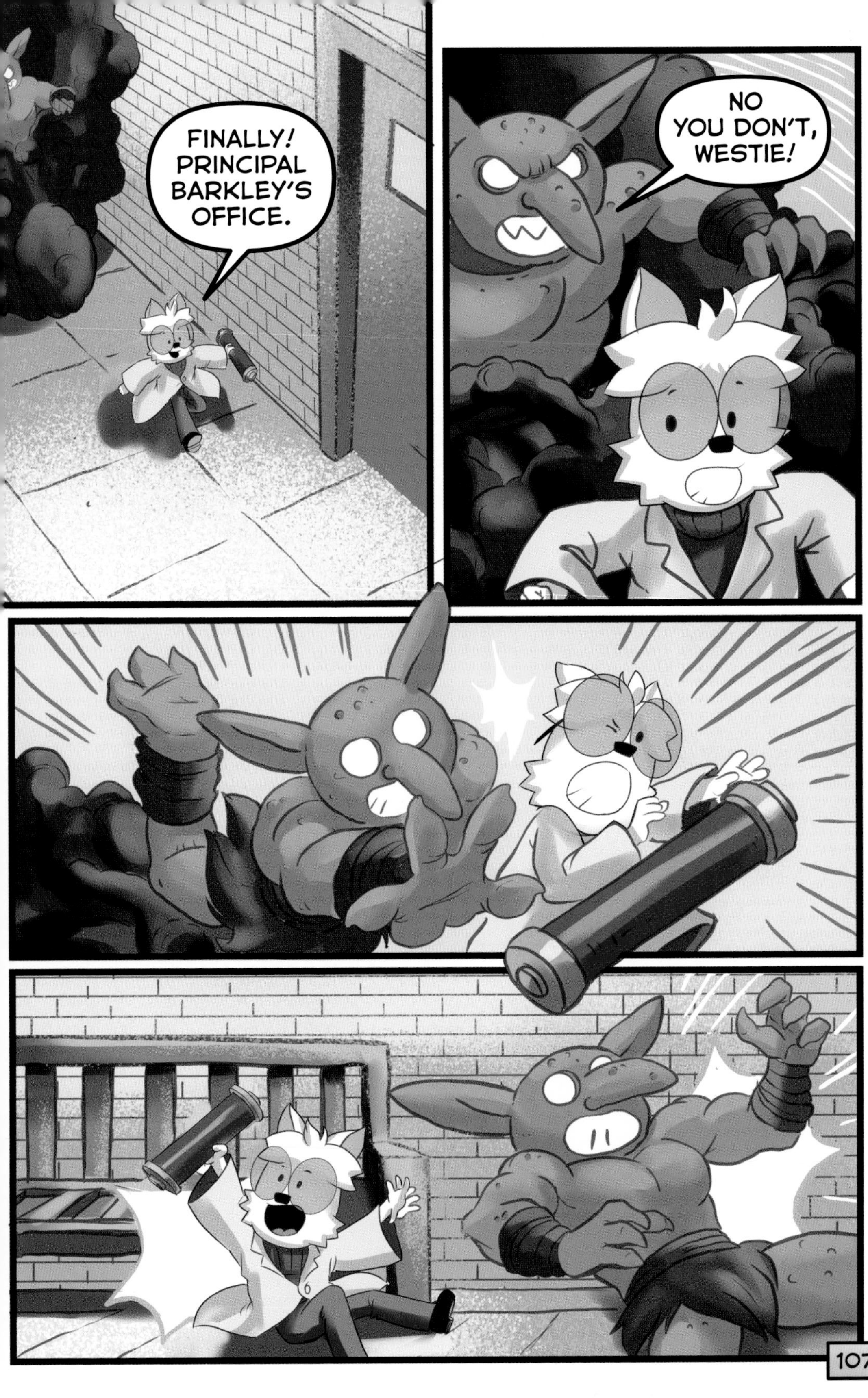
FINALLY! PRINCIPAL BARKLEY'S OFFICE.
NO YOU DON'T, WESTIE!

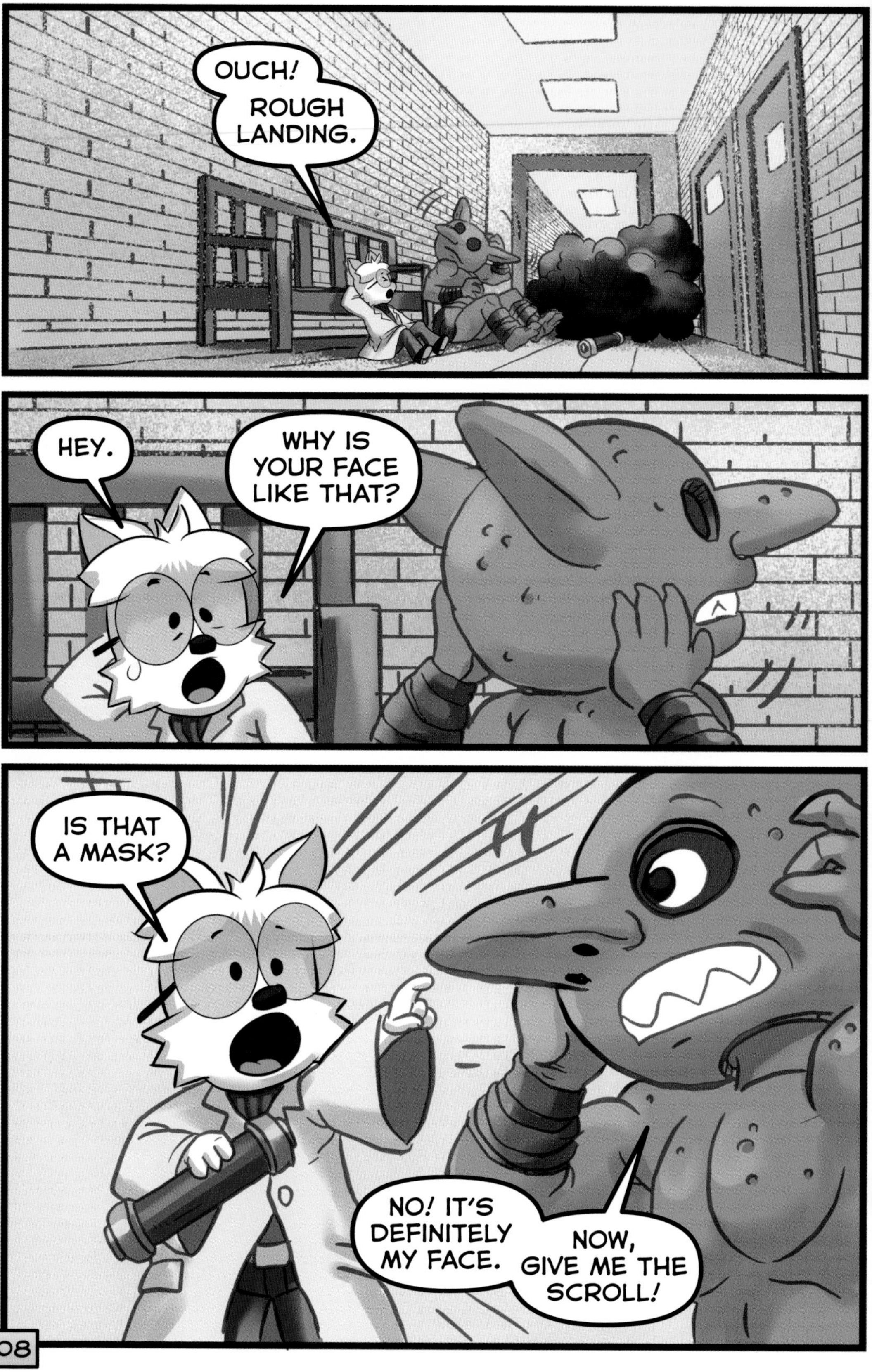

OUCH! ROUGH LANDING.
HEY.
WHY IS YOUR FACE LIKE THAT?
IS THAT A MASK?
NO! IT'S DEFINITELY MY FACE.
NOW, GIVE ME THE SCROLL!

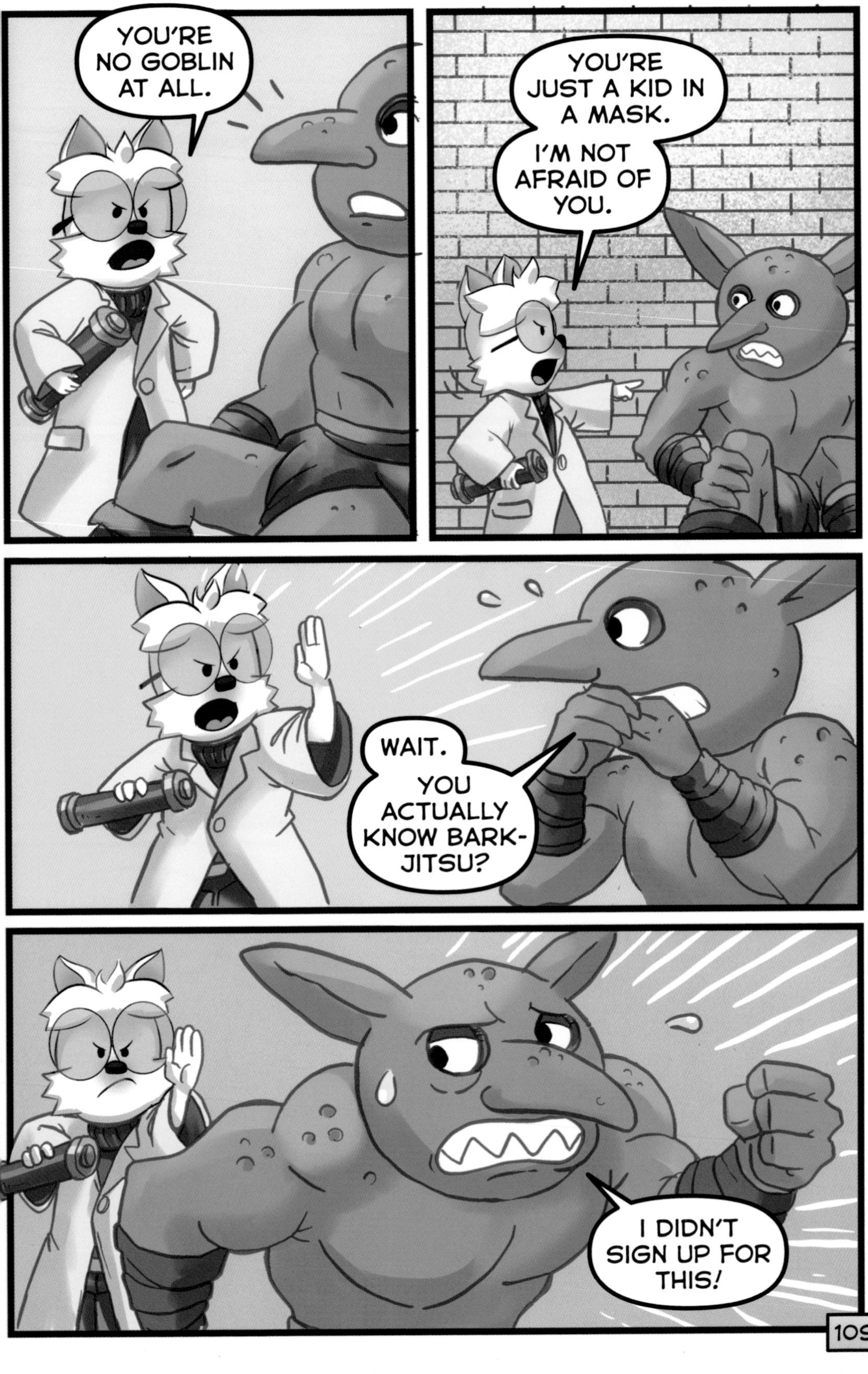
YOU'RE NO GOBLIN AT ALL.
YOU'RE JUST A KID IN A MASK.
I'M NOT AFRAID OF YOU.
WAIT.
YOU ACTUALLY KNOW BARK-JITSU?
I DIDN'T SIGN UP FOR THIS!

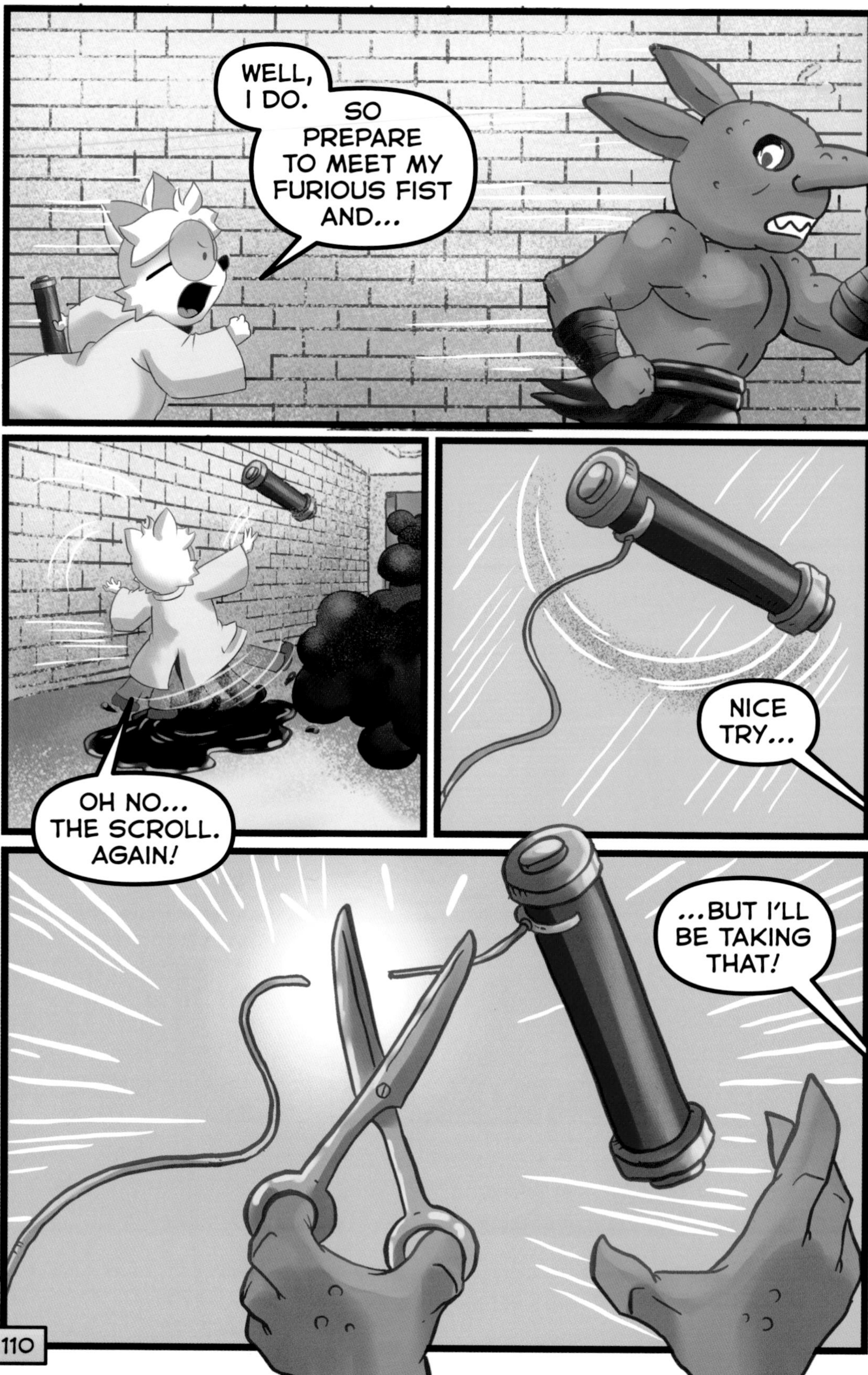
WELL, I DO.
SO PREPARE TO MEET MY FURIOUS FIST AND...
OH NO... THE SCROLL. AGAIN!
NICE TRY...
...BUT I'LL BE TAKING THAT!

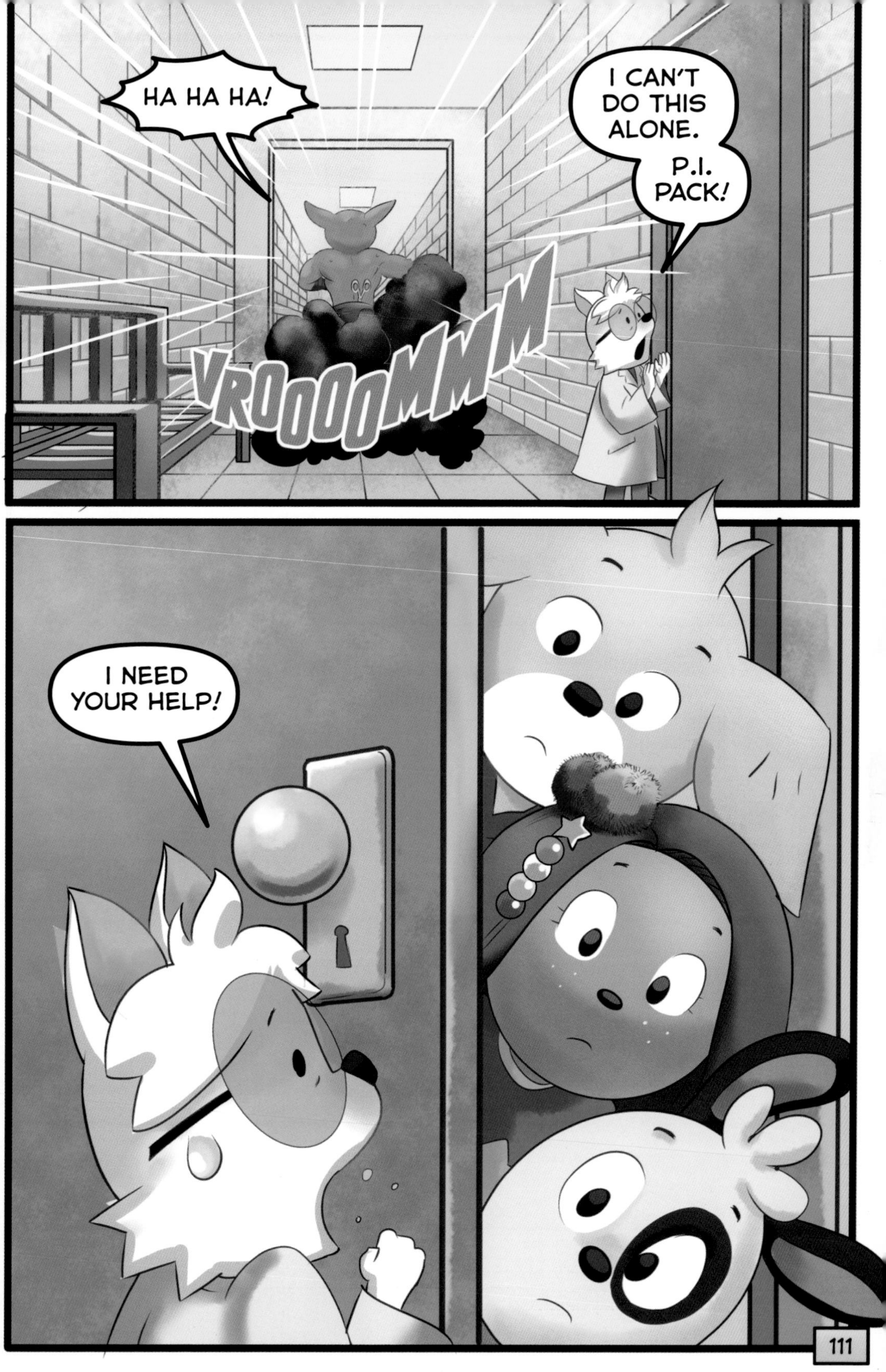
HA HA HA!
VROOOOOMMMM
I CAN'T DO THIS ALONE.
P.I. PACK!
I NEED YOUR HELP!

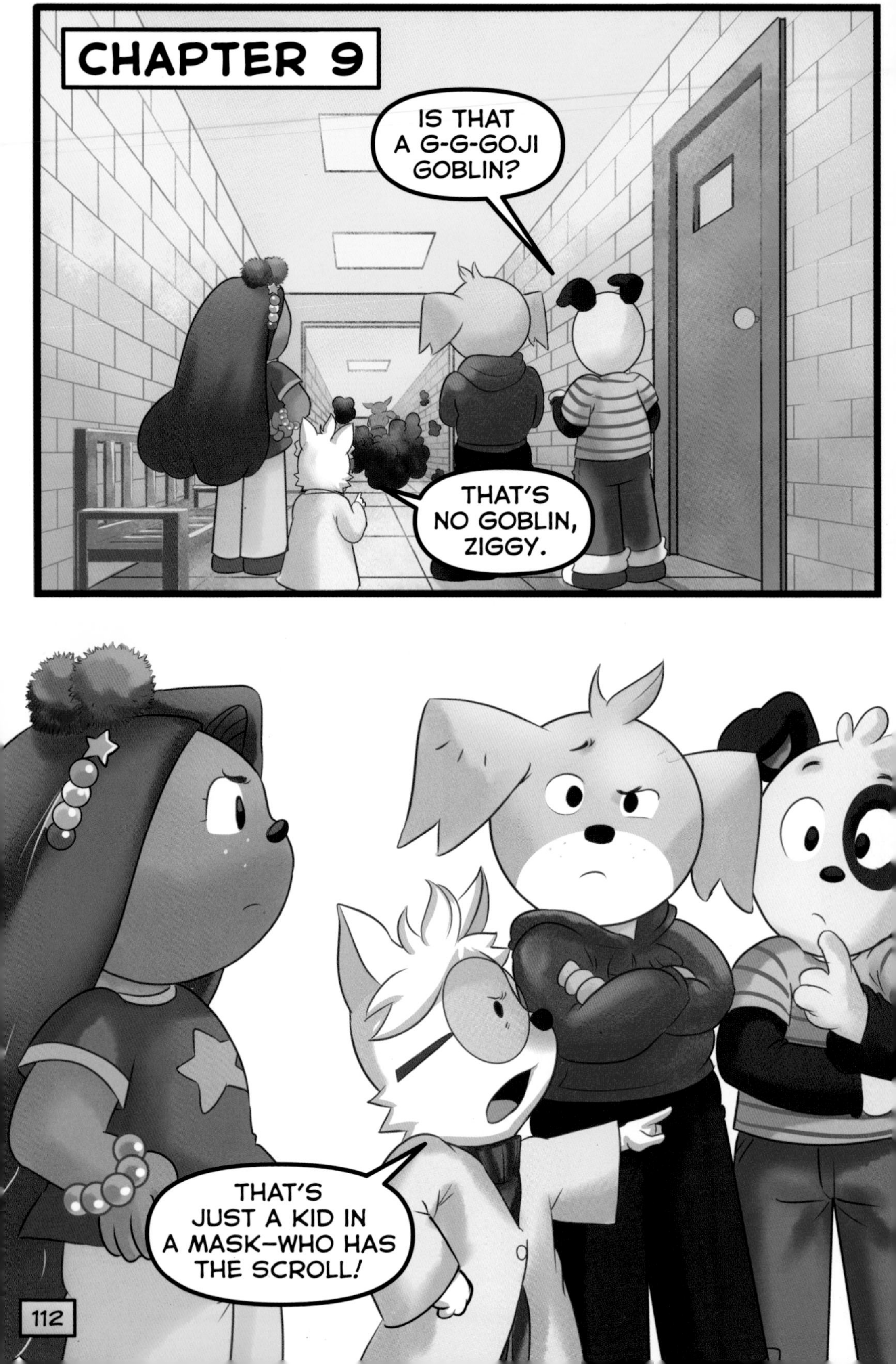
CHAPTER 9
IS THAT A G-G-GOJI GOBLIN?
THAT'S NO GOBLIN, ZIGGY.
THAT'S JUST A KID IN A MASK—WHO HAS THE SCROLL!

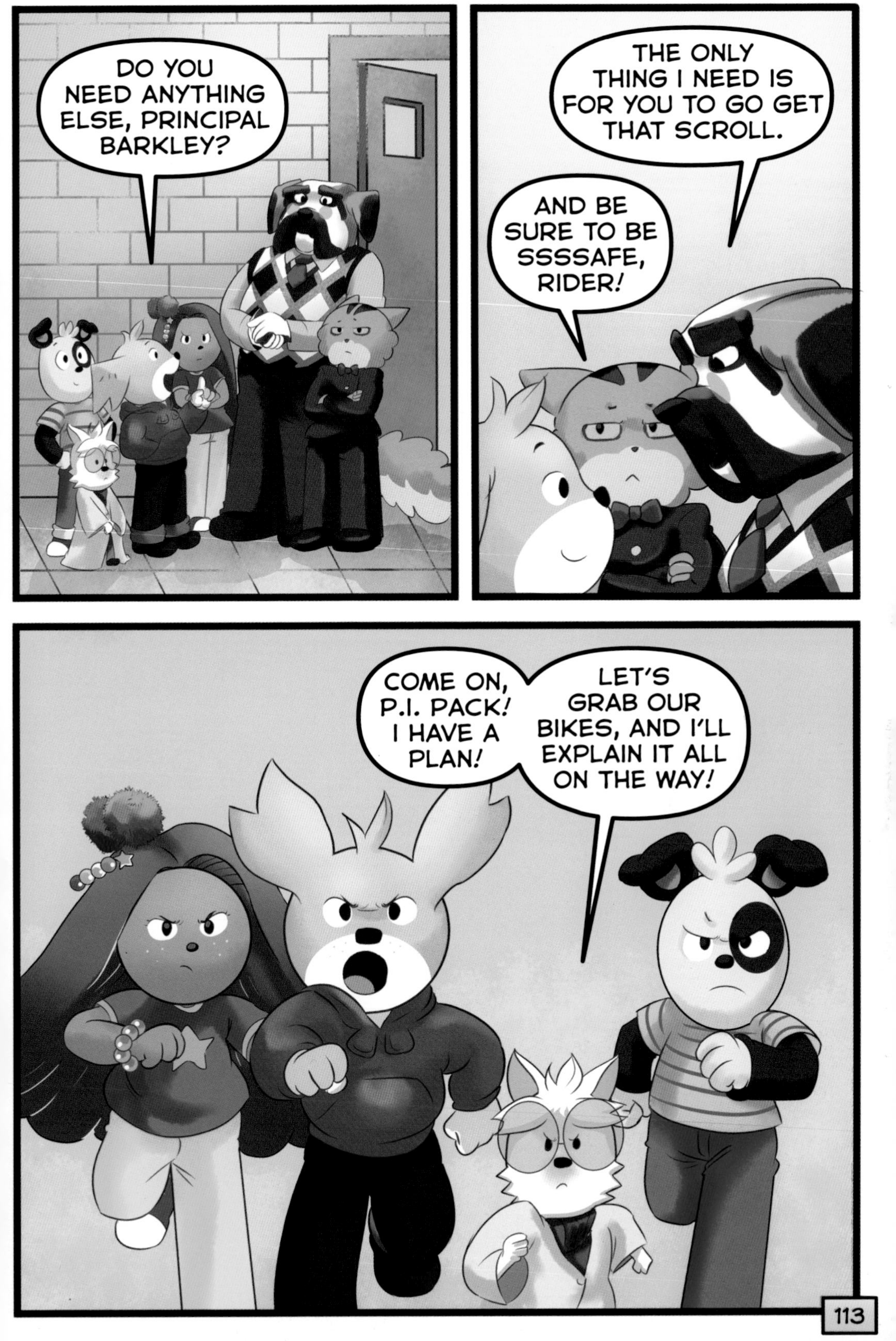
DO YOU NEED ANYTHING ELSE, PRINCIPAL BARKLEY?
THE ONLY THING I NEED IS FOR YOU TO GO GET THAT SCROLL.
AND BE SURE TO BE SSSSAFE, RIDER!
COME ON, P.I. PACK! I HAVE A PLAN!
LET'S GRAB OUR BIKES, AND I'LL EXPLAIN IT ALL ON THE WAY!

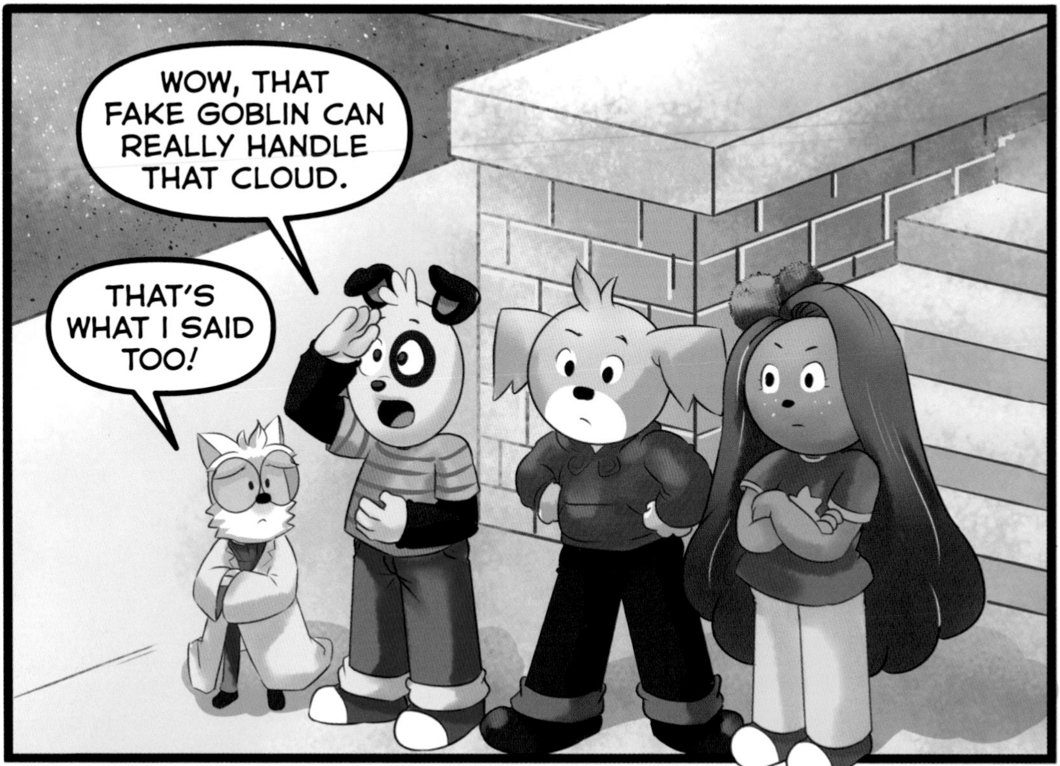
WOW, THAT FAKE GOBLIN CAN REALLY HANDLE THAT CLOUD.
THAT'S WHAT I SAID TOO!

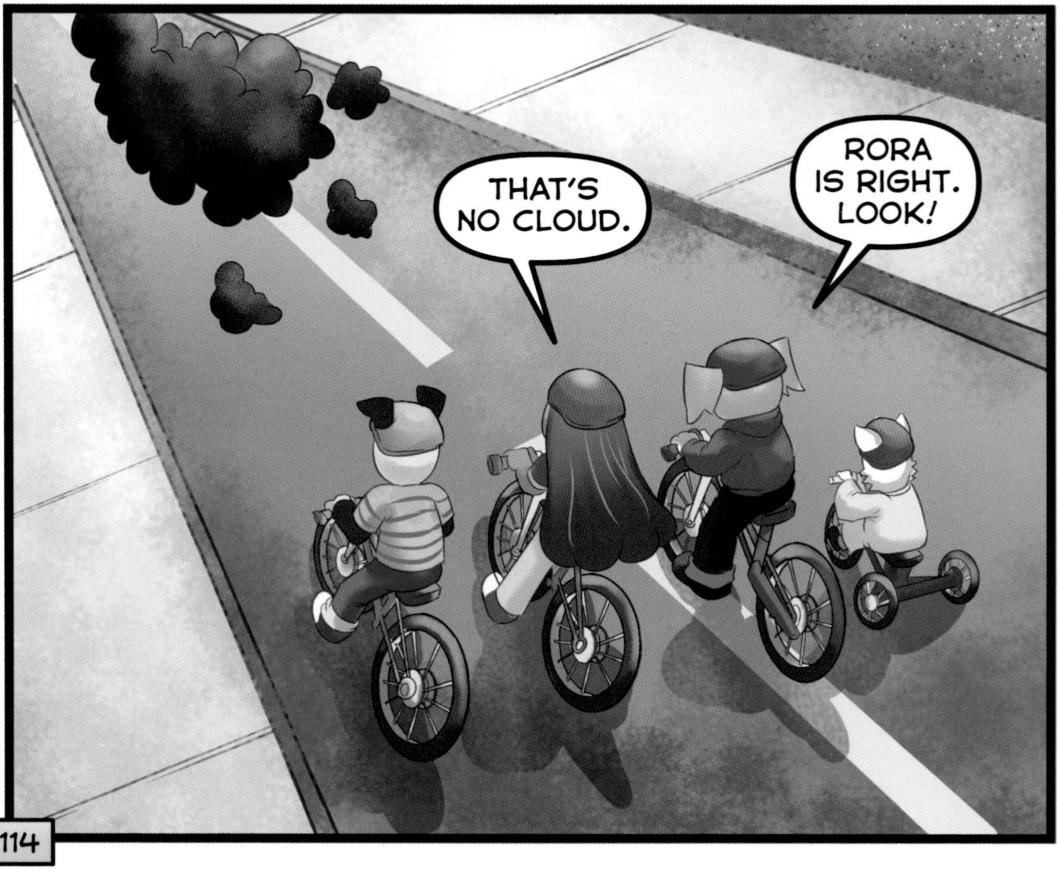
THAT'S NO CLOUD.
RORA IS RIGHT. LOOK!

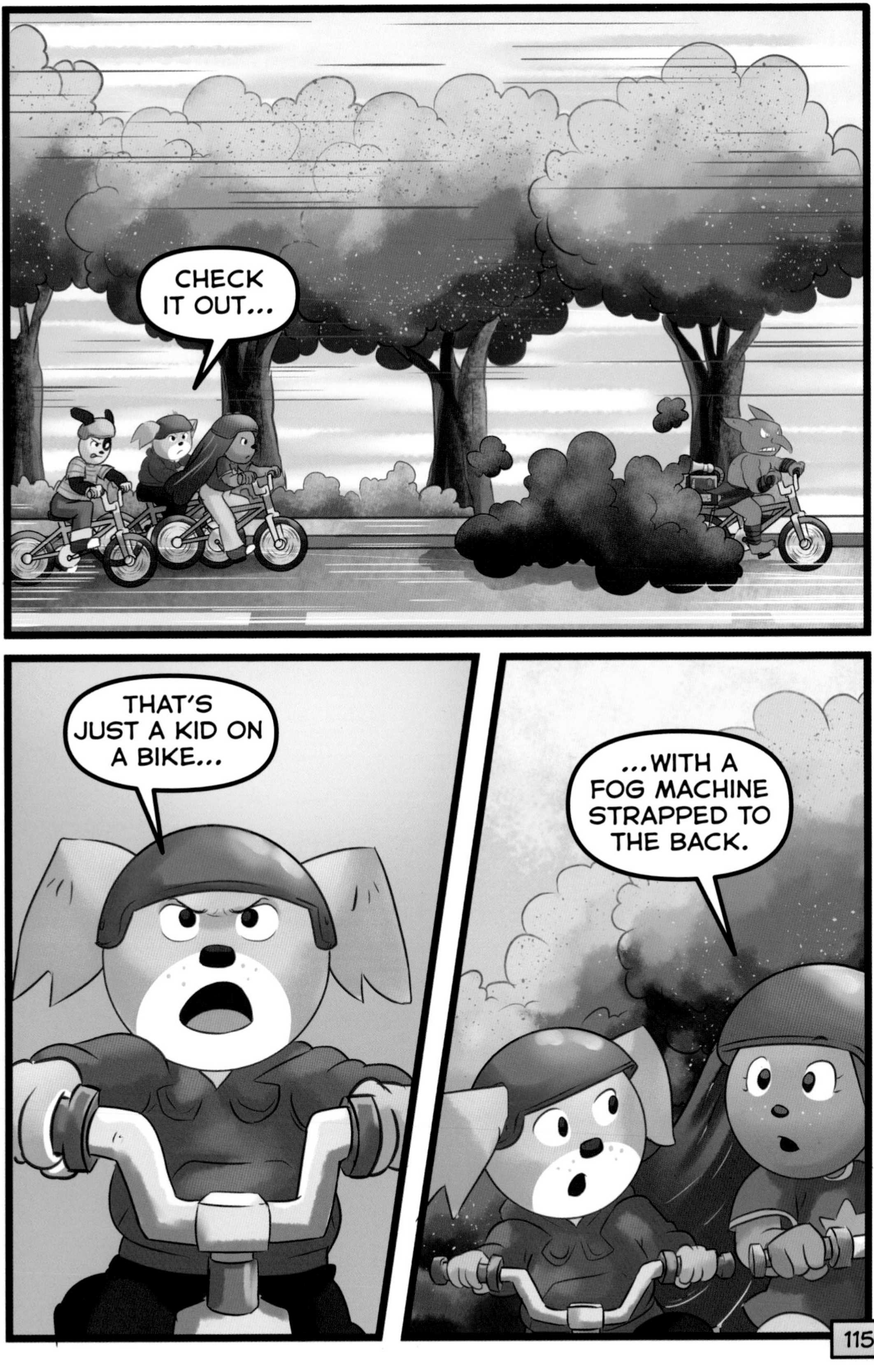
CHECK IT OUT...
THAT'S JUST A KID ON A BIKE...
...WITH A FOG MACHINE STRAPPED TO THE BACK.

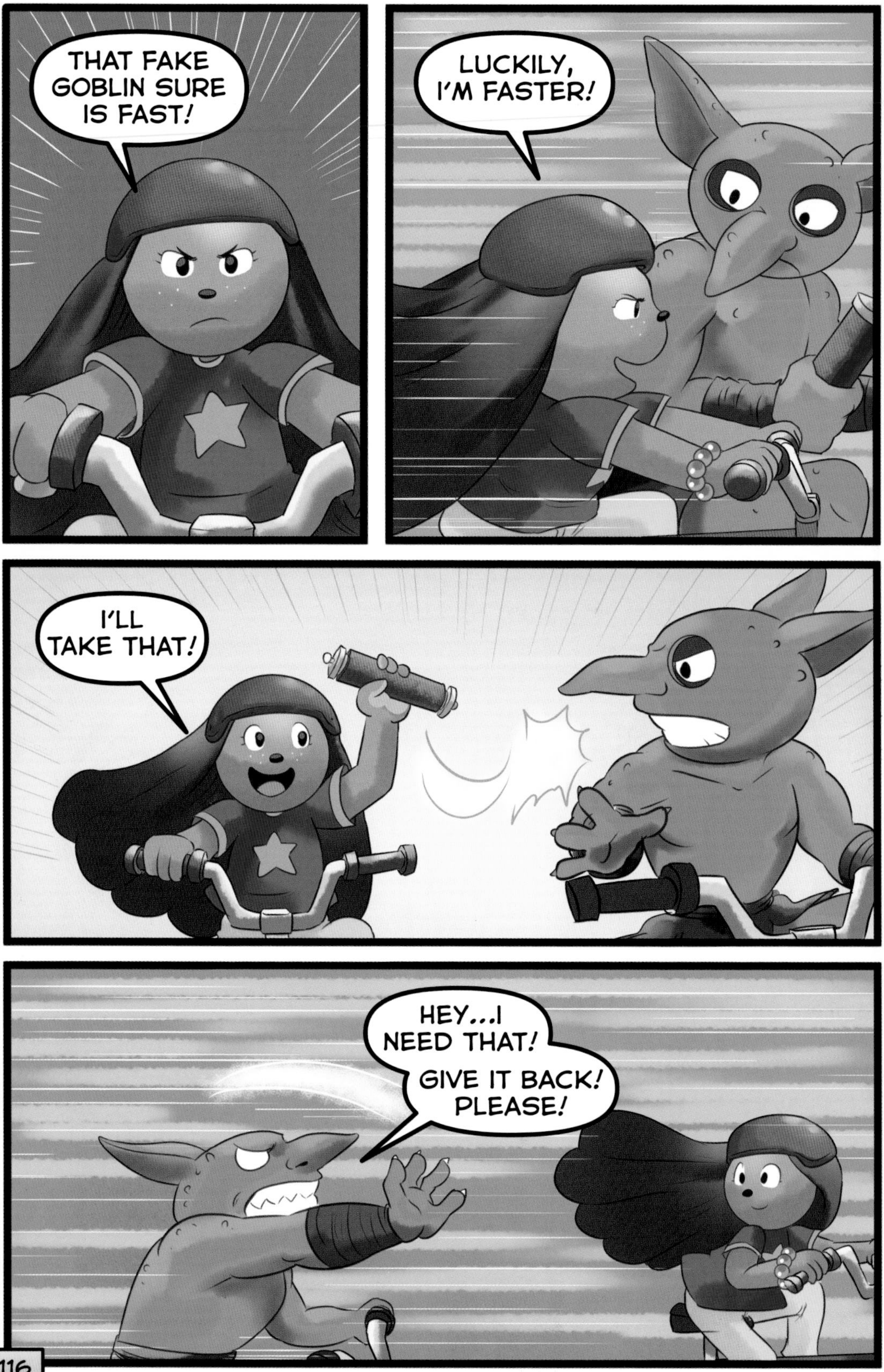
THAT FAKE GOBLIN SURE IS FAST!
LUCKILY, I'M FASTER!
I'LL TAKE THAT!
HEY...I NEED THAT!
GIVE IT BACK! PLEASE!

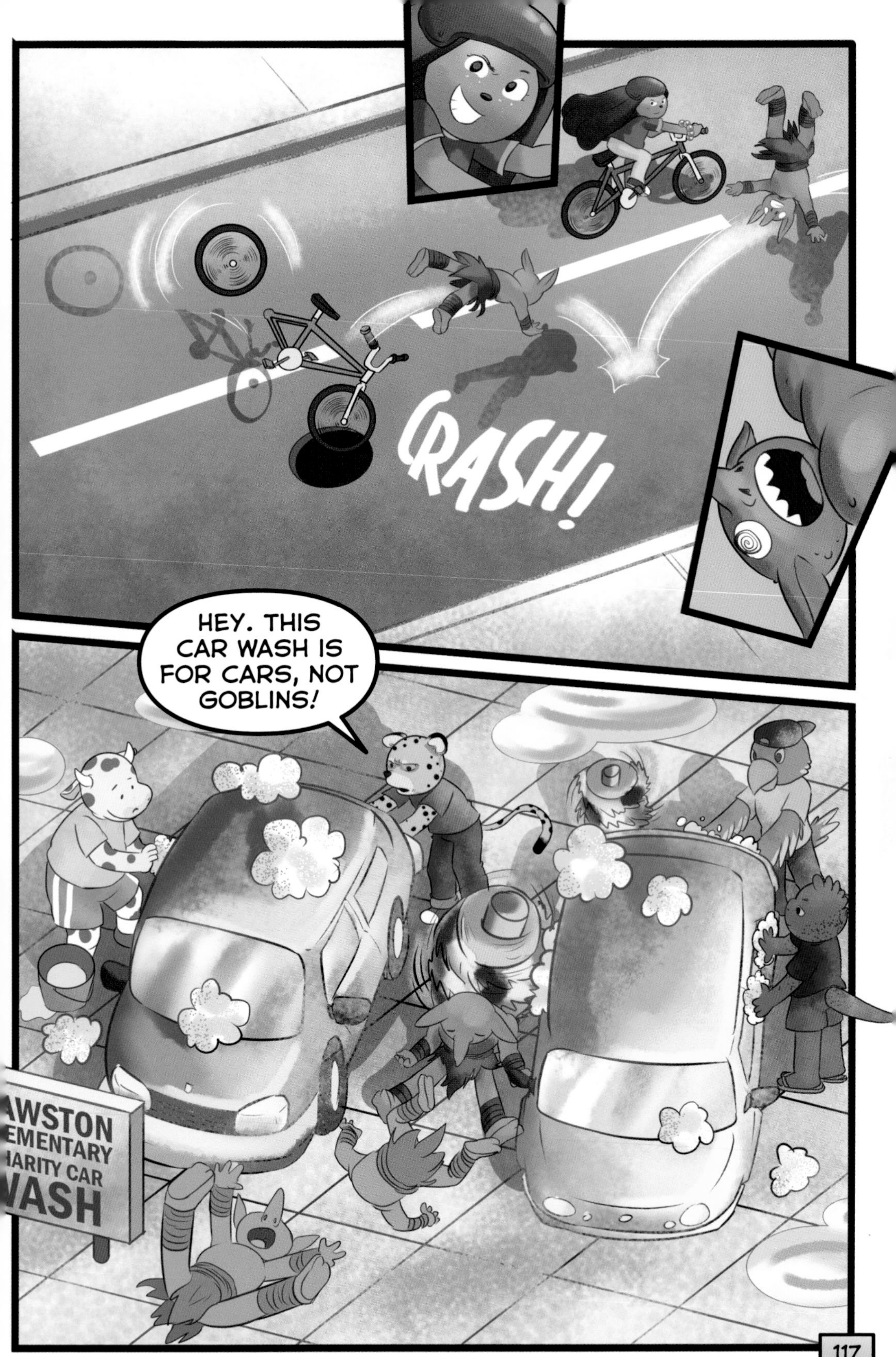
CRASH!
HEY. THIS CAR WASH IS FOR CARS, NOT GOBLINS!
AWSTON
EMENTARY
HARITY CAR
WASH

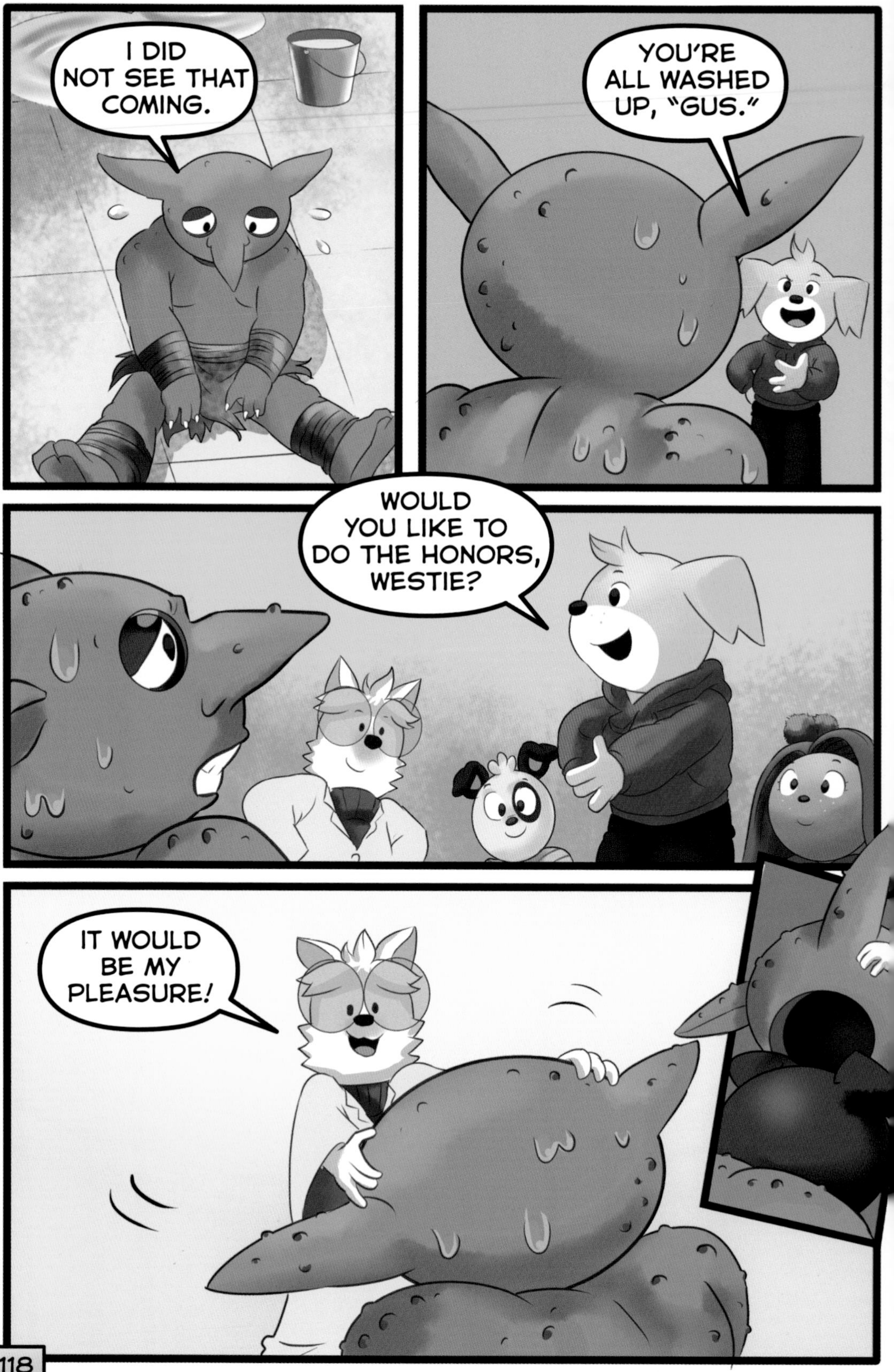
I DID NOT SEE THAT COMING.
YOU'RE ALL WASHED UP, "GUS."
WOULD YOU LIKE TO DO THE HONORS, WESTIE?
IT WOULD BE MY PLEASURE!

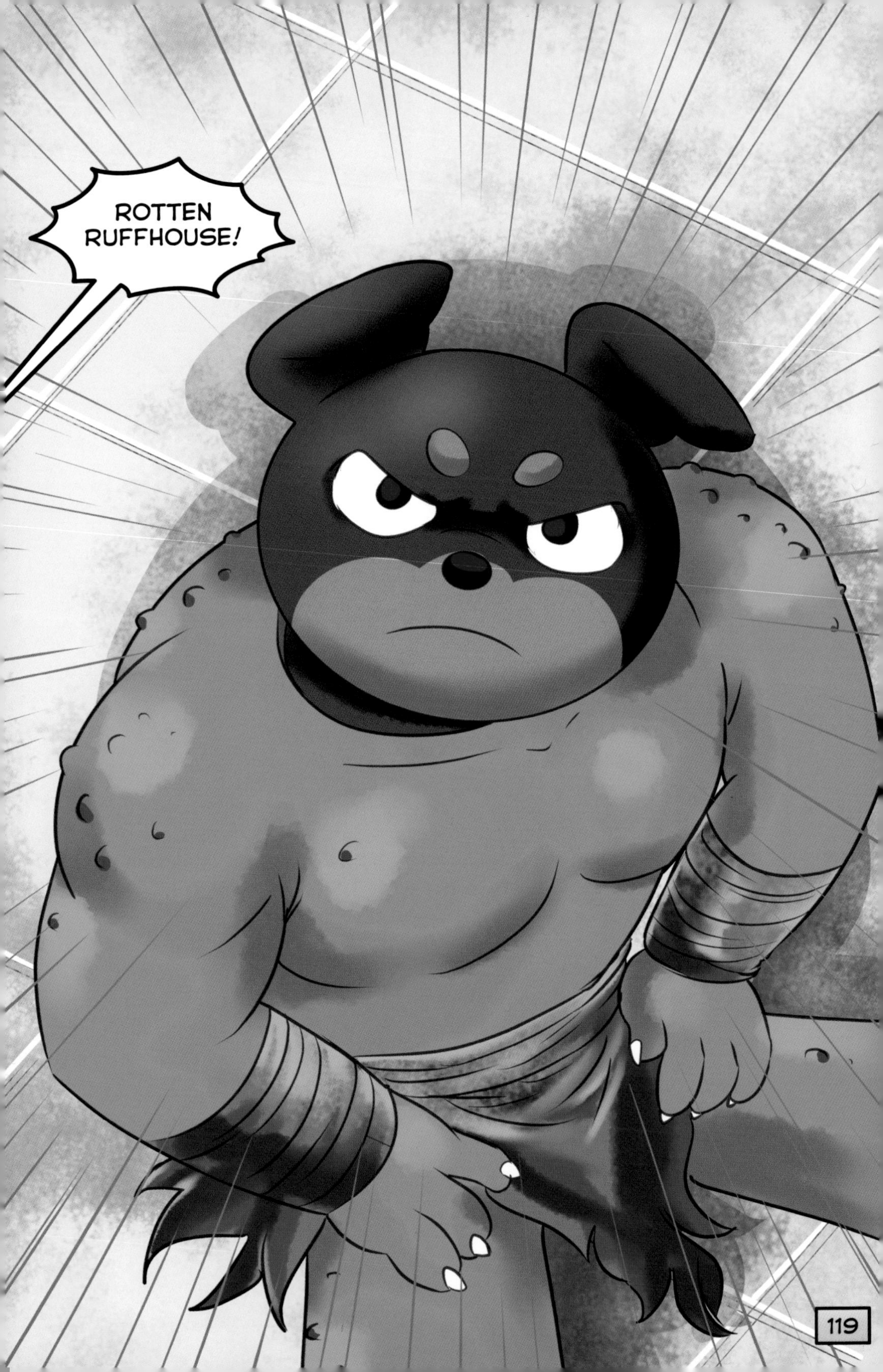
ROTTEN RUFFHOUSE!

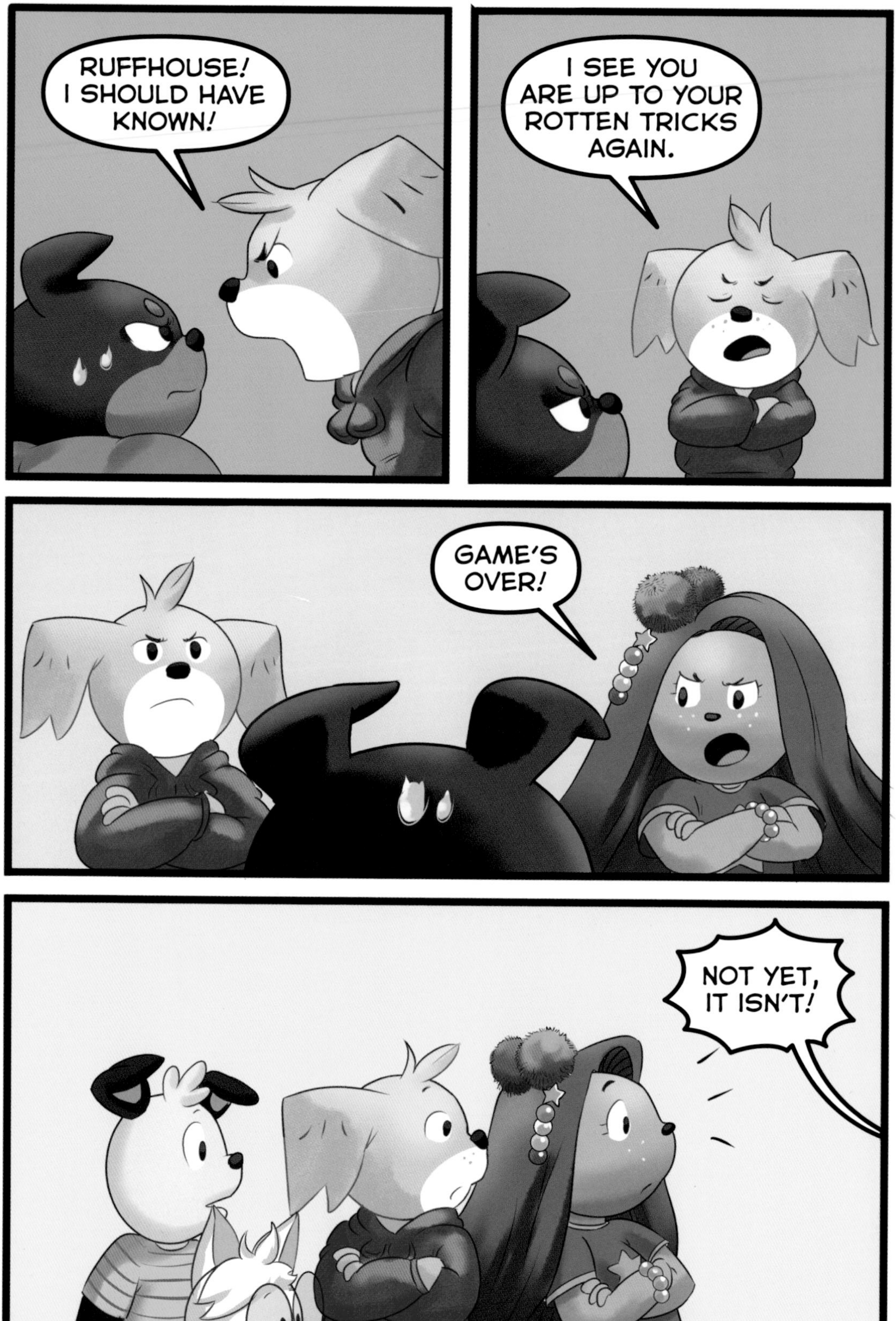
RUFFHOUSE! I SHOULD HAVE KNOWN!
I SEE YOU ARE UP TO YOUR ROTTEN TRICKS AGAIN.
GAME'S OVER!
NOT YET, IT ISN'T!

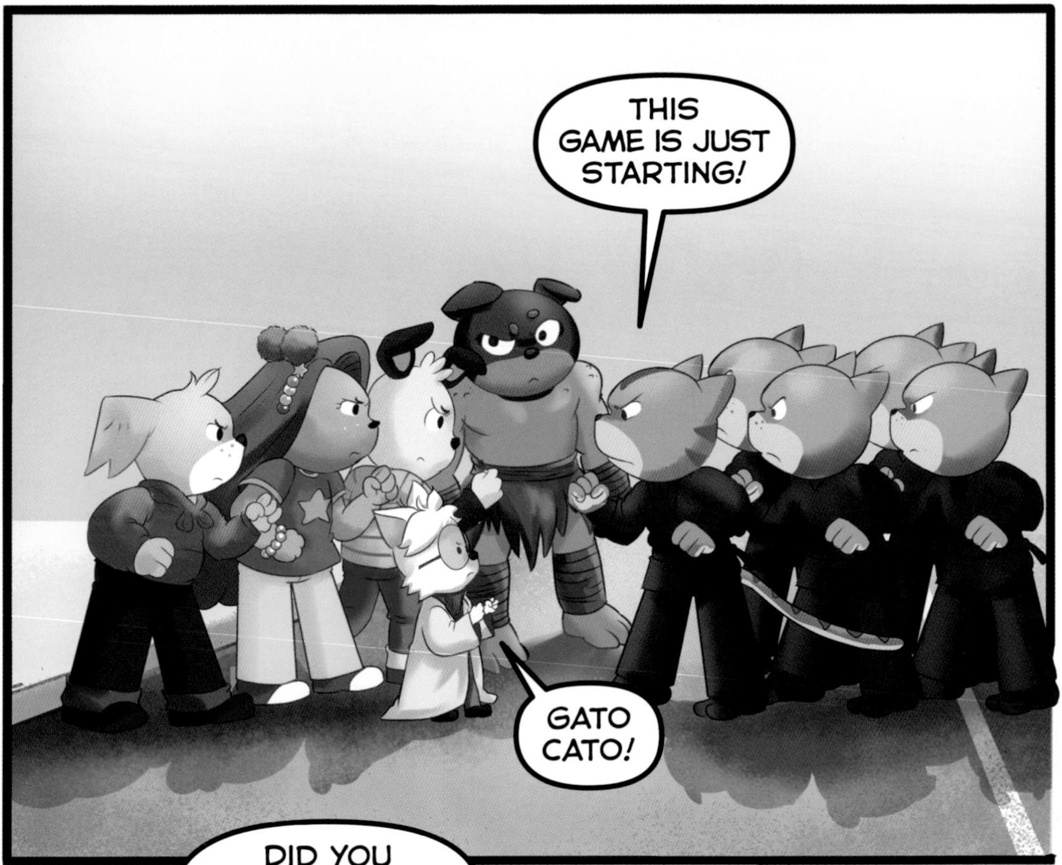
THIS GAME IS JUST STARTING!
GATO CATO!
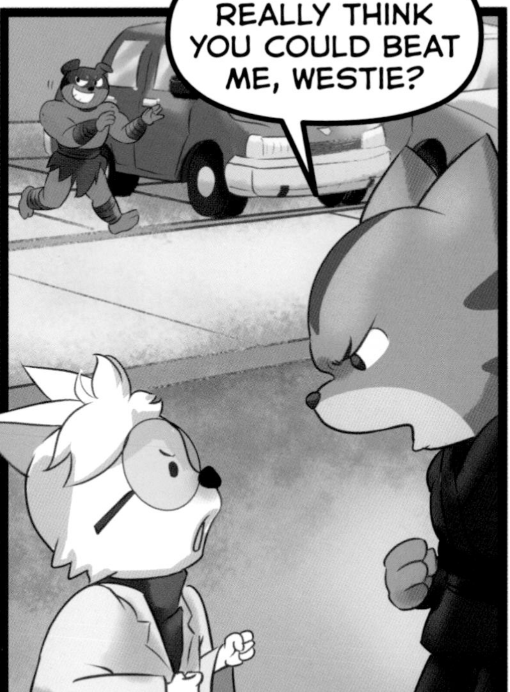
DID YOU REALLY THINK YOU COULD BEAT ME, WESTIE?
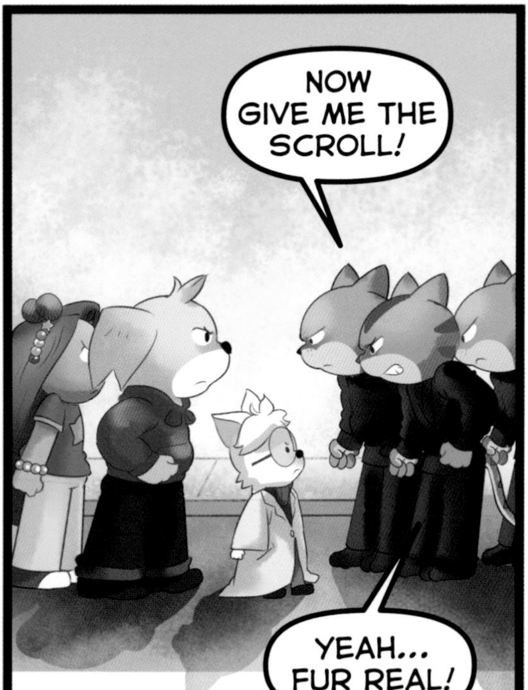
NOW GIVE ME THE SCROLL!
YEAH... FUR REAL!

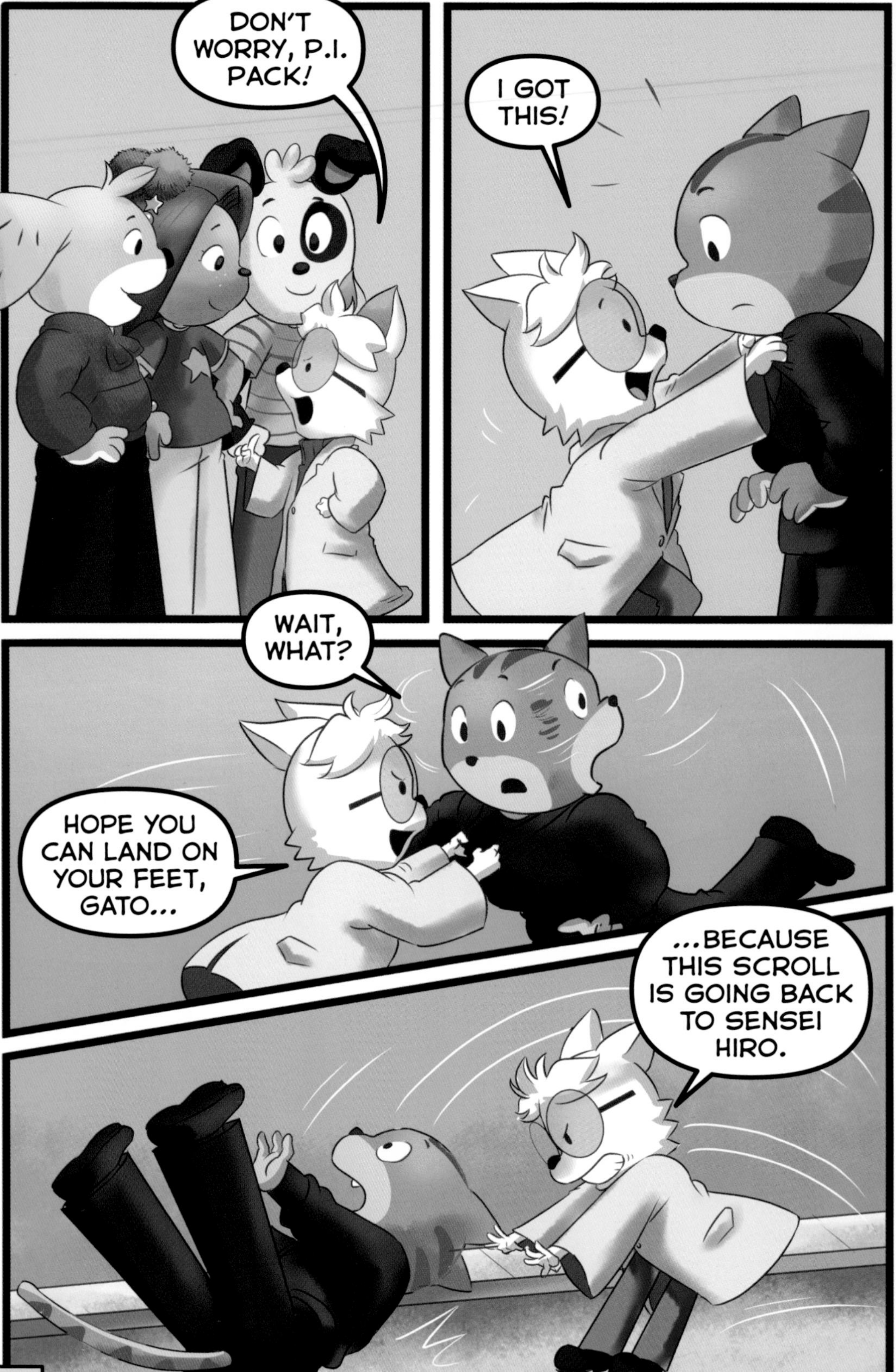
DON'T WORRY, P.I. PACK!
I GOT THIS!
WAIT, WHAT?
HOPE YOU CAN LAND ON YOUR FEET, GATO...
...BECAUSE THIS SCROLL IS GOING BACK TO SENSEI HIRO.

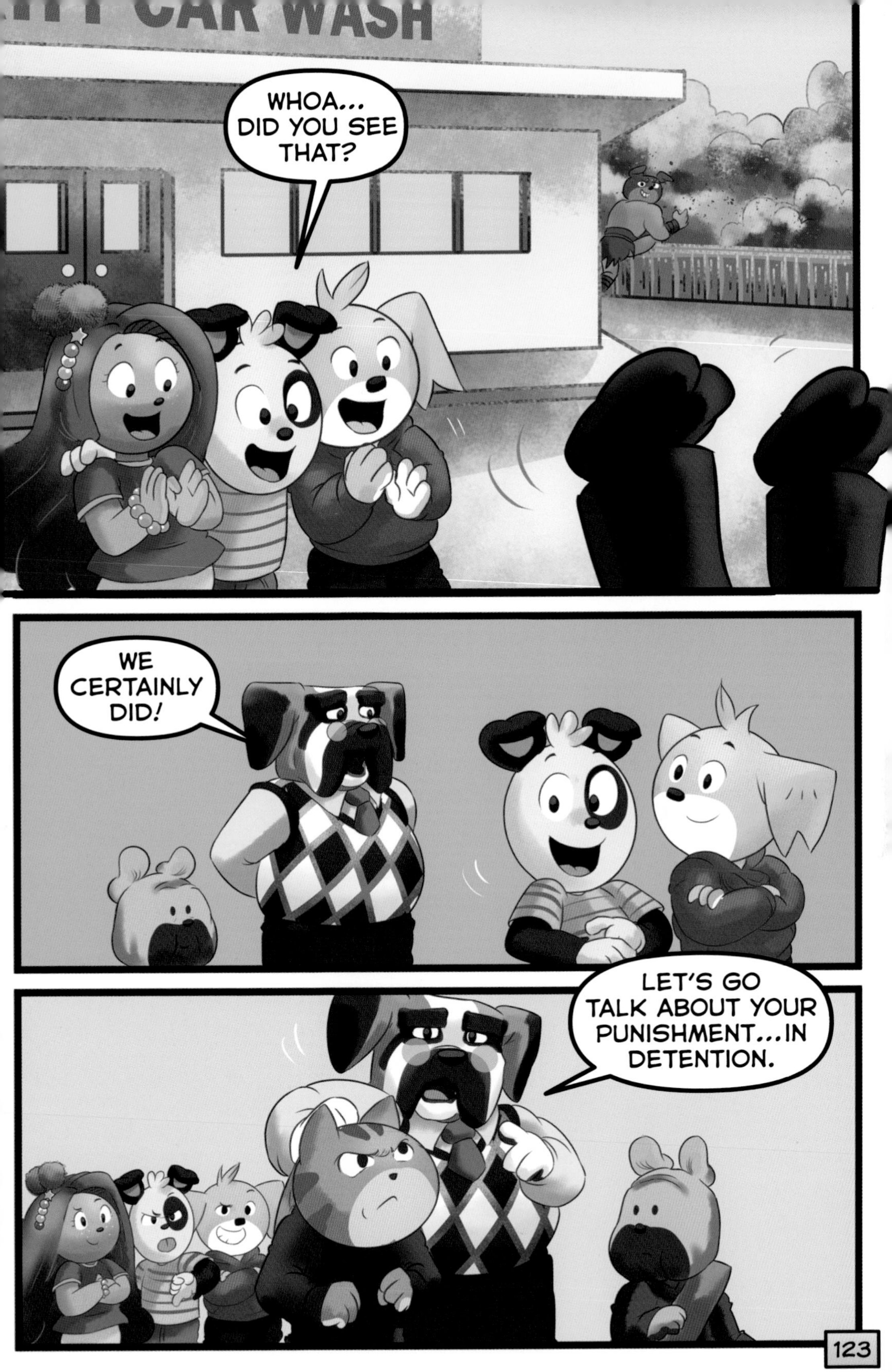
CAR WASH
WHOA... DID YOU SEE THAT?
WE CERTAINLY DID!
LET'S GO TALK ABOUT YOUR PUNISHMENT...IN DETENTION.

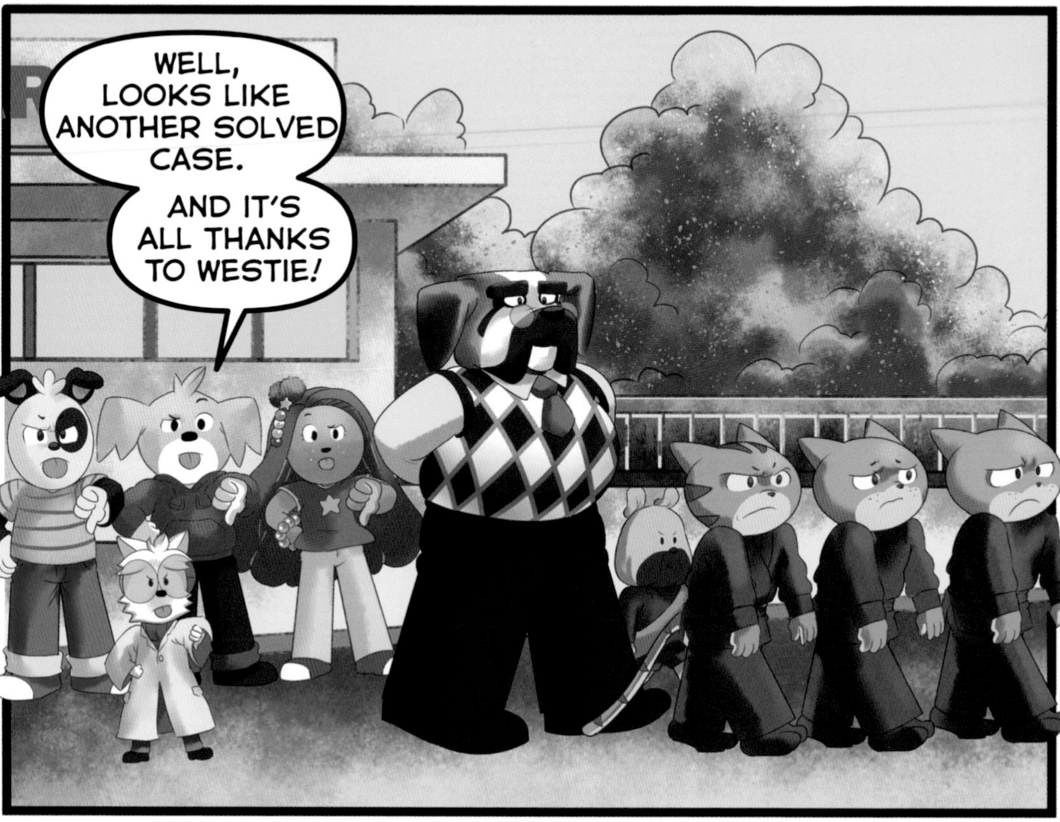
WELL, LOOKS LIKE ANOTHER SOLVED CASE.
AND IT'S ALL THANKS TO WESTIE!

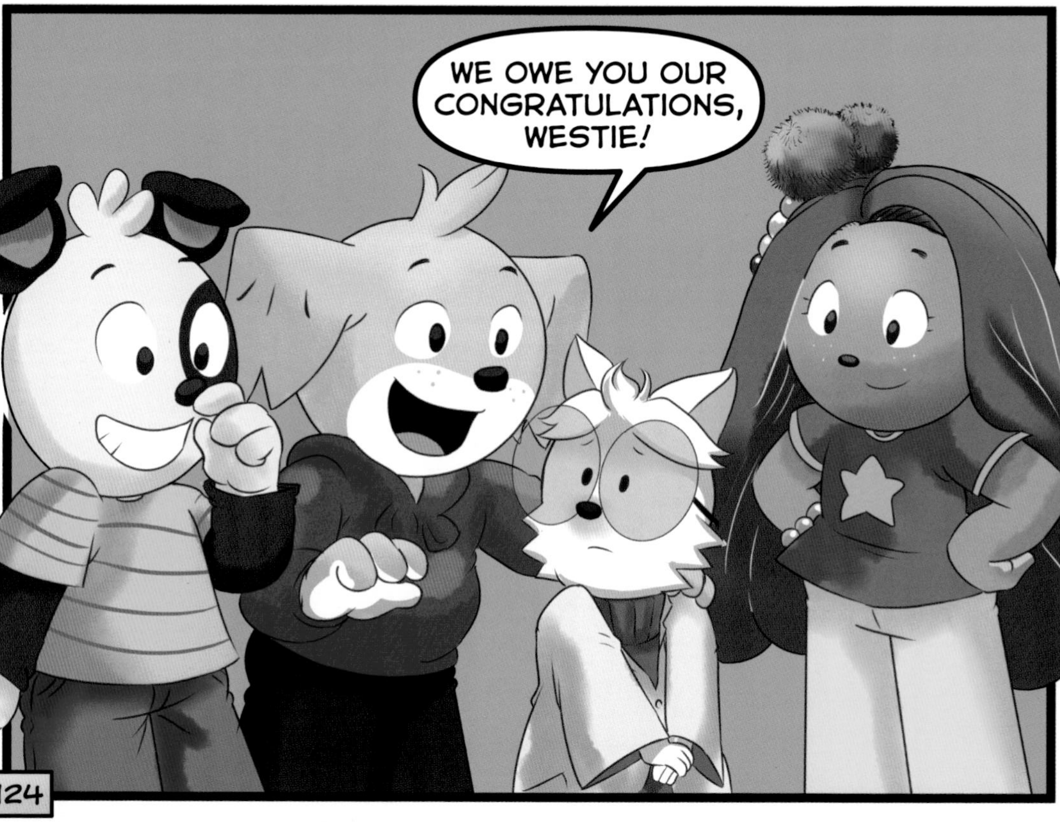
WE OWE YOU OUR CONGRATULATIONS, WESTIE!

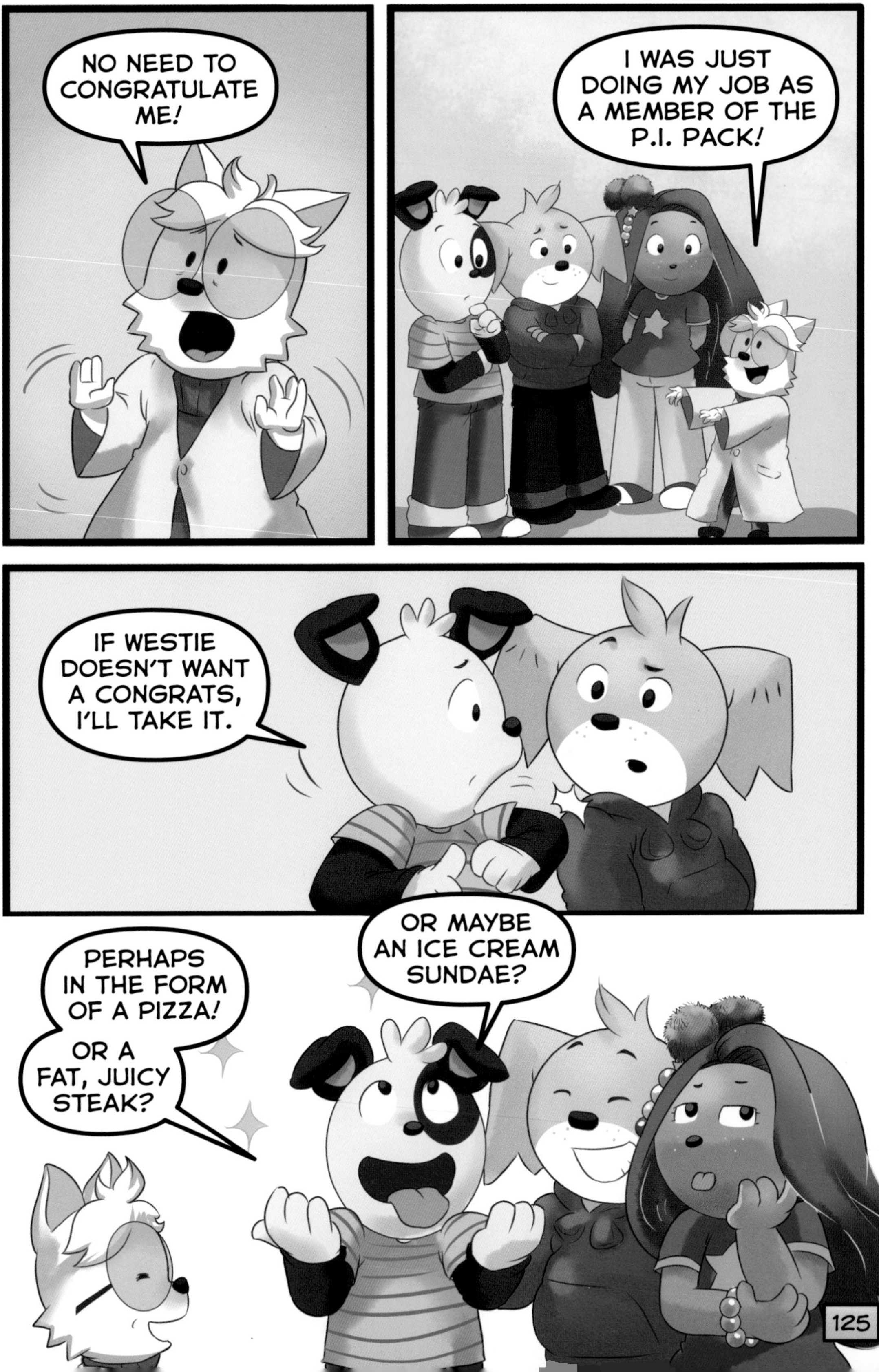

NO NEED TO CONGRATULATE ME!
I WAS JUST DOING MY JOB AS A MEMBER OF THE P.I. PACK!
IF WESTIE DOESN'T WANT A CONGRATS, I'LL TAKE IT.
PERHAPS IN THE FORM OF A PIZZA!
OR A FAT, JUICY STEAK?
OR MAYBE AN ICE CREAM SUNDAE?

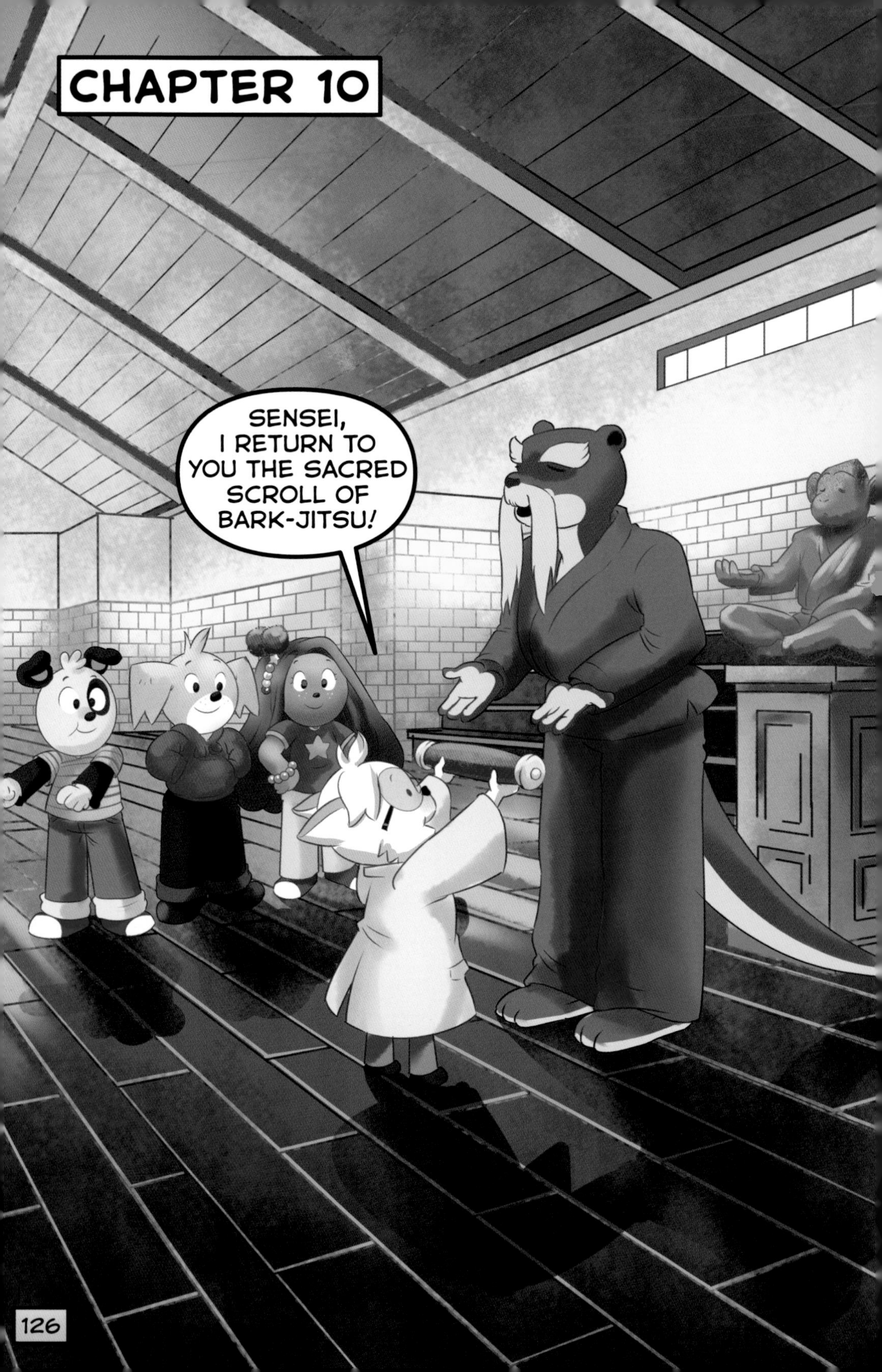
CHAPTER 10
SENSEI, I RETURN TO YOU THE SACRED SCROLL OF BARK-JITSU!

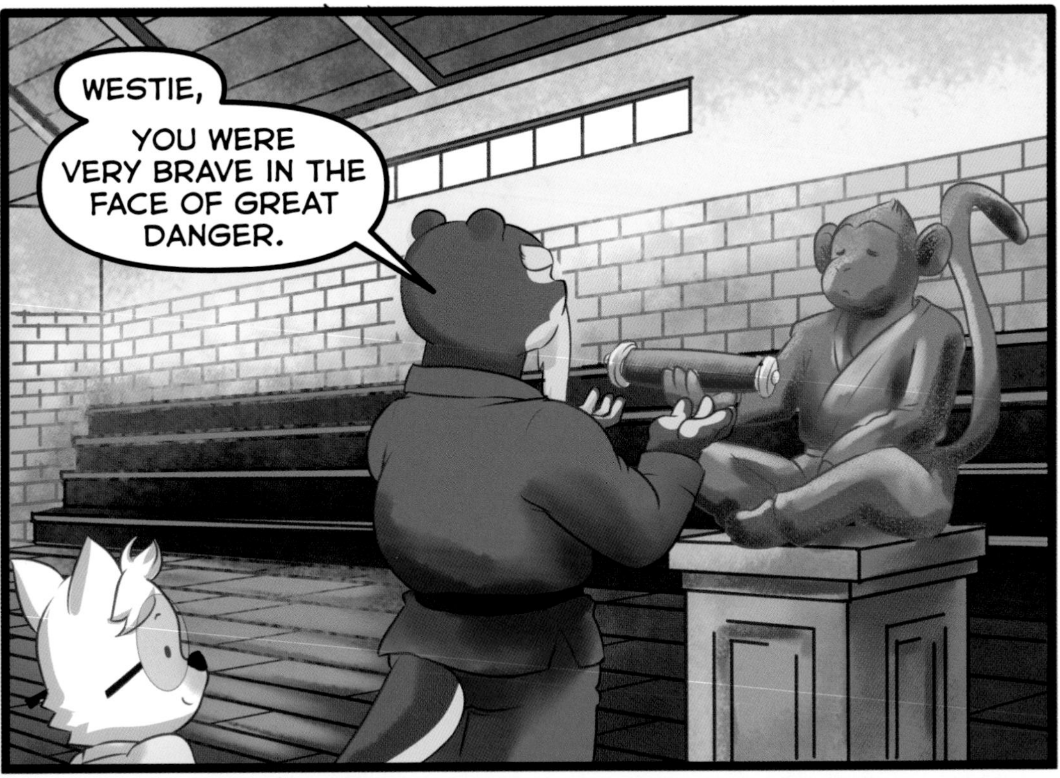
WESTIE,
YOU WERE VERY BRAVE IN THE FACE OF GREAT DANGER.

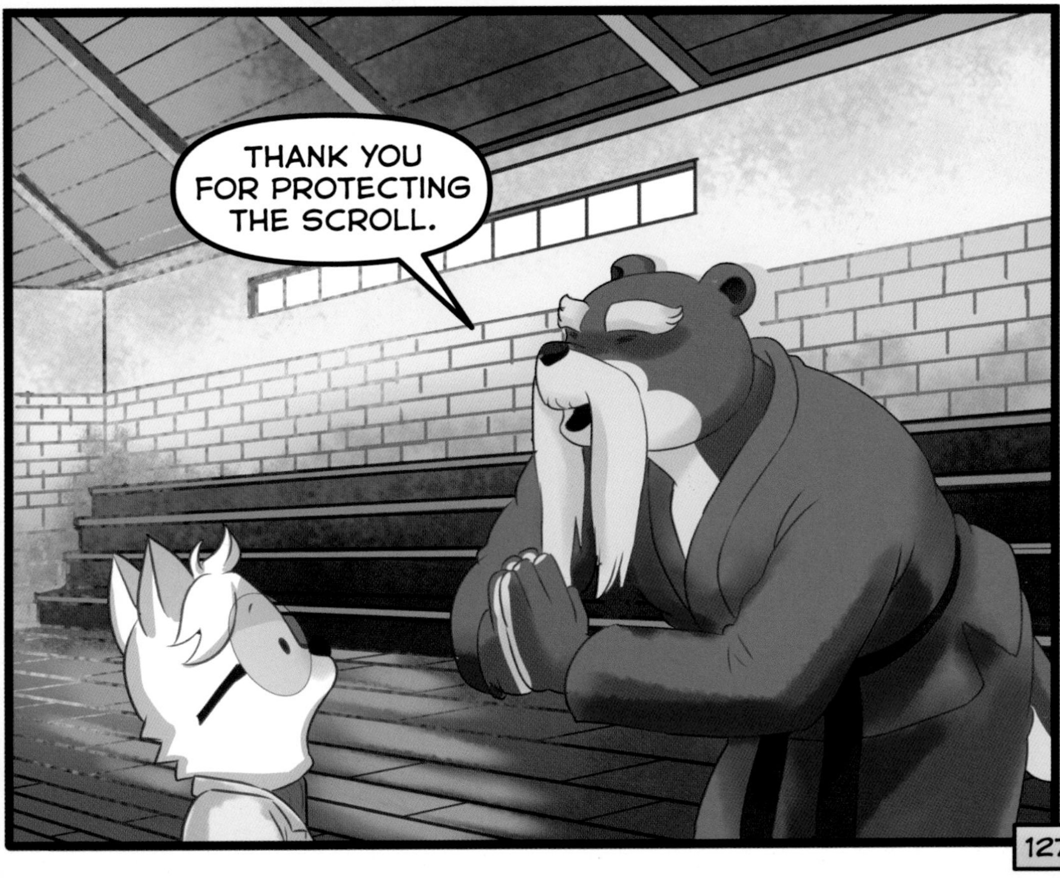
THANK YOU FOR PROTECTING THE SCROLL.

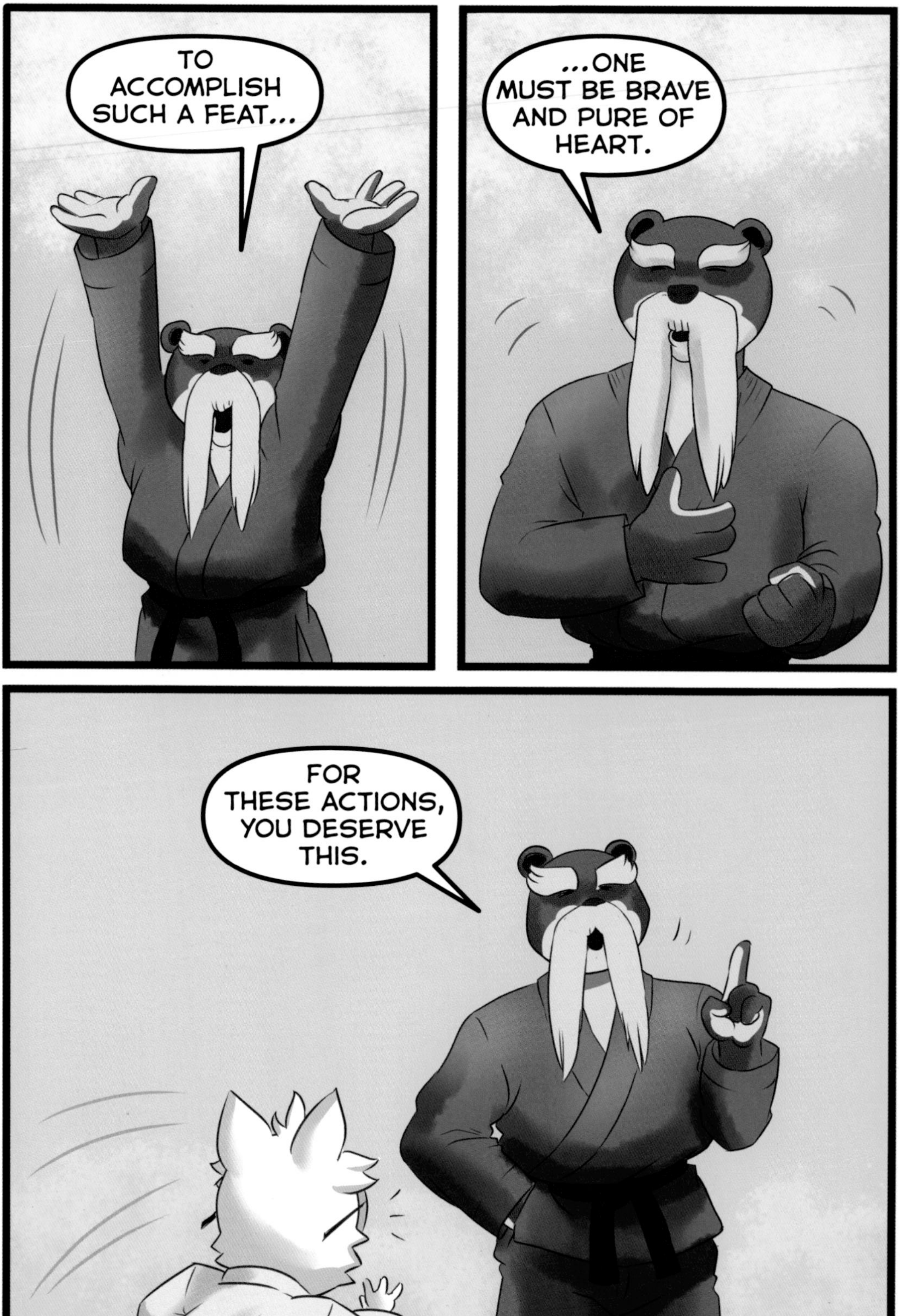
TO ACCOMPLISH SUCH A FEAT...
...ONE MUST BE BRAVE AND PURE OF HEART.
FOR THESE ACTIONS, YOU DESERVE THIS.

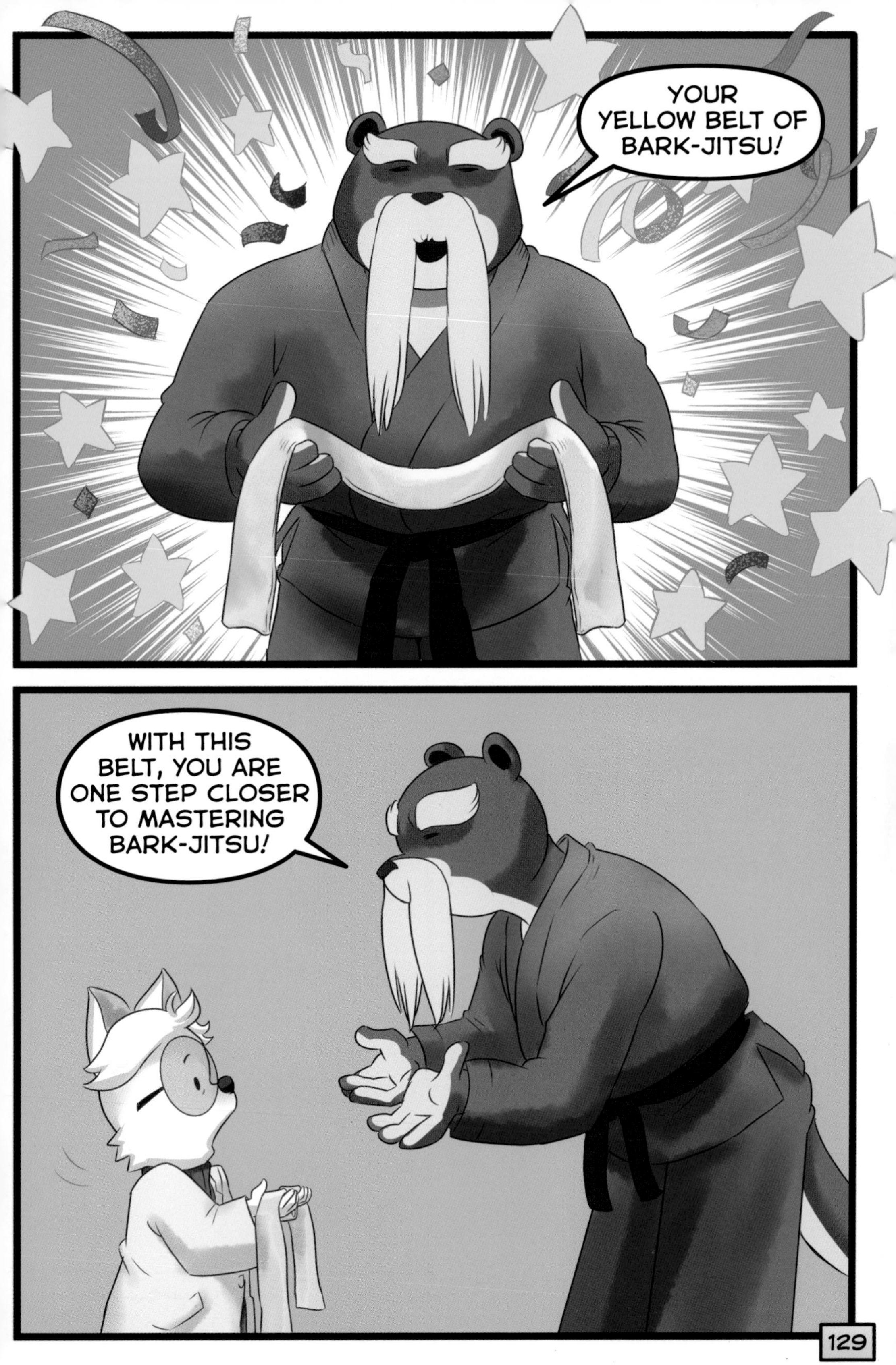
YOUR YELLOW BELT OF BARK-JITSU!
WITH THIS BELT, YOU ARE ONE STEP CLOSER TO MASTERING BARK-JITSU!

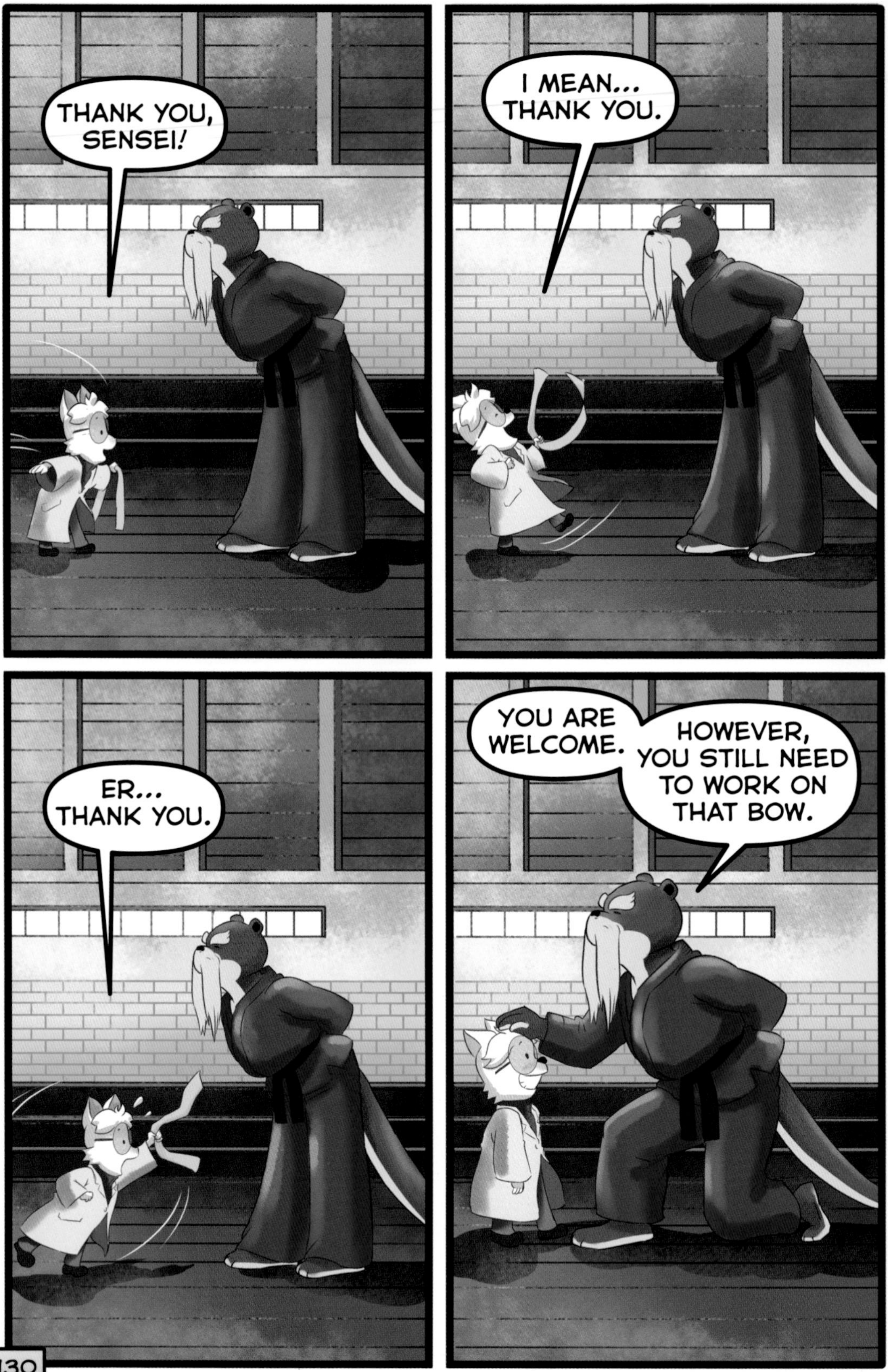
THANK YOU, SENSEI!
I MEAN... THANK YOU.
ER... THANK YOU.
YOU ARE WELCOME.
HOWEVER, YOU STILL NEED TO WORK ON THAT BOW.

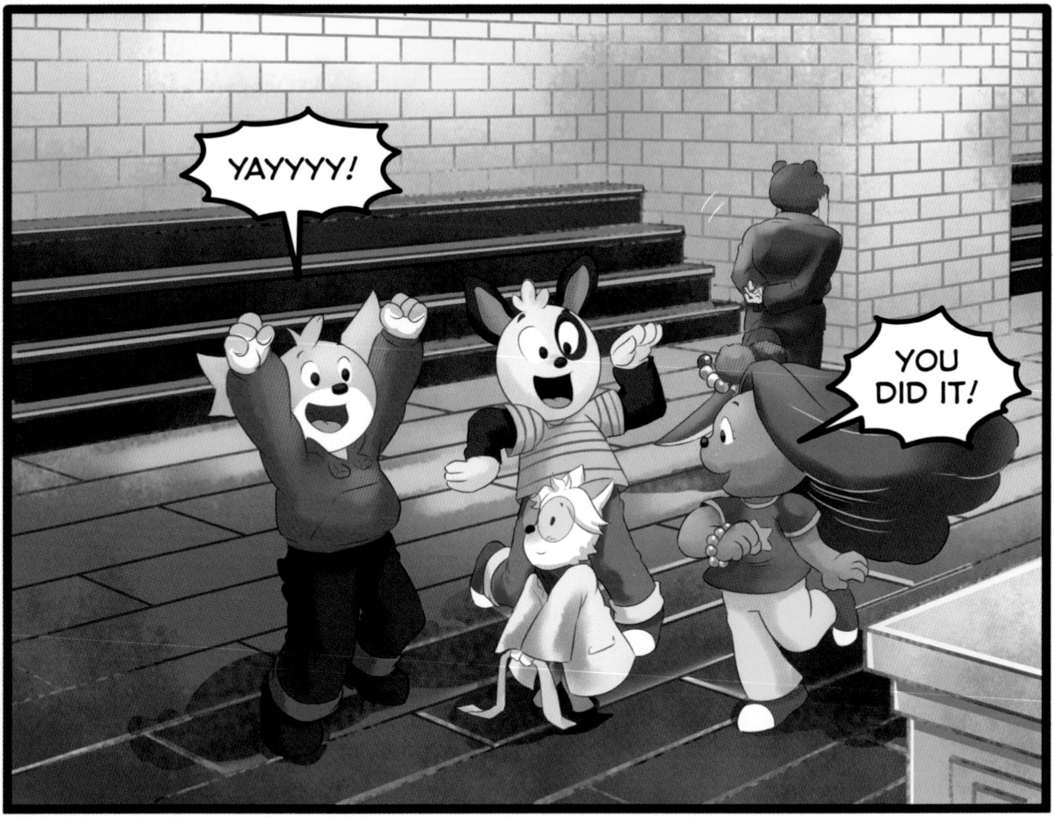
YAYYYY!
YOU DID IT!

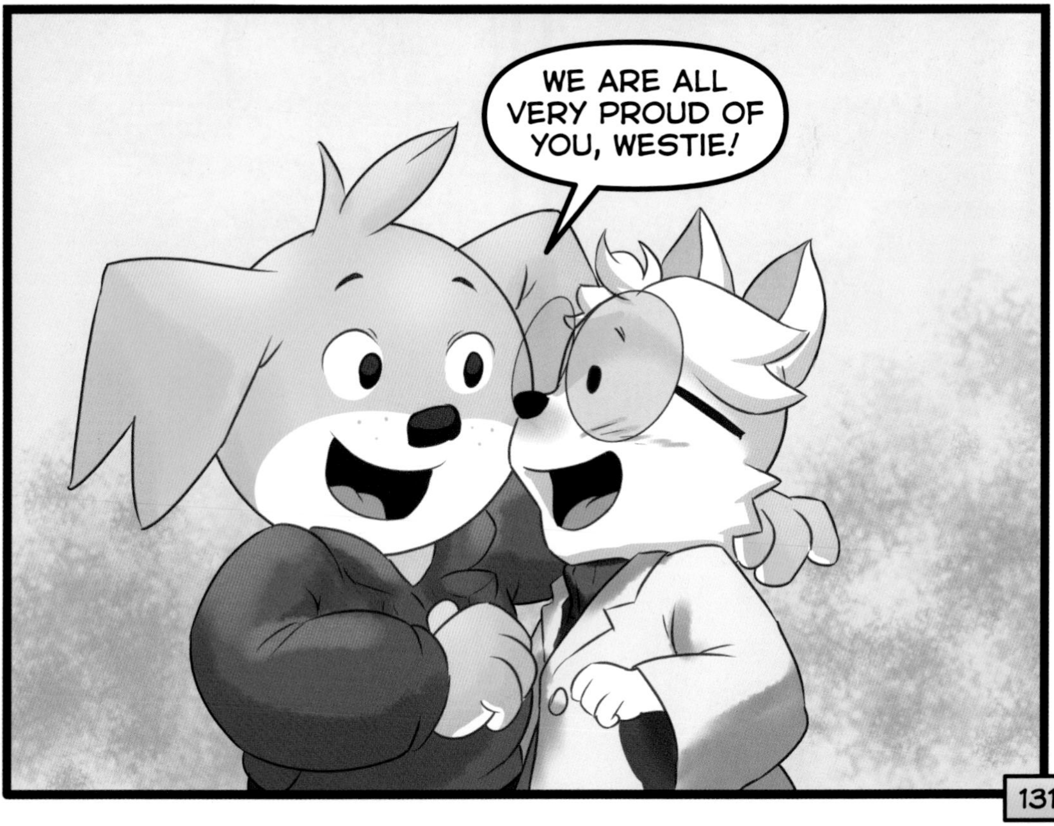
WE ARE ALL VERY PROUD OF YOU, WESTIE!

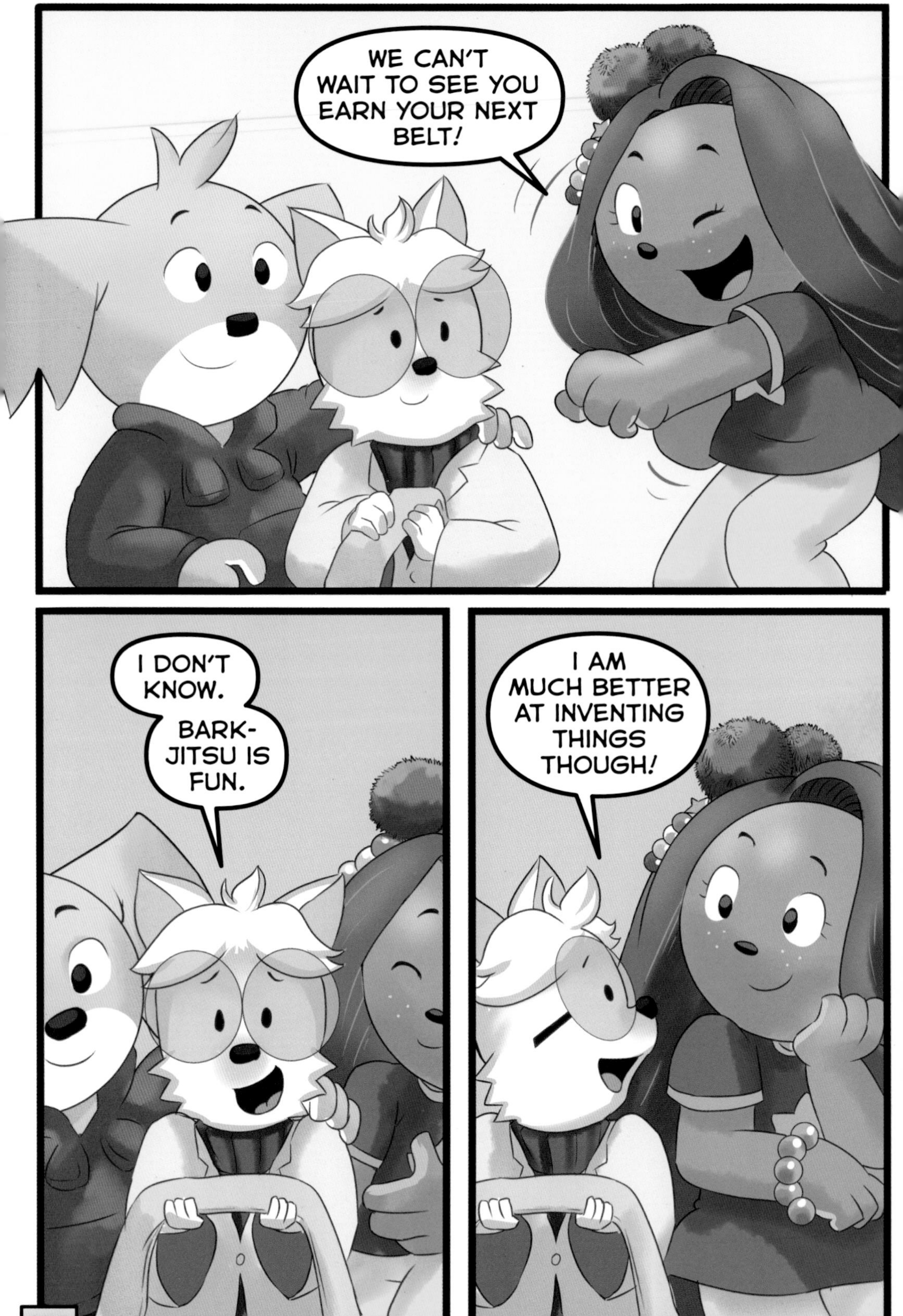
WE CAN'T WAIT TO SEE YOU EARN YOUR NEXT BELT!
I DON'T KNOW.
BARK-JITSU IS FUN.
I AM MUCH BETTER AT INVENTING THINGS THOUGH!

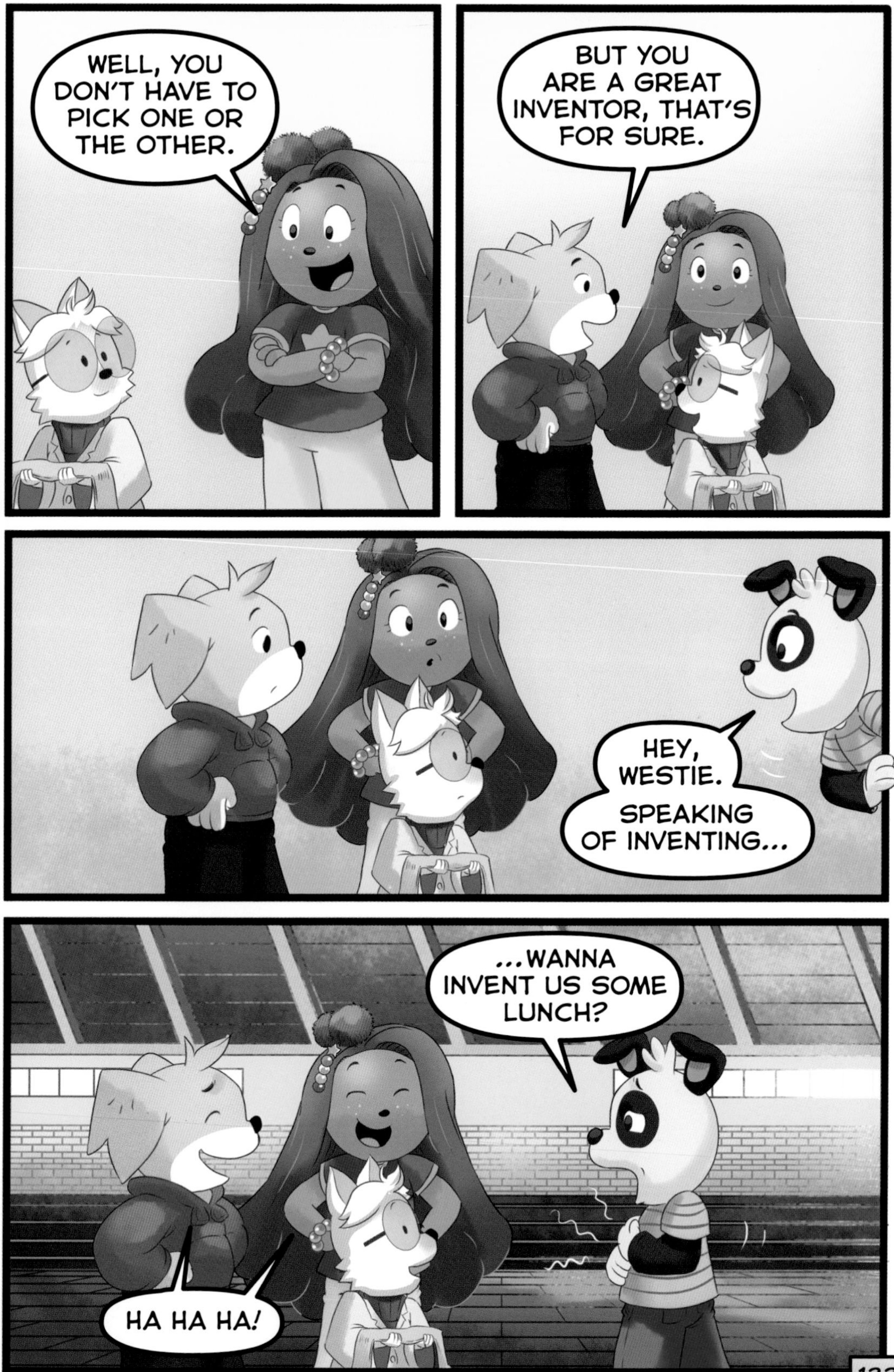
WELL, YOU DON'T HAVE TO PICK ONE OR THE OTHER.
BUT YOU ARE A GREAT INVENTOR, THAT'S FOR SURE.
HEY, WESTIE.
SPEAKING OF INVENTING...
...WANNA INVENT US SOME LUNCH?
HA HA HA!

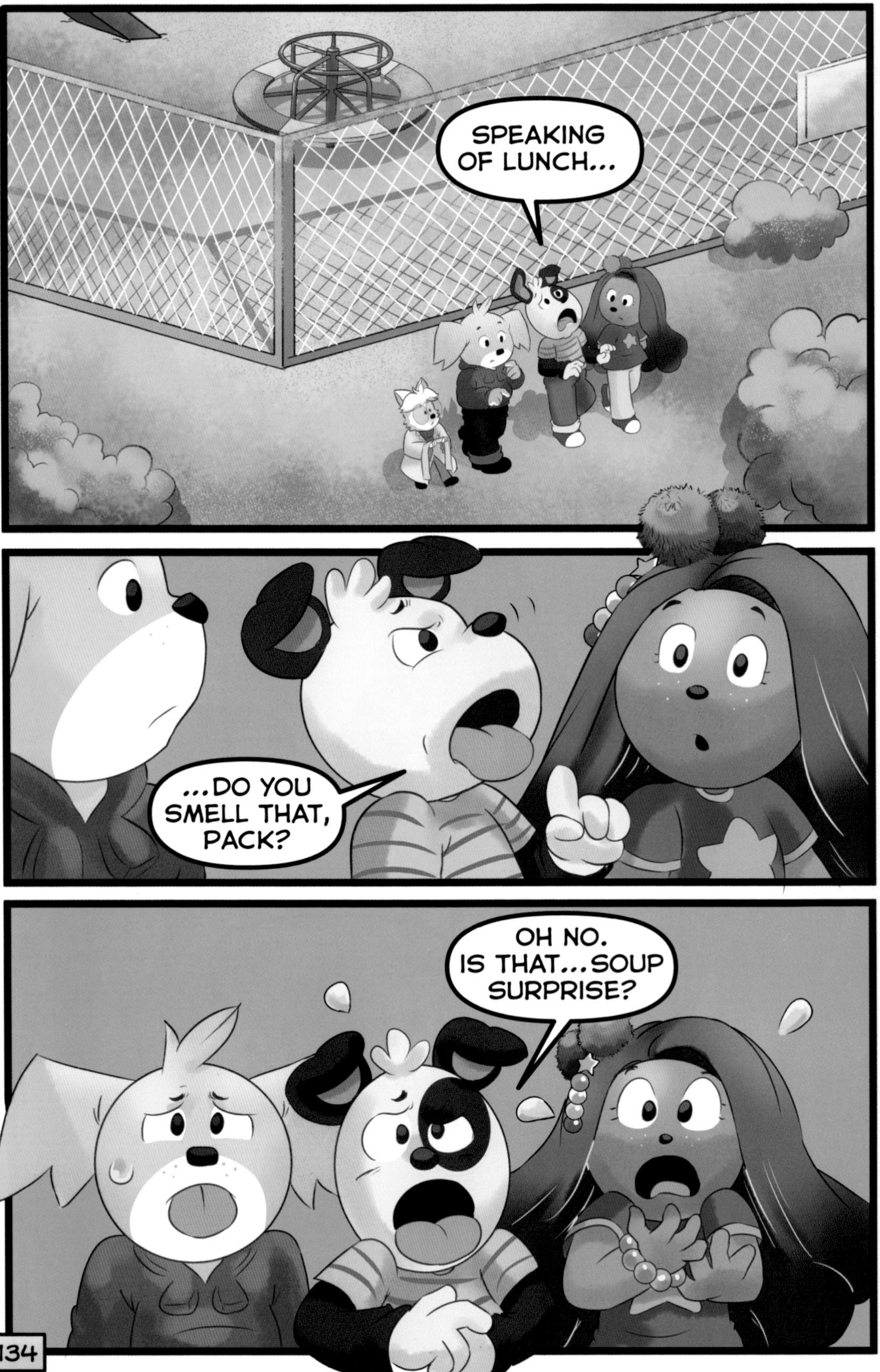
SPEAKING OF LUNCH...
...DO YOU SMELL THAT, PACK?
OH NO. IS THAT...SOUP SURPRISE?

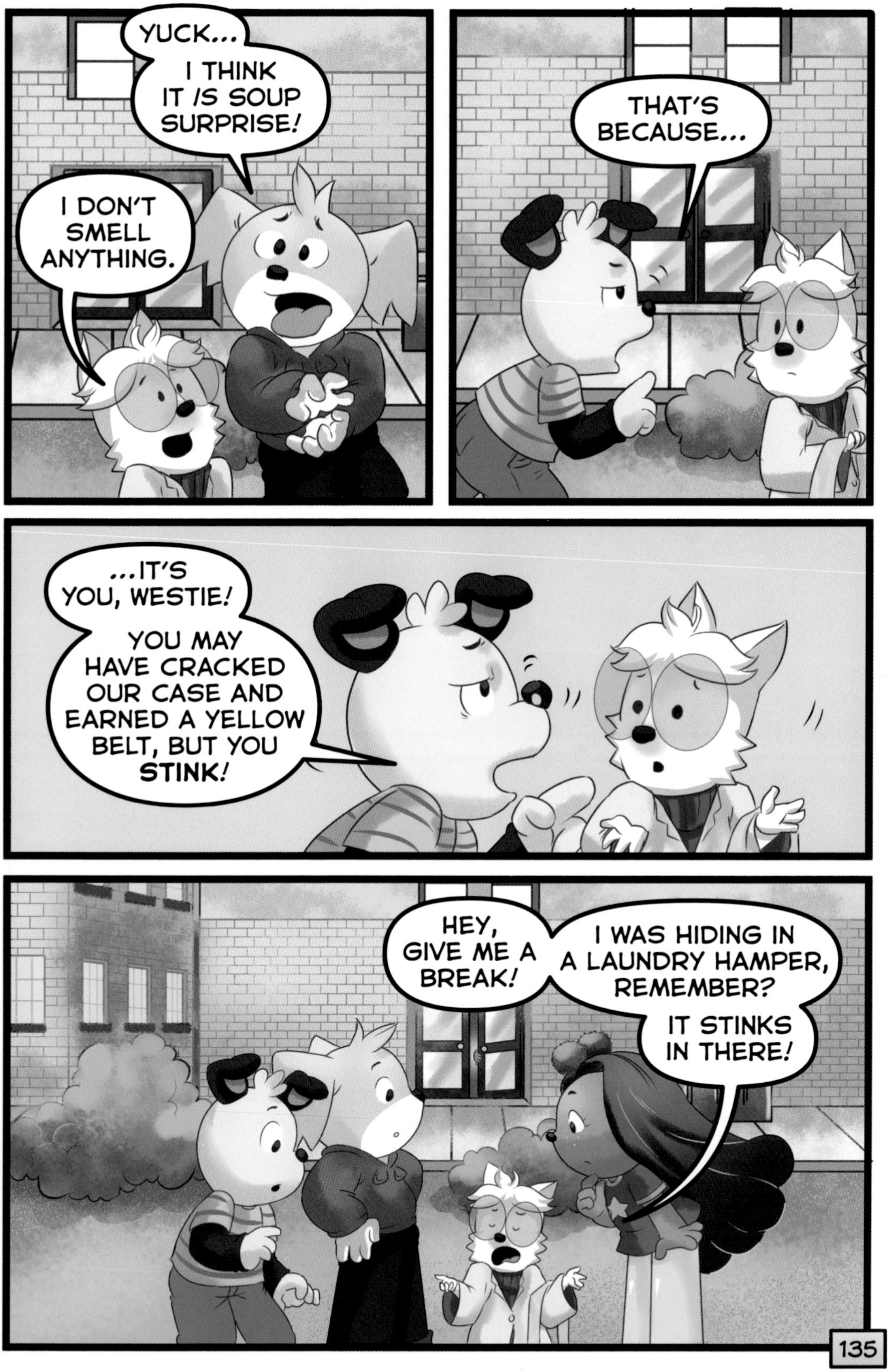

YUCK...
I THINK IT IS SOUP SURPRISE!
I DON'T SMELL ANYTHING.
THAT'S BECAUSE...
...IT'S YOU, WESTIE!
YOU MAY HAVE CRACKED OUR CASE AND EARNED A YELLOW BELT, BUT YOU STINK!
HEY, GIVE ME A BREAK!
I WAS HIDING IN A LAUNDRY HAMPER, REMEMBER?
IT STINKS IN THERE!

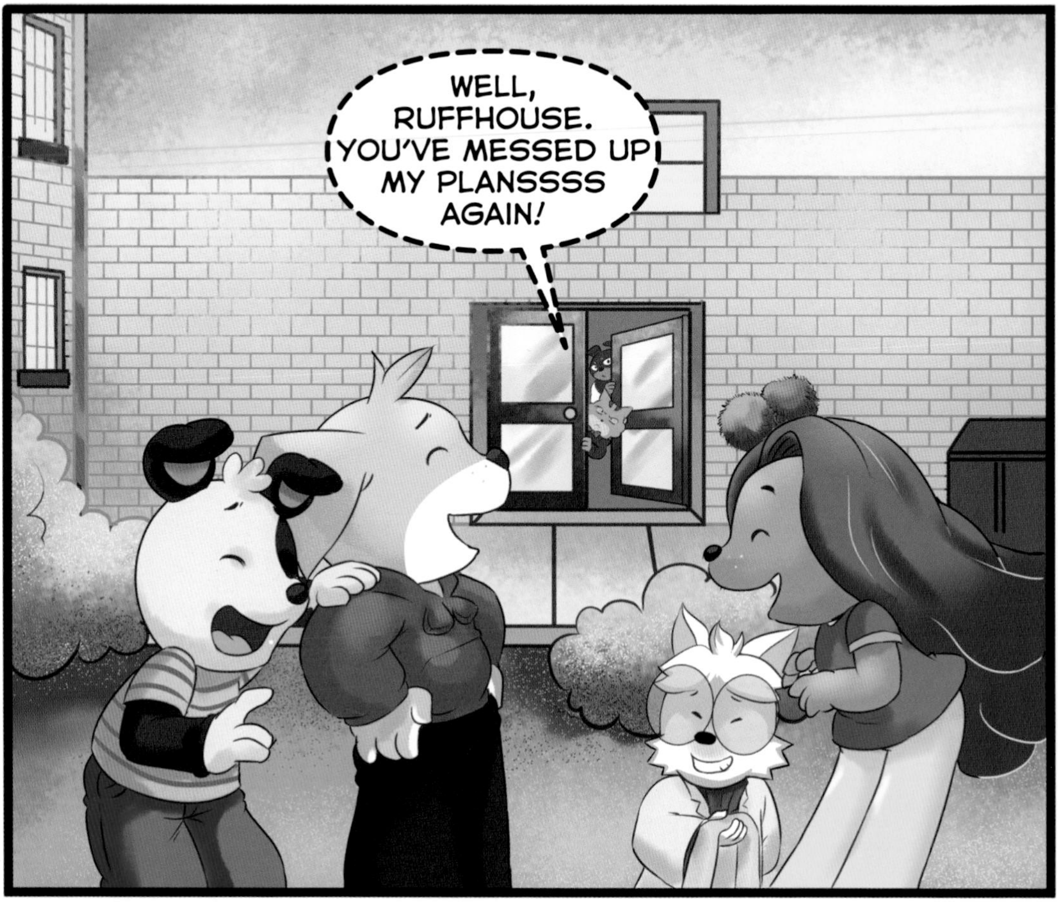
WELL, RUFFHOUSE. YOU'VE MESSED UP MY PLANSSSS AGAIN!

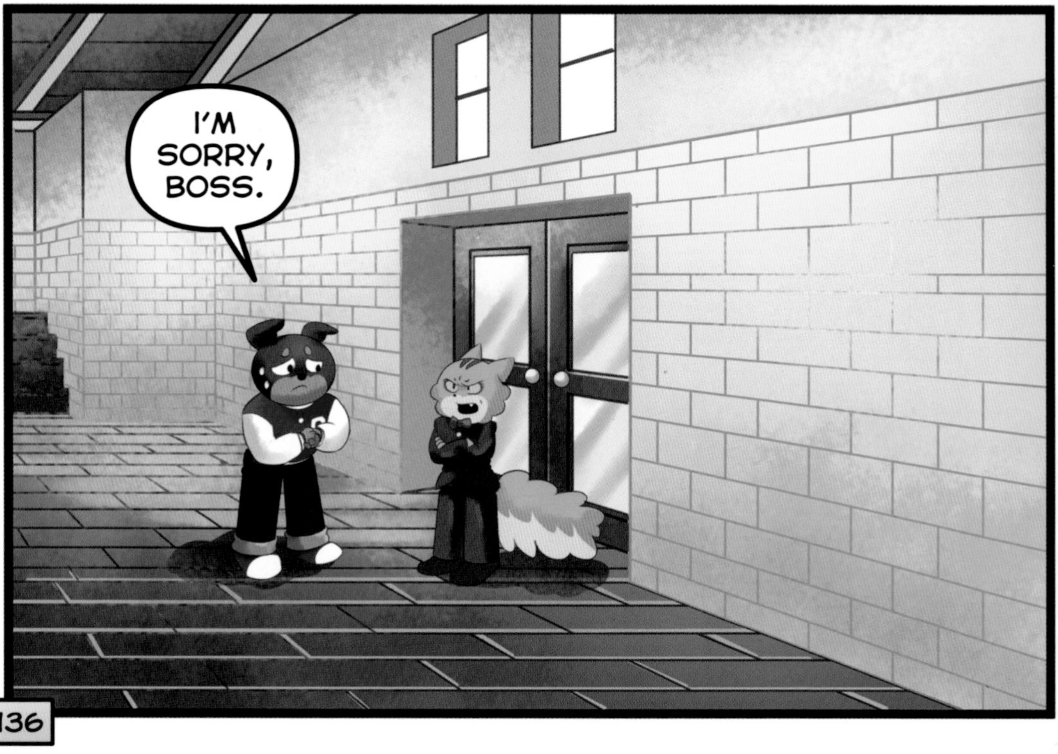
I'M SORRY, BOSS.

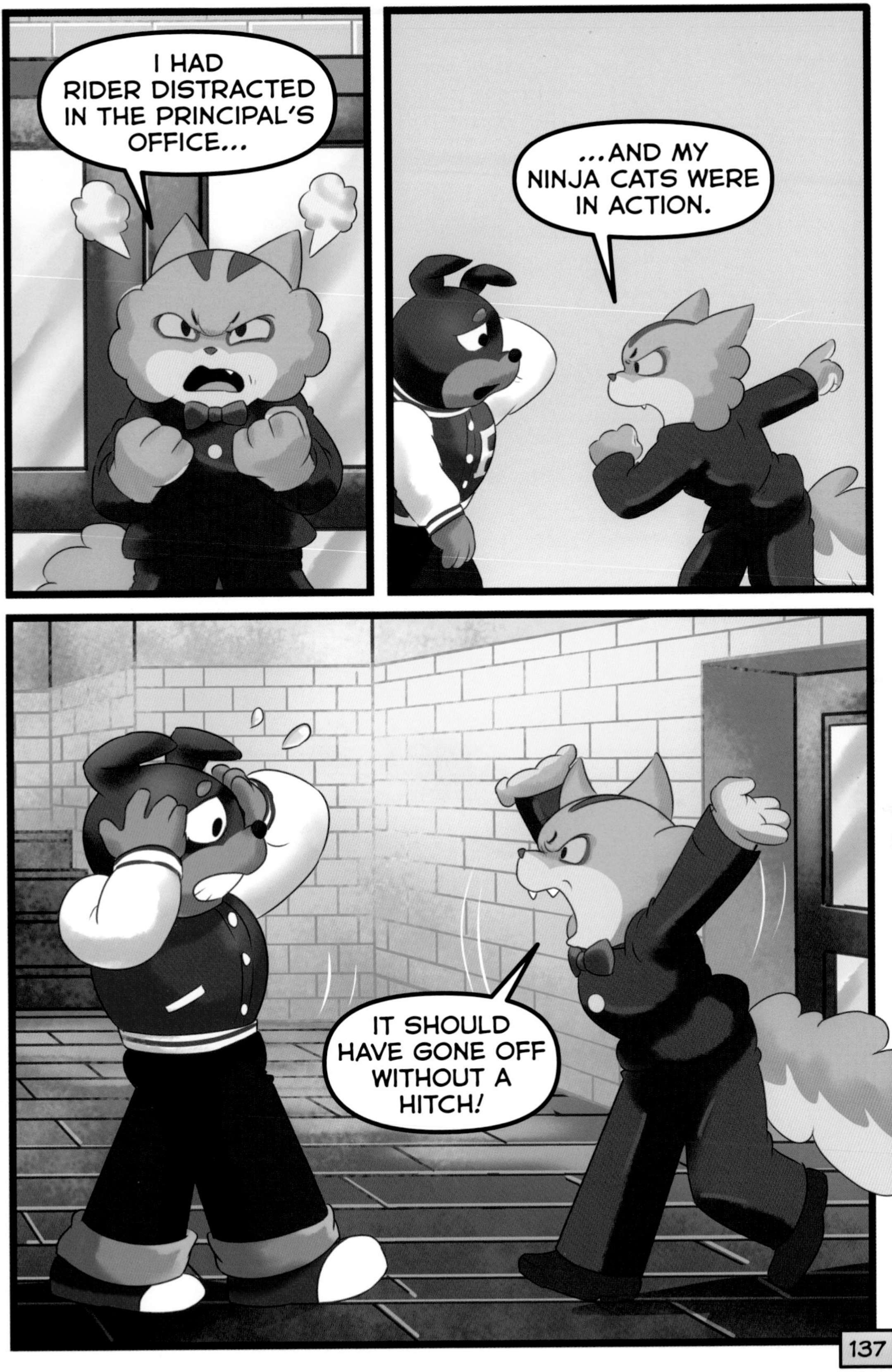
I HAD RIDER DISTRACTED IN THE PRINCIPAL'S OFFICE...
...AND MY NINJA CATS WERE IN ACTION.
IT SHOULD HAVE GONE OFF WITHOUT A HITCH!

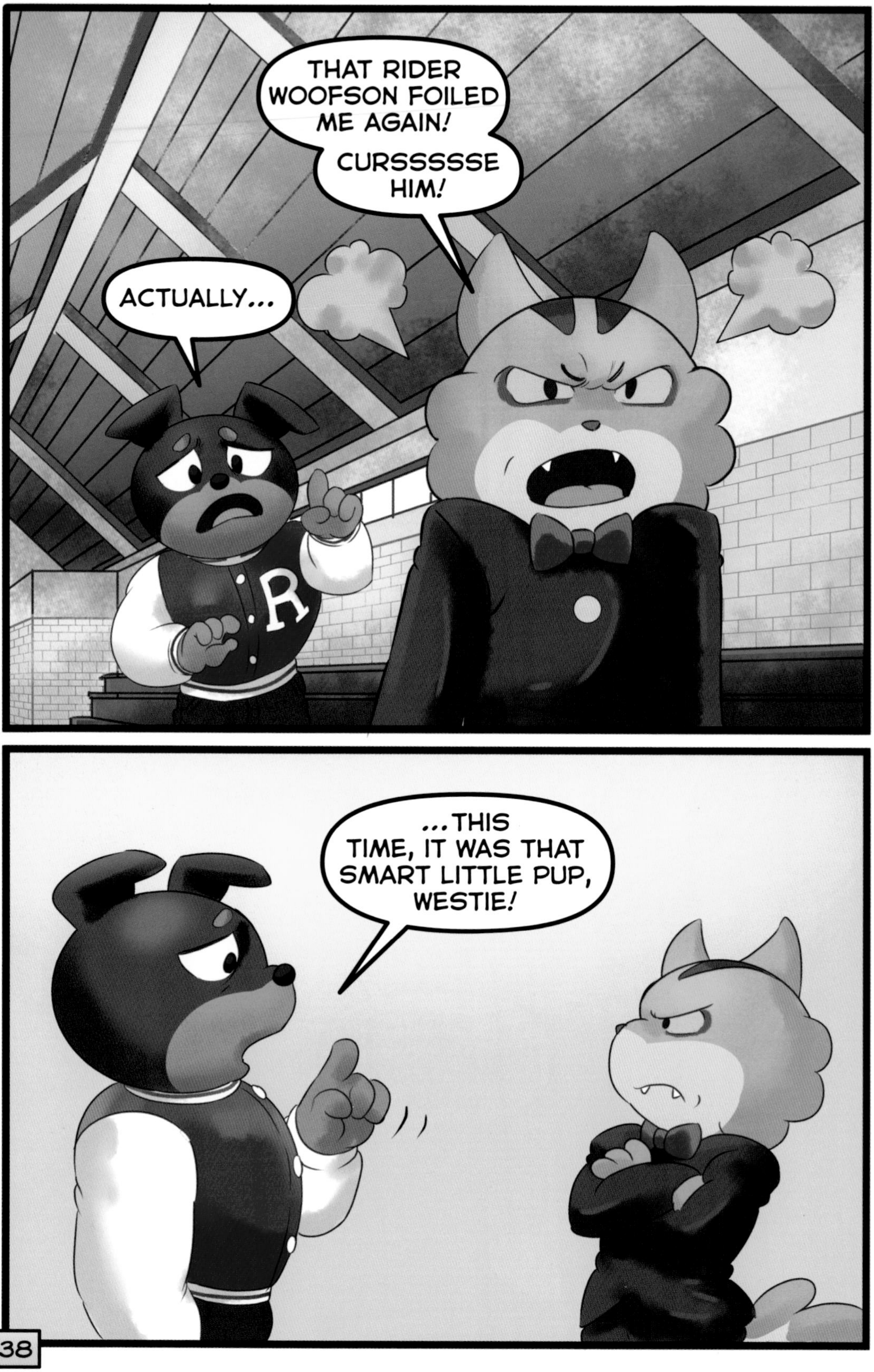
THAT RIDER WOOFSON FOILED ME AGAIN!
CURSSSSSE HIM!
ACTUALLY...
...THIS TIME, IT WAS THAT SMART LITTLE PUP, WESTIE!

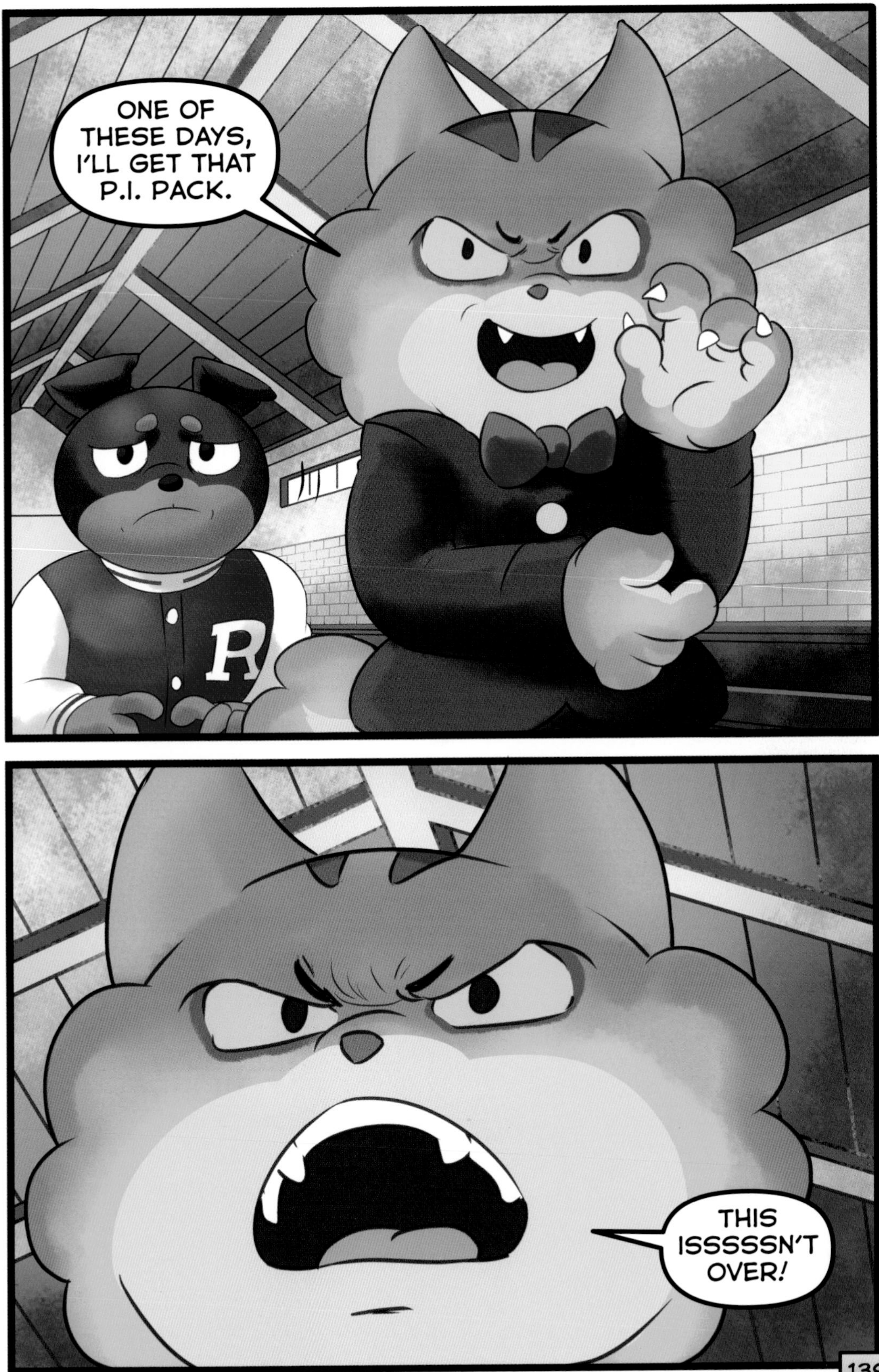
ONE OF THESE DAYS, I'LL GET THAT P.I. PACK.
THIS ISSSSSN'T OVER!

A NEW CASE AWAITS IN THE NEXT INSTALLMENT OF

Graphic Novel
PUP DETECTIVES
FEATURING...
THE MISSING MAGIC WAND
ZIGGY
FRENCHIE
MATTY MEOW
5

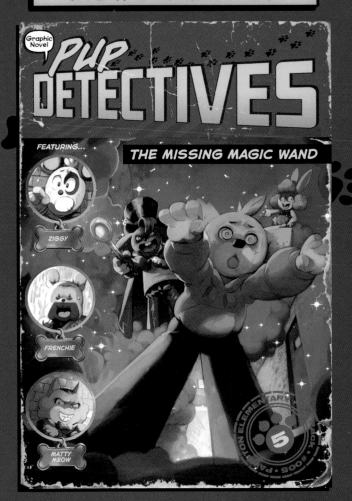

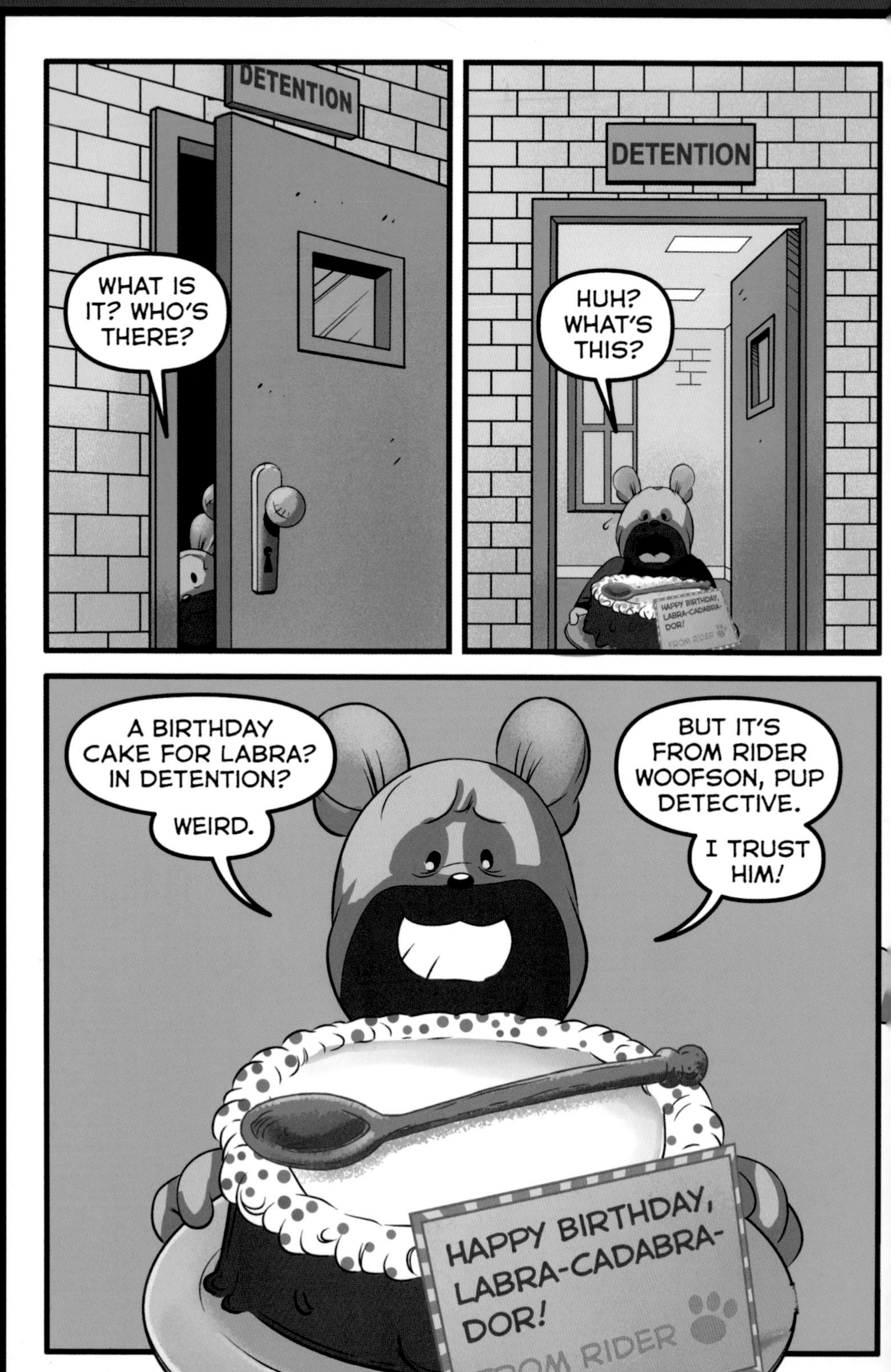
DETENTION
WHAT IS IT? WHO'S THERE?
DETENTION
HUH? WHAT'S THIS?
A BIRTHDAY CAKE FOR LABRA? IN DETENTION?
WEIRD.
BUT IT'S FROM RIDER WOOFSON, PUP DETECTIVE.
I TRUST HIM!
HAPPY BIRTHDAY, LABRA-CADABRA-DOR!
FROM RIDER

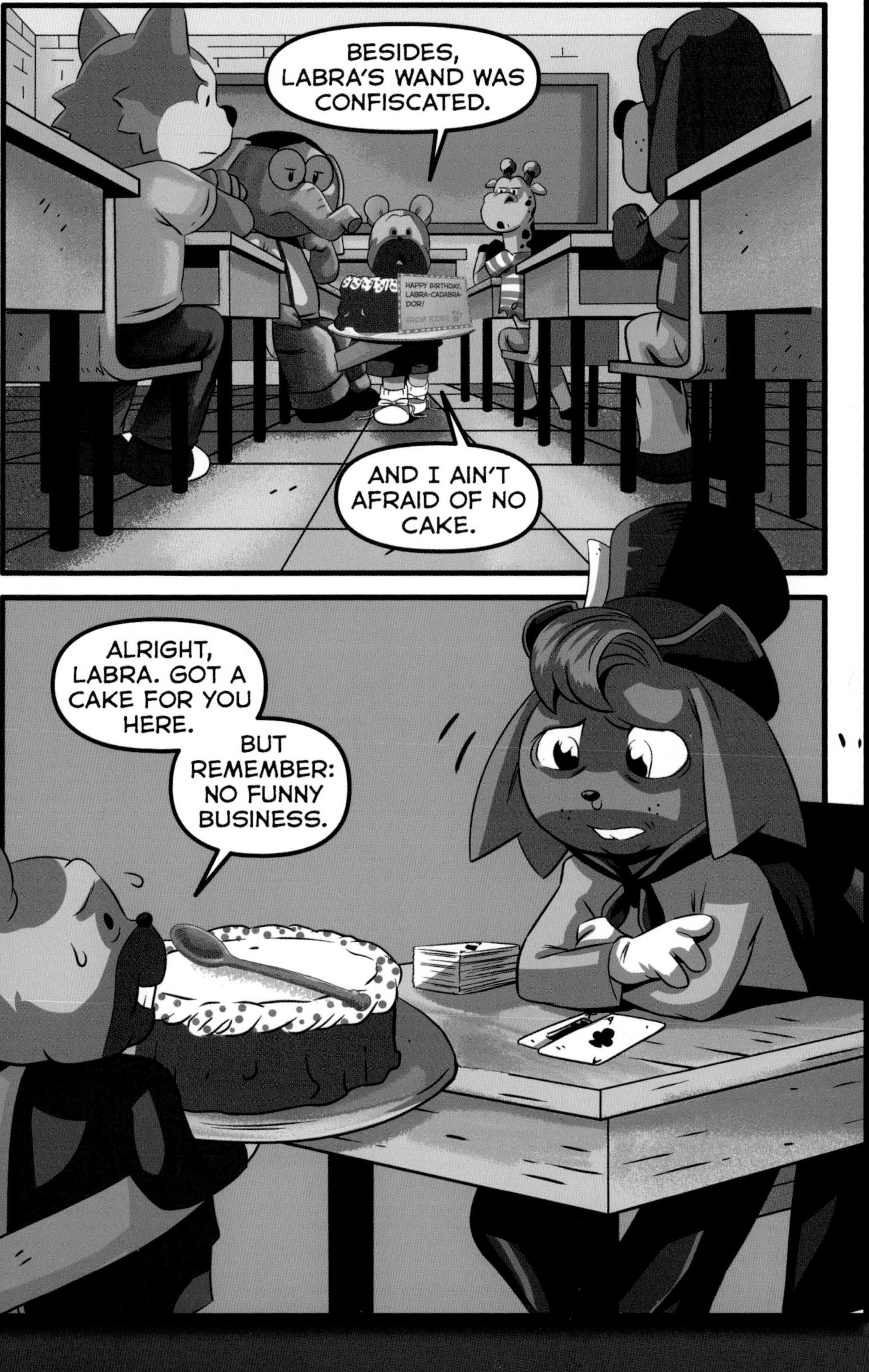
BESIDES, LABRA'S WAND WAS CONFISCATED.
HAPPY BIRTHDAY, LABRA-CADABRA-DOR!
AND I AIN'T AFRAID OF NO CAKE.
ALRIGHT, LABRA. GOT A CAKE FOR YOU HERE.
BUT REMEMBER: NO FUNNY BUSINESS.